F. Sionil José

VIAJERO

Solidaridad Publishing House
531 Padre Faura, Ermita
Manila, Philippines

Acknowledgment:

I am grateful to the University of the Philippines
Writing Center and to the Rockefeller Foundation
Study and Conference Center (Bellagio)
for their fellowships which enabled me to write this novel.

—FSJ

Published by
Solidaridad Publishing House
531 Padre Faura, Ermita
Manila, Philippines

Cover design:
Irwin Nicanor José

"Lift Every Voice and Sing"
by James Weldon Johnson
and his brother, Rosamond.

Cebuano document:
Asuncion Cenabre

ISBN 971-8845-04-6 (bp)

ISBN 971-8845-05-4 (np)

For Brigida and Steve Bergkamp

Books by F. Sionil José

Novels
PO-ON
TREE
MY BROTHER, MY EXECUTIONER
THE PRETENDERS
MASS

ERMITA
GAGAMBA, THE SPIDER MAN

Novellas
THREE FILIPINO WOMEN

Short Fiction
THE GOD STEALER
WAYWAYA
PLATINUM
OLVIDON
DONG-AO

Verse
QUESTIONS

For Children
FIVE STORIES

Non-Fiction
NOTES ON LITERATURE

CANTO DEL VIAJERO
Por Jose Rizal

Hoja seca que vuela indecisa
Y arrebata violento turbión,
Así vive en la tierra el viajero,
Sin norte, sin alma, sin patria ni amor.

Busca ansioso doquiera la dicha,
Y la dicha se aleja fugaz:
¡Vana sombra que burla su anhelo...!
!Por ella el viajero se lanza a la mar!

Impelido por mano invisible
Vagará de confín en confín;
Los recuerdos le harán compañía
De séres queridos, de un día feliz.

Una tumba quizá en el desierto
Hallará, dulce asilo de paz,
De su patria y del mundo olvidado...
¡Descanse tranquilo, tras tanto penar!

Y le envidian al triste viajero
Cuando cruza la tierra veloz...
¡Ay!. !no saben que dentro del alma
Existe un vacío do falta el amor!

Volverá el peregrino a su patria,
Y a sus lares tal vez volverá,
Y hallará por doquier nieve y ruina
Amores perdidos, sepulcros, no más.

Vé, viajero, prosigue tu senda,
Extranjero en tu propio país;
Deja a otros que canten amores.
Los otros que gocen: tú vuelve a partir.

Vé, viajero, no vuelvas el rostro,
que no hay llanto que siga al adiós;
Vé, viajero, y ahoga tus penas;
Que el mundo se burla de ajeno dolor.

SONG OF THE WANDERER

Dry leaf that flies at random
till it's seized by a wind from above:
so lives on earth the wanderer,
without north, without soul, without country or love!

Anxious, he seeks joy everywhere
and joy eludes him and flees,
a vain shadow that mocks his yearning
and for which he sails the seas.

Impelled by a hand invisible,
he shall wander from place to place;
memories shall keep him company—
of loved ones, of happier days.

A tomb perhaps in the desert,
a sweet refuge, he shall discover,
by his country and the world forgotten...
Rest quiet: the torment is over.

And they envy the hapless wanderer
as across the earth he persists!
Ah, they know not of the emptiness
in his soul, where no love exists.

The pilgrim shall return to his country,
shall return perhaps to his shore;
and shall find only ice and ruin,
perished loves, and graves—nothing more.

Begone, wanderer! In your own country
a stranger now and alone!
Let the others sing of loving,
who are happy—but you, begone!

Begone, wanderer! Look not behind you
nor grieve as you leave again.
Begone, wanderer: stifle your sorrows!
The world laughs at another's pain.

Translated by Nick Joaquin

FOREWORD

FIRST, *let me make this clear—we had never intended to kill Salvador dela Raza or even imprison him. That would have been not just terribly unnecessary but a great waste. Alive he was very important to me personally—a man of such prodigious knowledge is a gift not just to the rebels but to the nation. I had merely wanted to question him in the most comfortable circumstances if that were at all possible and since he did not want to deal with us in any manner, and by his very actions revealed his hostility to the military, then his capture was my most important project since I became intelligence chief for the Central Sector. I knew from the very start that I was dealing with a most formidable intellect, not only highly honed in academe but urbane as well—his dossier had so revealed. He was also highly motivated—this much was obvious in the fact that he had returned to a country wracked by poverty and disunity when he could have easily stayed away. We would have been happiest to have him on our side, a man so committed to ends that demand the ultimate sacrifice.*

I am not even sure that he had joined the movement; if he had, it was too late in the day as it was obvious that it had spent its energies and was beginning to alienate the very people—the rural and urban poor—which it had regarded as its "sea"; its doctrinaire approach to the national reality

1

had caused many cadres to leave. But it seemed that his arrival breathed new life into the moribund movement. With his guidance he was soon rejuvenating the cadres, attracting bright new recruits from the intelligentsia as well as from the lower classes, the very same people who had flocked to the Iglesia Ni Kristo, and for the same social and psychological reasons about which I may have to explain later in another report.

The main articles in Brother, the major monthly publication of the movement, though bearing different pen names were mostly his—that is very clear to us who examined them, the unerring clarity of the prose, unlike the contentious and prolix analyses of the old guard pols; he exhorted the old cadres to develop a new nationalist fervor which the movement should have done a long time ago; but more than this, there was also a very subtle appeal to man's quest for God—a moral order which he clearly understood in all its philosophical ramifications. It was after all this same fervor, this same impulse in the common man to be closer to his Creator that makes fanatics of the peasantry. Perhaps it was this major consideration that drew him to this mountain.

I understood this early enough. My father who was a general in the army had recounted how the Colorums in the thirties, and after them, the Sakdals, had believed so much in the justice of their cause and God's forbearance for them, the little people, that they dared bare their breasts to the guns of the soldiers thinking they had become invincible. Such is the power with which faith endows the common man.

I had this perception reinforced when I was doing field work for my dissertation in Pangasinan and Tarlac, two areas where the traditional values of the peasantry often come in violent contact with the forces of modernism or, as my adviser often said, feudalism.

I would have happily stayed behind in the United States after Ann Arbor—there was an opening for me in one of the California state universities, but my father had pleaded with me to carry on the military tradition in the family because it was duty. So it was back to officers' school, a commission and a job wherein it was thought I'd be able best to use my special background.

A Ph.D. in the intelligence service? For the Philippine Army, this was really an innovation, but for the services abroad this was taken for granted. I read a lot of field reports, the arid jargon of the rebels and the secessionists, and in a way, I came to understand the wellsprings of their discontent. Salvador dela Raza understood this, too, and here was where both our minds were in full accord.

I first came across his name when a DPA—or deep penetration agent—made a report of the religious pilgrimages to the mountain, that up there was a very learned man, simple in appearance and very soft-spoken when he chose to speak, who at the same time argued with great force on such

2

esoteric subjects as hermeneutics or phenomenology. The DPA incidentally is a student at the state university in Los Baños which is close to the mountain, a graduate sociology researcher on faith healing and nativistic religions, all of which were getting cleverly entwined with the movement.

This immediately piqued my interest. In a conversation once with the former Huk Supremo, Luis Taruc, whom I very much respect and admire for his intelligence and commitment to social justice, he said that if he had been opportunistic, he would have built himself up into a rural guru, a faith healer with unearthly powers. That was already what many of the Central Luzon farmers believed at the time he was fighting the Japanese and making all those amazing escapes from the subterfuges and the traps his enemies laid for him.

I reserved this bit of background as a footnote on my paper on the guerrillas and rural images which I delivered at the MIT seminar on rural insurgency.

I would have wanted to meet Salvador dela Raza, to learn from him— this I must admit in all candor. Like Frantz Fanon's The Wretched of the Earth, his seminal work on revolutionary nationalism has been a must reading for those who want to understand the motive force of nationalism in emerging countries. It certainly made it more clear to me why our own revolution in 1896 failed. The book was widely acclaimed in academic circles, building for him a niche in the high councils of scholarship. Just meeting him in person would have given me great personal pleasure.

Having done field work among the Moncadistas in Mindanao and the remnants of the Colorums and the Sakdals, I also agree completely with the conclusions of Reynaldo Ileto in his classic work, Pasyon and Revolution, about how nationalism and the aspiration for social justice have gone hand in hand in galvanizing our rural oppressed. But how does one utilize these sentiments for political action at a time when the movement seems to have already been emasculated by revolutionary fatigue? After all, people get tired of violence. As Bertolt Brecht said, "even shouting about injustice hoarsens the voice."

This is the fundamental dilemma Salvador dela Raza had addressed. Ever since he came to the mountain, there was less military activity in the Central Sector. But the few documents we obtained as well as those cadres captured and interrogated showed that the movement was getting stronger and not weaker as we had originally thought.

From the mountain came this clear voice, infusing new strength to those who flagged, calling for a union with God who was also in the soil, in the nation and with those who worked the land. Education, he also seemed to say as well, is the true precursor of social change. Pro bono publico and civic spirit, all-embracing in a society, is the key to progress. This may be a simplistic interpretation of Salvador dela Raza's core teaching and I

3

may be wrong, but it was a unique approach to a revolutionary situation that continues to exist—and here I am extremely objective—because the poor are still poor, even poorer, while the rich get more oppressive and richer.

The efforts to photograph him were futile; at one time I thought we already had a good picture but, as with the other photographs, his face was blurred. From the description of our informant, Salvador dela Raza was in his fifties, of medium height and average build with no distinguishing features. In other words, he could blend with any crowd. In fact, there were some in the mountain who believed he had supernatural powers— that he could disappear at will into the foliage, or among the rocks. At most, we have one of those quasi-portraits worked out with graphics. How do you picture eyes that are full of sympathy unless you meet the man himself, talk with him to feel the grip of his conviction, the warmth of his friendship?

I have long recognized the difficulty in establishing identity. This is why in the selection of agents appearance is an important qualification, particularly for those who go out in the field. They must not be either too fat or too thin, their heads must not be bald and there must be few distinguishing features about their faces. An aquiline nose, a low chin, slit eyes, eyebags—these are easy giveaways.

And then, there is the intelligence, although it is often said that military intelligence is a contradiction. This is built by painstaking gathering of bits of information, the shaping of hard facts from jumbled pieces, the conclusions that can be drawn and finally, the plan of action to which intelligence has to contribute a lot for so many plans fail not because the will to action is absent but because the people go into terra incognito without knowledge not only of the place, but also in a much larger sense, of the objective. And sometimes such objectives are variable—they may not require elimination or possession because a transcendental objective might be behind it all.

From the beginning, the plan was to capture dela Raza and simply question him cordially. It was difficult to connect him with the cadres, with the death squads roaming Manila, for he was not in any order of battle and none of the new documents had clearly pointed him out as the new leader. At the most, his linkage with the party or the movement or any of its fronts was our speculation, mine most of all.

The exits to Raza where he often passed were closely watched. There were times he was supposed to go down to buy things but each time he melted into the green shroud, with the farmers or with the continuous stream of pilgrims seeking in the caves and crannies of the mountain solace, miracle cure and eternal youth. There were just too many of them, society matrons, foreigners even who were attracted to the Philippines for its faith healers and other exotica.

After several weeks of surveillance, we finally found his house high up on the other side of the mountain, close to a ravine, and accessible only by one path. It could not be seen from the air unless one knew the precise location for the house was not all that big—a hut rather—and it was difficult to get close to it without being noticed by the people in the other houses way below, farmers who had clearings planted to vegetables, root crops and highland rice where there was some level ground. It had continuously amazed me to see how resilient mountain people are, how they could live on such meager harvest. We were to find out later that among the cassava and trellises of ampalaya and squash they were also planting the best species of cannabis and those herbs sold in Quiapo as medicine.

We acted immediately on this information. The teams were mobilized by nightfall. We had the place surrounded by 0500 hrs. A squad was stationed below the ridge just in case he had an escape route there, although we thought this was not likely unless he had a very long rope. We had studied that side of the mountain; it does not really show on ordinary photographs for many of the trees below the ridge are so tall, and from afar, the ridge is no ridge at all but the green top of trees. I have wondered why he chose to put his house there. He must have known that if attacked, he had only one way to go—down.

We sent up six flares when we were about a hundred meters away to signal to the secondary line below us and to announce our presence. It was still dark and everything around us had not taken shape—the trees, the small house invisible through the tree trunks. In afterthought, we should have waited for daylight but I didn't want him to escape. Unfortunately, two of the flares dropped quickly—their chutes malfunctioned and, as if towed by an unseen hand, they fell right on the roof of his house.

Remember, not a shot was fired, not one grenade was launched. It seemed as if the house was lighted instantaneously like a bonfire. A grass roof burns quickly in the dry season, and that was how the house burned, the flames quickly engulfing everything.

I had expected whoever was within to rush out and escape that pyre. I had really hoped he would run out and give himself up.

My men rushed forward but the heat was very intense, so we could not put out the fire or salvage anything. It was all over in less than an hour. It was now morning, cool and pleasant. The solid wooden posts still stood smouldering but the house, its walls were now all ash, as was the grass roof which had blazed with such quick ferocity. It was hopeless to piece together the flakes of papers, and books, folders, notebooks. They would have yielded so much information, not just about the movement but about this unusual man, his thinking that was the fountainhead of the new Jerusalem. There were also plastic and metal remnants of what seemed like video and electronic equipment, melted into unusual lumps and shapes,

5

perhaps a computer or a wireless receiver and transmitter. We had to wait for expert opinion from our engineers so we could find out the depth of sophistication with which he was functioning.

I have some knowledge of Buddhist mysticism, and though I am not a great believer in all that esoteric stuff which we associate with parapsychology, faith healing, the supernatural, still I must relate my amazement when I looked closely at the charred remains of the man—nothing really but a lump of charcoal with a human shape, compact but recognizable.

The morning sun shone through the wilted trees. I saw them then, the myriad crystals encrusted in the body, irregular in shape, some round, some like diamonds, each no bigger than a fingernail—there were many of them, some red, some blue, others yellowish or whitish, like bits of solid gum. They were cool, almost like ice, and almost weightless. I gathered them and placed them carefully in a plastic bag for examination in the lab. I was so excited knowing that these crystals were the man, his greatness or holiness, the essence of his manhood, the meaning of his life. This much I remember from my reading. With great haste, I went to Manila to the lab. Who would believe now what I had seen? The plastic bag where I had put those crystals—no, there was no hole in it. The crystals did not liquefy or evaporate—they simply disappeared!

Close to the charred remains of Salvador dela Raza—I was sure it was him—at his side, as if before he died he wanted to be sure that we would get it, was this black container like a small safe. It was made of some fireproof material but very hot so we dared not touch it. It was not a bomb—with that heat, it would have exploded. It was heavy; when we opened it finally, it was lined with something like asbestos. Within were five computer diskettes. I hastened to have the diskettes transcribed thinking they were a series of important documents. I was not disappointed. They were one man's account of his labyrinthian passage. I have purposely retained the title Salvador dela Raza himself gave his memoir, VIAJERO.

Simplicio Verdad, Ph.D.
Colonel, NISAP, AFP

1

IN GIVING shape to this book, I have arranged the chapters, incidents and the narrative structure to provide consistency, a pattern which shows that the conception of this story is a totality that involves me both as person and as persona. I have also used fictitious names and places to protect people who have been very generous to me.

To whom is this work addressed but to my countrymen so that they will share with me my long and tedious journey in search—oh, such a dreary cliché!—of my beginnings.

Terrible doubts as to the authenticity of my being had cankered me—is a creature of flesh enough? Or a man, born of other men, my genes from some distant and dried-up spring. Or was it a bog, instead?

Bear with me then, dear reader, my personal agony knowing as all men do that they cannot really reach out with certitude to the past and say, this is where it all began. In God's hands perhaps? But God has no time, no place, no memory. This is so often true with us, devoid of the memory which gives us our truest identity. I have travelled, but in another sense I have never really left the place where I was born.

All over the world, in airports and bus stations, in shopping malls and under the garish lights of entertainment marquees, I have seen the faces of my countrymen—solemn, sullen, steadfast, stricken with pathos—men and women who have come from the sulky recesses of the provinces, from the slums of Manila and the smug comfort of middle-class neighborhoods. They are everywhere, I am now sure, even in the glacial isolation of the arctic, the pitiless deserts of the

Middle East, the raging seas of the North Atlantic. Ah, my countrymen, dislodged from the warmth of their homes, to make a living no matter how perilous and demeaning, to strike out in alien geographies and eke from there with their sweat and their cunning what they can. I have seen them lambasted in foreign newspapers, ridiculed and debased by those who do not know how it is to be Filipino, how it is to travel everywhere and yet hold ever precious and lasting this memory, stretching across mountains and oceans, of my unhappy country.

This is my story, it is also theirs—and, maybe, yours.

Memory, help me!

But try as much as he did to think back, always this pit without a bottom wherein he was suspended, and all around was darkness thick and impermeable like raw opium. Above was a dot of light which he must reach if he was to be free. Towards the light visions of the past recurred in flashes again and again: running, always running; war, shooting, hiding. Blurred images, his mother's face, all forgotten, his father's face as well; his mother telling his father: *take him, you can run faster.* Narrow streets, still narrower alleys, the shouts *Hapon, Hapon*—he clung to his father's head, propped as he was on his shoulders; his father's heavy breathing, running, his father putting him down in a corner under the awning of a huge building, *do not leave this place, I will come back for you. DO NOT LEAVE!* then a mass of people swallowed him and he was lost to them, merged with half-naked men swaying and holding above their heads—through mists, shouts, heaving and pushing—this gaunt figure of a black man with a beard, agony disfiguring his face, blood from a crown of thorns oozing down his forehead, and on his shoulders as if it had weighted him down to his knees, this huge black cross.

Then men in uniform with guns, shouting, foreign in visage and language—they were shooting at the crowd and men were falling and rushing about and that was when he was pushed inside this huge building, candles burning inside, women in dark veils on their knees. He cried and screamed, *Itay! Itay!* and a panic which he will never forget suddenly shrivelled him. He crawled into a corner thinking that here he would be protected as people milled about. More shouting that echoed long and loud and afterwards, he fell asleep.

When he woke up, his stomach was churning and the night was complete. He started to cry again. *Itay! Itay!* what did it mean?

8

He remembered the word only too well, but it was meaningless now, there was no one to hold him, feed him. He slept again, shivering now for it was cold as it had never been before. Daylight, and the dead were cleared from the wide plaza. Was his father among those killed? He couldn't go there to look. Afterwards, toward midday, people streamed into the churchyard, some with carts drawn by horses. They unloaded leaves, weeds and small rocks— some colored white and dull red. They passed all these to vendors around the church. He had no more tears but he continued to sob. A lightness suffused his bones, a feeling of being totally alone. Then this old man came and asked why he was crying. He had a kindly face, almost like that of the wooden figures in the church. He felt no fear at all toward this strange old man who extended his hand. He grasped it immediately. "Itay, itay," he said softly and the old man said, "He is not here. What is your name?" Readily, he answered, repeated what his father and mother had always called him, "Badong."

"Do you know where you live?" the old man asked. The boy shook his head.

"Your father's name, or your mother's?"

The boy looked dumbly at his inquisitor.

The old man smiled. "How can I help you if you don't even know your parents' names, or where you live?"

There were others now. They understood him, that much he could see in their faces.

"I am hungry," he said softly and someone immediately gave him a piece of white coconut meat which he bit into at once.

"I will take him," the old man said, holding his hand. Gladly he went with the old man. At last someone would take care of him.

They rode in a calesa and clattered out of the wide plaza, empty now of the soldiers, the shouting crowds—now a vastness of asphalt burning under the morning sun. He slept most of the way. When he woke up, they had long left the city—all around were brown, stubbled ricefields, splotches of black where the straw had been burned.

Soon, it was dark. With the night, the smell of a land that had been baked by the sun filled the air; he would not forget that smell, nor the scent of newly cut grass, or the earth blessed with rain at last. The old man unhitched the calesa and on broad stones, he cooked their evening meal. They were in some plaza of a name-less town, the lamps of houses in yellow frames around them. He lay on a piece of sackcloth and sleep came quickly. He woke up, the sun a shock on his face, breakfast of hard chunks of cold rice,

9

and hot coffee warming his insides. Throughout the uneven ride along empty stretches of road, he dozed off again, and still again, the brightness of the land, sky and the air itself now a haze in the mind. Slowly the land turned green. They were going up a narrow road and ahead loomed this mountain, and the trees, huge and brooding.

They got off the calesa which, together with the horse, the old man left in the yard of the last house by the road. "We have to walk," the old man said, taking him by the arm. The road had ended and they were on a trail, grass in the middle, the twin and parallel indentions made by wheels half-covered with weeds. In a while, he was tired—he had never walked this far before, and he was also thirsty and hungry again. When he could no longer go any farther, he stopped, sat on the ground and started to cry.

"I will carry you," the old man said, hoisting him up on his shoulders.

The old man walked for a long time. The tree trunks became stouter, taller, so many of them clustered together. They rose, a canopy above them, blotting out the sun. It was dim underneath; they had quietly entered a green world, breathing and embracing them, and above and everywhere, birds were twittering. In brief bursts of light, the sun shimmered through, dancing in splendor on the leaves and branches.

Then the canopy thinned, and they broke out into the open and giddy sunlight. The sky was large and blue. They were on a narrow plateau, with some houses roofed with grass, the plots planted to crops he could not recognize, other than that they were green and leafy. He looked back and was surprised—they had climbed very high and the plain fanned out below them in a thralling sweep of brownish green, the villages below in splotches of many hues.

The old man stopped and let him down. He pointed to a small bamboo house far up ahead atop a ridge, still larger trees like sentinels towering around it.

"That is your home now, little one," the old man said.

It was as if their arrival had been announced, (by the birds, the beasts?) for in a while, a woman appeared in the doorway. She was young, exuding a fragility and a glow, as if she had in her being the capacity to imbue with grace anything she touched or breathed upon.

The old man said, "That is my daughter. Her name is Mayang."

They went up the house floored with bamboo slats. A cubicle adjoined the middle of the house, and to the left, a small kitchen

10

with clay water jars, an earthen stove and cooking pots. The woman held out her hand as he went up the ladder. He waited for her to speak, but she did not utter a word, maybe because words were not needed. It was enough that her handclasp was warm and warmer was the smile upon her face.

Again, he had dozed. It was dusk so soon, a fire was leaping in the stove, the rice pot started bubbling and the woman went to it and took off its lid. Still no word from her.

"Why does she not speak?" he asked finally.

The old man looked at him earnestly, and then with a slow shake of the head, said, "Mayang—she cannot see, hear or speak—but she knows you are here, she knows so many things, sees so many things, too, which both of us will never be able to see."

"She is not blind," he said in protest. "I know, I know!"

The old man smiled at him. "She is...and she is your mother now..."

"And you, my father?"

The old man continued, "No, Apo Tale—that is me—I am now your grandfather."

Through inexorable time, cobwebbed, misted, tortured, these were the only names he would long remember: Mayang, Apo Tale— names that evoked love, compassion and everything that was good and eternal, blessed with God's understanding as he was to know what understanding was, for by then he understood both—the God of this mountain, the God of the plain below, the same God who ruled the skies, who made the plants grow and the flower to become the fruit.

He would remember, too, the evening meal, something he never had before—the rice was fragrant, the vegetables sweet, and what were those dark things that looked like flowers? He would soon see where they grew, mushrooms as large as the cover of the pot. Mayang knew where to find them in the forest, their benificent provider.

They went there the following morning. Mayang led him, held his hand firmly lest he lose himself in the dank green embrace of foliage and vine. She fingered the leaves of plants, plucked their small berries and large pulpy fruits; she could feel with her feet the weeds which she uprooted and placed in her big bamboo basket. Then they came upon a clearing and Mayang sat on a boulder veneered with moss, half-buried in the loam. Close by was a spring, the water pure and clear, ceaselessly flowing into a tiny stream. She sat quietly; after a while, she turned around as if expecting something. They came as if a call had been hurled into the ether and they had heard it—two does, their bodies aquiver and glossy, a couple

11

of deer, their horns a dull brown in the light, and wild pigs, their tusks white and sticking out of their snouts like knives, and birds of many hues and sizes, twittering and surrounding Mayang and him—these creatures of the forest were without fear, at ease in their human presence, particularly the does who had snuggled close to the woman, so close she could touch them, caress them and wordless with wonder, the boy stretched his hand, too, to confirm if they were real, for he had never seen such beasts or fowl before. To each, Mayang gave a bit of the mushrooms she had picked up earlier and they ate it, their heads raised in supplication. He raised his head, too, and looked at this woman, and her eyes were shining sightless though they were. Years and oh so many years afterward, he would remember this scene and marvel again and again for it did not happen just once but several times, and if it was all a dream, then it was a dream that lived; if it was reality then it was a dream that he had so completely witnessed that it all became a part of himself, entwined with the fibers of his own being long after he had grown up and had become cynical about magic and the arcane ways of the world.

THEY NEVER went back to the church and the wide plaza; he never saw the place again till much, much later—but this is going ahead of the story. Apo Tale had left that morning and returned at dusk the next day with a bottle of salted fish sauce, matches, thread. The things Mayang had gathered—the leaves, berries, shrubs and lengths of vine, some of them with thorns—were in a corner to be brought to the city again the following day. He knew for sure then that they possessed powers magical and unexplainable.

Apo Tale also brought back from the city stories of hunger, of emaciated city folk butchering cats and dogs and even gutter rats that they had trapped. But here in this mountain redoubt they had, it seemed, everything they needed. Rice, cassava, bananas from the clearing below, even fish from the pond that was always fed by the spring up the slope, the same spring that irrigated the vegetable and rice plots. He learned from the old man how it was to plant, to watch the seed break free from the dark soil, a tiny green thing. "You will also grow into a man," Apo Tale told him.

THEY HAD NO visitors. Sometimes people were way down the slopes working their way up, but somehow, they never reached the house. Then one night; the rainy season had started and the frogs down by the spring had filled the night with their croaking. Moths had entered the house and died in the crackle of flames at the kitchen

12

stove and dusk had quickly deepened. He had a slight fever as he had played in the spring too long and had lain in the cubicle where the pillows and the rice bin were.

The oil lamp that hung from a rafter had long been extinguished and the house was totally dark, but used to the darkness he could make out the old man asleep by the door and Mayang in the middle of the house. He was wakened by shouts, by commands in a language guttural and strange, all the while a sharp beam of light flashed around the house. From the door of the cubicle, he saw them come up—six of them in shapeless trousers, all of them with guns—he knew their shape by now. They were the same men who had fired at the crowd near the church—how could he ever forget their bearded faces? Apo Tale and Mayang, now roused from sleep, cowered before them. Now the beam of light rested on Mayang's face. They laid their guns on the floor and went to her. By this time, Apo Tale started shouting as one of the men tore at Mayang's blouse. A man aimed a gun at the old man and in a flash of red, he saw the old man's frightened face as he sprawled on the floor. He quivered then lay still. Mayang fought them but they were six and stronger. He could not see anymore what they were doing. He rushed to the window at one end of the little room and jumped out. He had hardly stood up when a beam of light cut across the emptiness ahead of him. The sound of the gun was like thunder but he was not hit. He ran onwards to the ravine and slipped, letting his body fall, scraping the earth and the rocks, until he hit the ground. He lay there for some time, the trees a dark, protective veil above him.

When he woke up, it was day; the fever was gone but he felt so weak, he thought he was dying. He raised his hand to a sliver of sun and realized he had become very thin. He tried standing up but couldn't—it seemed as if his whole body was some empty pot or a hollow length of bamboo. It rained the day before but now the ground was dry and the sun which drenched the trees was high. It splashed on the ground, it danced in patterns of silver. He felt dizzy so he squatted until the dizziness passed. Then it came, this hunger so unbearably sharp it felt like his stomach was being gnawed by huge rats and his insides were being wrenched away, shred by shred. He couldn't climb the ridge—it was much too steep, and to get back to the house, he had to walk a distance to where the ground rose. He chanced upon a papaya tree laden with fruit, some over-ripe and eaten by birds. He reached out and started eating, skin and all until he was full, and feeling better, he sat down as he started feeling drowsy so he slept again. When he woke up, the day had cooled and the westering sun already cast long shadows on the

13

ground. In a short while, the place seemed familiar. He was not mistaken—the house of Apo Tale was close by, up the rise of ground among the trees.

Then the thought came—it was no nightmare that had happened the previous night. Was Apo Tale dead? And Mayang, too, dear mother and provider, whose smile was the grace of life itself? What had happened to them...the men who had barged into their house—surely they were the enemy against whom they had no defense. *Inay, Inay*—the words shaped in his mind—*Inay*, he cried and ran towards the house as the afternoon quickly deepened and an eerie stillness suffused the forest.

Even before he could get to the house, he could already smell that sweetish odor of putrefaction that soaked the air, assailing his nostrils with unforgettable power, he felt nausea come again.

He went up the bamboo ladder, the stench much stronger now, as if it were some wave that engulfed everything. Apo Tale and Inay Mayang were in a corner, their legs bloated, their faces dark and beyond recognition. Then something moved within them. The dead coming back to life? A ghost that had possessed them? He stood transfixed and gasped. Two big lizards which had been feeding slithered out from under the corpses, looked at him then fled to the kitchen and jumped to ground.

The leftover food in the kitchen had been eaten by creatures of the forest. On the shelf where Apo Tale kept their things, there was still a box of matches, the kerosene bottle was full. He opened it and crying softly started pouring it on the bamboo floor, splashing it on the grass roof, and finally emptying it on the corpses. He realized long afterwards, this was also a ritual of farewell. He couldn't bear to look at them whom he had loved so much, who had given him a home. How long had they cared for him?—a year, two years—he was never conscious of the passing of time as if days and nights merged into some endless breathing and playing and eating—that was what he remembered most, the food in the house, the sweet vegetables, the mushrooms, and the small eggs of birds or whatever they were that Inay Mayang brought back from the forest.

He lighted a strand of grass which he had pulled from the roof. The grass burned quickly. He watched the roof of the kitchen burn, first into a grey whorl and then into crackling flames that forced him out of the house and to the yard.

He wanted to be close to the burning house but as the sides and the roof started to burn, the bamboo posts crackling in the fire, the heat forced him farther away, to the trellises of ampalaya and squash. Smoke and ashes from the burning house rose, swirling in the air.

14

The last ember died at dusk and he could now go to the mound of ash, and among them, the clay pots and the stove lay in shards. He had forgotten to look into the rice bin and now the rice lay in a heap of black beads. And where the corpses lay, what remained of Apo Tale and Inay Mayang were two mounds in the shape of the human body and on top of both were so many little crystals, some in the shape of beans, golden yellow, blue, white, purple—all glowed then dimmed with the night. He put them in his pocket and wondered afterwards how he could have lost them when much, much later he remembered.

He walked on, down the trail to the black, edgeless plain below, the night dusted with stars. In a while the fever returned and it seemed as if his whole body were immersed in scalding water, then in a pool as cool as the spring above the clearing where he had seen Mayang rest so often, and the deer drinking their fill.

Perhaps, just perhaps, he had died then had come to life again, or he had gone to sleep like he did at the bottom of the ravine. When he woke up, the night had passed, the world was astir; he could hardly lift his arms—there was no more bone to them. He looked around him. He was inside a wide, cavernous cave—not a house or if it was, it was indeed a strange house for it had no windows, only a door from which light poured in. He was frightened for he was immediately surrounded by big, black men with short kinky hair, all of them in dark green uniform. Some had rifles—he knew them by now. When he stirred, a big man not as dark as the others peered down at him. He felt the big palm press down on his forehead then feel his pulse.

Years afterwards, he was to hear how it had happened, how he finally came to, and how Captain James Wack, who was fairer and taller than all of his men, had come forward, smiled at him and reassured him that he was safe.

The man who was going to be his father asked although he did not understand it then, "You okay, kid?"

They were all Negroes, in a quartermaster unit of the U.S. Army, and they had bivouacked at the foot of the mountain in the small village of Raza. They had heard of Japanese stragglers in the forest above them and Captain Wack had organized a platoon to reconnoiter and capture the stragglers. They had marched the whole day, deep into the forest, high up where it was cool and the trees were huge. They came across some houses, small waterfalls and strange caves, and some clearings farther up but all the people had fled to the town or to Raza, where the American troops and some guerrillas were stationed.

15

Captain Wack's squad came across the boy asleep on the trail, feverish and emaciated. They thought he was dead but he was still breathing, at times moaning. In the camp, after a few days of care, he was well. He had nowhere to go so he stayed and came to be known as Buddy, the mascot, the captain's six-year-old orphan. He had told them his name was Badong. They asked about his parents—they are dead, he said simply; the Japanese killed them.

He knew no English, he hadn't gone to school at all, so they taught him. He was a fast learner and was soon talking with them in their own language which he realized when he grew up was a kind of dialect.

All those days were a pleasant haze but he would always remember his first bowl of oatmeal with sugar and cream, the canned fruit, corned beef, spam, the heaps of food the soldiers cooked, most of which they gave away to the people of Raza, mounds of powdered eggs, bread and peanut butter, and oh so many gallons of Coca-Cola. Within the year, the war ended and the Negroes left town in huge trucks for Manila; they encamped in a wide field away from the city—so many tents like the ones they used in Raza. And one afternoon, he was placed in an olive-green duffel bag and told not to move or make a sound. He thought he would die, unable to breathe in that bag, how hot it was, and thank God, it was not too long, for when the bag was opened, he was inside a wide room together with the soldiers and they were all laughing, tousling his hair, and saying he was on a big ship and would soon see San Francisco.

He was told not to venture outside the room. He could hear the splash of water, feel the throbbing of the ship, which soon grew stronger and the whole room seemed to vibrate; that night soon after, the captain took him out—they were out at sea, the water black and limitless around them. He asked the captain if he could go out in the daytime, when the sky was bright; yes, he could wander around the ship. He never saw the ocean before and now he was astounded by its breadth, so vast, so very much alive with the waves that heaved and flattened out in bubbling valleys, and the flying fish that lifted from the water, skimming the surface, glinting like a bolo, before swooping back into the sea, the porpoises below the prow swimming ahead, weaving and playing—and the promise of America across the ocean.

By now, he was used to the onslaught of oatmeal, the cartons of milk, dried fruits and mounds of mashed potatoes. In the mornings after breakfast, he would go to the steel deck and scan the limitless expanse, water all around, the air so clean and fresh it filled his lungs like liquid life. The days lengthened, and he no longer waited for

16

the morning when he could go out for there was nothing to see but the sky, and that grey, heaving mass of water wherever he turned. It had become cooler, too. "We are nearing San Francisco," the captain told him.

The men stirred; everything again into those bags and steel lockers, everything—and when they were finally ready, back he went into a duffel bag together with some laundry. It was no longer warm as it was the first time—in fact he felt cold but not for long for when the duffel bag was finally opened, he was in the back seat of a car.

"We will go home now, Buddy," the captain said. Driving the car was a beautiful fair-skinned woman, Captain Wack's wife.

HIS NEW home, his new country, the soaring, stone buildings, the many cars in the wide, wide streets, the big white and black people and among them, people brown like him, too; small men with wide-brimmed felt hats, and baggy trousers and jackets too big for them, and so much food, not just in the big house where Captain Wack took him, but everywhere, in the food shops. And on the sidewalks, people always in a hurry.(America, America—he kept repeating to himself; you are a promise, and much, much later on, he would also add, and a curse.)

The Wack house in San Francisco's Pacific Heights, an inheritance, was in an affluent neighborhood. The house was built in the thirties when construction was still superior; the materials were the finest that could be had, brick and redwood timber, a tile roof with a sweeping slant in the back and a grand view of the bay in the rear. The front yard was flanked by rhododendron bushes, their rose and pink blossoms brilliant in the California sunshine. The front porch was veiled by wisteria, the flowers a violet cascade down to the very lawn. Attached to the house in the rear was a small apartment; it was once Jim Wack's study but it was given to Buddy when he was in college so that he could have privacy and get to the house without bothering anyone, which was hardly necessary for the house was so big it had all the space and the silences necessary for solitude. When the apartment was given to him, he could not appreciate it for it seemed as if Jim Wack were excluding him from the family. Only much later did he realize the need for it when as a student at Berkeley, the privacy was not just for himself but also for the friends who visited, and the girls who by then were a pleasant though not frequent company. He could lock the door to the living room—a sure sign that he wanted to be alone and not be bothered. It became his sanctuary.

17

IN THOSE formative years in Pacific Heights, insulated as he was from the rigors of having to earn a living, he came to know three women: Jessie, his sister, who would be for a long, long time a precious companion, critic, and a lost and forlorn friend; Roxanne, his mother, and Serena, the girl he met in college.

Jessica was born four years after he arrived in San Francisco and her birth was greeted by Roxanne and James Wack as a miracle; like her husband she was close to forty and no longer in the best age for childbearing.

When he was already in high school in San Francisco, Buddy got to appreciate his father more. James Wack was really incredible. He obtained his Ph.D. in anthropology from the Sorbonne shortly before the Nazis entered Paris. It was difficult for James Wack to uproot himself from Paris. This city had given him the freedom from discrimination, a freedom he couldn't get in America, and the company of white women, too. He wanted to join the French Foreign Legion but was dissuaded by Roxanne in the United States who said she would marry another man if he stayed away another week— he had to rush home and claim her for he knew that Roxanne meant every word she said. The marriage was somehow arranged between her father, a successful doctor, and his father. But he also loved Roxanne from the very first time he met her.

James Wack was not all that dark—he could have passed for a South American, a Cuban or a Brazilian with his curly brown hair, his straight nose. Mediterranean or Spanish, Buddy would describe him later. Like most light-skinned Negroes, James Wack had often passed for white where it was necessary, since he was not one to wear his race on his shoulder and dare everyone to knock it. When he was with white Anglo-Saxons, he spoke the standard English of the middle class, but when he was among his own people, then his language adapted easily, a language which soon enough Buddy also mastered.

James Wack was also embarrasingly affluent through no effort of his own. His father, a graduate of the Mahara Medical School in Nashville, Tennessee, had a very successful practice. Moreover, oil was discovered in their family farm in Oklahoma. And to complete the doctor's good fortune, he had produced two patent ointments— a skin bleach trade-named "Lait," which made the skin lighter through constant use without doing any epidermal harm, and a pomade, "Strait," which unfurled kinky hair for as long as it was continually applied. Both were selling very well, more in the North than in the South, and in the Carribean, Brazil and cities in Africa. James Wack's assured income enabled him to travel at will. At one time, even before the Negroes were avidly searching for roots, he had gone to Africa. He was very disappointed at what he saw and he returned fully conscious that he was not African at all. He was thoroughly American.

Mrs. James Wack, Roxanne, entertained neither curiosity nor consuming qualm about her ancestry. It did not bother her that she was Negro; she could pass for white and that was what she often did. Only if one looked hard enough did one notice that her red hair was slightly wavy, but of course that could easily have been a hairdresser's doing.

She was tall and graceful, unlike most Caucasian women who seemed to have little grace; a quality which in no manner demeaned them, but really set them apart from the Oriental women who, Buddy later observed, always seemed so feminine even if they were ravaged by work.

He remembered being scooped up in her arms when he got out of the car. She was so full of life. It was not she who was in that coffin at the mortuary. The professor explained later what had happened, how she was mugged and dragged into an alley in East Oakland across the bay where she had gone to visit a friend, and was stabbed when she fought back. They never found the killers but a group of Negro boys who were in the vicinity said it was a couple of Negroes who had done it.

The professor remained affectionate and ever attentive to his and Jessica's needs but he had changed so much, the easy laughter that came to him, and now, these silences which even as a young boy Buddy knew he must not sunder, the many times when the professor's eyes misted particularly when memories proliferated their talk.

Shortly after the death of Roxanne, James Wack brought to Pacific Heights a full-time housekeeper, a newly graduated Mexican nurse. Porfiria Castro, diminutive, twenty-four years old and an orphan, with very Indian features—an aquiline nose, high cheekbones and a happy disposition and dedication, tending to a distinguished academic, a growing boy and a baby who would be pampered. A room in the first floor was converted into a nursery and Porfiria's room was beside it.

Unlike her parents, Jessica was brown. She could easily pass for a Southeast Asian, with such wavy black hair and the merriest eyes—even when she was sad or angry, she always managed to look pretty.

"You are not my brother," she had shouted at Buddy once. "We have the same color, but that doesn't mean a thing—so don't go around calling Daddy, Daddy. Only I can call him that!"

19

Legally, however, he was now Captain Wack's adopted son, although he bore the name Salvador dela Raza.

"HOW DID I get my name, Dad?" he asked James Wack one morning; they were over the Oakland Bay Bridge, the canvas roof of the Chevrolet coupe was down, and the cool air whipped around them. Below, on the first level, a train blew its whistle, a shrill, whining, echoing blast, the rumble of its wheels shaking the bridge slightly. He had mused afterwards, looking at the magnificent bridge from a distance, its huge suspension cables slung across the lengths of pylon that straddled the waters, and though seeing it almost every day, he did not cease to be awed by the overwhelming megalithic construction.

"Your name is your own," James Wack said, turning to him. They had spent hours in offices where the Captain had filled up forms and Buddy was photographed and asked how he liked it in the United States. To all the questions, he had merely grinned, although he would have wanted so much to say he felt so safe unlike in the mountain that evening when Mayang and Apo Tale were killed.

He was silent for a while, then James Wack continued evenly, "It is all legal now, you are now my adopted son, you are now an American citizen, too. You may change your citizenship in the future if you want, but for now, no one can drive you away from here."

"How did I get my new name?"

Jim Wack continued: "I did ask what your real name would be if, as you said, everyone called you Badong, and they told me, the Filipinos I asked, that most likely it would be Salvador. And the family name—you came from the village of Raza—that is why it is Salvador of Raza. Badong is not easy for us to say, so you are Buddy—just as you were called in the army, remember?"

He nodded. There was no mistaking the logic of his name, Buddy.

BUT WHO are my parents? And from what subterranean core of the earth did I come from?

One evening when he was in senior high, the year before he was to go on to college, he was asked by his history teacher which part of the Philippines he came from. The lesson that day was about World War II and the liberation of the Philippines, that very time in which he had lived and which he remembered best, soaked from bits and stories that James Wack had told him. He couldn't give an answer, for he really did not know then where Raza was.

James Wack was in his study—he had been writing and his library was always in disarray, the books piled on the oak reading table in

20

the middle of the room, markers of yellow paper stuck in them. He switched on the lamp focused on the Rand and McNally wall map of Southeast Asia, the Philippines in the middle. For a while, he tried to read aloud the names of places, islands, then he asked, "Dad, please show me where Raza is."

James Wack rose from the writing desk. He had been working the whole afternoon; he stretched his arms, then strode to the map and pointed out where it was; there was of course no name because maps do not carry the names of small anonymous villages. James Wack took a red pin from his desk and stuck it on the map. He held Buddy by the shoulder and said, "Now you are interested in your beginnings. That is very important, and it can also be very frustrating..."

He had, after that, gone to the study many times, stood before the map as if it were some precious ikon, and gazed at it, wondering what the place looked like now, reliving those days as he knew them, hazy though they had become, and Apo Tale and Mayang—were they just vivid images from a dream?

And one evening, when memory was brightest, when it seemed as if he could pluck blurred images out of the cosmos and give them shape, he sat down and wrote to the parents he never knew and to Apo Tale, to Inay Mayang:

Soon I will be eighteen, an adult in America, and though this letter will never reach you—how could it when I don't even know your names, if today you are still alive. Father, you could have died in that plaza where the soldiers shot the people, you could have been one of those figures prostrate on the asphalt—this I recall only because if you were alive, you would have come back for me. And, Mother, where are you, who are you? I long for an explanation of myself, to seek knowledge of where I came from, but all I have are these fleeting shadows.

But dear Inay Mayang and Apo Tale—I do know you, I do remember your faces although they are not clear now, and most of all, I remember the forest, and the mountain, and the spring where those animals drank their fill, where they seemed so unafraid but only because you, Inay Mayang, were there.

And so I ask again, and still again, who am I and where did I come from? I now have a piece of paper with my picture on it, my name as it was given to me, not by you, my father or mother, but by a man who cares nonetheless. All that I retain of the child that I was once are what these eyes have seen, a tall building with a cross—a church, I know that now, and after that, a mountain covered with trees, the earth planted to living things, a dark forest alive with creatures that did no one harm, a small house at the edge of a cliff, and those two wonderful people who fed

21

me and took care of me. I remember waking up on the ground, the sun high in the sky and blinding me, and big, dark men smiling, their white teeth framed by thick lips... And this is as far as I have gone for much as I would like to go to the farthest memory can take me, there is nothing there but a rimless void which I hope I can fill someday...

WHO AM I?

I look at my reflection in the pool and I see a brown man with an inquiring face, eager to know, to taste all the juices of the earth. I came upon myself not knowing wherefrom I came, but I do suspect it was not from an eternal womb, the hollow of a bamboo? Or of the sky? I am alone, yet I know there are likenesses of me, with the same bone and muscle, and hungers that cannot be assuaged. I must also stand alone, for this is what all men must do, if they are to prevail in the wilderness.

I was made to wander; if I had wings I would have soared to the highest my wings could propel me, but with my feet, I must now go as far as they can lead me.

I have seen this face and it belongs only to me, but I will also recognize it everywhere, for it is the face of a traveller, a seeker, even if he moves not a muscle or an eye, for the mind is what travels farther than what the flesh with all its frailty can reach.

But where will I go and what will I become? Is there a niche somewhere in the desert or in the jungle into which I can fit? and where I belong, where I will die, this the surcease I have always sought?

ALL THOSE YEARS engendered remembered bliss—how quickly they vanished like smoke up the chimney—grade school, high school, summer camp, vacations in the east, trips to the national parks, Yosemite, the Grand Canyon, he had them all imprinted in the mind, and most of all, how quickly did Jessie grow.

By then, the San Francisco house did not seem big enough. James Wack often brought students home, mostly Negroes. He was involved with the civil rights movement. Like the many Negroes who fought in the war, he was determined to clamor for change peacefully, to demand of America the rights that were truly his. His children must not relive the damnation of his experience. But at the same time, he did not ease up on his teaching, the papers he had to write about folklore and the history of his own people. He belonged to that generation of European scholars involved with the beginnings of civilization, tribal societies and their food and habitat, who also asked those value-loaded questions about the ethics of progress. His tenure at the university had allowed him very little teaching chores as his probity and scholarship focused more on research and writing. The study on the ground floor was always cluttered with his things, clippings that had not been filed, and stacks of magazines and newspapers and artifacts of "primitive" living from Africa and South America.

Jessie grew up with this mess, the empty rooms her playground. At twelve, she was a woman although childlike, her enthusiasms, her tantrums and playfulness.

Jessie's complexion was clear, with no blemishes and those pores sometimes as big as pinheads that are often spread on the whole skin surface of some black women. She had a nimbleness of foot and did not walk into a room but bounced into it.

She disregarded privacy, his as well, for she would barge into his room in the house, or into the apartment in the rear without even knocking. She was also physically strong; when the spirit moved her, she would challenge him in arm wrestling at the breakfast table, on the porch, in his bedroom, and brought all her will and strength into the contest, her face reddening as her arm became a brace of iron, her face contorted, and then slowly, ever so determinedly, she would press his arm on the table, keep it there while her face became wreathed with triumph and she would break into peals of adolescent, mocking laughter.

The first time, he decided to humor her and let her win with not much difficulty. She had slammed his arm instead. On the second and third times, he decided to teach her a lesson, but she won two out of three bouts, and there came a time when he said he wasn't going to waste his energies on stupid contests.

He brought her things, a bag of Hershey's Kisses, a teenage book scrounged at some bargain counter, plastic geegaws and pins and she would hug him in simple affection.

She was now almost as tall as he and he blamed his genes for not growing any taller. Her black hair was glossy and her eyes were bright even in those moments when she was peeved or sad. Buddy was her constant companion, her "big brother," and it was to him that she also confided her "crushes," and the early problems of color that she was soon aware of, which Buddy came to realize earlier though not as keenly for all along, he knew he was not born in America, and his beginnings were to be found across the ocean.

For all their affection for each other, Jessie envied Buddy; her father talked so often with him, guiding him. Buddy could see the pleasure in Professor Wack's eyes every time he went to him and

23

asked questions not so much about the past but about the broader issues of how events are shaped. And one afternoon, James Wack came upon Buddy in the study reading aloud the poetry of Langston Hughes:

I've known rivers:
I've known rivers ancient as the world and older than
the flow of human blood in human veins.

My soul has grown deep like the rivers.

I bathed in the Euphrates when dawns were young
I built my hut near the Congo and it lulled me to sleep.
I looked upon the Nile and raised the pyramids above it.
I heard the singing of the Mississippi when Abe Lincoln
went down to New Orleans, and I've seen its muddy
bosom turn all golden in the sunset.

I've known rivers;
Ancient, dusky rivers.

My soul has grown deep like the rivers.

"This is the story of humanity, Dad," he had said when James Wack asked what he thought of the poem. And Buddy wasn't even eighteen then.

Jessie could not elicit such attention from her father. But she was his daughter and Buddy was only an adopted son. It came to Buddy early enough that this was one way he could endear himself, to grow up in his father's image, to be interested in what interested the professor.

And the Philippines? It was some dismal and distant shadow which had no claim on him other than as a casual subject for study, if only so Professor Wack could see, indeed, that this young, brown boy had the makings of a searcher too, as James Wack had always been.

2

SERENA FONG was Chinese, but was thoroughly a California girl for she was born in San Francisco's Chinatown. Her parents ran a small grocery on Stockton Street near the Sacramento corner selling Oriental food. Her parents and another sister lived in the apartment above the store. Like Buddy, she was a senior at Berkeley majoring in history—she in East Asian, and he in Southeast Asian. She also helped in the shop, preparing the Chinese vegetables, or filling up the containers with dried shrimp, mussel, abalone, and other exotica that make Chinese food.

Serena was three years older than Buddy. Like many girls of her generation, she was very sports-conscious and had been in the university decathlon team. She would have pursued sports more were it not for the rigors of study. In her tennis outfit, her legs were well-shaped, and her bosom was best complimented by the silk cheongsam she sometimes wore; though Serena was thoroughly American, there were instances when she liked to be Chinese, to revel in that identity.

They had met at the East Asiatic Library at Durant for both wanted the same book, Karl Wittfogel's *Oriental Despotism,* and they had asked one another why the interest in the book.

They went out Sather Gate, into the square and from there to a coffee shop across the street for what had seemed like one of those casual campus meetings. They talked till it was really dark and Serena had to catch the late bus back to San Francisco. He had a Porsche convertible and he took her home instead.

Again, they saw each other till it became obvious to both that there was more than just intellectual curiosity between them. Soon enough, that kind of casual physical contact, the touching of hands, the affectionate kiss that easily became an intimation of something which both wanted, and so it did happen finally, two months after that first library meeting.

Professor Wack was lecturing in the east, and had brought Jessie with him. Except for Porfiria, the housekeeper, the big house was all his. (On this afternoon, Serena was in a quilted, blue silk Chinese coat.)

"If my folks find out that I was here with you," she told him knowing she would stay at the apartment the whole night, "they'd surely kill me. Oh, they're so old-fashioned!" Serena prided in being modern, in being able to make decisions for herself, but just the same she had to abide by the wishes of her parents who wanted her to date only Chinese boys. She was so interested in the history of China, a history that Buddy had started to get interested in for he knew it was not Magellan who had "discovered" the Philippines as had appeared in history books.

He had read on the Philippines, anthropology, archaeology, and one of the Berkeley librarians, who was from Manila, was most helpful; she even told him of the New York Public Library and the collections at Yale and at Ann Arbor which he could explore.

A cold February evening. He had been working on his history paper on Chinese contacts in archipelagic Southeast Asia. By then, he had also started taking Mandarin lessons in the evenings, convinced that to know Southeast Asia, one must know China, Buddhism, and even Hinduism. Serena was a great help; not only could she read and write Chinese, she was also a competent Mandarin and Fukienese speaker.

She was comfortable in his embrace, maybe because he reminded her so much of some distant ideal, some South Sea youth, wearing a sarong, a wreath of flowers on his head, something she saw in an old movie with Dorothy Lamour and Bob Hope, and still again, the islands and the languorous spell they had cast over so many westerners—Conrad, Maugham, and she had read them all.

"The Chinese diaspora has been an ongoing process for centuries, Buddy," she said as she nestled closer to him. San Francisco

26

winters can get cold; she wore a dark red, quilted Chinese coat over her yellow dress. Buddy had not turned on the heat; Jessie had challenged him not to do so, that this was one way he could build resistance to the greatest physical pressures. Jessie was very right; the body could be conditioned, like the mind. But he was not going to lead an ascetic, spartan life. The circumstances in the Wack household would not permit that.(Growing up in America had taught him not just to appreciate comfort but sensuality as well.)

"Would it be possible to find documents of Chinese efforts to colonize archipelagic Southeast Asia in the old records—if they can be found in the many remote and inaccessible Chinese archives?"

"Sure, if the Communists allow it," she said. She had cousins who had tried to escape from China. Some made it to the United States and others were waiting it out in Hong Kong.

They talked about themselves. "I have no memory," Buddy quickly admitted. "You see, I am without a past, I don't know who my parents were although I do know who took care of me when I was young. And then my father came along." He told her about Professor Wack.

She was surprised. "Of course, I know of him," she said, her eyes sparkling. "He is one of the best cultural anthropologists in the country. I heard he lectured in French to a visiting group from the Sorbonne."

"That's where he got his Ph. D.," Buddy said matter-of-factly, used as he was now to hearing such encomiums about his father.

ANOTHER day, in the late afternoon, the sky was cloudless, porcelain blue, and the Berkeley hills ahead were a darkening wall of pine and eucalyptus. They had left the university library full of questions. Seated in the square beyond Sather Gate, they sipped coffee from paper cups.

"I am filled with a great curiosity about the people to whom I belong, my tribe—to put it plainly. I wish I could say that my father was this and my mother was that—but I don't remember them. And now, here I am, truly alone."

She touched his hand. "I know that feeling," she said, the sympathy shining in her eyes. For the first time, Buddy realized that Serena Fong was beautiful.

"What is America but the sum total of the contribution of its native peoples? And its immigrants? The Boston Brahmin—the aristocracy as they would like to be called—who are they, Buddy, but immigrants, too? This is a nation of immigrants! So don't feel out of place in this country because of your race, your color."

It was, of course, comforting to hear that from Serena. "Look," she said, "tomorrow, I want you to see Locke—that's where my grandfather used to live—he built a house there."

He picked her up on a cold morning at their store in Chinatown and they quickly got out of the city environs—the new freeways were a great help. The softly rolling hills were quickly turning to gold again as the sun burnished everything. Only the week before rain had fallen in torrents, creating landslides in the residential areas that had begun to clamber up the low mountains.

Towards Stockton, a heavy fog blanketed the land, grey and pervasive, soaking everything with permeable lead. But the fog did not last long and when it finally lifted, the sun shone bright on the green but fallow fields. Towards Walnut Grove trellised vineyards, shorn of their leaves, spread out.

"You know, of course," Serena said, looking at Buddy briefly, as she pointed out to him where they should make a turn. "The Chinese built the railroads, they were brought in from China—coolies—by the thousands."

"The way it was with the Filipino migratory workers," Buddy said. "Although that was in more recent times."

Serena did not need a road map; she had been to Locke several times, particularly when her grandfather was still alive and had refused to leave the house he had built.

One of the tributaries of the Sacramento River came into view, a wide grey swath, on both sides the levees the Chinese had built in the twenties. "My grandfather worked here for years, and when he had saved enough he didn't only build his house, he also sent for his wife and children from China."

In the yards of some of the farmers' homes, orange trees laden with yellow fruit stood like bouquets, and beyond, the orchards of Bartlett pears in even rows, leafless as of now, the new branches sprouting from their tops like a forest of orange arrows.

Locke was a huddle of wooden frame houses, listing and inconsequential from down the levee. They eased down to what could be its main street, more wooden houses with wooden balconies looming over them. He parked the car before a battered building that could have come straight out of a Hollywood western, only this was real for people were still living in it.

"My grandfather and the other Chinese used to live in Walnut Grove close by, but the whole neighborhood burned down—I don't know how, but they say it was because the Chinese were not liked...I don't know, you hear all sorts of things, even now, and that's why they moved to this place. Then it seemed so far from everything, so that they could live as they wished."

She guided Buddy down a boardwalk, and at the end, this wooden house, now occupied by another family after her grandfather had died. She pointed out to him the Chinese character her grandfather had carved on one of the posts. "That's my last name," she said.

Driving back to San Francisco, the fog had lifted completely and the jade-covered hills shone in the sun, "I'm so glad you took me to Locke," Buddy said. "Looking at those levees, I'm sure they had protected the Sacramento delta from flooding and assured the farmers a good crop every year."

"There's wonderful fishing there, too," Serena told him. "Striped bass, sturgeon...have you ever seen one?"

Buddy shook his head.

"It's a big fish, sometimes over a hundred pounds. Its eggs—that's what the Russians make caviar from."

"We'll have to go fishing next time," Buddy said.

She laid her hand on his thigh and pressed it, the pleasant sensation coursing quickly through him. When she looked at him, there was merriment in her eyes, and a promise as well of better things to come.

She told him afterwards about how her parents still talked about the old home in Amoy before they migrated to the United States in 1939, how they had saved and persevered to set up the grocery and how, after so much hard work, they were able to buy their own store, and a farm in nearby San Joaquin...

But that was not all; she told him, too, how it was to return to China, as did some Chinese Americans who wanted to help, who ached to prove their Chineseness by being supportive at least of the Chinese experiment. And at eighteen, she had to see for herself.

"I don't know if you consider yourself American," Serena told him. "I know you grew up here."

"Since I was six. I was brought here," he said, recalling the troop ship, the humid quarters below the deck, and his first enthralling view of the ocean, the total blackness on starless nights.

Serena was a sympathetic listener; where, after all, does life start? He was risen from nothing, as when he woke high up in the mountain, and still again when he fell down the cliff into the warm bosom of the earth, and yet again, when he woke up in a cavern surrounded by big black men.

At night, when he was alone and the noise of harried living was stilled and he could hear only his breathing and the beating of his heart, he would close his eyes and remember, remember—what are the images that have lingered in your mind, in the depths of your soul? Always, Apo Tale and Inay Mayang, always, an old and kindly man, and a woman so beautiful she was now just a dream. He would doze off and when he woke up, the questions still rankled.

He was seeing Serena quite often then, and by Christmas 1960, he had also developed with her an intimacy so exalting not so much for its physical completeness but because it gave him, finally, something solid to cling to, unlike in the past when even with Professor Wack and sweet Jessica, he seemed to float in limbo, trackless and without the points of a steady compass for they both seemed to come not from someplace he was completely familiar with, the earth he first strode on when he was born, and this was what Serena had then meant to him, the beginnings of a reality that must define itself soon enough, according to both their aspirations.

"It is such a cliché, Buddy, I wouldn't have told you if I didn't see myself in you, except I think your problem is more acute than mine," Serena said.

The communists had brought new hope to China; she was in senior high and, like many other young Americans of Chinese ancestry, was inspired to go there, to help rebuild the ancestral homeland. Many went not just from the United States but from all over the world, and particularly from countries in Asia where many overseas Chinese had sunk their roots for generations.

Three years of unremitting physical work and later, of disillusion for she realized soon enough that she was not meant to be there, that San Francisco was home, and not some dingy commune in Amoy.

"It was not the hard work, I quickly got used to that," she said, "or the fact that there were so many things they didn't even have, you know, simple flush toilets—these were minor irritations; it was that there, we were not allowed to be ourselves, and the time we were told crying was forbidden, I knew I had to go home. Rather, run away, first to Hong Kong and then back to San Francisco." Then she asked what he had dreaded to ask of himself.

"Do you want to go back to the Philippines, Buddy?"

For a while, he couldn't answer as a host of imaginings swooped into his mind.

It was not so often now that he had long talks with his father; it was wrong to interrupt the professor at his work and it seemed that as Jessie and he grew older, he had less time for them.

But Serena Fong had time, time to talk about the China she had experienced, time to relive those rash enthusiasms that had enabled

30

her to answer with a big yes when she asked herself: Do I really want to go to China and devote my life to it?

"I don't know," Buddy said finally. "There's really no reason. Why should I?"

"It's different out there, Buddy," Serena told him, remembering her own disillusionment, the brutal life in the agricultural commune where she had been assigned, the only overseas Chinese to be there.

"I realize that," he said, "but all that I know now are what I read in the papers, the magazines. I've even forgotten what it feels like to be in the tropics. Coconut trees, bananas."

"Are you homesick for all those things?"

He shook his head.

"When I was in China, I felt homesick for San Francisco, the wonderful weather, hamburgers."

"I don't even know what Filipino food tastes like," he admitted readily. "The first time I had a really full stomach, I had eaten all I could of dehydrated eggs, mashed potatoes, bread, peanut butter...."

THAT EVENING, after Professor Wack had showered and was in his library reading the papers, a glass of Jack Daniels by his side, Buddy went to him. James Wack had aged, his curly brown hair was now turning grey, and there were ridges on his brow. He had also developed a slight stoop, and his gangling walk now seemed to teeter and if he hurried, it seemed he would fall, a drunk unable to steady himself. But his mind had always been firm and fresh, and the new studies he was making on Africa as the cradle of civilization had elicited quizzical retorts—a part of the Negro effort to ennoble himself, and nothing more.

"Dad," he began when the professor looked up. "How important to a man, to a family or even to a nation is the past?"

It seemed as if Professor Wack had anticipated the question, a bright grin washed his face and, shaking his head, "A big question," he said patronizingly, mockingly in that often taciturn manner which Buddy by now knew as a kind of rebuke against those who were not serious enough. "Why do you ask?"

Buddy sat on the leather sofa across the table which was piled high with papers. "I'm doing history—you suggested it."

"You were beginning to ask the real questions, Buddy," he said, "Yes, but even if I hadn't encouraged you, you would have studied it anyway, on your own, not because it's important to your career but because you want to know..."

How right Professor Wack was! He now realized that, indeed, he needed no prodding.

"I met this girl, Dad."

"First time you tell me about a girl. Is it serious?"

Buddy smiled. "Not yet, but I like her a lot. She's from here, Chinatown. She's in history, too."

"Oh, like yourself. I should have known." The professor laughed slightly, approvingly.

"She heard you lecture on ancient and tribal medicine. She enjoyed it very much. I'm sorry I missed it. I should have recalled easily that when I was little there was an old man who knew a lot about herbs and other medicines from the forest. My grandfather..."

"Back to that holy mountain again?" Professor Wack stood up. In his Donegal tweed jacket, he had about him an aura of a man who had fully lived, the roughness at the edges already softened. "I wish I had had more time when I was in the Philippines," he continued. "I would have wanted to know more about the old cultures there, the Ifugaos particularly. When these old tribes—if I may call them that, although it is a bit patronizing—when they disappear, not by choice, mind you, but by the intrusion of modernization into their domain, many things will die, not just their way of life but their knowledge of the environment, their ancient medical practices. So now you have a Chinese girlfriend. One thing about Chinese civilization is that it is a continuum. Many of their old practices, particularly in medicine, are still in use today. Do you know how long acupuncture has been in use in China? For centuries and Western doctors are now just beginning to see its possibilities."

"I am convinced that the Filipinos—or the inhabitants of those islands—had contacts with Chinese and other Southeast Asian cultures before the Spaniards came," Buddy said with conviction.

The professor interrupted him. "Buddy, never say you are convinced until you have the document in your hand. Say you are 'of the mind.' In the event that you cannot prove your thesis, then there is always a way out."

It was advice he would never forget.

"Of course, you are very, very right. The Chinese traded everywhere—that is what contemporary archaeology is now revealing. They were a civilized people; they had moveable type a thousand years before Gutenberg. They imparted a lot of their technology to Southeast Asia. All the Southeast Asian and Pacific peoples were great seafarers. The distances they traversed on the open ocean—how could they have done it without the aid of modern navigation? And yet they did, with native wisdom. They knew the tides, currents, the direction of the wind and, yes, by looking at the shape of clouds, they also foresaw the weather. And most of all, they plotted the stars. Without a compass, yet they seldom went wrong...."

Buddy recalled the first time he experienced the ocean, its incomprehensible vastness, heaving, alive—how deep was it, and how wide? He was so shocked when one of the soldiers told him it was not drinkable because it was salty, but that it sustained life nonetheless.

Professor Wack sat back, stroked his beardless chin. This was truly his domain, this large library, the long oak writing table cluttered with books and folders, the reading lamp revealing the craggy face, and all around, the encompassing shadows of bookshelves.

Buddy was now equipped with the capacity to understand, to absorb, and make conclusions. Professor Wack would have wanted to be as black as the next Negro man on the street so that he did not have to explain himself. Oh, but to grow in a society where black was considered ugly, even evil, and everything good and beautiful was white.

What was he then? He recalled the Malay myth, how God had taken this piece of clay and molded it into a man, then put the clay in the kiln; it stayed there too long, and when he brought it out it was black. He took another piece of clay and molded it again, and this time, it stayed too short a time in the kiln and when it was brought out, the man was white. Then, he molded another piece of clay and put it in the kiln. Finally, the time was perfect and when he brought it out, it was brown!

Professor Wack had roared with laughter and when he had quieted down, he said that each race has its creation myth. "But the first recorded civilization in the world—something we can prove with data—was created by black people, when white men were still primitive food gatherers and hunters. You know so much of history but without a racial slant to it. Well, Buddy, would it surprise you to learn that ancient Egypt was a nation of blacks, Asians and Semites? Many of the pharaohs were black. I wouldn't be surprised if Cleopatra was partly black. Through the centuries, the men who wrote the history of Europe diminished then completely erased the black origins of European culture..."

Once again, cultural anthropology, how he had gone to Africa with a team from the Sorbonne who did not care if he was Negro, how he had happily spent all those years in Paris, well provided for by his father's largesse, to search for man's beginnings, and his. He luxuriated in freedom in France; in America he still had to seek it.

anthropology -

study of mankind.

33

"Even with our modern machines," he continued, "there is so little that we know of this past...must you spend your time looking for yours?"

"I don't even know where to begin," Buddy said. "Maybe it's just a fad, the Negroes going back to Africa, becoming Muslims. One thing sure, fad or not, it is very compelling—and interesting."

"So much can be found in the cemeteries of culture. The libraries. A great tragedy for scholars and for all men happened more than sixteen hundred years ago. Do you know, Buddy, that there was a great library in Alexandria? It was destroyed by fire. All that knowledge of the ages stored in scrolls—the scholars had to reconstruct from those ashes what we know of that past today."

So then, Salvador dela Raza, is that your real name? What is it that throbs in those arteries, what undeciphered messages are implanted in your brain?

IN THE summer vacation of his senior year, Buddy wanted to travel, not so much to see America but to go to places with a sense of discovery.

At breakfast one morning, he asked where it was best to begin. Jessie, having gulped down her orange juice, said brightly, "Wherever you go, take me with you, will you, Buddy?"

Professor Wack seemed to divine his thoughts. "No, Jessie," he said quickly. "You will be a distraction. A great burden. Maybe, when you are much older..."

Jessie pouted then left them. "Will Serena be joining you?" Professor Wack asked, a twinkle in his eye.

"Serena and I, we've tried the university library," he said. "It's very good, but there isn't much on the pre-Hispanic past of the Philippines. Serena reads Chinese..."

"Don't bank on that," Professor Wack said. "The old Chinese characters—there are so few truly trained scholars who can read them. Even the old scripts in any of the European languages—you have to have special knowledge to read them. But that is not the point..." He stood up and walked to the shelf at the far end of the room, and pulled out a copy of Pigafetta's account of his trip with Magellan. "There are clues here," he said. "Read it carefully." Then he brightened up. "At the Newberry way back, I came across an old Chinese document—it had been translated. Maybe, you'll find something there."

THEIR FIRST TIME in Chicago and in July, the city was broiling and the sun bore down from a cloudless sky in a fury that baked

34

everything. But thank God for the bursts of wind along the lake shore, particularly in the afternoons.

They had a room at the Allerton, a tall, dark brick hotel close to the library where Professor Wack himself had stayed. After a walk through the blistered streets, it was sheer bliss to be enfolded in its airconditioned sanctuary.

The Newberry was a short walk across Michigan Avenue. The librarian in charge of the rare documents was very helpful; she even showed them the vault where the manuscripts were kept, and she brought them out for them to look at with such care they seemed so precious and so fragile, sheets with blotted-out writing. They were even provided with a kind of pillow on which to lay the manuscripts so that they would not break.

Serena was pleased not so much for herself, but for Buddy. Now there was a tenuous link in the past between her people and his, just as there was now this bonding between them, strengthened even more here in Chicago's repository of some of the oldest testaments of Oriental culture.

"See, Buddy," she said happily, "it may not have been the ideal relationship; as with all relationships there were conflicts. Maybe when my people traded with yours, they drove very hard bargains. But I'm sure they brought a lot of things other than what they bartered. And I'm sure that even then, people being people..." she squeezed his hand under the reading table, "there were also personal relationships...more than this." She pointed to the text before them, the English in very quaint idiom for it seemed like a direct translation of the Chinese original. But the drawings of the early Filipinos were very detailed, their headdress, the exquisite jewelry and silk finery of the upperclass women, the simple loincloth of the lower classes and peasants, their lances and bows and arrows...

She turned the yellowed pages very carefully. "Imagine, going all the way to China to raid. What a warlike people yours must have been. All that passion. Now I know..." She smiled at him.

"But they did not take slaves. Or killed wantonly. It seems they went to war to avenge an injustice. They were honorable, upright—look at how the Chinese trusted them in trade. Leaving goods unattended on the beach..." Buddy said, the translation so lucid now.

LATER IN the evening, when Serena was asleep, her head nestled in the crook of his arm, it came to him with such brilliant clarity he suddenly came wide awake, the Newberry document like a living collage in his mind, and he wondered about the kind of life his ancestors had lived. His imagination was untrammeled—but he was dealing with reality, an island civilization with foundries for cannon, gold and iron, metalcraft, maybe Chinese-inspired, but just the same, a civilization which Spanish colonization had obliterated.

He slowly pulled out his arm from under Serena's head, careful not to wake her up, then went to the writing desk where his notebooks were; for the past many years since high school, he had kept a journal, recounting desultorily in it the thoughts and the events of the day.

Here was a unique story but how many Filipinos knew about it? Imbibed it in their nature? If the past can be inlaid in the living flesh, then the past becomes alive as well, perpetuated in the collective mind. He should now create the document as it must have been, frantic, frenzied with people, emotions. He thought of Apo Tale, of Inay Mayang—to her most of all should he tell this story, blind and deaf though she was, but alive still—so very much alive in memory. She couldn't die, all that beauty and grace are deathless; he would now write to her, how it was a thousand years ago, how it is today. Inay, I am now your eyes and your ears as well.

3

I AM PARBANGON, the Ulo of Daya, I salute you and all my subjects will do likewise—the brave citizens of this blessed land, now prosperous with trade and produce, ever ready to defend our ramparts with our lives.

Listen to my story, why my heart brims with sorrow, why I lost my most precious jewel, my daughter, Rang-ay. Listen and bear with me, a father derided by fate. I know now that leadership imposes a tremendous moral burden on he who leads; the decisions he must make will tear his heart out, for they could mean upholding tradition, the law, and at the same time hurting or losing someone loved so deeply. Here, there is no muddied thinking for the way is always clear and straight. Bathala, I could have easily turned to a byway and retained still my panoply of power, but I would have been recreant to my calling, my people. They may understand but they will condemn me in their thoughts. So then, Rang-ay, my beloved daughter, forgive me!

I have always loved the sea, its changeable moods a challenge in themselves for those who would dare its crests, its sullen depths the eternal enigma of those who want to sink into it but cannot, somehow, touch its bottom for who can measure the deep? Though the duties of office no longer permit me to go to sea, I still do when the call comes, as it did in the recent past when I journeyed up the coast and across the heaving waters, to bring my call for justice—others would call it vengeance—to the land of the Narrow Eyes.

37

As my father's son, I must do no less, do what is ordained not just by my calling, but by my blood. Those who dare now to question me—remember, I did not aspire for this lofty position but the elders chose me, confirming their judgment in my father's name. So I prostrate myself to Apo Daga, and feed from her fecund breasts, draw from her the sustenance that will make my people flourish and endure. As my illustrious father said, Life in all its mystery is the greatest challenge because it is in our hands to do what we want with it, to know ourselves fully, to explore the depths of the mind which we cannot completely do even if it is our very own.

And then, there is the sea—how to track it as far as we can to spread our commerce, even to those who were once our declared enemies. Unity! Unity! this is what my father had dinned into us Taga Daya and it was always with great difficulty that this had to be achieved for there are always ambitious men who think themselves more capable of ruling, braver in combat and more assiduous in the administration of government.

Thus, after many a season of planting and joyful harvest that filled to overflowing our granaries, of calm weather and ferocious winds, we have become united. Those of us whose skins are brown fight our neighbors no more although I could have easily waged war as my forebears had done to make our will prevail. Now, the old warriors shake their heads as they watch our young men grow flabby with prosperity and peace, no longer well-trained in the art of war.

I have always listened to the advice of the elders. As I myself grow old, I can see clearly that their counsel is not just the result of experience and keen observation; they are also always thinking of what is good for Daya, this precious land which we have made prosperous.

Knowing that peace must be preserved, I have not completely abandoned the techniques of the warrior as well as the finer attributes of diplomacy. But in everything I do for Daya, I have done so with a sense of justice.

Do not for once think that my family was never important to me, that I never put it above anything else; I love my children, my beautiful Rang-ay most of all for she was most virtuous of all the young women in Daya, she was the most skilled in the arts of embroidery and weaving. Rang-ay, my youngest, upon whom I had heaped so much love and attention, perhaps unfairly, but then, she was my only daughter since Apo Langit had blessed my wife and me with six boys, who in their time I know will also prove their worth not just as my sons and bearer of my blood, but as men of intelligence and virtue.

Rang-ay, wherever you are, at one with the spirits of our forbears, forgive this grieving father for what he had to do in the name of duty, honor and all the sacred edicts by which we have always lived!

It happened that year, during the start of the harvest season, when the bat-winged boats of the Narrow Eyes came again to Daya to trade. We had always welcomed them for they brought to us silk, porcelain, lead, tin and silver. With our foundries, we forged steel rims for their carriage wheels. We bartered or sold them ivory, pearls, amber, ebony and sapan wood.

The weather had changed so much—the last rainy day had passed, and now, a cool wind breathed upon the land, scented with the harvest which was spread in the fields but which would soon be gathered in sheaves and stored in our communal granaries.

Always a festive welcome for them just as they also welcomed us into their big boats—I, most of all upon whom all goodwill and authority resided.

They entered our harbor usually in the early morning but even before they rounded the point, their arrival was announced well in time with the beating of gongs whose messages travel faster than a man on his swift two feet.

This is now the tenth harvest season that this particular boat had come and we would meet them again—Old Scarred Face, his son and his crew— all of them fine men whose language, unfortunately, we understood but little. They did speak ours, though, slowly with heavy accent, and where there were no words, the hands, the eyes and the whole body spoke just as lucidly.

Old Scarred Face—I've always called him that since I first met him because of this deep scar across his right cheek, inflicted, he had told me, by pirates who had attacked his ship in the south. He always brought his youngest son, then a boy but now a grown and handsome man, very well-mannered and polite in his dealings, particularly in his regard for my daughter and her brothers.

As it always happened, they would lower a small boat, row to the shore where we waited. It was always I who went first and as it had happened in the past, I always brought with me one of my sons until Rang-ay who was but a little girl insisted that she visit the trading vessel, too.

Now Rang-ay was a young woman, already promised in marriage to Tured, the youngest son of the Ulo of Amianan. Like his father, Tured was also of noble bearing and as a young warrior was already skilled in the craft of combat, although such a skill had not been tested except in annual after-harvest games; our lands have had a long period of peace, revered and protected by all for our elders knew only too well the horrors of war as it had descended upon them in the past.

And so they stayed in our shores for seven days during which there was much intermingling, our people went to the beach to look at the goods they had brought, cloth, spearheads, dried fish, salted fruits, and yes, so many jars and plates. Often, these were unattended, and we just brought to the shore, too, what we traded in return: beeswax, gum, rice, dried meats. On the afternoon of the seventh day, they hoisted sail and left.

It was that night that we discovered Rang-ay was not in the house; by midnight when she had not yet returned, I was not alarmed; as had

39

happened often in the past, a girl her age often went to sleep with the other single girls in the house for maidens.

By the next day when she did not show up, I started worrying so I had my sons search for her. It was in vain. Late that second night, I gathered the girls who were closest to her and asked them what had happened, and one of them, the last who saw her, said she was in the boat of the Narrow Eyes.

Treachery! And I had trusted them, Old Scarred Face and his son, welcomed them to our shore without lifting a blade. Now, there shall be war.

I had one of my sons despatched to Amianan, to tell Tured what had happened. Rang-ay was promised in marriage to him, and as is the custom, he already had a lien on her. What happened to her was already within his responsibility; wedding arrangements had been discussed, the gifts between his parents and us exchanged.

In two days, Tured came. He was in great distress. He brought with him two dozen of the bravest warriors of Amianan, fully armed and provided.

The Narrow Eyes had a full two days start but speed was in our favor for our war boats could go faster than theirs with a good wind pushing us, while theirs seemed to wallow helplessly even in the briskest breeze. And finally, if there was no wind, we had rowers whose stamina had long been tested.

We had to make a lot of preparations for we were not only going to war, we were also venturing into waters we did not know other than what we had learned from Old Sirib, the helmsman, who had sailed the seas longer than any of us. When he was young, like some of our older seamen he had sailed to Champa, to Srivijaya, and to the land of the Narrow Eyes and those of the Hairy People farther in the North and had brought back stories of lands covered with ice, stories too strange for us to imagine but which we know were true, for Old Sirib was not one to concoct stories of such incredible magnitude.

No time was to be wasted but just the same, it took us a full two days to gather food, firewood and coconuts which would provide us with water and food.

Ready at last, the priestess gathered us on the shore, our war boats nearby; it was a morning clear as a mountain spring and her plaintive voice rose above us and our silence, imploring Apo Daga, Apo Init and all the spirits of our ancestors to bless our journey. Then the sacrificial pigs were slain, their blood soaking the sand, the meat we took with us.

Twenty boats, each armed with a brass cannon; twenty boats, five hundred men determined to wage war on the Narrow Eyes and rescue my Rang-ay. I prayed that she be unharmed, or as it had often happened, given *up for prey to the men in the boats, their lusts heightened by the prolonged absence from their loved ones.*

We were not at the mercy of the wind the way the boats of the Narrow Eyes were. Their prows were much too broad to cut the waters and to maneuver quickly. We followed the coast of all the islands, the open sea to our left, mapped out in the heavens by the stars. The wind was strong, our buri palm sails were bloated, the wind whistling in them. Old Sirib was in my lead boat, scanning the far distance to our right where landfall was, a dark strip in the night, the lights of distant villages burning.

Then the next morning, the wind suddenly died, the sea was calm like the unruffled surface of a pond. It was time for the rowers to work, their paddles glistening in the water as they moved in unison to the beat of the bamboo drums.

On the third day, there was no more outline of land to our right— it was time, according to Old Sirib, for us to strike out across that seemingly limitless expanse to the land of the Narrow Eyes. As if the spirit of the sea was on our side, now, a strong wind sprang and filled our sails. On some of the boats, the collapsible bamboo ladders were set up, mounted by our seamen long-trained in looking out far ahead into the water.

On the afternoon of the tenth day, their shouts erupted as one—land ahead, and indeed, towards the horizon, was this long serpent of low mountains against the sky, the huge domain of the Narrow Eyes about which I knew a little as we had all listened to the stories of Old Sirib. He had not only been there; he had served as guide to one of their captains in his youth and had learned of their strange ways, how they lived, traded and fought.

As we drew closer to the land, in the distance, still far from the shore was the boat of Old Scarred Face—I know its shape, its dark bat-winged sail. Would that be where my dear Rang-ay is held prisoner? No mistake about it, Old Sirib said; it had just come from Daya, so it was filled with produce and was deep in the water.

Once more, I gathered my headmen, my prospective son-in-law among them, five hundred seasoned warriors who had fought the pirates of Tausu and Achi, the slave traders who had often come to raid our shores. They knew how it was to fight in groups in our swift boats, or on land. Again, I explained to them the strategy I had refined with Old Sirib's assistance during the nights at sea, when looking at the stars that sailed across the sky, I would imagine how the Narrow Eyes would fight. We would surprise them, move against them in the safety and cover of darkness, three hundred men going ashore, a hundred to go deep into the country, and two hundred on both sides to protect our flanks; one hundred men to attack the boat, and a hundred men to stay behind at sea in reserve.

For many years now, we had perfected means of communicating with one another: We had water buffalo horns as well as conch shells for signalling by sound and all the warriors of Daya knew them. There was, however, no signal for retreat for each warrior was expected to do his duty to the very end.

As for signals to our boats in battle, we have them, too—we raised buntings of different colors, to call the boats together, to maneuver, to position them so that our arrowmen could fire volleys of iron into the enemy or crush them with our cannon.

The boat of the Narrow Eyes wallowed in the distance, hardly moving as the wind seemed to have become still. Which was all the more to our advantage—we would be able to attack at night. After our supper that night—we drank cups of cane wine, a good meal of leftover rice and roasted dried fish—we proceeded to paint ourselves black with finely ground charcoal mixed with coconut oil. Our allies from Amianan whom Tured had brought would be held back in reserve. Tured did not like this, but this was not his war nor that of his warriors. It was ours, and this he understood.

Before sunset, we had all our sails lowered so that from a distance, along the horizon, our fleet would not be sighted. Now, our splendid rowers went to work, our prows slicing neatly through the shallow waves.

The boat leaders who went to the shore to see to it that we would not be attacked from that part of the country told me later how it was—how easily they had roused the natives and drove them toward the interior to the sanctuary of their walled town. They had killed a few Narrow Eyes who had dared to fight back although I suspect that while they were all telling the truth, there was too much enthusiasm among them to have shown mercy to the poor devils who had become victims of our wrath.

I led the attack on the boat. Two lights, one on the stern and the other in the bow, unerringly guided us to it. It was about to cast anchor—the men on its deck were not aware of us; the sea around was dark, and we boarded it from the rear and seaward.

Did they not wonder at all about the sound of our conch shells announcing our regrouping? I heard it clearly—surely, the anxiety of being home must have been so great it rendered them deaf.

We swam—it was my first time in such cold water and I was numb and shivering when we started clambering up the side, while in the near distance, the arrowmen and the other warriors were ready if those of us who were boarding were repelled.

We had made no mistake.

We surprised them completely. Those who were on deck jumped into the water. Others ran below to get their weapons, but too late, we had swarmed like locusts on the hapless ship, and we slaughtered them in close combat, awkward and unprepared as they were. Old Scarred Face and his son tried to fight their way out but they, too, fell before our lances. Leaving them dead or dying on the deck, we searched the hold. A shout from one of my men took me to where Rang-ay was, cowering in a corner. She could not recognize any of us, painted as we were in black. In the glow of our torches, she looked frightened and helpless. Only when I called out her name did she know it was I and she rushed to me, trembling and in tears.

She was immediately lowered to one of the boats which had clung alongside the ship. Now, the men hauled away its cargo—that would be part of our booty, the grain, the cotton and all that they had brought back from Daya and elsewhere; we also gathered all their weapons, all the metal objects which we would recast in our foundries. When we had emptied the ship of its valuable cargo, we put our torches to it, first the sails which burned quickly. Those who went inland had breached the walls of their town. They did their work quickly, and returned to the boats and loaded them with their booty. We rowed away, the bamboo drums beating faster. We had lost ten men whose bodies we took with us; we did not want them defiled by the enemy; we will surrender them to the sea, giving them the honors due them. Thus, we withdrew quickly, the burning ship lighting the shore. When daylight broke, we were already far away in the open sea and beyond the easy reach of vengeance.

We had accomplished our purpose, there was no need to wage further war against the Narrow Eyes. They would certainly appreciate that we did not kill women and children, nor did we abduct anyone as slaves. Certainly we had achieved more than rescue Rang-ay. Five hundred men had crossed the sea and seen this vast, unknown country—it would not be unknown anymore to them or to our future helmsmen. This, in itself, was the learning that would do us well into the future.

All through the voyage back, the sea was kind and wind filled our sails so that not once did we dip our paddles into the water. Our booty included food, sauces, salted legs of pig, dried fruits unfamiliar to us. We ate them ravenously for they all tasted so good.

My jewel now safe in our midst, I pondered over what we had achieved, the wine of victory having been drained from our arteries. What had I done most of all? I had raised a war fleet and sent it across the sea to avenge the honor of Daya, to fulfill a pledge to the people of Amianan. But at the same time, I realized I had risked the lives of five hundred men, and for what? For my personal, familial interests which, because I was the Ulo, I had identified as the cause of Daya and my people. But was it really? Would I have done the same if Rang-ay had been a slave girl? the anonymous daughter of some lowly fisherman or peasant? Would I have gone myself to the land of the Narrow Eyes? I doubt it very much, and thinking more about what I had done, I was humbled to my very pores. I was not truly ordained leader of my people—I was just a simple father like all the others and realizing this, I looked at my men, at our many boats gliding with the wind, and I was filled with remorse, a searing hatred of myself which I will always carry with me, but which will always help me in making future decisions.

All through the voyage, too, my dear Rang-ay often cried, and her eyes were always swollen. Tears of relief, of happiness—that was what I thought they were, and why not? She was going back home to her people, to Tured to whom she had already been betrothed and to a future that was assured of order, and benificence. She would give me and my wife a handsome brood of grandchildren so that in my old age, I could look ahead to years of peace with Amianan.

But it was not so; the gravity of what had happened was missed by me entirely till after two moons when I decided it was time for the wedding to take place, and preparations must now start to confirm what had already been agreed upon by myself and Tured's father.

Her mother came out of the house that evening, rushed into the yard where I was talking with the elders, precisely about the marriage that would strengthen the bonds I had already established with the people of Amianan, bonds skillfully nurtured through the years so that never again should there be war between Daya and our neighbors.

"Come, my lord, my husband," she said, her voice anguished and shrill. "Ay, there is going to be no wedding."

"And why not?" I asked.

"Ask Rang-ay," she said. But I did not need to ask her; it was my wife to whom my dearest child had already told everything. She was not taken against her will by the Narrow Eyes—she had gone on her own free will, not so much because she did not want to marry Tured, that was one reason, but because she and the son of Old Scarred Face had had a meeting of mind and soul, and that she was now with an alien's child.

It all came clear as sunrise, those years when she was still a child, how I had brought her to the ship of the Narrow Eyes and often left her to play with Old Scarred Face's little boy. But they were children no more, and on remembering, clearer still were the times Rang-ay had waited in anxiety for the Narrow Eyes' ships to come.

For some time, I could not accept what was told me, and then it struck me viciously, the implication of what Rang-ay had done, the shame she had brought upon her parents, to Daya, and the heavy penalty—this she knew, I am sure—that she must pay.

It was much too grievous for me to bear; I did not want to see her, my precious daughter, but I had to.

She came to me, her face sad and pale, and the moment she started talking, I knew only too well that she also knew what had to be done.

44

"Spare my baby, Father," she implored. "He or she will have your blood, your grandchild it is, and when the baby has come, then what must be, must be."

How many days and nights passed in quiet anguish! I thought of ways to avoid destiny, to spare my precious Rang-ay. I could send her away and let her live, or altogether ignore what had happened, continue living and ruling. But people know, they can see, they will talk behind my back, perhaps even to my face. I will ask them to understand—to be in my place. I will ask them for compassion and the fathers and the mothers among them will not quibble, I am sure.

But I am the Ulo, who must live as an example, who must rule with justice! Duty is unswerving. Duty to Daya, to my people.

And so it happened the way Rang-ay wanted it; after the baby was born, it was I who handed her the cup to drink, the same cup into which we dip our arrows so that they would kill more surely, and before she was buried in the forest, away from all the honored dead of Daya, Tured had come upon my bidding, so that he could see her, so that he would know that what must be must be, not just for the sake of our honor, but for our lasting peace.

4

GRADUATION TIME at Berkeley should have been a happy event but wasn't for it was also a time for them to end it all—and part as friends, that was how Serena wanted it. It was a cool July evening as San Francisco evenings always are; somehow even when the rest of the country is simmering, the ocean breeze always sweeps away the pollution of factories and city smog and makes the San Francisco air fresh as well. But for Porfiria, the housekeeper, again, they had the apartment to themselves; Jessie was in summer camp in the east, and Professor Wack had gone to deliver a few lectures in the south.

Beyond the expanse of green lawn, across the darkened bay, the lights of upper-class homes in Tiburon glistened and at the right, Angel Island lay, a dark turtle hump on the water. From underneath the shadows of the Golden Gate Bridge, a passenger ship, all its lights ablaze, ploughed into the bay.

They were comfortably wrapped in each other's arms, domestic intimacy, the time for soothing reminiscence. It was she who broke it quietly. "There has to be an end to all the good things in life, isn't that so, Buddy? she asked, kissing him on the cheek and stroking his hair.

The question startled him; she had never spoken like this before, this premonition of the end was never made in all the times that they had shared. He gazed at her face, her cheeks pinkish in the light of the table lamp, her eyes now grave. "What are you saying, Serena? Of course, there has to be an end to everything—but the circle is endless, as good Buddhists will say."

"My Buddy, always so profound, when there's really nothing for us but this..." she teased him. Turning on her side, she lay on top of him—all that warm flesh and honeyed breath, and that playful smile on that ivory face. He encircled her tightly, affection coursing through him, warming him.

"There is much more," he said. "Look, we have the same interests. But that's not all. There is a sharing between us...This isn't the time to talk about marriage, but I want a life with you now that we truly know each other..." The whole world, his particularly, was at peace, and more so when Serena was like this, as close as skin to skin can be, as all the nerves that move the mind and heart can be. Until Serena, her eyes serious and probing, said. "I know you will always be secure even without me, even if I don't see you again..."

He held her up, cupped her face, her hair falling down and brushing against his face. Even in the soft dark, he could trace the blue veins on the ivory skin, down her breasts where they flowed— tiny rivulets of blue—around the sweet red raisins of her nipples. "What are you talking about, Serena?"

She eased herself slowly to his side and held his hand. For a while, she did not speak, as if she wanted every word clearly measured before it was uttered. "Thank you so much for wanting to share your life with me," she said, "but there is no future for us, Buddy. Does that sound too dramatic?"

He had tensed by then.

"I am getting married, Buddy—maybe next month." Then she said it, "I am Chinese, do not forget that, although I have so often told myself that I am American. And I am, too."

"Who is he?" he asked, his voice hoarse and dry.

"You don't know him," she said. "He is a distant uncle, third uncle you would say; he is my father's third cousin. You have this kind of extended relationship, too. Almost all Asians do."

"But I have no relatives—you know that."

"He is coming to San Francisco, and he wants to stay here, do business here. This is one way he can immediately get a citizenship— by marrying an American."

"I see," he said dryly.

"Don't be angry with me, please," she implored him, touching his face.

And why should he be? No second thoughts, no shrill rancor, she had given herself to him.

"There is something you must know, something I really don't tell people unless they are, well, as close as we are. It is all family. Do you understand, Buddy?"

How could he? To him, family was Jessie and Dad—Professor Wack, that is. There was no one whom he could call his relative—even they who are closest to him were not related to him by blood. How could he ever get that feeling of being closely knit with other human beings? Was it even necessary? Right now, she was the closest and dearest—family, she was family indeed!

He embraced her, all that smoothness and softness, as if this was the last time he would hold her. "Do you love him, Serena? Is there anything between you the way, I hope, there is something lasting between us?"

"No," she said quickly, with emphasis. "Not that kind of feeling at all. In fact, I've seen him only once."

"Then why? Tell me about him," he said, although what she would tell would only add to his hurt.

"There really isn't much to tell," she said, holding on to him. "I barely know him. But my family, and I, myself, owe him so much. More than you can imagine. You don't know how it was in China. You've read about it, but you don't know."

He rose from the bed and put on his plaid robe which was hanging on the bedpost. Outside, from the glass window, San Francisco was a giant casket of lights, and above the bay, the black hills of Marin County, the grey clouds scudding inland.

Serena did not get up. "Let me tell you then," she said, gazing at him across the room, "what it was like out there, in that vast, tortured land. My uncle—this distant relative—was high up in the party, Buddy. He was the one who helped my father get out early enough, and when I was in trouble there, and I wanted out, too, he was the one who helped me get to Hong Kong and from there, back to San Francisco. Now he is coming to America, and he has no intention of going back to China."

He rushed back to her, smothered her face with kisses, murmuring, "Don't, Serena. This is your life now. You can't throw it away because of gratitude."

She put her arms around him as tears started to gather in her eyes and roll down her cheeks, wetting his face. "I am Chinese, Buddy," she said quietly.

She freed herself from his embrace, his entreaties, and calmly started to dress. Wordless, he watched her, and when she had put on her coat, she went to him and kissed him. He wanted to drive her to Chinatown, but she held him back; she called for a taxi instead. She must go home alone and try and leave everything behind.

HE RESPECTED her decision, and though he truly missed her, he did not try to see her at the grocery on Stockton Street. And though he thought of her so much, he denied himself the temptation to wander around Chinatown. Once he saw her across Market Street, talking with a Chinese girl, and once again, at an Emporium sale, this time she was already big with child and holding on to her arm was the uncle who had married her, a short, fat man, balding and seemingly lost.

Then, one afternoon, driving around Chinatown with Jessie who wanted to have a mooncake, they passed Stockton. The grocery was now a dry goods store.

"I have to ask," he explained quickly. "That used to belong to Serena's father."

"I wondered why she never came to see you anymore," Jessie said lightly.

The man who was at the counter did not know where the former owners had really gone; the east, maybe to Boston...he had merely bought the shop from an agency.

He never saw Serena again although every so often, the memory of those days in the apartment in Pacific Heights, everything about her that was enshrined in the mind and heart, would come sometimes as a sweet deluge, sometimes as a twinge of reverie. But as time went by, and Serena was no longer a living throb in the breast, the times when he remembered were few, sometimes resuscitated by an item in the newspapers about refugees in Hong Kong and the bestial excesses of the Cultural Revolution.

HE HAD already seen many brown people like himself, immigrant workers in Market Street, office workers in neat suits in Montgomery where the big banks were. Almost always, he had thought them to be Filipino although they could have been Thai, Indonesian or southern Chinese. *unable to tell anyone's nationality*

He had also developed a fondness for fishing; with Professor Wack he would go on Sunday mornings to the rocks along Pacific Drive or just below the Golden Gate Bridge where schools of salmon passed in their annual flight to the inland waters to spawn. Orientals often sat with them—Japanese and Chinese retirees, and Filipino oldtimers who worked their lines with ardor for they were fishing not just for sport but for food. Their manner was always earnest, their patience stoic; these he saw as virtues for he had become impatient all too often and after an hour of sitting there without a bite, he would start wandering not so much with his mind but on his feet, climbing the higher rocks or walking in the sand where, as it often happened, he would pick up a stray crab to bring home, but only if there was no game warden watching.

HE WAS walking along Grant one afternoon, Serena no longer a blissful distraction on his mind. For the first time, he looked through the dirty glass window of the small, run-down hotel—a rooming house, rather. One of the old men playing billiards had turned to the window and briefly, their eyes locked. Briefly but something happened; Buddy recognized that face at once! He had seen it before in some distant time, perhaps in a forgotten dream. He went inside the narrow lobby which smelled of old leather and fatigued living. More elderly Asian men were inside, seated at the far end of the hall, playing checkers, or simply chatting. But it was the old man at the pool table who fascinated him and he watched the old man walk around the table, sure of himself, sure of his shots, the concentration intense and imprinted on the crumpled face. Then it came swiftly—that face could belong only to one man, Apo Tale!

It all rushed back in a flurry of images, the blessed yesteryears, the joyous days of early boyhood. He watched until he could hold his curiosity no more: he went to the old man dressed in baggy, dark wool pants and a nondescript flannel shirt. This extraordinary coincidence must unravel. "Sir, what is your name?"

The old man had seen him approach. His hair was white, like Apo Tale, and now the aged but affectionate eyes probed into him. "Telesforo San Agustin," he said, smiling, then went back to his game.

For some time, Buddy watched him play. The old man was good, that much he could see although he himself did not play the game.

He watched fascinated with each move the old man made. Truly, he seemed familiar, even the way he shook his head. No, this is not Apo Tale, Buddy reminded himself; this cannot be! In a while, the old man stopped playing. He put the cue on the rack by the wall and walked over to Buddy. "Do I remind you of someone? Your grandfather, perhaps?" he asked. "You have been watching me..."

"Yes, sir," Buddy admitted readily. "There was an old man who took care of me. His name was Apo Tale..."

The old man smiled and soon enough the smile turned into a wide grin, then into a hearty cackle. "I am called Tele, too," he said quickly.

"May I come again and visit with you?" Buddy asked. "I want so much to learn the language of the Philippines, your language."

But Telesforo San Agustin was not Tagalog; he was Ilokano, from Piddig, Ilokos Norte, and like so many of the oldtimers, he had come to the United States in the twenties to work first in the canefields in Hawaii and afterwards in the orange orchards of California and the salmon canneries of Alaska. He could teach Buddy only a little of the Tagalog he had learned from the other Filipinos but more of the Ilokano to which he was born.

The old man invited him to the coffee shop at the corner—one of those small but cozy places with round wooden stools before a long counter. A Chinese girl in white uniform across the counter greeted the oldtimer.

"I come here," Old Tele told him, "because of the siopao." The waitress without being told placed a cup of coffee and the white bun before the oldtimer. "Want the same?" she asked Buddy. The siopao should have been introduced to him much, much earlier by Serena.

"You will find this in the Philippines," Old Tele told him. And forthwith, he started to tell Buddy bits of his life.

THE SIXTIES and the early seventies were tumultous years that brought irrevocable changes as well as heart-wrenching and divisive issues in America. The Negroes—now they called themselves blacks— had finally brought the racial question to the hearts and minds of all Americans. San Francisco was of course different from most American cities—here the racial mix had long been made. It was a different kind of social cauldron; commingled in it was the recognition of homosexual rights—the fags, the homosexuals, now they were called gays.

Neither of these social movements truly affected Buddy. He was certainly very happy that so much of Professor Wack's efforts had finally been entwined with the black movement, although he now seemed so far behind as the blacks were radicalized.

The Vietnam War frightened him for like so many in the university he believed it was a war the United States should not have gone into. The square before Sather Gate, all the way to Bancroft Street, had been transformed into an open forum, and almost every day, the blather of speeches were spilled there, and crowds protesting, Make Love, Not War. These and other vaulting slogans were posted on walls; they adorned the stunted sycamores that palisaded the square. There was very little interest in the Philippines, in what the dictator Marcos was doing. America was in turmoil—there was no unanimity in the support for America's involvement in Vietnam. Indeed, looking back, no issue had so divided the American people more than Vietnam.

Some of his classmates at Lowell High had been drafted, and two dear friends, both black, had not returned. He was working on his master's and students were normally spared from the draft. Having identified himself with the blacks, Buddy could now appreciate their objections to the war, that it was one way by which white America was decimating the black youth, most of them unable to take advantage of the draft exclusion because being poor, they could not afford college. The draft then had a socio-economic bias and blatantly, it was working against the blacks. Worse, as an oppressed minority, they now saw themselves as instruments of a superpower imposing its imperial will upon a Third World nation. But who knows? There was no escaping the draft, unless one fled to Canada or to Europe and that was what many had done.

This was uppermost in his mind when he planned a trip to Spain, as his adviser, Professor Robert Scapini, and his teacher, Professor James Anders, had encouraged him to do. Scapini edited the *Asian Journal*; he was a political scientist of international reputation, having analyzed so much the political movements in the Asian region. His interests had also taken him to the Philippines several times as he followed closely the postwar developments in the country. The young Filipino American scholar had interested him for his conscientiousness and for the far-ranging interests that were similar to his. Professor James Anders of the Department of Anthropology looked at his student not as an aspiring scholar, bright as he was, but in a very genuine sense, the complete searcher who must be encouraged not just in his search but so that he would be certain of what he was looking for.

Both professors had forcefully argued that a scholar working on the Philippines cannot disregard the three centuries that Spain ruled the country. In fact, they told him to go to Mexico, too, for after all, until the opening of the Suez Canal, it was through Mexico that the Philippines was ruled.

5

EARLY ENOUGH, Buddy realized that the mind could be very eclectic in what it wants to retain, and though memory could be a wide pit, swallowing every minutiae cast into it, there were bits which were easily retrievable because they had been cast deepest. Jessica, Jessie—he had known her as a tiny, brown squirming thing, her cries filling the cavernous house, a protest perhaps, an announcement, too, that she was there. Indeed, she was always present in his mind for she grew up badgering him with her problems which became his because it was to him that she first told them—not to Professor Wack who was always seemingly lost in books.

Left alone with him when she was a child, he had looked after her well-being, fed her, read her the stories young Americans were reared in, and invented, too, from Philippine folklore and myths, the spirits that roamed the villages, inhabited big trees and took on the shapes of giant beasts. She had often argued saying these were not true, but she had listened just the same.

Now, Jessica met him at the driveway, distraught, all of her fourteen years smothered with a nameless gloom. There was even a slight tremor to her voice. "I've been waiting for you for two hours, Buddy."

He was taking a crash course in Spanish in preparation for his trip to Spain. He hurried out of the Porsche and with Jessica in tow, went to his apartment. Something was wrong—Jessica's face was so expressive, it was so easy to read her.

"You must promise me," Jessie said, kneeling on the rug before him and holding his hands. "Don't ever tell Daddy about this. Promise me, Buddy."

"I can't promise you that, Jessie," he said, suddenly alarmed. What horrendous secret will Jessie tell me now?

"But you must," she insisted. "This is just between you and me."

Jessica let go his hands and stood up; she walked to the window beyond which lay that perenially idyllic view, the marina below, and beyond, the shimmering blue of the bay, and across it, the bald, emerald hills of Sausalito. Without looking at Buddy, she went on. "I don't want to upset Daddy. I mean, this is a problem I don't want to share with him. I feel very guilty, Buddy, as if I had never really thought about him—or even you, always myself, myself, and now, I'm really in trouble."

"What do you mean?"

She turned around and faced him and in that instant, it seemed as if she would stagger and fall; but she steadied herself, and quietly, "I've been bleeding, Buddy—for the last two hours. Not much, but it won't stop...and I'm scared."

He rushed to her and held her; she began to sob, the grief wrenched out of her in short, quick gusts, and she clung to him trembling. "I had an abortion, Buddy," she whispered. "Oh, I am so scared. Oh, damn him, damn that whitey!"

He reacted out of pure instinct. "I am going to take you to the hospital. Now," he said, putting on the sweater he had taken off. "Go get ready, your things..."

"Don't you want to hear the rest?"

"I do, but not now," he said, urging her to hurry. "There will be time enough for that. It's your life we have to think of first."

All the way to the Pacific Presbyterian Hospital close by, she was silent, although once more, she reminded him not to tell her father.

At the emergency reception, he wrote down everything, answered all the questions; he would turn to her on occasion, and she would nod, head bowed, her eyes downcast.

In her room finally, the anti-infection shots given her, the bleeding staunched, he watched her slowly regain her composure, the color returning to her smooth, brown face, the laughter creeping back to the dark eyes. She asked him to come closer, and when he did, she embraced him tightly, whispering, "Thank you, Buddy. Thank you."

He drew away and looked at her. "I still can't believe it, Jessie. Whoever told you it could be done with a coat hanger?"

She pouted. "All the girls in school know that," she said.

Like he promised, he never told James Wack; when he arrived that night, Buddy simply told him that Jessie was sleeping over at a friend's house, and would be back the following day, the day she would be released from the hospital.

IT WOULD be his first time to leave the United States and as the day came closer, he grew more apprehensive, not so much about the trip, but that he would be away for so long and what would Jessie do next? She had not talked about what had happened, although she had told him it was one of the white boys at school, and that she had done it out of curiosity and for fun.

Come a time when the grievous immensity of what she had done would crush her; she had taken away a life already nurtured in her womb, and when she realized this, then she would be scarred inside, a vicious scar which only she could see, and no prayer, no money, no lover could wish it away.

"No," she promised him, "it won't happen again. Not only will I be very careful—you know, I'll just do it when I'm safe—but I will always make sure he uses rubbers..."

"There's got to be love, too," but how could a fourteen-year-old girl, fully developed as a woman but not yet emotionally mature, understand?

She asked him then what he had always found difficult to answer, the very same query perhaps that had led him to magnificent cemeteries of the past, the museums and the repositories of history.

"What is love, Buddy? How do you know when it hits you?"

He had to dredge into his own being. "It could be for a person, Jessie, from a man to a woman. Like it was with Serena. To love is to desire, but it also means wishing the other person, not just yourself, happiness. To be able to give a prized possession away, to sacrifice..."

Jessica laughed softly, almost mockingly. "I don't know that kind of feeling, Buddy..."

"I don't expect you to," he said. "But look at it this way, if Dad, or I, died today, would you be sad? Would you cry?"

Without any hesitation, "Of course."

"That's also love," he said triumphantly.

"What's so important that you have to leave, Buddy?" she asked suddenly. "I need you."

For Jessica to tell him now that she needed him gave Buddy this exultant feeling of well-being.

"I'll be helpless, Buddy. You know I can't just walk up to Dad..."

"You'll be all right," he answered. "Just learn to control yourself, your urges, your appetites."

"I want you here so that when I need you..."

"I've got to finish this study, Jessie. It's important."

"Fuck your history!" she said under her breath. "What use is it?"

But there was so much, much more than its use; the answer lay much deeper and it was what had led him to seek its definition and, perhaps, its purpose.

He was now ready to leave.

He had two grey Samsonite suitcases; they could easily be taken by mistake, so he stuck on all the sides the university sticker, and tied to both handles a small red plastic bouquet. Professor Wack, the seasoned traveller, gave him all these tips, double-checked what he carried, not just in the suitcases—notebooks, a white Olivetti portable typewriter, a Spanish-English dictionary, vitamins and remedies for colds, influenza, a sewing kit, clothes for cold weather—but also what was in his mind.

Ten in the evening, the plane for Washington would leave at twelve noon the following day. Professor Wack walked into his apartment with two glasses of cognac; he handed one to Buddy.

"I can't take you to the airport, Buddy," he said, a hint of sadness in his voice. "I have to be at the university. But Jessica can."

"No problem, Dad," he said. "I'll call for a cab."

James Wack, almost sixty now, his hair all turned grey, his jaw lax, seemed thoughtful as he took the easy chair by the writing table. "I hope," he said perfunctorily," that you will have a good stay in Spain—the Spaniards, they are a very proud, individualistic people, given to verbosity at times, and those highfalutin phrases. Don't forget, they once had an empire...And in that empire, they looked down on the Indians. In South America, in the Philippines." Professor Wack sighed. "So then, all of us who are not white are imprisoned in the concepts that the white man made. It is not a just world where color marks you at birth for degradation. My poor Jessica—so pretty, so alive, and so Negro."

"I'm colored, too, Dad," he said. "But I am smarter than most of my white classmates at the university."

"Stay in your place, son," the professor said. It was not often that he called Buddy "son." "That way you will not get hurt, like I have been so many times because I have money, because I studied in France where there is much less discrimination."

In all the years in San Francisco, even when he went to Chicago, not once did Buddy experience discrimination. But Old Tele, the Ilokano oldtimer whom he had befriended in Chinatown, had told him how it was in the recent past, the indignities that the migrant workers lived through, the lowest wages which Caucasian workers refused to accept, the primitive living quarters, and the anti-miscegenation law which prohibited Orientals from marrying white women.

"Now," Professor Wack continued, "if you go to the south, there is segregation still. You hear a lot of noise now about black being beautiful, then why is the devil colored black? The white man, he does not know of the prison that he has created for black people, he does not feel for he can never go beyond his skin, and get beneath the black man's skin. Look at me, fairer than most of my people, but there is enough blackness in me which I cannot hide. My hair, my nose, my mouth—they do not conform to the anthropological aesthetics that have been imposed on the world by the white man!"

Seldom did his father speak this way, the anguish of black, the tragedy of color. He looked briefly at his hands—they were darker than the hands of Professor Wack; in fact, Jessie's color was darker, too, than that of her father and her mother. The genes always surface through time, and there is no denying them and man's origins.

"I've profited from Negroes. And every time I am treated with deference, it is because I am less black, but their past is my past. And you don't know, Buddy, how the Negroes resent me, despise me, for being light-skinned. My lighter skin tells them my forefathers were treated special by their masters. My lighter skin tells them I belong to the few Negroes who were already free before the Civil War!"

But San Francisco was different—there were too many Orientals and dark races here. He could not recall one instance in grade school or high school when his being "colored" had invited discrimination, other than what children usually fling at each other—"you brown monkey," "you white monkey"; every kid who was precocious was some monkey, and it was no more but an expression of healthy rivalry.

"Times are, of course, slowly changing. When we found you Buddy, we were all blacks in that unit. We weren't trusted enough to fight, like the Hispanics and the Indians. Can you imagine? A hundred years after the Civil War when there were Negro officers in the Union Army? Lincoln went to war, Buddy, on a moral principle—that this nation cannot be half slave, that a black man cannot be excluded because of his color. That is America's strength, Buddy— the moral principle!"

Buddy listened intently. He was going to be all right, but what about his sister?

"I worry about Jessie, Dad," he said.

"I worry, too," Professor Wack said. "But she has to find her way, in her own time. Soon, she will know how it is to be discriminated against because she is black. The whites will snub her and the darker Negroes will shun her because she is fair—and pretty. She will get very lonely, with no real friends. You have to take care of her, Buddy. You have no deep-seated emotional problem because you know who you are..."

Buddy shook his head. "Drugs aren't going to help," he said sadly.

Professor Wack suddenly looked so forlorn, broken. A short distance from Pacific Heights, at Haight Ashbury, Jessica was with her crowd, the flower children, decking their hair with various blooms, their breath redolent of marijuana, their eyes glazed not with new-found faith, but with their highs.

Jessie often brought her friends to the house where they abandoned themselves; they were not filthy, just disorderly, their rucksacks, their flower books and talismans scattered everywhere, their sweet putrefaction and whatever else they smoked or drank now impregnated in the august mansion.

 And he was going to Spain, not so much to learn more about the history of Filipinas, but to know his own.

"What do you think I'll find in Europe, Dad?" he asked finally.

Professor Wack smiled wanly. "Jump out of your skin, Buddy. Get underneath the skins of the Indians, the Filipinos whom the Spaniards abused. You will find what you already know—but go just the same so you will be confirmed. There is in the history of colored peoples a lot of sorrow. Imagine yourself an African slave transported to South America. But there is also a lot of forbearance and courage. This is all that history is really about—our own lives, but in a different time and place..."

He had always felt kinship, remote though it may be, with the black man, and with his father, that kind of ennui and unspeakable helplessness for being, in a sense, colored, too; but this only because now, he lived in a land where white had other values, where it anointed people with status. Epidermis! Epidermis! How could it mean so much, when underneath, all blood was red?

6

BEFORE LEAVING for Europe, Buddy visited the Library of Congress and the National Archives in Washington for a week, then the New York Public Library for another week to familiarize himself with their Southeast Asian collections and whatever materials they also had on Mexico. It had taken him a year to do his masteral thesis on Japanese modernization and its impact on the Philippines and Indonesia, a project Professor Scapini had advised him on and which enabled him to study Japan as well at a time when, with its victories early in this century over China and Russia, it had drawn the admiration of Asian revolutionaries. Now, this interest had truly broadened into the Ph.D. program he was to pursue in Spain— Revolutionary Nationalism: The Philippines and Mexico. Professor Anders had told him to focus on the Philippines—that was a formidable enough challenge. Mexico could be the subject for a future study. As Buddy saw it, this ever-widening interest would include Indonesia and Vietnam. He was thirty years old, healthy and without financial encumbrances. Moreover, he had some talent for languages and next he would tackle Bahasa Indonesia and Dutch, then Viet-namese and French. He had also been assured of a position at the university; with the backing of an academic giant like Bob Scapini, this possibility was there for the grabbing.

First London, Paris, then Frankfurt. London was wet and bleak and the English and their horsey faces were homogenous, as were the French—a small people—and the big, ruddy-faced Germans. He had expected a lot of bowlers and umbrellas in London, but there were few. London, like all the other European cities, seemed so effete, so lacking in the physical vitality that America had a surfeit of, and after the soaring dimensions of American cities, he had to delimit his scale of vision as he surveyed the bleak, grimy cities of the Continent. Even Paris, which James Wack was so enthusiastic about, was physically grim—none of the neon glitter, the spanking shine of American cities. He was staying in the most expensive hotels and dining in gourmet restaurants and, as expected, English cooking was awful; kippers for breakfast was interesting enough, but kidney pie was an abomination. And there was no secret at all to French cuisine—it was the sauces that made all the difference. After three weeks of European cooking, he longed for the freshness and honest simplicity of American fare—sweet corn on the cob, a thick slab of Porterhouse steak, baked Idaho potato, and crisp California salad.

IN MADRID on a precious October morning; Frankfurt where he had stopped for several days was green, well-tended lawns, the leaves of the poplars and sycamores turning into yellow and gold, and the woods of pine dark green against the grey autumn sky—and now, this barren earth scabbed with ochre, and he recalled at once what he had read of the poor Spanish land. The drive from the airport to his hotel at the Gran Via, the heart of Madrid, was not just an introduction to the aridity of the countryside, an entry into terra cognito; the Philippine past was somehow sprinkled with this soil, and with the Spanish character and all its vices.

He did not tarry in Madrid; a week was enough with visits to the Prado, that august museum and gallery where all the grandeur of the Spanish past was entombed, its violence and treachery. He recalled Picasso's Guernica at the Museum in New York that belonged to the tradition of men like Goya. He visited the Naval Museum, too, and stood in awe before the models of the early ships that had dared the vicissitudes of the mighty oceans.

The train to Seville took almost the whole day—there was this ineffable slowness compared to the pace in Germany. Was this lassitude due to Franco's heavy hand over almost everything?

The countryside was just as bleak; after the train pulled out of the station, nothing but the wasteland of rock and arid plain, the land over which Don Quixote travelled about, until towards the late afternoon when the train broke through the grey mountains, the fabled city of Cordoba, then the green of Andalucia welcomed him, the orange trees now far more abundant than the bushes of olive marching up the scraggy hillsides.

His room at the Hotel Colon in the heart of Seville was done in the traditional voluptuousness of European hotels, comfortable and ensconced in roccoco snobbery. Professor Wack's letter of introduction to the librarian, Doña Aurora, of the Archivos General de Indias would assure him of assistance—so many times had his father's academic contacts been of help to him. The evening he arrived, shortly after he had unpacked, he went downstairs to the lobby, a magnificent cavern dominated by an iron chandelier, and at one end the bar was already full; dusk had filtered in but it would be a long twilight for the Andalusians, like most Spaniards, would tarry till about ten in the evening when they would finally dine.

He decided to take a walk and discover the city. The hotel was fronted by a small square, at one end a tobacco kiosk and at the other, the beginning of San Eloy—a narrow, crooked street as almost all the streets in this part of Seville were.

For the next two hours, he meandered around, peering into the shops which were still open, into the cafes which were beginning to fill. He could make out the sounds that emanated from them, words in Spanish whose intonation was quite different from the Spanish spoken by Porfiria Castro, the housekeeper, but he was glad that he could understand everything. The crash course in Spanish was worth it, and more than that, it enabled him now to look into the character of the people as their language revealed themselves to him.

He did not want to waste time so the following morning he walked in the general direction which he was given: to the right, until you see the cathedral—you cannot miss it—and indeed, it was a landmark not just in Seville but in all of Spain.

He found himself being drawn to churches, to cathedrals, maybe because one of his first conscious images of the world was that of a church, not as a place of worship, but as a refuge. And wherever he went, he entered them, cathedrals of whichever faith. To him, they exuded man's deepest longings, their feeble reaching up to the firmaments in celebration of their humanity and of God. They were also one measure of a civilization's achievement, the lasting pinnacle of imagination realized. Though built for worship, they had become ultimate examples of a people's ability to construct and embellish their faith. And here in Spain—there was such an infinite profusion of them; even the smallest chapels were wreathed with the splendor of carving, gilding, of glittering crystal and the finest brocades. It was much later, looking back as he always did, that he recognized the magic pull of these churches was not of devout religious inclination

61

but by the accident of his being orphaned and lost in the vestibule of a church.

He decided to go to the cathedral first, knowing now that the building across from it would be his place of work for the next few months. He had gotten it from somewhere, maybe from one of the oldtimers in California, that if he entered a church for the first time, he could make a wish and it would come true...

These Gothic cathedrals—they were really massive and built in such exalting design, but it was very dim inside, except for the golden glow of the baroque altars, the unctuous luminosity of a thousand candles flickering in the shadows, and on one side, the altar, a priest, the pews empty, celebrating a solitary mass.

I wish that Jessica is well, that she be delivered soon from her vice, and that she will be able to achieve a personal sense of well-being.

He realized, having made the wish instinctively, that Jessica was the dearest person to him, and though it was not possible, he hoped he could finish soon enough what he had to do so he could hurry back to San Francisco.

Across the street, the Archivos General de Indias is a large, square building of granite, with a little plaza in front. An old man at the door told him to go to the second floor where, at the reception, he handed the letter from Professor Wack. He was directed to a small anteroom through which he could see a wide reading room, with people poring over documents in huge brown folders. Most of them had a pile of notebooks and were writing down what they were reading; others seemed to have difficulty deciphering what was before them because they constantly referred to some dictionary.

She broke into the room, a middle-aged woman, buxom, severe of manner, and immediately asked him in staccato Spanish what he wanted. He handed her the letter and upon reading the first line, the businesslike mien changed immediately into a warm, even friendly, manner as she inquired how Professor Wack was, that she hadn't seen him in so long a time, but of course, she would always remember what a fine gentleman and magnificent scholar he was.

Doña Aurora asked what he wanted to see, explaining that the Archivos had a special bibliography on the Philippines. It was very possible, considering the number of materials in the archives, that there may have been items in the other folders that had been overlooked, but he was welcome to look at all the documents.

She led him to the reading room—the sala de investigadores—and was immediately given a seat, Numero 40, and a library card. All he had to do was fill out the form and one of the clerks would go to the long, high shelves where the documents were filed and would then bring out for him whatever he wanted.

So they are all here—the three centuries of the empire, from South America and even California, to the vast uncharted Pacific, three centuries crammed into these yellowed parchments tied with a piece of white string, some already flaking and falling apart, the ink in them still legible, the fine scrawl of quills, the ornate loops and exaggerated flourishes, as if each document was meant to be some valued title, the honorifics, the magnificent signatures of bishops and cardinals and yes, of princes and kings.

The crash course in Spanish, the conversations in Spanish with Porfiria—now, they served him but yet weren't enough. Like his father said, he would have difficulty deciphering the documents for they were in archaic Spanish, and it was more than a dictionary he needed, but an expert in the old Spanish idiom.

The Philippine bibliography was very helpful; it had only recently been prepared—in fact, as Doña Aurora explained late that afternoon when she invited him for a cup of chocolate in one of the cafes close by, the archives had only a handful of trained archivists, that she was the first professional to give a sense of order to the place, and that more were being trained. It was absolutely possible that many documents were not yet properly indexed, but most of the official documents of the royal government had been assiduously catalogued and perhaps in the near future, as more technology and funds were available, microfilmed, too.

It was not the expense; he was tired of hotel food, of hotel ambience. He wanted a more personal experience, the possibility of mixing with the natives. He found the apartment in San Eloy in the second week, having already surveyed the entire neighborhood as he took the other narrow streets, all of which converged on the square before the hotel. He wondered how he had missed it; he had passed the old four-storey house with its glassed-in balcony and iron filigree every day; it merged so well with the other houses, it did not stand out as all the old houses had similar balconies, tile roofs and window shades that slid down.

Six in the afternoon, the siesta almost over, and very soon, all of Seville would be in the streets promenading, gossiping. The narrow street seldom saw the sun unless it was high noon, and the October sky was a blue metallic sheen above the red roofs. He had banged the brass knocker several times, and he was about to turn and leave when the door opened. She was a handsome woman, perhaps in her late thirties, or very early forties. Before he could speak, she asked brusquely, Chino? He shook his head, trying to smile, and again, Japonés? No, he said, Americano.

She was about his height, slim, with an almost angelic face, her eyes gypsy dark and bright. She studied him all the while, and when he pointed out to her the "for rent" sign above the door, she opened it wide to let him in. "It was vacated only this morning," she said. The tenant had stayed for a year, a man from Peru who, like him, had been doing research at the archives.

FELIZA MANAGED the boarding house, actually their old residence handed down through several generations. In the European tradition, she was the filia hospitalis; her mother had managed the house but the old woman had died and Feliza had to take over. Buddy's room at the top—there was no elevator and it was up four flights of a musty, sagging staircase of ancient wood—a studio apartment, with its own bath and kitchen. A tiny patio in the rear opened to the backyards of the other houses, laundry, abandoned furniture, potted plants and children playing and raising a racket below. Feliza lived in the penthouse—if it could be called one—above his room, which explained why it took her so long to get to the door. It would have been more logical for her to occupy the ground floor room, but it was occupied by an old gentleman, a retired naval officer whose only exercise, Buddy noted afterwards, was to go out in the late afternoon, to "paseo" the narrow, rambunctious streets before going to his favorite cafe and from thence, home.

October, and the strangling heat of summer had been completely dispelled, a summer that in this part of the country could be viciously hot. The orange trees along the streets were heavy with ripening fruit. Grapes, pomegranates, cherrymaya and fresh dates from across the sea—North Africa—filled the fruit stalls.

Capitan Jimenez, the retired naval officer, had told him within the first month of their acquaintance, of Cadiz, the magnificent port of Andalucia. Twice he had taken the train to look at the ancient port from where the ships of Spain, the caravelles, the galleys that traded in slaves, and the merchant ships set sail to discover the new world and build an empire as well. He had wandered around the old port, the houses packed together in the narrow peninsula, the quays alive with fishermen and perhaps smugglers, too. And in the afternoon, he took the Talgo back to Sevilla, which remained uncrowded, until it reached Seville two hours later and there the rush to fill the seats began, and around him eddied viajero Andalucians.

If he did not cook his breakfast, usually Spanish ham, eggs and milk, he went down to the cafe across the street where, at the counter, he would be served chocolate so thick and hot that the churros could stand in it. Then, at ten, he would be at his seat No. 40 in the sala de investigadores, ready to tackle whatever document his methodical reading demanded.

Sometimes, he went to the huge, glass-covered shelves to help Señor Dominguez of the staff who brought down the documents, mummies that never came to life, discolored by time, but with many stories in them yet to be unravelled.

Just as James Wack had described to him earlier, he saw in the Spanish search for spices a continuum, the eager and compulsive reach for the wealth of the East as an extension of European imperialism, far more extensive than the outreach of Rome or Byzantium. Surely, after the spices, there would be other products of Asian lands that would be craved as history had already abundantly shown— sugar, coffee, coconut oil, tobacco, and opium—again, the stomach and the senses declaring with unfaltering direction where expansion must proceed.

Walking home in the afternoons, as autumn slowly drifted into winter, cold but never with a hint of snow or frost, he sometimes meandered down to the river to watch the boats and the tourists. He had already visited the Alcazar several times, had lunch in a cafe within the old Moorish palace, and gazed at the filigrees in the ceiling, all those relics of Muslim art that had been left behind in this citadel. Many a time, too, he was lost in reverie. What can history teach? Dates, the lives of men who betrayed themselves so that they could achieve a paragraph or a page in the books. But people easily forget and they act out their own destinies without looking back, motivated as they are by passions that corroded their hearts. He was, however, enjoying himself, learning so much but as a voyeur and nothing more. Surrounded by all those documents, some of them so precious in their detailed descriptions of places and people, he marvelled at the tenacity of the old bureaucrats, not just to their friar orders or to their kind but to the act of recording in minutiae what they had witnessed or done without an inner eye focused to the future, that they were writing for people like him, immersed now in self-discovery.

By now he had gotten to know some of the researchers, most of whom were from South America, some from Britain and the United States, scholars working on their masteral theses or doctoral dissertations and here he was reading and in no hurry at all to finish with his Ph.D., his time uncluttered by reports or meetings.

He had also by then struck a friendship with his landlady, Feliza, who volunteered every now and then to cook dinner for him. There were only four boarders in the house and looking after them was no real chore—she had plenty of time for herself, to go shopping, to take those long walks specially in the early evenings when all of Seville seemed to be in the streets. She also had a standard question, "Have you found it yet?" to which he replied always with a smile and a vigorous shaking of the head. She was used to having scholars around, sometimes they stayed for as long as a year, and usually, they were good guests, seldom imposing on her or bothering her with personal demands. They had gone together one early December evening to her cafe close to the church on Jovellanos Street and while they drank manzanilla and nibbled tapas—marinated olives, deep-fried squid, anchovies—she told him it was not difficult to trace one's ancestry. There was an office in Seville, as well as in other cities where, for a few hundred pesetas, one's ancestral background would be traced. "Did you know, Salvador," she told him, "that my great, great grandfather lived in Manila?"

Kinship again, he took her hand impulsively and pressed it. She let him. "There were letters," she continued evenly, "and I remember having seen them—my grandmother...I don't know how we lost them. It was such a long time ago—but the house, we saw to it that it would remain with us."

"How did you find out that a relative was in Manila at all— and so long ago?"

She smiled. "Time does a lot of things. There is continuity some- times, and there are always records, bits of paper, or something more permanent such as what you are reading now from the archives. But what really is important is if such things matter to you, if they can be used in your life."

He saw her then not just as an anonymous housekeeper, but a person capable of perception and perhaps profundity. "You are a very lovely person, Feliza," he blurted out, wondering afterwards why at that exact moment, he said it. "And certainly very smart. May I ask why you live alone?"

A dark cloud—was it gloom, sorrow or anger—immediately shrouded her face. She compressed her lips, and shaking her head, she told him, "Maybe, I carry a burden too heavy for me to bear and can't throw away." Then quickly, the humor came back to the brooding eyes. "Maybe, I have not found the right man after all these years..."

CHRISTMAS CAME; the telephone connection was very bad, but somehow, he managed to get San Francisco. Porfiria made a domestic report in Spanish. James Wack had been in the hospital for a couple of days, a heart murmur, but he was well and was at the university. Jessica was in the east, with a new boyfriend; she had called and was fine.

The long holidays came to an end and in the first week of February, he came across a new batch of documents, No. 351—Reales cedulas sobre materias gubernativas suelos, hospitales e Islas Marianas, 1580-1838. The Marianas was a way station on the Pacific route, there could be something there, the Nueva Filipinas, that would pertain to Filipinas itself. By then, he had gone over so many reports, royal orders, and communications between Madrid and Manila, and he already had some picture of how tyrannically the Spaniards ruled as well as how the natives reacted to that rule, and the first faint stirring of nationalist thought.

He had gone in the morning chill for a cup of hot chocolate at the cafe across the street, having given the borrower's slip to Señor Dominguez who had, by now, understood what the young American was trying to do, a formidable task could take years, as it had for so many other researchers, not because they had no course nor direction, but because they wanted to know everything that happened during those three centuries that Spain had ruled their lands. Everything! How could one cram all these centuries into those notebooks, but then, these people had already lost track of time for they were in the most adventurous and exciting of discoveries—the discovery of the self!

When he returned to his seat, it was there on the table, the usual bundle of documents tied with a piece of string. It seemed older than most of what he had seen, and from the film of dust at the edges, it was a sure sign that no one had bothered with this batch, perhaps for a hundred years!

He started slowly, carefully, so that the documents would not stick to one another and tear. Who would want to know about an obscure Pacific island like the Marianas? Perhaps, among the fifty or so researchers hunched over their work, it was only he who was here with all the time to be desultory.

He glanced at each page, most of them frayed at the edges, and also darker where they were exposed to dust and light. The perspicacity of the clerks, the administrators who prepared these always amazed him—here they were all clearly noted, the accounting of funds, the decisions, the orders.

He had not yet gone through half of the batch; it was almost closing time and that rich, mellow Andalucian twilight was upon the city. He was about to close the big folder, tie the string, when he noticed sheets of the same old and flaking paper folded together.

He opened it—it was not in the Roman alphabet, but in some phonetic script, Tamil perhaps, Burmese; certainly it was not Thai or Balinese, he knew them by sight. Maybe Bugis—Indonesia after all belonged to the same cultural orbit.

And then, it struck him and it all came rushing back, what he had seen of the old Philippine phonetic scripts that the friars forbade the early Filipinos to use when they introduced the Roman script. That inverted bean, that nervous squiggle—was it Tagalog, Ilokano or Cebuano? If only he was in Berkeley now, he could be sure. He took the documents and rushed to the office of Doña Aurora.

"I am sure, señora," he said excitedly, "this is an old Philippine script. I do not know how it got mixed up with documents from the Marianas."

The librarian studied them under the lamp on her desk, a beatific smile on her face. "You never know what is in this vast ocean of information," she said. "Do you want to find out"?

"Of course," Buddy said. "May I photograph it and send it to people I know who will then be able to identify and read it?"

IT WAS eight p.m. in Seville and almost noon in San Francisco. Jessica answered the phone, the connection this time was very clear. "I thought you were in the east, Jessie,"

"Was, Buddy," she said, a hint of anger in her voice. "I've been back for some time. He was just after a good time at my expense."

"Oh, Jessie, I am sorry."

"I'm such a poor judge of character," she said dolefully.

He was gushing as he told James Wack about the document. "It was buried there, Dad. Nobody seems to have bothered with that bundle, for decades even. Or if someone did, he chose to ignore it."

"Slowly, Buddy. Tell me what you think it is, how I can help you."

He told James Wack how he had enjoyed discovering the high quality of the island civilization and getting to know the early Spanish efforts, how he had hoped to gain insights into the history of Filipinas—before the Spaniards came and wrought havoc on the native cultures...And now, this document. He was convinced it was similar to the old scripts he had seen in the Newberry collection, in Berkeley itself. He had permission to photograph them in the morning, he had bought a Leica M3 in Frankfurt with three extra lenses, one precisely for photographing documents, and in another day, the enlargements would be ready. Surely, there must be a scholar somewhere who could read the script, translate it even...

James Wack was silent.

"Dad?"

"Yes, I have it!" James Wack came over the line exultantly. "At an Asian Studies conference way back in the fifties, he made a comparative study of ancient Javanese script with the Malay and Filipino scripts. He should be able to do it—get in touch with him immediately at the Asian Studies Institute of the University of the Philippines. Professor Adda Bocano..."

DOÑA AURORA helped him set up the documents. The morning sun flooded the room. He had not used the Leica for something as important, having taken the usual touristy pictures, the opera house at Frankfurt, the museums in Madrid, and now this—and his spirit lifted.

The glossy enlargements, eight inches by ten, came the following day. Even Doña Aurora was impressed—he had become a photographer as well. "You must promise," she told him, "to tell me as soon as you hear what the translation says."

The pictures were sent by air.

In a week, a cable arrived from Manila; now Professor Bocano wanted more details, where he found the document. There was some skepticism in the man, he knew only too well how several so-called documents purporting to be basic records about the Philippines were exposed by him as either forgeries or fictions by charlatans who wanted to give Philippine history a new drift. He had studied in the past some such documents, some of them in copper, attesting to the literacy and high degree of scientific proficiency of the early Filipinos. But this script was specific—it was Cebuano, and the Cebuano words were still very much extant, in actual use to this very day. He had realized in just one day that he had a document of great significance; it ended once and for all the controversy about where this Enrique had come from, this slave of Pigafetta who, in actual fact, was the first to have gone around the world.

So many had searched, and it was Buddy who had triumphed.

Within a month, he received the Cebuano, Spanish and English translations; there was no doubt about its author—both Magallanes and Pigafetta were mentioned in it several times. But the document was incomplete. Surely, Maisog, the man who wrote the document, attempted more than to describe what had transpired in Cebu and Mactan islands, or the voyage across the Pacific. Did the name, Maisog, mean anything? Professor Bocano explained: In ancient times Filipinos named their children after virtues, the dawn, happiness. Maisog meant courageous. It would be up to Buddy to fill the gaps.

Unya usa niana ka adlaw may usa ka tawo

nga maalam, usa ka magsusulat nga taga

Venezia nga ginganlan ug Antonio Francesca

Pigafetta mipalit kanako sa bili nga usa ka

gatos ka bulawan nga dukats — nagpasalamat ako

niini — tungod kay nakahibalo man siya ug diin ako

maggikan. Miingon siya nga kinahanglan mouban ako

kaniya sa paglayag paingon sa Pulo sa mga

Lamas pinaagi sa Sidlakan, ug ang mamuno sa

among paglayag maoy usa sa mga bantogang

manlalayag sa maong panahon, si Fernao de

Magalhaes, usa ka Portuges. Si Pigafetta magtala

sa tanan nga among makita ug mahiagoman.

Excerpt from the Enrique Document as decoded by A. Bocano

7

ALL MEN, *hearken! This is to let you know that this humble vassal, Maisog of Sugbu, should be addressed* Primus Circumdedisti Me *by the earth, when we finally reach Sugbu. But who would do me—a brown man of anonymous origin—this exalted honor?*

Now, as old age approaches and my bones are brittle, my breathing labored and slow, I know that I have to set down my thoughts, my remembrances, of what I have seen and visited through these many years. No less than my Lord had said that I should do so. I have had an inclination to write this down in the language which was taught me, which I now speak with utmost fluency, but I think it best to write it down in the language to which I was born, with which I grew up and this is now what I am going to do, although I am not sure at all what it is that urges me to write down these thoughts of a man who has left his native land, who will most likely never go back to it. Here in the mind and heart, I will always be Maisog of Sugbu although my Lord and all those who know me now say I was baptized a Christian, and I am now Enrique de Malacca even Enrique Negro. There are others named like me, illustrious princes like Enrique de Navigador, but no matter, this name is now mine.

In writing this down in the script I learned when I was young, and in my own tongue, I know that I will not be able to say everything I want to say—I have so forgotten through the lack of usage my own language; alas there is no one here in this great and bustling city who knows my language, who knows my handwriting—just I, and my lord to whom I tried to teach my language as well as my script but who had not really taken to both with the same dedication as he has with his writing.

To begin. My father and mother tell me I was born that year a mountain to the south of Sugbu blew up and sent a huge wave to our very shore, smashing many a seaside community and drowning hundreds of our people; for days, the bloated corpses were washed back to our shores; for months, too, the sky seemed darkened with ash, and the sunsets were never as glorious as they were then. It was a year, too, that the harvest was very good and our granaries were full.

My boyhood was a happy one. My father was a distinguished member of the court of the Raja—he had so many times helped defend our land from the pirates who came in swift boats, pillaging and abducting our children and women to be sold as slaves in the bigger islands in the south.

As a boy, much of my time was spent learning our old songs and epics, handed down to us by our elders and teachers. I also learned how to write, a most tedious process which I failed to recognize then as important, till much later when I realized that everywhere I went, it was the important people who wrote, and the slaves and others who did not know how to read or write were doomed to remain that way.

We were also taught to navigate the seas around us by men of wisdom and talent, who had sailed far, to the lands in the north where there was ice in the mountains, to the south, and the far countries which were ruled by leaders with skins fairer than ours. And then, there were the techniques of war to be learned as well, but I was never meant to be a warrior for I was meant, I suppose, to be a sailor, a navigator, having memorized as I did the landfall of different islands, different nations, the coming of the good winds, of the cruel seas, whipped by typhoons. I learned them all, for we have always been a nation of traders as well and the craft of the sailor is hammered into us as a matter of course, even before we learned how to sail.

Even as a boy, I already knew that when I became a man, I would be married to Ma-anyag—she whom my parents had chosen, who was not only beautiful and talented in verse and music, but as my parents had every so often hinted, so that our two families would be united. It was a choice which both of us had accepted to be as natural as breathing, and though we were not yet married, it would appear as if we were already husband and wife, for it was seldom that we were not in each other's company.

We went one morning to a spring in the rim of the forest as had happened in the past, we had often gone there to swim in the cool, clear pond which the spring fed. We had just finished, and were putting on our clothes, when we were attacked by six men, their bodies painted black as most warriors were when they went to war. We did not have an enemy;

we had a truce with the Maktan people, were in an era of peace and prosperity, we had never thought we would be in danger. They marched us into the forest, our hands bound, and at the other side of our island, they had hidden two boats under a canopy of trees.

Ma-anyag was put in the other boat and I never saw her again. Perhaps it was just as well. I was taken to a far-off place, from one island to another, under very close watch, sometimes without food and water, until we reached a prosperous city, with many boats from different countries. I recognized it at once as the port of Melaka, and there, I was sold as a slave.

Ma-anyag, I was sure, suffered the same fate, and worse, for with all that loveliness, she was first defiled in a manner that I do not want to think about. The slave market was close to the sea—a huge, walled square to which I was brought together with the others. There were several enclosures to which prospective buyers went, bargained with my captors beyond my hearing; then they came to me, looked me over, naked as I was, and so were the women, the children, who were captured in raids. Some of them were dark-skinned.

Those who had not come to terms with their condition were bound hand and foot, and some were flogged, their wounds open and bleeding. I could only look at them with sympathy, for there was no mercy here. We were not people, we were merchandise. The man who bought me—I understood everything that was said, although the language they spoke was slightly different from my own. I had a talent for languages, and could speak— from conversations with traders and sailors—some of the languages of the islands around us. I was going to serve in the household of the Honorable Muhammad Saleh, Trade Counsellor of the Sultan of Yuhur. He was so glad that I could speak some of the local languages and that I could also write—skills which I did not exhibit to my captors but which they suspected. They knew by my bearing, I was no common peasant.

I wanted very much to escape, to return to Sugbu. Ma-anyag would no longer be there, I realized this with bone-deep sorrow, Sugbu would no longer have any hold on me.

My new master was a most civilized man; I told him all he wanted to know about where I came from; he had never been there, but had heard about it, and because I knew how to read and write, he said that after two years he would grant me my freedom, but only if I would work for him, help in his business, particularly since it was growing. He had more boats than he could handle, more goods to tranship, up and down the waterway, and even beyond for there were, on occasion, bigger ships with bigger sails, white men manning them, very black men working in them, coming as they did from a far country where there was ice not in the mountains alone but all over the land during certain times of the year. Someday I would cross these great distances.

I often had the urge to go back to Sugbu; on occasion, our boats passed that way, and I often sought news about my parents, about the town where I was born. I could get but little and none whatsoever about my beloved Ma-anyag.

In the meantime, I had gathered knowledge about spices, nutmeg, cinnamon, pepper, cardamon, ginger—all the things that the ships from far away had come to Pasai to buy. Transhipments were also made to the land of the Narrow Eyes, to Siam and Champa. So much trade went on that I was always busy.

I also came to realize what importance spice had in European society. It was a measure of status. At a festive table, only the richest had it in abundance and it was not just to flavor the food or to preserve it—it was used to add distinction to wine, to desserts. The more pungent the dish, the higher the social rank of the host. Spices were gifts of royalty, of the upper classes to one another. No wonder then that they craved it, no matter how expensive. And the Venetians, with the vast amounts of pepper they brought to Europe from India, profitted the most. To them, pepper were "the seeds of paradise."

Although I was not much of a mapmaker, I tried to make some, a portolan—an account of landfall, nautical experiences, useful only to those who go to places already known, but useless to those who probe the unknown. I gathered maps drawn by others, men I trusted because they had very good reputations. These were not public knowledge—many of the sailors kept their secrets to themselves, of passages to take, the dangerous reefs and currents to avoid, and most important, the position of the winds that could push the boats from their appointed course. Much of this knowledge was instinctive, and could be earned only by experience.

I had, by then, done a lot of sailing, all the way to the ports of India, and on each trip, I always brought back to my benefactor tokens of my respect and gratitude for his benevolent treatment.

Sailing back to Pasai from one such trip, I was surprised to find Muhammad, my Pasai lord, waiting for me at the quay. A foreign ship, its sails furled, was there. The moment we had cast anchor, he called me and said—I must now join the white men in the big ship. From his tone, I understood that I had no choice, he had "sold" me to them as their translator and their guide in the waters of the region. I was extremely vexed, but did not show it. I owed the man so much, and besides, here was the opportunity to go farther into the open sea.

You must go, he said in parting; and when you return, with all the new things that you will get to know, you will have a place with me, by my side, and you will be rewarded handsomely. I will make you, he added with much earnestness, one of my sons-in-law.

The man had five fat and useless daughters, good only for childbearing.
The fate that I would return to, I was sure, would not be so demeaning.

We stopped finally in Lisbon, and I watched in a shipyard the caravelles being built, boats bigger than what we had. Carpenters made the hulls, each rib and plank carefully sawn so that they would fit. The logs were brought in from the nearby forests and were from a species of trees which we did not have for they grew straight and round in the trunks unlike many of our forest trees which were shaped irregularly.

Once the planks were laid, the sides were packed with hemp from our part of the world, then it was welded with the wood with a kind of thick black oil which was heated; in this manner, the hull of the ship becomes impermeable. I also watched them draw their charts, indicating where the wind blew and in what direction, so that although we could sail against the wind, it was much better just to follow it although sometimes, it would take us the longer way.

We sailed to Africa; followed the coast, sought the wealth of that land, gold, so much of it as it was also in Sugbu, and slaves—men and women and children.

I was puzzled and at the same time drove to heart man's cruelty to his fellow beings, maybe, in this case, because they were not white; but then those who sold me into slavery were like myself, of the same visage and color.

Then one day, a man of great knowledge, a chronicler from Venezia named Antonio Francesca Pigafetta bought me for a hundred gold ducats— my price had truly appreciated—because he knew where I came from. He said that I should go with him on a voyage to the Spice Islands by way of the east, and that the captain of our fleet would be one of the greatest sailors of the age, Fernao de Magalhaes, a Portuguese. Pigafetta would record everything that we would see and experience. He was also a crafty man, amassing information not just for himself and for knowledge, but I suspect for his superiors in Venezia which was, itself, a powerful trading city. But he trusted me enough to show me copies of secret maps, those of dela Cosa and a few others showing the routes to Oceanus Orientalis and Oceanus Chinensis—regions I already had passed.

By then, I could speak a little Portuguese and Spanish, and though I had some difficulty, I could understand both clearly. I did not want to forget the language I was born to, and many a time, I would speak it, translating the Spanish and Portuguese words into Sugbu, saying them aloud when I was by myself, and only in my head when I was with others. That was one way I could be closer to the land I had left.

We faced many difficulties even before we started out. I had heard there were many sailors who were jealous of our captain, jealous because he was able to present before the Spanish King an audacious plan to find a new route to the east.

We had prepared for weeks, cheese, biscuits, beans, dried fish and meat, provisions that would in principle last us half a year even, but we did not consider the vicissitudes of weather, of strange climates and prolonged expanses with nary a breeze stirring our sails.

We sailed out of Guadalquivir, the "Great River" of Andalucia, on September 20, 1519—five grand ships, the Victoria, the Trinidad, the San Antonio, the Concepcion and the Santiago—the Armada de Molucca. We were a motley crew, Arabs, Chinese, black men, white men—and one brown man from Sugbu.

I will not dwell on the horrible hardships that afflicted us—these have been well recorded by my master, Pigafetta, the strange people we saw like the giants of Patagonia, the patos sin alas (penguins), the terrible hunger that we suffered, the disease that decimated our ranks.

Of the voyage, I treasure most that morning when we reached what seemed to me familiar waters, the clear blue sea, the palm trees, and soon enough, from the island came five small boats, the very same I used to take out to sea.

The men shouted greetings in the language to which I was born, and soon, we were babbling, unmindful of the men who were now on the rails, listening to us. After more than thirty years—I was home, not an old man, but a young boy again!

Distant places, the sea, will always lure me, and I will never deny it. But life is short, and a person like me can take in only so much knowledge which, in itself, is of little value if it is not used. What good are the languages that I have learned? the geographies that I have witnessed? They will be nothing but stories that I will tell, and of course, I will tell them, for this is what I was destined to be, a storyteller to my people, so that their minds will be broadened, so that their eyes will see beyond the horizons before them.

I had thought that having lost Ma-anyag forever, seeing too that all my relatives—my brothers and sisters and my parents—had all gone their ways or had died, I should be at home in the distant lands where I have travelled and learned of other ways of living and worshipping. But that can never be for not only am I not white, but also because home is where I was born, where memory has chained me. Sugbu, Sugbu—all the magic that can be intoned is in your name, my precious island, my island of long-repressed dreams, welcome me back into your bosom!

Let me tell you about the captain of our ship; a man of stupendous learning and skill, courageous, and all of us held him in awe and respect. He was also a very good soldier, although as it was shown by the Raja of Maktan, he did not know enough strategy in dealing with a new enemy.

Let me now comment on that skirmish—I wouldn't dignify it as a battle although it resulted in the death of our Beloved Commander, our Great Helmsman, leaving us all orphans of this ocean, grieving the irreparable loss of a dream.

The Raja Lapu-Lapu of Maktan and his people were often at war with their neighbors. They were feared for they were great fighters, capable of incredible audacity and courage, as well as of infinite patience and cunning. These qualities, I am sure, were developed by the harshness of their land, mostly rock underneath that veneer of thin soil. Thus, they were great sailors, too, and traders and fishermen, but it was really with their weapons that they survived and conquered.

Our Beloved Commander should not have, in the first place, been drawn into a local quarrel which had festered for so long, the quarrels over trade, over territory and what else that sometimes marred the relationship between the people of Sugbu and Maktan. But our Beloved Commander was certainly flattered by Sugbu hospitality, the readiness with which the Hari and his family and so many subjects had willingly prostrated themselves before the Spanish king's envoys, before the Cross; they were all easily mesmerized, too, by our ships, our superior armaments.

Raja Lapu-Lapu taunted our Commander; if the Hari of Sugbu was an easy convert, he and his people would not be. Moreover, he was not going to pay tribute.

So it was that the Commander decided to teach the Maktans a lesson—an exercise I objected to with great shaking of the head for they had never really faced the Maktans in combat before.

I told them that even in my boyhood, their excellence in combat was already well-known. With their wooden shields, they could form an impregnable barrier to warriors attacking frontally or in the flanks. They could rain clouds of arrows on a charging mass; as individual fighters they were disciplined and skilled for they trained early in their youth.

But who was I to be listened to by men in higher councils? I was just a slave who happened to know their language and the language of Sugbu and Maktan.

None of our small boats, certainly not the Victoria, could get close to the shore—the shallows extend quite a distance, a long, wide barrier of rocks, reefs and other obstructions but which, in low tide, could be crossed on foot.

The Maktan warriors were scattered in the shallows, just a handful of them, but at that distance, our cannon would be ineffective, the muskets and arquebuses would miss them, too. And they seemed to know this.

They faced us, yelling taunts: Uncircumcised devils! Hermaphrodites! and everyone, upon a signal, would bring out their male instruments and urinate. Or, they would turn their backs to us and squat, as if to defecate, and point to their rectums, repeating those obnoxious words that, addressed to any man, would mean a challenge to combat.

I translated all of this, relayed this to our Beloved Commander and Helmsman. But he ignored me, blustering, "We will teach these infidels with the sword. That is the only thing they understand."

I ran to my Lord Pigafetta, entreated him to stop the Commander, but they were already armored, they were already lowering the boats which would take them to the shallows and the shore.

This is what the Maktans want, I cried; they want you to fight in the ground of their choosing. Oh, my masters, I fear for you because you do not know them, their treachery, their cunning.

But they would not listen; they were laughing, singing, joking.

And thus did it happen; from the deck of the Victoria, we saw what the Maktans did; so many of them had hidden behind the bushes in the shoreline, and when our Commander and his soldiers were finally in the shallows, too far from us but not on land either, the enemy simply poured out in force, surrounded them, raining poisoned arrows and iron-tipped lances on them. Our Beloved Leader and his men were able to fire their muskets, but how quickly could they reload? We watched it all, helpless, because even if we went to their succor, by the time the battleground would be reached, the Maktans would have retreated and this is what they did, having done their best, having killed our Beloved Leader. Our men retreated in hysteria and disorder, leaving the body of our Commander behind. We never recovered his remains.

Grief filled all of us, and I grieved, too. Our Beloved Leader was kind-hearted, suffering the same tribulation which all of us had suffered in the long voyage. But I have always felt that, to a man, they who came from Iberia looked down on us, so-called infidels, people who are uncivilized, uncouth.

They were defeated—for that was what it really was—because they were arrogant, because they always assumed their arms, their armor, were superior. What could these naked natives possibly do to harm their precious white skins, and with what? But the Maktan warriors knew what they were doing, they had looked at these strangers not with awe but with curiosity and without fear—and thus, it was easy for them to know the enemy's weaknesses.

I was, therefore, torn between my loyalty to my Commander and my secret feelings of pride that I came from this place. I found kinship with the people of Maktan and wished myself an ever-loyal subject of their king. I recalled my own pitiable condition, a chattel, a man not free, living apart from those of fairer skin. I should not be here on this alien vessel but out there amongst my kin; they had fought not just for their honor, but also for mine.

8

DID MAISOG or Enrique of Sugbu return to Europe to be the old man he described himself in the beginning of his memoir? Or did he stay behind as Pigafetta had indicated in his writing? The document itself, as Buddy had now built on it, was not very explicit, but there was one clue to Buddy's unflinching conviction that, in the end, Enrique did not return to Europe by way of India and the Mediterranean. He had seen enough, but more than this, he wanted to be a teacher, a storyteller, and his audience was his own people.

Buddy could leave Seville now, or Spain altogether; in the last six months, not only was he able to satisfy many of his curiosities, and become confident with his Spanish, even pronouncing the z as *th* the way the natives did, unlike the Spanish of Mexico or of Latin America.

Feliza held him back.

By then, Buddy had become familiar with the other tenants, the retired naval officer on the ground floor, Don Esteban on the second floor, with his wife, a portly woman who went to the church on Jovellanos Street every day, Geronima Piedad, the short, stubby scholar from the University of Mexico who was researching the galleons...They never left the house or arrived at the same time, and Gerry Piedad—as he called her—sat at the other end of the sala de investigadores in the times that she was there; he suspected that she had an Andalucian lover, the elderly gentleman who sometimes visited her room, who often went out for a walk with her.

He had found Feliza very helpful, even going out of her way to take him to the places he needed to visit, the stationery shop, the public market towards the river where he could get better meats and fruits. She had an ostensible reason, of course; she was learning English and was glad to teach him the correct Spanish idioms. She did not talk too much about her family. She had two brothers, one of them an engineer in Madrid, and another, a banker in Bilbao, both of them married, with lives of their own, and here she was, the youngest, stuck with this house which her parents had entrusted to them never to sell, because it had been their house for so many generations.

Spring finally, and though the cold still gripped the land, that grip had loosened. The sun bore down with more warmth, and orange blossoms filled the air with fragrance. Feliza said she was going to Cordoba which Buddy had passed on his way to Seville, but which he had not yet visited, although he already knew about this magnificent Moorish city that was once the capital of the Moorish kings. Would he like to come along for the weekend? She had gone to school in Cordoba, had friends there, and there was this long weekend with really nothing much to do in Seville.

Buddy was pleased for by then, he had already gotten to enjoy her company, her vivacity which, having read a little about Seville, seemed to have been influenced by the gypsies.

They arrived in the early afternoon. At the train station, she immediately started making phone calls. The three friends whom she thought she would surprise were not in—they had gone elsewhere for the weekend, too.

They walked over to the center of the town, the streets as narrow as those in Seville, and found a small hotel close to the Cathedral which had a vacancy—but it was only one room with double beds. Buddy was not going to subject her to embarrassment by suggesting that they take the room, but it was she who did it, saying it was foolish to go looking further, when there was already this one which was not only centrally located but also cheap.

"Are you embarassed?" she asked him, laughing, when they were shown the room, with its tall window open to the square which was now bustling with people. One side was dominated by a huge and ancient cabinet that had started to list with age. Extra pillows and blankets were folded in the lower portion. A washstand was in the corner, close to the window, of dubious style as well, and beyond the washstand, was the bathroom with its old tiles now cracked in places.

They went out in the twilight, and though he was tentative about it, she let him when he held her hand, just like two old lovers in a city where nobody knew them anyway. She knew Cordoba and she showed him all there was to see in the center of the town, the remnants of Moorish architecture. Later in the evening, she took him to a cafe where there was fandango music, and in another half-hour, a wiry woman with stern, dark eyes came out, clicking her castanets and stomping her feet to the magic cadence of a guitar. "It bores me," Feliza said. "But I know you have not seen one yet or you would have told me."

They had codfish for dinner, and somehow, he had never gotten tired of it. Shortly before midnight, when his fancies had started to bedevil him, they went back to the hotel.

He was only too conscious of it when she locked the bathroom door as she prepared to take a shower. So, she does not trust me after all, in spite of our apparent closeness. I will respect that, he told himself. He slipped out of his clothes, and in his underwear, he lay down on the wide bed, the bedcover over him—these Spanish beds, they were unusually wide. She took a long time in the bathroom and when she was through, the long afternoon walk had exhausted him and he had already fallen asleep.

Feliza woke him up with a demand, almost harsh, "Move over, Salvador. They have turned off the heater and I am feeling cold." And without any further explanation, she slipped under the sheet beside him.

For an instant, he thought he was dreaming, then he realized that this was Feliza indeed, her scent swirling all over, her softness, her skin touching his skin, cold at first then finally, the warmth of intimacy as only couples in copulation could experience. He slid his arm under her head so that her face would be close to his, and when she turned to face him, her body now facing him as well, he brushed her lips in a tentative kiss. She drew away quickly. "None of that," she said coldly. "None of that, please."

He was now fully awake, and had begun to stir; the many months of celibacy giving way to this engorgement. He did not know the Spanish word for celibacy, so he asked her.

"Celebe," she told him.

"Months for you, for me it's years," she said with a laugh, thrusting her thigh between his legs so that she could feel him where he was now most sensitive. He asked her if she was a virgin, a doncilla—he knew that word—and again, that easy laughter that implied neither yes nor no, rather, as he interpreted it then, why don't you find out.

He could not go back to sleep, but Feliza was soon quietly snoring. He slipped his hand under her nightgown and started fondling her breasts—they were small and very firm. She had wakened and had grasped his hand, but she did not remove it from her breast; she pressed it instead.

She could not sleep anymore, either. "Tell me about your women," she said. He told her he had none but she immediately said she did not believe him. He had known very few women, but if she wanted to know to whom he was most devoted, it was to Jessica, his sister in San Francisco, now beset by so many problems.

For a while she did not speak. He thought she had gone to sleep again, but she sighed, turned to him and kissed him. "My poor Salvador!" she said, "You will be searching forever, because the past is past and it can only have some meaning if we give it that meaning. We live for today, and perhaps, for tomorrow, too—if we have the time."

He wanted to savor her lips, her mouth, her tongue, but she would not let him; she put her hand over his face and said, that is enough. In a while, the Andalucian dawn crept into the room, subtly for the drapes were drawn, and finally, they went to sleep.

It was high noon when they woke up. When she stirred, she seemed shocked that she was in his bed and she rose hastily and rushed to her own bed, lay there for a while without saying anything, then she finally got up without looking at Buddy who was, all the while, looking at her with avid interest. She took her time as usual in the bathroom, and when she reappeared, she had regained her composure. "Let's go have breakfast," she said casually.

They went down to the cafe across the street and had churros and chocolate. They spent the whole afternoon sightseeing, talking, and back at the hotel that night, Buddy had expected her to share his bed again, but this time, Feliza seemed comfortable enough with the cold although Buddy was sure it was colder on the second night than on the first.

He was not too sure of himself, and he restrained himself from asking her to join him again. Unable to sleep, his mind wandered in reverie and remembrance, and again, as he often did in the past, he asked himself what he truly wanted to do with all the money and the opportunities his father had given him. He had finished his master's in Asian history, in another year, if he put his mind to it, he could do his Ph. D. too, but if he did this, it was no longer just to please James Wack. Did history really matter to him that much? He had come to Seville, yes, for there was much to see here, but more than this, he came to Europe to enjoy himself, live fully, have all his senses pleased. In a way, he was no different from Jessica, who truly lived for the moment, and like her, too, what was there to live for? Their paths had already been mapped out, paved, strewn with roses, and there was not a worry for them other than what tomorrow might not bring.

IT HAPPENED in Seville the following day after they had returned to a house where their absence had not been noted at all. And it was just as well for Buddy did not want too many personal questions asked of him. He was finally awake, but when he opened his eyes, everything in the room seemed dim. And worse, he did not seem able to move his arms, his legs; the most he could do was turn his head. Feliza! he cried, Feliza! but it was hardly a voice that escaped him; it was more of a gurgling sound. Louder, Feliza! Feliza! He could hear the door opening, a stab of red across his blurring vision, someone bending over him, asking, What is wrong? You are not well? It was Feliza at last, dear Feliza. Call a doctor, he whispered. Doctor, that much came clearly out of him. He could feel his strength being drained, the life ebbing out as if from a cracked casement; he was not going to die—not now, not now, and then everything was lost, a deep void without a rim.

When he finally regained his senses, he was in a white hospital room, empty save for a steel table with trays and bottles. He pressed the buzzer beside his bed, and in a while, a nurse came, smiled at him and left immediately. She returned with a tall, lean man in white, a stethoscope like a necklace around his neck. He smiled at him, and immediately felt his pulse. He spoke to him casually in Spanish, "You were in a coma for two days," he said. "We do not know what is wrong with you. We have done all sorts of tests. We can only guess—how do you feel now?" Buddy described the uncanny sensation of a thousand needles pricking him earlier.

"Paresthesias," the doctor explained.

He heard everything, understood everything. He raised both hands, wiggled his toes—his sense of locomotion had returned. He tried to rise which he did easily. He was in a white hospital smock. "I feel fine, doctor," he said, assured that he was really well now. "And hungry," he added.

Feliza came at lunchtime with sausages and grapes. Two other doctors came, asked him a lot of questions, his history, any ailment

or serious infection in the past, any hereditary malady in his family—
to which he replied as best as he could. The results of the tests came
and all of them attested to his good health. Good health? But he had
been in a coma, he had lost his sense of hearing, his sight—and he
was in good health?

"I have suspicions," the first doctor said, "but I cannot confirm
them, unless I get to see you regularly. When you get back to San
Francisco, I suggest you have a thorough check-up, the nervous
system, the spinal cord—and do let me know what they find. I have
yet to encounter a case like yours."

He had not jotted down anything in his journal for the past
several days. Now, he had something important to record, the
weekend in Cordoba, his coma and confinement in the hospital, and
above all, this riddle, this woman, this challenge of Feliza.

He took her the night he was released to the restaurant of the
Hotel Colon—she said she seldom went there although it was in the
neighborhood for that was where the social butterflies went and she
was not one, although she had been to the coffee shop many times,
sometimes to meet friends.

"I am very grateful to you, Feliza," he told her, holding her hand.
"So very grateful. I could have just died there if you hadn't come
and brought me to the hospital."

"You spent a fortune," she told him for it was she who made
the arrangements. "I am very relieved that you could afford it."

Money had never concerned him; there was always more than
enough when he needed it. "All the money in the world cannot pay
for the care you gave me," Buddy said. The nurse and the doctor
had told him how Feliza, his "novia," had looked after him. In the
glow of the crystal chandelier, he could see the blush color her
cheeks and for a while, she fidgeted with the napkin which she had
already knotted. He took it away from her, smiling. "Thank you,
Feliza," he repeated.

It was a short walk to the house in San Eloy. The shops along
the street had already closed, but a couple of cafes were still open.
Before they entered the house, he whispered to her, "I will come up
to your room very soon."

In reply, she pinched his hand, the sharp, sweet pain coursing
through him quickly. "Wait for me," she said. He waited for her,
listened to every sound from the room upstairs, a turn of the lock,
a knock on his door; sometimes, he drifted into brief snatches of sleep,
and woke up from them, wondering if she had gone to his room
and finding him thus, no longer bothered to wake him up. It was

84

finally light when sleep could no longer be warded off, and he succumbed to it.

Buddy promised himself that she could never take advantage of him again, trick him into waiting or believing. Dour of spirit, he left shortly after waking up, just at the same time that Gerry Piedad was also starting out. They walked together to the Archives. "I haven't had anything yet, not breakfast, not lunch," he told her, in fact invited her to have something before both of them went to work. They stopped at a cafe close to the cathedral, and ordered coffee, bread with a generous spread of anchovies for him, and for Gerry a ham sandwich.

He did not want to pry—this he never did. It was not the first time they had been together; she was not really doing research, she told him, she was merely reading up on the galleon trade preparatory to writing a series of articles for some Mexican magazine, and in Seville primarily for a vacation—a long one for she had been in the San Eloy house for more than two months.

She was surprised at his little interest in the galleons when, as she explained, they were the most fascinating of all sea trades, three centuries crossing the Pacific and back, at a time when navigation was an adventure that could culminate in disaster, or death.

Gerry Piedad was short and brown, most probably with Indian parents, but her English, although she was educated entirely in Mexico and had visited Los Angeles only for a month, was impeccable. Her eyes were large, her nose rather flat, and her lips were full; she was not homely for sure—in fact, there was about her a charm that grew on anyone who talked with her as he was doing now.

Briefly, he wondered about the tall, middle-aged Spaniard who he sometimes saw in her room, sometimes walking out of the apartment arm in arm with her. They made such an unusual pair—the thumb and the forefinger—and for a while, he mused over the possibility of a clandestine relationship.

On the fourth day that he did not see Feliza, aching as he did to see her, Gerry knocked on his door; he had spent all day at the Archives—late afternoon and he had just taken a shower, hoping to go out that early evening for a stroll, and dinner in one of those restaurants near the river. "You haven't seen Feliza yet?" Gerry asked, standing at the door and not bothering to come in.

"Should I?" he asked nonchalantly.

"She asked about you," the Mexican said. "She has been very ill."

He bolted out of his room and rushed up the flight; Feliza's door was ajar and without knocking, he went in. She was propped up by a pillow, her face so pale it seemed as if there was not a single drop of blood in it. He sat on her bed as she stretched her arms to him, and hungrily, lovingly, he embraced her.

"I am sorry, Salvador," she whispered. "It happens every month, but this time it was so bad I spent the whole night doubled up in pain. I thought it would be over the following day—it usually is...I feel better now. In the morning, I will be fine. I will keep my promise tomorrow night."

HE TIDIED up his room, bought some apples, pomegranates, oranges and placed them in the fruit bowl on the reading table. In the tiny bathroom by the door, he placed a couple of fresh towels, a new cake of soap. There were also fresh pastries, a carton of milk. She did not say when she would come, maybe before dinner.

His door was ajar as it always was, and he busied himself, arranging his notes. She entered his room so quietly, he really didn't realize she was already there till she placed a hand on his shoulder and he almost jumped in surprise. He stood up and tried to kiss her but she pushed him away and walked to the door, locked it, then she went to him. It was she who kissed him, all the passion that would have been spent the week before, now revived, ever-fresh, collectible.

He would never understand Feliza. If only a while ago she was so joyously and eagerly entwined with him, now she pushed him away as if he was spoiled meat and all that was detestable. Though she was still very warm there was this glacial coldness now in her whole being, more imagined perhaps than real. Her face was no longer caressingly sweet but disdainful and harsh. She rose quickly and just as hurriedly put on her clothes as if she was afraid to be caught in her nudity in this strange room. He stared at her, not knowing what to say, perplexed and at the same time worried that he had done something unconscionable, an irreparable breach of courtesy perhaps?

Did she resent having left himself in her? But she was safe and it was, after all, what she had wanted.

But she did not leave the room after she had dressed. She combed her hair leisurely, then sat on the chair by the open window. Below them in the street, the drifting talk of passersby. She sat wordless, staring at the low roofs of the houses across the street. Then she bent her head and began to cry, not loud but in stifled sobbing that shook her, so he rose hastily, put his shirt on and went to her.

"Did I do something wrong?"

She did not turn to him. "You don't know what you have done, do you? You don't know?"

He embraced her but she pushed him away with such sudden vehemence it shocked him. So he stood away from her, gazing at her, studying her and her grief which had mysteriously come from nowhere.

"You don't know what you have done," she said softly, careful not to have her voice carry through to the other rooms below. "I have been virtuous, in a state of grace..."

"But you weren't a virgin," he remonstrated, and was at once sorry that he had to make this pronouncement so explicitly. "I didn't do anything you didn't like."

Still sobbing quietly, she flung at him, "You have led me to sin. Sin. Sin! I will be damned."

He went back to her and held her by the shoulder, expecting to be rejected brusquely, but she let him hold her, and when he pulled her back to bed with him, she acceded, still sobbing quietly, and lay down beside him. He let her cry out her grief or her anger, until she was quiet, then he turned on his side and bending over her, looked into the eyes that were now swollen, and he kissed them both, murmuring, "Feliza, I don't want you to be unhappy..."

She did not speak. The sounds of the street below were stilled, and in the rooms underneath, everyone seemed to have retired for the night. "I will be with you till morning," she said evenly, trying to smile as she rose and once more disrobed, her back to him gleaming like alabaster in the light. When she finally lay beside him, her nearness filled him with a feeling of completeness and all the imagined glory because he had persevered and waited.

GERONIMA PIEDAD knocked on his door in the morning, and Feliza who was not yet up had wakened with a start. She clutched at the sheet, terror-stricken, and pointed to the door.

"Yes," he said tentatively.

"It's me, Salvador," Gerry said in an unusually eager voice. "I have an important thing to show you. Not at the Archives but some place just as interesting."

"I will be down in a moment," he said. He listened to her footfall fade down the wooden stairway. Speechless, Feliza was still clutching at the sheet. Buddy started to laugh softly. "What if you hadn't locked the door last night and she just peeped in as she sometimes does?"

She giggled, got up and started to dress. "I will make breakfast," she said, and proceeded to the small kitchen.

Gerry was waiting in the foyer at the entrance. With her was her middle-aged Spaniard in a dark blue suit which, on closer scrutiny, was of very fine material, but the style seemed dated, as if it was a turn-of-the-century suit.

"My father," Gerry introduced the gentleman to him. His hand which he extended quickly in a handshake was cold but the grip was firm. He had blue eyes, and now, he realized that Gerry's eyes were also blue, though she was brown like him.

His suspicions were all unfounded, ridiculous even. There was a very long and complex story which Gerry must tell him, but for the time being, he would just glean from their presence the answer to his unspoken question.

They did not go to the Archives. They walked toward the river, and in one of the old buildings close to it, they went through dim corridors, quiet and sepulchral, with heavy wooden doors on all sides, the old stone floor having been trodden on through the years now undulated in places, the veneer of clay already eroded. The whole place smelled of preserved dust and that pervasive odor of things old, decaying and forgotten.

At one end of the corridor were several offices, with people in them, not one of them young. In the last room was a well-ventilated office, with antique wooden chairs and a large desk.

"My office," Gerry's father said. It was an old shipping company whose glory had long passed, but it was still creaking along, as there were still many properties to be watched not just in Seville but in Mexico, and yes, in Filipinas as well.

The coffee came, freshly brewed and strong and its aroma filled the room. "Geronima told me last night that you are from Filipinas. I was there, of course, a long time ago. In the thirties, and I commanded a ship which went to Cebu, to Macau and Hong Kong and of course, Manila... Early on, we were in the galleons, too. The epic voyage, the wealth they brought. Nothing like them in the whole of maritime history!"

He led them to another room in the huge relic of a building, and they were there, old files in folders tied with pieces of string like they were at the Archives. So many mummies that would perhaps come to life someday, disfigured by time, atrophied even, but could be revived in the mind at least.

"You are welcome to them," Gerry's father said. "I hope you can come here and look. I do not know much, but I'll try and remember."

But being a voyeur he was here to enjoy himself, to let time beguile him into new dimensions of living. With Feliza, Seville now had a new meaning, sensual, not historical. He cannot participate in the past; better amnesia for it denies the past, and everything that is pleasurable is now, or in the future if it were a blank.

Again, he was being drawn into another facet of history; again, his interest was stirred. The Enrique chapter was over, he had learned of the seafaring endurance of his people and the knowledge had given him pride, fulfillment even. But there was still so much to know. Would knowing transform him? He had been involved and this was what James Wack had hoped would happen.

That night, Buddy wrote to him. "Dear Dad, I had hoped that I would soon leave Seville, having had that generous stroke of luck with the Enrique document, but now, I can see that there are things here that hold me back. Today, I got interested in the galleon trade, having met an old Spaniard whose ships once sailed not just to the Pacific but the Atlantic. I cannot seem to let go, being in this treasure trove..."

Professor Wack would delight in his letter, feel justified in having nurtured this orphan; indeed, how often had he wished that Jessica would acquire some interest other than pursuing the pleasures of the senses.

But Salvador dela Raza did not indulge in self-delusion; Seville had captivated him, there was so much precocious ebullience in the city, every time he walked out of the San Eloy house in the morning, that antique charm was his for the taking, infusing him with a vitality that must be vented.

Heaps of material on the galleons were in the Archives; others were scattered everywhere in Mexico and in Spain, in the various houses of the friar orders, in Filipinas, the friars who were in the trade and had profited from it immensely, and all the way to Peru which the goods from the Orient reached.

Gerry Piedad did not know her father had been in the Philippines before World War II, commanding a merchant ship; in fact, she did not know much about her father other than he was in Seville, at the address her Indian mother had always kept. He was upright, and through all the years since he left Mexico, he had sent money to his child. And now, she was visiting him for the first time. As a girl, her mother had worked in Acapulco where she met the handsome officer. She had since then moved to Cuernavaca, a resort town below Mexico City. "I went to school there—a sunny place for shady people," Gerry described it to him. "Next time you go to Mexico, visit our place."

Now, Gerry's father talked with him on occasion and asked about the Philippines. He surprised the old gentleman when he said he had never been there.

Gerry's bounding enthusiasm finally prodded him to read more on the galleons. It should not be a Mexican without real training in historiography who should do it. "It is so incredible, Salvador. There I was, a little girl in Acapulco, listening to all the stories of these ships, wondering about the Chinos—that's what all of you were called. You built and manned them. It should be you, not I, Salvador, who should write the story. It was your people who were responsible for this epic trade—not the Spaniards, not the Mexicans; they just profited from it."

Gerry Piedad introduced him to a Peruvian scholar, Julio Martin Vargas, who was researching the effects of the galleon trade. "It all but abolished the silk industry in Mexico," he said. "The silver mines—they were developed just to support the trade. And the ostentatious tastes of the South American elites. There are many lessons to be learned from the trade."

"It's a great story, Dad. I have to stay longer," he wrote Professor Wack.

9

"There is not an Indian in those islands who has not a remarkable inclination for the sea, nor is there at present in all the world a people more agile in maneuvers on shipboard, or who learn so quickly nautical terms and whatever a good mariner ought to know...They can teach many of the Spanish seamen who sail in those seas...There is hardly an Indian who has sailed the seas who does not understand the mariner's compass, and therefore on this trade route there are some very skillful and dexterous helmsmen....

—Francisco Leandro de Viana

WHEN I WAS thirty years old, after fifteen years of apprenticing for my father who was then a master carpenter, I was myself made into a master carpenter recognized as such by the viceroy and all the powerful royal officials who managed the galleons. The year was 1710 and I had already been working in the Cavite shipyard together with my fellows from Macabebe. That is where all of us came from—thirty carpenters, most of us related, brought to Cavite by my father. Because Macabebe was quite far, we settled in Cavite, close to our place of work.

We could not be overlooked, in fact, we were easily identified. When I was a boy, a smallpox epidemic swept through our part of the country.

91

My father and all of us in the family—actually no one in town was spared—were afflicted. Many people died including my only sister. Others in the work camp also had had smallpox, but our scars seemed bigger and deeper, and these scars which are all over my body had always made me feel that I am unspeakably ugly, no woman would look at me a second time, which is why at an age when I should already be husband and father, I am not.

My father was a very good teacher. When we were not building ships, we were often in the Walled City building handsome houses with stone walls, tile roofs, and solid wooden floors and panels. We were most valued, however, for constructing those hardy ships that sailed to Acapulco and brought back wealth to Manila. We were also better educated than most Indios; I attended the escuela in Cavite and got well beyond the cartilla; all of us spoke Chabacano which is simplified Spanish, but my Spanish was adequate and I could read construction plans just as my brother, Arcadio, could read navigational charts.

Don Carlos Paz directed the building of the new galleon. My father had worked for him; he told Don Carlos that I could already do the job. I did not know that Don Carlos had been watching us all the while.

At the time, it was getting to be more and more difficult to build the galleons in Cavite; good timber, molave and the like, were getting more scarce in the Bataan and Cavite forests. Bringing them to the shipyard required so much labor. This was one of the sources of Indio discontent, those who were not skilled like us were forced into the tedious job of cutting the trees, the timber, and hauling the logs on rollers by carabao to Cavite.

Don Carlos decided that we should go to Pangasinan, to Sual, which had a good port and was also very close to the forested mountains where good timber grew in abundance. Don Carlos was short, balding, with a face that seemed in perpetual scowl...his manner was impatient, imperious, and he was extremely loud in his curses and commands. The peons called him El Tigre, but to those of us who knew him, my father and my relatives, he was a tiger without fangs—El Tigre sin colomillos. He carried this whip which he threatened all the time to use and, of course, he would have those lazy oafs chained; it was like this in Cavite—the poor peons were whipped, their backs infected often where the whip had broken the skin, the ankles of those in chains bloodied and oozing with pus where the iron had bitten into the flesh. But this was not our fate; like the Sangley craftsmen, we were indispensable. The poor peons who often tried to escape were hanged if they were caught. All too often then, by the gate to the shipyard, an unfortunate Indio would be hanging for days.

El Tigre was never a tyrant; if he were selfish or cruel, we would never have been able to go to Acapulco for it was only the favorites of the viceroy, the archbishop or the rich merchants, who were elected to go and make a fortune even if they were not capable seamen.

My father had gone to Sual much earlier, and he had supervised the cutting of the trees, identified those that were sturdy, molave, and all the fine hardwoods, and they were then sawn and dried. By the time we arrived with our families—the building of the ship took more than a year—much of the timber we needed was ready, and my father then left the master carpentry job to me and the supervision of a hundred carpenters and a couple hundred forced-labor peons.

We laid the keel close to the shore with magic rituals which would enable the ship to defy punishment at sea. A great festivity, too; priests all the way from Vigan came and blessed it, and Don Carlos donated six cows to be butchered for the workers. Under the repartimiento system they were required to bring their own food. But Don Carlos saw to it that they were well-treated unlike in Cavite. El Tigre was a difficult and exacting taskmaster. If there was any work which he did not like, which was shoddy, he would have it repeated even if it delayed finishing the ship. He saw to it that the best materials were used. The sails were woven of the best cotton in the Ilocos, and cut and sewn there, and the hemp for the ropes were spun right in his presence because he wanted them tightly twined. Perhaps, his reasons were not just to make a beautiful ship. We learned that he was also going to New Spain to pick up his betrothed from Leon; though almost fifty, he had remained a bachelor.

When finished, we painted her white and may she, in her pristine nature, ride the waves with grace and cleave through bad weather like a tempered blade. On her prow, above the stately forecastle, the life-size image of Sta. Teresita garbed in blue, her arms outstretched as if to beseech a smile from the heavens.

The workmen then pushed the ship down the slipway to the water. We boarded it with our families and returned to Cavite where it was fitted with cannon from the foundries there.

We had built two galleons in Cavite earlier, the Rosario and Santissima Trinidad, big ships but the Teresita was even bigger—we had added two feet to all the dimensions of the keel. When finally afloat, the ship, my father told me, would be over two thousand tons, perhaps the biggest ever.

My father had begged El Tigre to take us. How many Indios have had the opportunity to sail on these beautiful ships? But above all was the hope that when we returned there would be a small fortune for all of us, as all those who had sailed were thus rewarded.

The great ship was ready; El Tigre promised my father he would take me as master carpenter and six of my relatives who would be with the crew. They had no training in seamanship, but they had been building these boats for so long they could man them. It was March, and very hot; they started loading the boat at its mooring on the Pasig, just below the walls of Fort

Santiago—porcelain, jewelry, gold, the finest silks, the products of the Orient and what else I could only guess. Written on each shipment was the prayer, "Dios llevandolo en sacramento"—God bring it to safe harbor. We went on a pilgrimage to the Virgin of Guadalupe, to the Santissimo Rosario in Intramuros, and that first week of May, we walked to Antipolo to pray to the Virgin and finally, to the patroness of the galleons, Our Lady of Porta Vaga in Cavite, whose image, much earlier in November, was borne across Manila Bay.

The seventh of May, an auspicious day; the Archbishop came and said mass on the ship, and all of Manila was there on the riverbank. Bands were playing, rockets were fired, the sails were unfurled, and we were on our way, tarrying not lest we would be overtaken by the typhoons of the rainy season.

The seven of us, servants of El Tigre, were all apportioned jobs. As master carpenter, I was in charge of repairs on the ship. My younger brother, Arcadio, was taken as a servant of the pilot, a mestizo who was now on his third trip. My other cousins were to serve in the kitchen, on the deck, whichever job was assigned to them. Arcadio was the happiest for he was on deck most of the time, bringing out charts, working the wheel in accord with the compass or as ordered by the pilot. He had always wanted to be a seaman, a pilot even, if such a high position was not denied the Indios.

Even in good weather, according to the pilot, it was difficult to go through the string of islands that blocked the way to the open ocean; the currents were swift, and sudden squalls and strong winds could buffet the ship off course. But in three weeks, we were finally in San Bernardino, then free from the green gauntlet, and we broke through the Embocadero into the seemingly trackless Pacific.

As Filipinas vanished behind us, the wind filled the sails; they billowed and pushed our boat, the masts and the woodwork creaking, stretching, bending to where the wind took us. In the mornings, everyone would be on the deck, watching the sun go up, the sea heaving around us. A hundred passengers, some of them soldiers, some of them functionaries, friars returning to the Peninsula. They were on the first deck and we were at the bottom, among the cargo, sleeping where our bodies could fit.

Then monotony started its slow, deft siege. The crew, my relatives— we always had something to do, cleaning, washing, cooking, but the passengers could only gossip, play card games, or read if they had such lofty inclinations. And on days when the air was still, the ship stood there on a glasslike world, a cloudless sky relieved at night when the stars swarmed out. It was oppressive below, the foul odor of the bilge beneath us would whorl and engulf us, but we got used to it. And if the ship capsized and sank, it was also safer below than to be on deck. We realized this soon enough.

Our first typhoon struck during our second month at sea, at a time when our water was already running short and the water constable had to ration it. First came the squalls and we were thankful for now we could bathe in the rain and that is what all the passengers did, crowd the deck in various forms of undress. We had also spread large woven mats to capture the rainwater and funnel them into the empty jars. But the squalls were a prelude to stronger winds, the pilot warned, and we furled the sails, but now, I do not think it was done fast enough. To go up the riggings lashed by the wind, to keep the giant sails furled, nothing could be more dangerous even for the bravest sailor.

The wind clawed at our puny ship, and now the waves as big as mountains came; they loomed before us, to our right, then crashed down. Twenty men, including six passengers, were washed away from the deck. We who built the boat were shaken—could it stand such punishment? The Dominicans, the Franciscans on the second deck and the passengers were praying, their novena drowned by the howling wind. The front mast snapped and crashed down on the forecastle, partly demolishing it.

Whenever a huge wave hit the side of the boat, it would list so much the masts would almost hit the water. We feared the boat would now sink, but it did not. Nor did the sides give way—we had built this ship from the strongest hardwoods, and as the English pirates found out, even their cannon could not penetrate the hulls; their cannonballs were uselessly embedded in the woodwork.

Five days of hell during which we could not cook and therefore could not eat, nor could we sleep. Finally, the typhoon spent itself.

We thought our problems were over, then a cousin came up screaming, saying that there was a leak and water was rising in the hold. El Tigre and I rushed to investigate and sure enough, water had risen in the hold. I had to find the leak and plug it before the ship was flooded.

We enlisted the help of some of the seamen, particularly those who could dive, and we scoured the hull for several hours, examining each plank methodically, feeling where the water was coming in. All these in the dark, with the dim light of a lantern or two. All these in foul-smelling water, for the bilge had mixed with the leak, all these by diving and feeling out the hull. We had built the Sta. Teresita well; none of her ribs had cracked. I found the leak, not a hole but a gash where the caulking, having been battered by the waves, had given way. We formed a relay to draw buckets out while I plugged the leak feverishly with pieces of cloth.

There was so much to do, and I now realized that I had only six men to work with; the mast must be braced, the forecastle fixed, although I did not really see any value in maintaining its height—it was a hindrance to navigation and was nothing more than a concession to the ship styles of the day.

We could proceed with the voyage on two masts, slower perhaps, but we could not go on with a ship that leaked and I was in fear that the next storm would do more damage to the hull.

El Tigre was very pleased; he said I had saved the ship; the mast was repaired in three days and we were in full sail again. He was now optimistic. "Segundo," he said. He always called me Second, and my father Primero, or First. "When we get to Acapulco, you and your compatriots will have a thanksgiving feast."

But Acapulco was still weeks or months away. From those who had already made this crossing, there was more travail to come and I hoped to God we could bear it.

The others did not. In a few more weeks, the dread diseases of scurvy and beri beri began to take their toll. Our food had greatly diminished, the biscuits rotten with bugs, the rice and the meat already decayed and rats were all over the place. The beans, the cheeses were so badly attacked by vermin, some of them clung to our bodies and created boils and infections. People started to die, and the priests were always busy, listening to confessions, administering the last sacraments, performing burial liturgies as the corpses were pushed to the sea.

The sun shimmered on the still waters; no breeze, nothing moved. In the depths, even the demons that lurked beyond the reach of men had gone to sleep. The sky was pure blue, emptied of clouds. We waited for those señas, the signs that would tell us the coast of Baja California was near, but much as we scanned the waters, none of those signs appeared.

We were now throwing into the sea twenty corpses every day, men whose teeth had fallen out, whose bodies were bloated. Our food was running low, and what we ate was no longer fit for human beings, scraps of dried fish with vermin in them, dried meat that had turned foul-smelling, crawling with maggots, but we ate them because death by starvation was the alternative.

Then the breeze stirred; it had also become cooler.

On the last week of the fifth month, a cry erupted from the lookout. Señas, señas! We all rushed to the deck, the few who had survived, and looked at the islands of matted grass, and sea lions—it was my first time to see them. And soon, seagulls, porras—yellowish strands of kelp—and up ahead, the thin outline of land at last, Cape Mendocino in California.

Fresh water, food, oranges, fresh fish—but these came too late for many. When we finally reached Acapulco, of the hundred or more who boarded in Manila, only fifteen survived. Still, recalling some stories of tragedies on this trade route, we were much, much luckier, unlike that galleon that came in—a ghost ship, with everyone on board dead.

96

Acapulco! The Spanish dream, gold and glory and all those fantasies that have fired the Iberian imagination, sending these white men away from their homeland to achieve their destinies, their illusions.

I had not witnessed the loading of the ship in Manila, and now I realized how much cargo was stashed everywhere. The man in charge of the cargo manifest was dead, so it was El Tigre and myself, and Fray Marcelino, the Dominican friar, who helped in disposing the goods at the feria; seeing to it that the prices indicated in the manifests were clearly recorded. Gold, jewelry, ornaments, silks and other products from the east—they were all there and there was not enough for the wealthy Spaniards of New Spain and their cohorts who wanted them. The feria lasted for a month, and in the meantime, there was no rest for us. We had to make sure that the leaks in the ship were well-plugged, that all weak planks were replaced or strengthened. We had to clean, smoke out the vermin, kill the rats and make the cabins livable again, free from the stench of disease and doom.

One afternoon, in the midst of all these efforts, El Tigre took me and all my Macabebe relatives in a carriage close to the mountains that surround Acapulco, to a large hacienda with a big house of many rooms. He had a small calf roasted, all the sherry and tequila we could drink. He assigned us each to a room. I was too full of food and wine to notice the pretty Indian girl that had come in. In my stupor and satiety, I had instantly fallen asleep.

If on the start of our journey, he was apprehensive, wondering if ever those English pirates would attack us, now El Tigre was almost sure that they would, divested as we were of our cargo, but loaded with so many boxes of silver pesos. A new man in the boat had the specific duty to watch over them. We were lighter, we could sail faster. We loaded ballast, those granite stones used for paving the streets of Intramuros. Even before we sailed out of the harbor, El Tigre ordered the troops to drill, and the cannoneers to prepare a series of broadsides which they did when we were finally in the open sea.

On the day that we lifted anchor, again there was mass. El Tigre's betrothed arrived, a beautiful woman with skin as fair as the rose, and eyes that sparkled. She was not even twenty, I think. I had never seen a girl as pretty as she. She had an Indian servant girl, short and squat and very protective. She followed her mistress wherever she went. No one among us talked with her, more out of respect than anything. It seemed her Indian maid was also anxious to keep all of us in the crew away from her.

We had a hundred and fifty passengers, some two dozen of them friars who were going to join their orders in Filipinas. We were never short of men of the cloth—they would minister to our needs during the voyage, which Arcadio told me was shorter this time—a little over three months—and not as perilous as the trip to Acapulco.

We were also well-provisioned.

Indeed, the wind was on our back and though at night we should not have sailed, we did, the pilot confident of the way. Seldom did we encounter heavy rains and high seas, just the gentle wind which bloated our sails and pushed us on.

Barely a month out of Acapulco—then, it struck. First, it was the women passengers. They complained of high fever, of vomiting, and finally, little sores that ripened into pus broke out all over their bodies. One of the priests immediately knew what it was, the dreaded pox that had decimated whole populations in Europe and America Sur. We did not know what to do. One of the priests told us to fumigate the ship, which we did, careful that the fires we started did not spread. We began again the sad ritual of throwing to the sea the many who had died, and so it went on for days as the death ship ploughed on. As on the voyage to Acapulco, the sad ritual was repeated; in the morning, each cabin was visited, the light in the lantern by the door extinguished, and the bodies of the dead were brought out.

On the first week of the third month, the pilot himself died. El Tigre was frantic, frightened, I could see that in his face. How to guide the ship back to Manila now? He was not a sailor; he was, after all, a builder, a merchant. And though he often looked at charts and maps, like me he did not know how to interpret them. Then, like his wife and her Indian maid, he too fell sick—he could not even go out of his cabin as his fever raged. The fate of the ship was now entirely in our hands, in my brother Arcadio's hands. Arcadio was grim-faced, but was determined. He had had many talks with the pilot, he had studied the charts and knew, of course, that the way back was different, but was it possible for someone like him to know the track in the ocean the way the pilot did? He had studied it for years, and had served on these boats so long, and here was Arcadio, now our only hope. Almost any moment now, El Tigre could die. I was at my brother's side always, looking at those charts, wondering if we were truly headed for Filipinas.

One of my boys in the kitchen made a headcount; of the two hundred passengers, only forty were left. But, thank God, El Tigre, his wife and her maid were still alive, though very ill and unable to leave their cabins.

At first, I wondered when the pox would strike us, and if we would survive it. My fears were banished when a Franciscan friar who had recovered from it, came to me and said, now he was immune, too, as all of us whose faces were pocked were immune. He was one of the five who had survived as all the other friars had died.

We slept through nights discordant with rasping breath, the scurrying of rats on the funereal hold, an occasional shriek of despair, or hunger, from the crew, most of them too weak to do their chores. Above, a clear sky hovered above the ship, and around us, the translucent waters so quiet and still, untouched by a ripple of some distant wave or flurry of a lost wayward wind. The lamps fore and aft burned bright marking the length of this wooden coffin glued, immobile, on the dark, smooth surface of the ocean.

Now just twelve of us remained.

Then, slowly, we could feel a subtle change in the weather—it was getting cooler, and Arcadio said this was to be expected as we ventured into higher lattitudes. That was what his teacher, the pilot, had told him. Soon enough, however, the weather seemed tropical again. We finally sighted land to the left—a long coastline in the distance.

That is Luzon, Arcadio said with great certitude.

He steered the ship closer to the shore, and soon enough, several small boats came to us. We were not wary anymore. If this had happened on the way to Acapulco, we would have been fearful—they could have been hostile islanders, cannibals even. But the boats that surrounded us were familiar; they carried Indios like ourselves, fishermen mostly, and they shouted greetings.

El Tigre stumbled out of his cabin and clambered on deck, so thin had he become! It was his first time in the sun, he was well but very weak, and his face—now marred by scabs of black—was extremely bright. He knew this part of the country, of the port close to Ciudad Fernandina, Curimao, it is called, and we went there, anchored quickly, and then rowed ashore to hear mass, to give thanksgiving.

After all those weeks of uncertainty and danger in the open sea, how exhilarating, how joyous it was to tread again on firm ground, to feel the earth under our feet and walk straight, and not sway on seasick legs on a yawling deck. Most of all, no foul weather could threaten us now and if on the way back to Manila we were to chance upon some storm, we could always hug the shore.

El Tigre had thought of sending fire signals all along the coast but that was, as he said, inconclusive and could even be misunderstood. Better to send a horseman to Manila to bring the news that we were bringing in the Sta. Teresita, and that we were also harbingers of so much bad news. We had new provisions, bathed in fresh water and feasted on young corn, papayas, banana, plenty of fresh fish and pork. El Tigre recruited under repartimiento twenty young Ilokanos to help so that we could have some rest; they were all very pleased to join and realize their dream of seeing Manila.

More than a week later, we sailed into Manila Bay, and to our mooring at the bank of the Pasig. Again, a multitude awaited us, bands played, rockets swished in the heavens. We had brought for those who had invested in the trip so much profit, the silver that supported Manila and its enterprises. I was assured that my relatives would also get something. I did not doubt that—El Tigre was a man of honor.

When his wife came out of her cabin, her face was shrouded with a veil. I could only look at her Indian maid, her skin now covered with pale scars because the scabs had just lifted. What a tragedy for one so young and beautiful! But as the years went on, El Tigre was very devoted to her; she gave him half a dozen children, all boys. He never sailed on the galleon again, other than invest in it. He retired to Laguna with his family, bought a big hacienda there. He was widely honored for his courage, his wisdom and skill in bringing back the Sta. Teresita. And the merchants in Intramuros whom he had made rich never tired of talking about his courageous exploits, and they always feted him whenever he visited the Royal City.

But he knew—all the five Spanish survivors knew—the full story and none of them can ever take away from the seven of us Indios this knowledge of how we persevered and triumphed.

10

IN SEVILLE Buddy's formative ideas on history, on exile and revolutionary nationalism, became more lucid. At the same time, several questions had begun to form in his mind, impinging upon him the uniqueness of the Spanish conquest of the archipelago, the subjugation of the Indian empires and civilizations of America Sur.

The South American empire had been liberated by Simon Bolivar, but the Philippines was still very much a Spanish colony, its native elites desiring not freedom from Spain but equality with the Spaniards and seats in the Spanish Cortes.

How would it be if those three centuries were compressed into three hours, a long movie reeled backward, images jumping in profusion, in disarray, exploding, merging, flowing in squeaks and squiggles, and when finally over, what would it leave behind? What did Spain leave behind? The Spaniards, as they themselves have indelibly embossed in history, are a cruel people and this cruelty is what they had left, not Catholicism which has become a grievous lie though unknown as such by the multitudes worshipping those wooden images. A lie, too, is the humbling piety because underneath the penances and scented rosaries is the forgotten agony of those they had bludgeoned with the cross. This then is the sum of it all, the distillation of centuries, this legacy of cruelty encrusted in the lands they had plundered, its grand hypocrisies shaping the people, particularly their leaders. And entwined with this cruelty was grasping, corroding greed. The native peoples easily succumbed and submitted themselves to the lash and, thereby, became infected themselves.

How was this warped, gnomish Spanish personality formed? Where did its authoritarian impulse come from? The intolerance? Where but from those centuries of the Spanish Inquisition. And here in Seville, Buddy saw so many priests in black soutane in the streets. Even the smallest churches bore the baroque effusions of the past, the carvings in ivory, marble and wood. But somehow, he knew that all these could not quite erase the ignomiy that, here in Seville, the Inquisition had so profoundly left behind in the persecution of the Moors and the Jews and their descendants, the vehemence against "Jewish leprosy" as voiced loudest by Cardinal Mendoza, the archbishop of Seville. Here, the great fortress Triana on the banks of the Guadalquivir was transformed into the bastion of the Inquisition, here in Seville was the "quemadero," where the heretics were burned. And the Royal Couple, Ferdinand and Isabella, they who sent those gallant seamen in their voyages to the New World, they themselves were the grand patrons of the Inquisition. Surely, no single institution has shaped the Spanish psyche more than this aberration. Hossanahs then for the irredentism of the Basques, the Catalans and the host of maverick Republicans who kept alive the spirit of inquiry and liberalism. Now, under Franco, the faint reverberations of the free spirit were repressed but surely, the pendulum would swing the other way. It did so less than a hundred years ago when Indios like Marcelo H. del Pilar and his writers in *La Solidaridad* were in Spain, arguing for reforms in Filipinas and they had found a receptive audience among the Spaniards.

The elites of a colonized nation usually inherit the vices—not the virtues—of the colonizer, and this truism was now blatantly evident in the elites of the former Spanish colonies, in Filipinas as well, where power was mostly in the hands of the mestizos, who in turn discriminate and look down on the native population. The Indios, Buddy was convinced, were willing victims long after the conquistador had gone, and the legacy of cruelty and intolerance still prevailed. In many ways, he now came to realize, there was not much difference between the black Americans suffering white prejudice in the United States and the Indios of Filipinas under their elites.

At the Archives, Buddy met a lanky, young Jesuit, Jack Macher, who was working on what he termed the Propaganda Movement. Buddy had spent with the American scholar several pleasant and engaging hours, drinking sherry, eating tapas and discussing how Philippine nationalism was finally given its context by an innovative group of young Indios—almost all of them from wealthy mestizo families—studying and living in Europe. It was the middle of the nineteenth century, Spain had a liberal government and in the Philippines, the schools that were once the special preserve of the Spaniards and the wealthy mestizos were finally opened to the Indios—three centuries of Spanish rule and what could Spain show? He knew from his reading that it was not correct to judge a situation in the past from the perceptions of the present. With Father Jack, he looked at the Indios in Europe; they represented the first truly Western-educated Filipinos. It was a time, too, when Spanish liberals in and out of government wanted reforms in Filipinas.

"But it is difficult for me to understand," he told Father Jack, "why they chose to be identified with Mother Spain, why they sought equality with the Spaniards, and seats in the Spanish parliament."

"That was a matter of strategy, too," the young Jesuit said. "Towards the end, remember that they gave up such ideas, that they realized there was no alternative but freedom from Spanish rule."

"I also could not understand why, in spite of the villification they suffered from the Spaniards, the racial insults that they did not have the mental capacity for intellectual development, they did not mount a revolution outright. I see now, of course, that in the social hierarchy of the times, the Spaniards were on top, and they were right below them. In that position, they were above the masses, the peasantry."

Father Jack added, "More important than social positioning is that they created the consciousness of a Filipino nation. The three priests, Gomez, Burgos and Zamora whom the Spaniards executed did it first with their ultimate sacrifice. The idea of a Filipino nation developed from there. And Rizal, more than any one of them, with his novels and writings truly inspired the Revolution that was to break out later."

Buddy recalled the Filipino exiles in the United States who had fled Marcos. Some of them were truly in fear of their lives, but a lot more used Marcos as an excuse to justify themselves, to glorify themselves even, by giving their exile a patriotic color when they were merely running away from challenges they couldn't cope with, to live in the comfort of America.

Of the exiles in Spain, as Father Jack said, Rizal was the most important. He was also the acknowledged leader, the rennaissance man—a medical doctor, a poet and novelist, a scholar, a painter and sculptor. He dominated the exile community in Europe. His family in Calamba, Laguna, had difficulties with the Dominican friars who owned the hacienda where the Rizals lived. Rizal had encouraged them to organize, to fight the friars and bring their case to Spain itself. He had argued that if Filipinas was indeed a part of Spain, then the Spanish courts should have a say on matters such as this. The friars in the Philippines who had long been the real holders of power did not want this to happen for it would mean the diminution of their power. And many of the conservatives in Spain believed that to open Spanish institutions like the Cortes or parliament to Indios would mean the beginning of an independence movement.

At Berkeley, Buddy had seen so many books and pamphlets about Rizal. In fact, there was a Rizal industry churning out all sorts of scholarly work about the man, the tritest details about his life, his loves, his letters and soon, his laundry bills. Not that the man did not deserve it—he did, he epitomized all that was heroic in the Indio. But Rizal was a supreme egoist who prepared for his place in history, who saw himself as a leader of his people and proceeded to play that role. In this, the Spanish tyrants were on his side; pre-cisely by executing him, they elevated him to his pantheon not just as martyr but as national hero, admired as such even before the Americans came and confirmed him.

Buddy was more fascinated with another exile, self-effacing, capable of heroism as well, and that was Marcelo H. del Pilar, certainly older than Rizal and most of the students of his generation in Spain.

Del Pilar was sent to Spain by the Manila Committee which, like him, felt it necessary at the time to propagandize for reforms in Spain itself, the Spanish government having been changed into a more liberal one, capable of compassion and willing to listen to the complaints of the Indios. The newspaper, La Solidaridad, was the main organ of the Indios for this purpose—it came out twice a month in Spanish and though primarily directed to the Spaniards in Spain, it was also addressed to the Filipinos at home. Del Pilar edited it.

The exile community in Europe was, in a sense, representative of the Indio elite. Almost everyone came from wealthy families—it required then, as it did now, financial means to send a young man to Europe. Many of them, much to the annoyance of Rizal who was always lecturing on moral rectitude, lived lavishly, gambled and chased women, but there were also those who did not have such sensual inclination nor the money.

What does it mean to be an exile? More and more, Buddy was being confronted by the phenomenon. Was he himself one? an exile from his own self? or now that he was in Europe, an exile from the plenitude of America? America had an exile tradition, the writers who went to Europe before World War II, his father himself, seeking in France the freedom denied him in America.

And there is that exile who has never left his native land, who has shut himself up in a mansion, a shell, a prison, uninvolved with the humanity around him, as if it were some distant swamp of smells and unseen dangers surrounding him but unable to touch him, because in body and in mind, his defenses are secure. Or such an exile can, on occasion, with patronizing reluctance, leave his sanctuary and go down to feel the outside, to experience vicariously its varied tastes, and having done so, hurries back to the comfort of his old habitat. Such an exile does exist, a voyeur in the turmoil of the world, an excursionist—and thinking thus, Buddy was shocked that this very person, this very creature whom he detested, was actually himself.

He read about the quarrels of the exiles, marvelled at their passion and florid prose, at their grandiloquent gestures, Rizal most of all, proclaiming unabashedly their love for Filipinas, and more so because they were far from her, far from the tribulations that bedevilled the Indios who could not leave.

He could imagine himself easily as Marcelo H. del Pilar, take on the great man's persona, live the excruciating pain, the vicious loneliness and disappointment as only del Pilar could feel; indeed, of all the exiles in Europe at the time, he was the most tragic figure and with him and him alone, Salvador dela Raza identified completely.

The Hotel Manila was close to the Cathedral and on Sunday afternoons young people gathered there, singing and dancing in a circle, their voices bright and vibrant in stark contrast to the austere darkness of the cathedral interior. Watching them, Buddy had mused how it must have been in another time, when an Indio was here, lonely and homesick.

Reading the letters of the exiles, particularly del Pilar's, he recognized their anguish, the stringent pull of memory that Buddy himself felt for those fractured images of his early boyhood. How he wished that del Pilar had kept some journal which could now be retrieved so that all he had to do was translate it.

11

ON THIS, *my last year in Spain I think, I am filled with misgivings not so much about myself, although this is already starting, but about my compatriots. Are they here more to enjoy themselves, to savor the pleasures of the bedroom with Spanish women, to waste their time gambling, rather than attend to the festering wounds of the motherland?*

Those friars! They have been our lascivious corruptors and to think that they had come to bring us the blessings of Catholicism! How often had they seduced and despoiled our women, searched our homes for evidence, manufactured or real, to prove heresy and treason—to them, not to Mother Spain. They have jailed us, tortured us, confiscated our properties and left us to starve. And here in Mother Spain, their tentacles reach out to us. The news from home continues to tell us of their mendacity and their abuses. And all we can do is write against them, tell those in Spain who will listen to us, that across the seas, in that colony named Filipinas, the legacy of Spain is rotting, because those who are in power are not true to the faith.

The life of an exile, even if one had enough money, is never easy to justify and this is what Rizal had raised before the entire community and inferentially, myself. I see our role so clearly, the instructions of the Committee which sent me here are unequivocal: Talk with the authorities, argue with them, show them the necessity of immediate reforms in

Filipinas—if the country is to progress and to continue being true to the legacies of Mother Spain.

###

I had to move to another rooming house today, this in a much cheaper place in the city. I know that I should not do this, but I have difficulty meeting the rent, and I am living now on a much smaller allowance. Many a morning, I wonder if I will have enough to eat. I envy my richer countrymen, particularly those who have a continuous flow of money because they can spend so much time talking in the cafes. I cannot join them, my poverty does not permit it and much as I need their charity, it is difficult for me to accept it. That I have sunk into this pitiable state is so demeaning. If I were back in Bulacan, I would not have to undergo this. But I know, even though they never told me, that my family does not see why I had to leave, why I had to come to this distant land to write. I tell myself it is for Filipinas, but I think I was not truthful enough to myself, that I also wanted to travel, to experience other lands not just for myself, my education, but so I would know what it is at home that we do not have, how we can better ourselves. In this sense, I hope that my wife, my family, will eventually understand—truly, I left them for Filipinas.

I envy Rizal, not for his intellectual prowess, not for his leadership; I envy him for though Calamba and his parents have a very strong hold on him, he did not leave behind a family dependent on him. He has the freedom to move at will, to stay in Europe as long as he deems it necessary. Maybe, men like Rizal are precisely what Filipinas needs—men unswerving in their loyalty, undetracted and undeterred by the trivial pull of home and family.

###

I received today a peso from my dearest daughter; only eight years old and she had saved this so I could return home. For someone so young, it is a lot of money and she could have bought herself a dress, a pair of shoes, whatever her young fancy wishes. How I miss her, and her sister, too, oh that they could be with me so they can sit on my lap while I tell them stories the way I used to.

I do not think there is any sense anymore in my writing to my own relatives, my friends, for help—I know they are in great difficulties, too, perhaps much greater than mine and they also have to face the anger of those friars whom I have attacked.

But my daughter, she writes such good, polite Tagalog. I am quite sure my wife dictated it to her. I have reread the letter so many times, I can hear her voice, feel her presence—I am very sorry, dear Father, she says, but this is all that I have saved, all that I can give so that you can come home.

And so I ask myself again—this I do so many times—if my being here is well worth this helplessness. I tell myself it is not, that I must live for myself and work for myself and then I realize how selfish I am, how utterly devoid of the sentiment that had borne me so well before. Filipinas, you are the dearest mother I cannot deny. And I remember again the skies of Malolos, how clear and blue they are in the mornings, and when the sunset comes, how glorious it is. And the harvest season, the fields amber with ripening grain, the air scented. And Christmas after that, the noche buena, the family feast—lechon, cheese, stuffed chicken, and pork adobo—just remembering already fills me, and I can go to sleep.

I wander around the city, through the narrow streets of Barrio Chino, and proceed to the Ramblas where I take a seat. I watch the people file past, well-dressed, well-fed.

But I have hoped too much that it is here in Spain, here where power begins, that perhaps I can persuade those who wield it to understand the aspirations of my people for the equality, the dignity, we deserve. I have had sympathetic listeners, but there are also those who are on the side of the friars, who will always regard us as inferior, as children who must always be led, because we are brown, because we are a vanquished people.

Graciano Lopez Jaena is dead, the last days of his life spent in penury. He had dissipated himself with drink. I had warned him against it. He was such an eloquent speaker, he could move to tears or enrage his listeners. But he was careless and he exaggerated or adorned facts. When I warned him about his rhetorical excesses, he always waved me aside, "Marcelo, these Spaniards do not know any better." But suppose they did? That would destroy the credibility of our cause...In the end, he also proved most difficult to us in La Solidaridad. He wanted so much to be a member of parliament, his overriding ambition embittered him and he started attacking us, questioning our motives and our decency. But let it be—patriotism comes in many guises...

I am very grateful to Ferdinand Blumentritt who has also written in La Solidaridad such brilliant and well-argued articles about Filipinas. As a European, his articles carried more weight than the articles we wrote. Too, his reputation as a scholar is unblemished. Vicente Barrantes, an *academic who had served in Filipinas, had written articles deprecating the Indio's capacity for intellectual discourse. This was the general view of so many Spaniards who looked down on us; now here comes this famous European scholar to our defense and lauding as well Rizal's Noli which had been attacked in the Spanish newspapers by the friends of the friars.*

###

I arrived in Spain much ahead of Rizal and, because of my age, because of what I was doing, the Filipinos had looked up to me as their leader, a position which I did not seek but which, of course, pleased me. Those were the days when La Solidaridad had financing, when there were Spanish officials in the highest places sympathetic to our cause. When Rizal arrived, he immediately assumed that, because of his prestige, he would be the leader. On many occasions, he had also preached to the Filipino community a high degree of morality, of avoiding wine and women. I agreed with him but most of us knew, of course, of his affair in Vienna. I did not want to antagonize him, not once have I written anything that was not favorable to him, for I always felt that we should be united in our struggle for reforms. He wanted, however, to impose his will, to have La Solidaridad under his command which, of course, I could not grant, first because I cannot; it was the Committee in Manila which had given me that position. There was an election and, of course, Rizal won, but that election was so unnecessary. It served nothing but fracture the community. I did not want that election—he could have just stayed on and became the leader. His victory was hollow, he knew it and we knew it. And what had it served him in the end but disunity? I think he recognized this but it was too late— the lines had been drawn. I did not let the division stop me; I continued asking him to write for La Solidaridad just as he had done in the past. I recognized always the contribution he had made to the movement—he was an important part of it.

Then Rizal started talking about returning to Manila. Now, he criticized not just the policy of La Solidaridad but, above all, how it carried out its objectives. There was great validity in his argument, that the real fight for Filipinas was in the country itself, close to the sick man, and not in far-off Spain. I can easily agree with that position, but we were already in Spain, we already had established not just an organization but also a newspaper. Will we close everything then? For me, the fight should be continued in Spain as well, to continue doing the most that was possible.

Rizal left. I begged him just the same to continue writing for La Solidaridad. In the past, he and so many others had written for it and brought prestige and credibility to the newspaper. I recognized his greatness, but I also saw he was ambitious and wanted to dominate everyone. But we needed him, and it was a very sad day when we had to part ways. I think that in the end he understood me and was very careful not to attack me, that all the while he expressed his respect for me. I had done the same but somehow, I cannot quite erase from my mind this flaw in his character, his insufferable self-esteem and determination to lead, and to lead alone.

###

I spent all my money yesterday to pay the printer and even that was not enough. It is so difficult to keep a regular printing schedule when I do not have the money to demand it, and it was so understanding of him to realize what I am trying to do, and he agreed to release the issue even if I had not paid him in full. How will the next issue ever be published when I cannot even make a down payment? I can see my countrymen, who used to be so supportive, flagging, even questioning now the advisability of continuing the paper. Some of them began to agree with Rizal that it is better to carry the fight for reforms in Filipinas, rather than pursue it here. Maybe they are right, but I still see the necessity of fighting here, arguing our case, for this is where, after all, the decisions affecting Filipinas are going to be made. Or have the friars already established so large a power base here that they cannot be uprooted anymore?

###

I did something very shameful yesterday. I haven't had a smoke now for three days—three days of sheer agony—and I picked up a cigarette stub from the sidewalk. I lighted it surreptitiously and inhaled deeply, savoring the smoke as it coursed through my system, invigorating me. I looked furtively around to see if someone had noticed me, but it seemed that no one did.

###

I think this is the fifth week now that I have felt feverish in the afternoons, and my cough, too, has worsened. I know what I should do— have good food and rest. I have all the time to rest, but the good food— how can I ever afford it now? I do not want to be beholden always to my countrymen for even the most basic of needs, but it is only when they take me out to some cafe, or to some festivity that I can really eat, and this is not often. My stomach is sour, I know my breath is foul, and this throat is blocked by phlegm and, most of all, that I should see a doctor. I have done that once—and I cannot afford to go again. I know what I will be told.

110

Mabini's letter arrived confirming the message he sent by cable way back. La Solidaridad *must now cease publication. It is being confiscated in Manila and all those who possess it are punished with imprisonment and confiscation of property. Mabini tells me the Committee will no longer send the one hundred pesos monthly that I need. That I must go home. My fare, oh I am so sorry to say, had been sent and spent—a matter of honor and social obligation for me. Poor man that I am, I am also an ignoble sinner...*

###

If I were home, I would most probably be able to prescribe some medicinal plants for myself. There are so many of them which we have not been able to develop because we do not know of these plants, and even if we did know, we are so used to <u>Western medicine.</u> *When I get back, I will devote some of my time to this and perhaps establish a pharmaceutical firm to propagate them. Take the common banaba, for instance—it is so abundant in every part of the country; its leaves, its flowers when they are boiled, drinking the stock is a good cure for so many internal disorders, for a bad kidney, for problems in the urinary tract, in the stomach. We tend to look down on our herbolarios—we even call them brujos—but there is a lot of experience in these people, experience with medicinal plants which they use in abundance. This must be recognized as one way by which in the future we can develop a pharmaceutical industry that is ours.*

###

I have not been able to leave this room for three days now; I am so weak and when M visited me yesterday and offered me a little money, I could hardly hold back the tears not so much of gratitude but that there is still someone in this city who has not deserted me. It is very difficult to admit, but it is true that I have perhaps fenced off some people with my thinking, with my implacable hatred for the friars, and here there are so many who are their friends, who would swear by their mothers' lives that they have done Filipinas good. Where have I failed? Why haven't I been able to fan alive the flame—or is it just an ember—of love and sacrifice for Filipinas in them? With all their money which arrives regularly from Manila, what do they do? The cafes, the gambling, the women.

I owe it to my family, to my neighbors and relatives who are always living in danger, and to the many more like them, my countrymen who cannot breathe the free air, who cannot speak like I do, who cannot act like I have acted. But have I really done anything to redeem my race?

111

I look around me, right here, and see my countrymen in exile acting as if there is nothing at all wrong with us, with the way we behave. They seem so far from it all.

It is perhaps too soon to tell, but I can see it clearly even now—the enemy is not just the friar and his Indio acolyte; he is among us, the wealthy Indio who profits from whoever is on top, who cannot transform himself into a Filipino.

###

Events in Filipinas have overtaken us. I learned that a new and very active group called the Katipunan has been established, and that it was ready to lead a revolution. I knew it had to be that way eventually, that we would have to fight not for equality with the Spaniards but for freedom from them. If they were a just and liberal people, this would not have been necessary—but they refused to listen, and their friars in Filipinas will hang on to power as long as they can. Nobody gives away power or privilege unless they are forced to, unless they are bloodied into letting go. So it must be then, freedom, not equality. Rizal understood this, and if I did anything at all for Filipinas, I think it is to point out the way, perhaps slowly, but all of us who wrote for La Solidaridad, we have surely been redeemed.

My dearest wife, my daughters—my brothers, I can feel life slowly ebbing away from me. I can see you in memory, not just you but my unhappy country, and I do so deeply regret that I cannot help you, or bring you the triumph of my cause. But, my God, I have tried; with all my heart, my mind, and soul—I have tried!

12

PORFIRIA called him at his Barcelona hotel. The connection was bad but audible enough to carry through the housekeeper's frantic anxiety. "Buddy, thank God, I reached you. The professor—he is in the hospital, in a coma."

His throat immediately went dry. "Slowly, Porfiria. What happened?"

As it always was when the housekeeper was excited, her English was interspersed with Spanish. "I am helpless, Buddy. I cannot do anything. And Jessica, I cannot find her. I am just una pobrecita housekeeper. You must come home, Buddy. Pronto!" She began to cry.

She related between sobs how she was vacuuming the living room when there was a loud thud in the library. She went in to investigate; Professor Wack was on the floor, froth dripping from his mouth. She had the steadiness of mind to call an ambulance from the nearby Pacific Presbyterian Hospital and followed when she couldn't find Jessie.

From the airport a day later, Buddy proceeded to the hospital; Professor Wack had suffered a heart attack and was not allowed visitors. But this was his son so he was led to the intensive care unit; the professor was surrounded by machines, wires and tubes connected to his nose, his mouth, and his arms. The verdict of the attending doctors was bleak; Professor James Wack had reached the end of a fruitful and exciting life.

113

After his visit to the hospital, Buddy went home and headed for Jessie's room; she must have an address book somewhere, a list of places for her supply of drugs, the friends who fed on her endless benevolence. Her room was locked, just as Porfiria had told him, and when he knocked, there was no reply.

He looked through the keyhole and saw Jessie's legs on the floor. He stepped a few paces back then rushed the door, ramming his body against it. On the third try, the latch broke.

Jessie was unconscious. Over her dark, glossy hair, she had on a flaring Afro wig as wide as a Mexican sombrero. When he felt her pulse, however, it was still beating. Her room was in a mess and it stank. Vomit was all over, on her clothes, on her face. He carried her to the bathroom and put her under the shower, but she did not revive. He quickly filled the tub with warm water, washed her, and dressed her like a helpless baby. Then he carried her down to her car and drove to the hospital where her father was.

She had overdosed so they pumped her stomach until nothing came out but water. Buddy told the doctors she was on drugs, there was no sense hiding it.

Jessica regained consciousness two days after her father died but had to stay in the hospital for a few more days to recover. Buddy did not tell her that their father was dead, not till he was sure she was truly stable. She was surprised why he had returned.

He took her home; still so weak he carried her to her room, now antiseptic and clean. Porfiria had really worked on it. She lay on her bed glumly, Buddy watching her. "I must have been a mess, Buddy."

"More than a mess," he said. "No one can make you get a hold of yourself, Jessie. God, I've tried."

She stared at him. "Keep trying," she said, pouting.

"You're lucky I was the one who found you. I had to clean you up..."

She smiled gratefully, "What did Dad say?"

"Dad is dead, Jessie. While you were in a coma. We buried him yesterday—there was no way you could have made it to the funeral service, that's why we didn't tell you. It was for the best..." He couldn't continue for Jessie rose and crumpled on the floor, animal cries torn out of her and like some mad woman, she started to beat the floor with her fists.

Buddy went to her, held her, calmed her, explaining what had happened, why he had to rush home.

"He hated me, didn't he?" she cried. "I was jealous of you, he liked you so much, and I—he hated me!"

"No, Jessie," he said, embracing her. "He loved you, much, much more than he loved me. You are his real daughter. Me, I am just adopted, Jessie. But I loved him, truly loved him, he was the father I never had. When will you ever understand these feelings? There's just the two of us now!"

The following week, in the late afternoon, about half a dozen people, all sober of mien, came to the house ostensibly for tea. The reading of James Wack's will did not take long; there were no disturbing questions, no recalcitrant comments. It was a simple will to begin with. Half of the estate would go to a trust fund for Jessie and Buddy. Its income would be divided equally between them, and what they had not spent at the end of each year would revert to the fund.

The other half was judiciously divided between the university, the Booker T. Washington Foundation, and something for Porfiria to see her through old age. The house was not to be sold; it would pass on to the two, Jessie and Buddy, who may want to live in it. If it was to be sold at all, the proceeds were to go to the university, if the university had no plans to convert it into a residence or office.

At the dinner table that evening, with Porfiria serving them, they asked her what she planned to do with her money, if she would retire. But Porfiria said she would continue on the job—unless, of course, they had other ideas.

Alone together finally. Jessie started to weep, the tears falling down her cheeks, her face seemingly glazed with sadness. "I am sorry that I was so bad. I should have been kinder to him, the way he had been so kind to me."

"To us," Buddy said.

She rose and went to him, knelt before him and held his hands. Her eyes were filled with entreaty. "Help me, Buddy. I want to start anew, not for myself but for Dad."

I KNEW of death's finality when I was very young, when the Japanese killed my father, then Apo Tale and Inay Mayang. But when I wept over my real father's failure to return, I did so not out of sorrow but in fear of being left alone. Roxanne's death—my mother's death—taught me what sorrow was; though I was but thirteen then, the tears came unbidden and seemingly without end. She had loved me; every child knows this instinctively when he is hugged or brought close to a warm and beating heart. Jessica had come by then, my dear sister, her real offspring, but her love had not diminished, nor James Wack's. But she was gone and banished forever was her effulgent presence. What could I remember of her? Oh, so many things—the visits to the supermarket when she always got more cereal than we needed and only because she knew I wanted the toys inside those boxes, the sweater she knitted for me, the honey-flavored cookies she baked when she found out how much I loved them, and her frequent admonition: "Buddy, take care of your sister..." Now, Dad is gone, too, his luminous lessons, his affectionate prodding.

As a little boy, I can hear him even now: Let me smell the sun upon your young skin, the breath and promise unsoured as yet by age. May the truth be yours and though lies rampage, let them pass and let your eyes be clear as they are now; my vision becomes you.

But all I see now is a world grown dim by my father's passing. I embossed in my mind and heart the hymn the black chorus sang:

> Lift every voice and sing
> Till Earth and Heaven ring
> Ring with the harmonies of Liberty
> Let our rejoicing rise
> High as the listening skies
> Let it resound
> Loud as the rolling sea
>
> Slowly the ground we trod
> Bitter the chasing rod
>
> God of our weary years
> God of our silent tears

They loved him, too, as all of us who were within the ever-widening penumbra of his wisdom. I can see more clearly now how he stood steadfast for us; our rights are now ours but only because men like him prevailed. I see him now in his greatness, and I in his shadow owe him this everlasting shade. And knowing all these, an enormous grief encompasses me. Again, I weep.

BUDDY TOOK Porfiria with him on a brief visit to Mexico six months after his father's death. Porfiria hadn't been to Mexico in ten years. Would Jessie manage by herself for two weeks? She promised she would but just the same, in those two weeks, Buddy called sometimes twice a day. He discovered that in Mexico Filipinos also had left their imprint. He also found in the archives that there was a Filipino, an officer at that, in Emiliano Zapata's revolutionary army.

The first five days were spent in Mexico City, then they went midway down the plateau to Cuernavaca, and after that, to Acapulco.

Geronima Piedad whom he met in the boarding house in Seville was getting married in Cuernavaca to Julio Martin Vargas, the Peruvian scholar who was also at the Seville archives. And Gerry's father was visiting Mexico for the first time in so many years. An unexpected reunion; it was Gerry after all who got Buddy interested in the galleons.

The surprise in Cuernavaca, however, was Feliza. Seeing her again immediately resuscitated all the remembered feelings, the transient ecstacies; she had put on some weight but the beauty had not faded, nor the smouldering eyes that greeted him with candor. He would have embraced her but with all those people, all he could do was grasp her hand firmly, longingly, until Feliza withdrew it, aware of Gerry and the rest looking on.

"Some reunion, isn't it?" Geronima Piedad said, insinuating laughter in her eyes.

But for all the apparent warmth with which Feliza welcomed him, she eluded him in his efforts to be alone with her. She also refused his offer to take her back to her hotel. She was a tourist, she said, visiting some of the scholars who had stayed at her house, first Mexico City, then Lima, Bogota, and finally, New York. She did readily accept, however, his invitation for dinner at the hotel where he and Porfiria were staying.

Alone with her at last on the restaurant terrace which overlooked the city, the cool night air redolent with the fragrances of jasmine and assorted blooms, he asked about her life, the ancestral house in Seville. Her reply astounded him; for some time he could not say anything.

"When I get back, Salvador," she said, pride shining in her eyes, "I will become a novice. I have decided to become a nun."

All that beauty, that vivacity, to be shut up in a cloister. "Are you sure about what you are doing?"

"Of course, I am sure!" she said emphatically, the corners of her mouth curling in anger and determination. "I should have decided on this much earlier, but there were distractions..."

They had barely begun with their lengua. The margarita and the sangria, too, were not touched. They were here to talk, to reminisce. From below in the hotel lobby, the tinny music of a mariachi wafted out to them, "if to your window a dove flies..."

"I am sorry, Feliza," he said after a while, "that I had to leave Spain like I did, without the proper good-byes. After Barcelona, I really wanted to go back to Seville. But my father, I told you, I had to rush home. I wrote to you..."

She nodded.

"You did not bother to reply. Several letters, Feliza."

Again, the downcast look. "What is there to say?" she asked. Then, "The house, Salvador—I sold it. My brothers—they did not really care. It was only I who had a sense of family, of the past..."

"I will always remember it, my room on the fourth floor. San Eloy, the shops close by...come and visit us in San Francisco."

"Of course," she promised. "I know San Francisco is lovely—but it is for the best that I stay away..."

He understood and did not ask her to explain. From the restaurant terrace, they strolled into the hotel's lush, brightly lit garden, poinsettias in profusion everywhere, the bougainvilleas clambering over the high stone walls. In the dark shadow of a great tree, he took her hand and drew her to him.

"I would like very much to hold you," he said, pleading. "And kiss you just once more..."

She recognized the fragile moment and smiled. "Since I won't see you again..." then she clung to him and kissed him, a lingering, trembling kiss, not of passion but of good-bye.

JESSIE was very glad to have him back; she welcomed him effusively and with a plateful of honey-flavored cookies.

They had finished dinner—Porfiria would do the dishes, so they went to the living room, so vast and devastatingly forlorn now that there were just the two of them, her crowd as well as her lovers having departed long ago.

She brought him a glass of cognac which he did not really relish but drank just the same, "How was it, Buddy?" she asked, not really wanting to delve into his academic pursuits.

"I am much closer to the core," he said, "but still must do a lot of digging."

"I wish I had your steadfastness," she said, smiling wanly; her eyes rimmed with a melancholy that cannot be banished, but which briefly lifted when she smiled, "I don't have an interest that can last..."

He listened to her always, sometimes tediously, always feeling her hurt. "I don't want to fall in love again if I can help it, Buddy. Isn't it rather funny, that it is always the physical aspect of it that interests me?"

"It is not unusual, Jessie," he assured her. "Much of what we think is the ideal kind of love always ends up that way, because love has to be expressed physically."

"I'll be more careful, more selective, that's all."

"That's not too easy to do," Buddy reminded her. "Soon, the senses take over. And when that happens, then a new threshold is reached. A new relationship..."

"The last was very bad," she said, rising. She went to the table at the far end of the living room and picked up a sheaf of notes. "Tomorrow, after you have gone over these, I'll tell you all about it."

She handed him the letters, messages, mostly telephone calls. He leafed through them quickly—some notices from the university, from colleagues, then he saw the note from Old Tele—three of them, asking if he could see the old man. He glanced at the dates; they were written more than a week ago.

"Anything important?" Jessie asked.

"An old friend. He had worked in Hawaii, the West Coast, all his life. Once he returned to his home in the Ilokos, but he came back...I wonder what he wants. He has never asked me to see him. It was always I who wanted to see him."

He was a week too late—Old Tele had died, a massive stroke, and they had already buried him. The other oldsters took him to the third floor, to Old Tele's room, a cubicle rather, impregnated with the smells of dour living, with faded Philippine posters—an elegiac harvest scene, a Manila sunset—stuck with thumbtacks on the wall. His old iron cot was without sheets, the faded mattress stained with dirt and whatever had gone through the sheets and colored it a deep brown in places. A small writing table was in a corner, close to the window with a shade that no longer worked for it was permanently down. By the writing table was a bookcase filled with books; he looked desultorily at the titles—some Marx, Steinbeck novels, poetry by Negroes and Latinos and old copies of *The New Republic*, *The Progressive* and Philippine vernacular magazines. By the bookcase was a wooden chest with worn-out hotel stickers. The old men said the wooden chest was to be left in his care, that was Old Tele's wish. They opened it for him. It contained some old clothes which Buddy immediately gave away to the men who wanted it, the jackets in very good condition, and beneath them, a batch of letters, notes. Old Tele had kept them all, and Buddy must make use of them now.

He brought them back to Pacific Heights and for the next few days, pored over them, the life of a man who was braver than most, who had borne witness to an America that was morally shrivelled, and to a time when there was no justice for people like Old Tele.

13

I WAS sixteen years old when I went to America. I lied about my age—
I said I was eighteen—because I was anxious to see the country about which
I had heard so much. Money to be made easily. White women, the ultimate
experience for any young and virile man.

My parents were tenant farmers. They farmed two hectares of riceland
in the barrio of Asideg, that is in Umingan, in Pangasinan province. It
belonged to the richest man in the town, Don Alfonso Cacab, a mestizo
who stayed most of the time in Manila, his lands supervised by an encargado.
I am the oldest in a family of six—I had gone to the elementary school
in the town, which is about three kilometers from the barrio. I walked that
distance every day. During the rainy season, I sometimes had a whole banana
leaf for an umbrella. I did not want to bring the palm leaf raincap to school
as I would be laughed at by the other children.

I was able to finish grade five I could read very well, and speak English,
too. I found this to be an asset later on for it opened to me so many doors
in America, education, for instance, and knowledge which I had earned, much
more than the arrogant white men who managed us.

I recall that day we left for Manila. The day before my father butchered
the pig that we were supposed to sell for the coming school year. Tuition

for my younger brothers and sisters. But I was leaving and had to have a farewell party. We fed the neighbors and the morning that I left, they were all lined along the village road waiting for the bus. It was a tearful parting—I looked at the familiar faces, my poor mother crying, at the barrio houses with grass roofs. And Aning who told me she would wait. I was supposed to be away for only two years—I did not realize it would be so many years before I would see my village and my brothers and sisters again. It was also my first time to wear shoes; they were rubber. By the time we reached Manila, my feet were blistered. It was just as well, for in the boat, I had very little need for shoes.

It was a big ship, with a big funnel. We were not allowed to go up to the deck; we were in the cargo hold below where there was very little air. It was very hot. I thought I would stop breathing. We were fed bread, not rice, and at first I enjoyed it very much because in my barrio, we never really had bread. And it was my first time to eat spinach, too, and mashed potatoes—it was all so new and wonderful, but not after a week during which there was hardly any change in our food.

One night when everyone seemed asleep, I got up and walked up the stairs till I found the door to the deck. It was completely dark but for the lights of the ship; the sky above was dotted with a million stars and the sea seemed calm for there was not a sway in the ship. I could hear the splash of water as it ploughed onward. Now, I knew what it meant to be free, to breathe the fresh air, not the hot and stinking poison down there where we were all packed, some sleeping on the steel floor for there were not enough cots for all of us. We were almost all Ilokanos, farmers like myself, and the discomfort was a burden that we could all bear. I sat on the deck, filling my lungs with that cool air, wondering how it was in the village that I had left—Aning, all sweet fifteen of her; we had talked of living together some day, particularly when I would return with enough money to buy a couple of carabaos, and even a pig, perhaps, to be butchered for our wedding. We had embraced one afternoon, behind a sprout of grass, there by the irrigation ditch where she was doing some washing. She had let the saya wrapped around her fall. I had fondled her breasts, the thunder in my heart I could hear. She had touched me—but that was all we could do, for in the near distance, the neighboring girls were coming to do the laundry, too.

Sprawled there on the deck, thinking of Aning and our future, I fell asleep. I was rudely wakened. A big white man who was apparently one of the sailors had kicked me in the ribs and it hurt. I had never let anyone white or brown hit me before, and quickly rising, I did what a small man can do—I kicked him in the testicles so hard he doubled up screaming in pain. I ran back to the door that led to the hold below.

Soon there were six of them, all white men, with pieces of wood. With the head man who brought us to the ship, they started demanding who it was that had gone on deck. But no one pointed me out. For that, I was grateful. I told the men in Ilokano that there were about a hundred of us and only six of them. We will surround them, I said, and if they attack us, then we jump them—all of us. And that is what we did, surround them without saying anything. They got scared; they cussed all of us—*samobabits*—and that day, they did not feed us. The manager did not want to arrive in the United States with a load of dead laborers so the following day, they gave us food.

That incident made me think about justice, how all too often, there was no way the little people could get redress other than in fighting together the way we had acted as one. Why did they not betray me? Because I was Ilokano? Because I was a laborer like them? Whatever, I realized that there could be strength in the little people if they united.

I had heard so much of Honolulu but we did not go there. We had been at sea now for two weeks, apparently sailing in calm weather—and then, just before we got to Hawaii, a storm tossed our ship. We all got seasick and we vomited everywhere. Our quarters were already smelly, and with our vomit, the stench was almost unbearable.

It was such a pleasure to walk out of that hell boat when we were finally landed in Maui, one of the islands in the Hawaian group. Not a day was wasted—the moment we were taken to the sugar plantation and assigned our quarters, we were made to work immediately, cutting the cane for it was already late for milling. It was difficult manual labor, having to slash and bend, slash and bend the whole day.

Toward July and August, it turned just as warm in Hawaii as it was in the Philippines and as we were close to the sea, we often went there to swim and fish. My compatriots who came from farther north and who had lived by the sea, all would gather the seaweeds on the shore, small things like worms, and we would wash them and eat them raw, with tomato, sliced onions and salt. By then, those who had come to Maui earlier had already planted saluyot, eggplants, and all the vegetables we are used to at home so we had dinengdeng every so often.

There were no Filipino women but there were whores in town and gambling and cockfighting in the plantation. I kept away from them knowing that I had to send money home, or save it so that I could get married to Aning after my contract was over. I loved her so much, I promised myself I would stay a virgin till we got married—and that was not difficult to do because I felt that I had to reserve myself for someone I really loved.

By the second year, toward the end of my contract, I had put on a little height and weight. It was at this time, too, that I received a letter from Istong, my younger brother, and he mentioned in passing that Aning had eloped with someone from town, and had gone to Manila. That same evening—it was Saturday—I joined the men who were going to town.

The brothel was run by a Chinese. He had about a dozen girls, half of them white, who were always busy it was difficult to get one immediately. All of us, even when we were in that stinking ship, had fantasized about white women, what supreme pleasure and crowning experience it would be, even if we had to part with our whole month's pay for just that one moment.

I was extremely fortunate because that afternoon we were early, and were, in fact, the first customers. My first white woman kept me waiting for an hour—she was asleep and when she woke up, she took her time getting ready. I had expected her to be like those movie stars whose pictures we see in the newspapers and in cinema posters—Clara Bow or Mary Pickford; well, she was not young anymore, maybe forty and more than twice my age, but she was white and blonde, too, with a large mouth and tits that bulged out of her tight dress like two big squash. She must have weighed about three hundred pounds.

She ordered me to take off my clothes at once while she also undressed. She tossed her robe, then lay on the bed, all that white blubber, and without any further delay, she spread her legs and said gruffly, "Make it quick, boy."

Toward the end of my two-year contract, Asiong, another countryman from Umingan, told me to go with him to California. He said there were more jobs there, and better pay as well. White women were also more readily available, and if I wanted to experiment a little, Negro women, too.

It was now well towards what the Americans called the Depression—there were very few jobs, even for us, but because we took any job that came by, we did not suffer so much. And one thing, we never went hungry. Americans do not eat the head of a pig, fish heads. They are so wasteful, but we are used to simple living, and I think most of us who were working in the farms never really missed a meal.

Our living quarters—bunkhouses—were never comfortable. They were narrow, walled with tarpaper, and cold in the winter. The toilets were in a separate shack and we went only when the need was urgent in pelting rain, in bitter cold. We persevered.

By this time, too, I realized how necessary it was to be educated. Whenever we moved, following the crops all the way to the salmon canneries in Alaska, I was always looking for libraries, or night schools where I could enrol.

It was in this manner that I met Laura—she was a brunette, rather short for an American, with the prettiest smile I ever saw. She was a librarian in Stockton and I suppose that she realized, much as I loved reading, I was in the library often because I wanted to see her. After three months,

I finally found the courage to ask her if she wanted to have some coffee with me after the library closed. Surprise of surprises, she said yes.

I wanted very much to marry her—I did not want to leave Stockton, I was prepared then to take another job, clerking maybe, so that I could be near her, but we knew it was not possible. There were laws in California then prohibiting intermarriage of the races.

By then, too, I was deep in work, organizing the farm workers not just in Stockton but wherever there were Filipino stoop laborers—that is what we were called. Oh, we had many problems, betrayals, threats, bombings and more than once I had to go to the hospital for treatment. I survived them all, and realized that in America, one must fight for one's rights. Two of my comrades were not so fortunate; they were killed. Investigations— but not much came out of them.

When World War II came, I wanted to join the Filipino regiment but they found out that I had defective eyesight—so I had to work again in the farms.

Laura and I could have gotten married after the war—things had changed by then, but she felt it was not necessary. It was enough that we were together when I could manage it, when there was some respite from my organizing work.

By this time, too, she felt it was too late for her to have a baby. When she did not want to marry me but still wanted to continue the relationship, I was extremely disappointed, hurt even, but I could do nothing to change her mind. We sort of drifted apart though we remained friends, but something between us had withered, and died.

Filipinos will always be themselves; though uprooted from their native land, they bring with them the island customs. Where many Filipinos stay, fiestas are celebrated and a Miss Stockton Philippines is "elected" in the traditional manner—by how much money she and her supporters gave to the organization. Though prohibited, cockfights are held in the remoter areas where it would be difficult for the police to arrive without advance warning.

Jokes particularly about us Ilokanos are many: my favorite is about a younger brother who cannot speak English well and goes to California to work in the vegetable farms with his brother. He goes to town for the first time and he asks his brother what he should order in the restaurant. Easy, the brother says; just say hot dog and coffee.

In the bus to town, he keeps repeating, hot dog and coffee. After six months, he complains to his brother that he is tired of hot dog and coffee, and since he now has some money, he wants a different fare.

So the older brother instructs him: tenderloin steak smothered with onions, vegetables, french fries and coffee. On the bus to town, he has difficulty at first remembering but finally, masters the sequence: tenderloin steak smothered with onions, vegetables, french fries and coffee.

The moment arrives, the waiter asks him what he wants, and he says: tenderloin steak smothered with onions, vegetables, french fries and coffee.

The waiter smiles: I got that, sir. Now, how would you like your steak?

He repeats, tenderloin steak smothered with onions, vegetables...

The waiter interrupts him: Sir, I got that. But how would you like your steak!

He looks dolefully at the waiter and mumbles, hot dog and coffee.

I DECIDED to visit the Philippines in the late sixties, in the manner of the oldtimers who returned. They brought with them their life savings, married younger women in the province, and settled down to the easy life of a landowner.

They were very surprised at the consulate when I went there to have my old passport renewed. Why hadn't I become a citizen—that supreme status which all immigrants aspire for? I had, of course, asked myself this question so many times. I could not find within myself a truly satisfactory answer. So I went home with a green card—the intention to become a citizen retained, but deferred. Perhaps, in time, I'll be one. If it's only a question of knowing America, or passing the citizenship barrier—I know I could easily do these.

Having lived this long in the United States, to be a citizen is the most logical thing. There are so many advantages, but then I have been a permanent resident and I have had nothing to complain about. Maybe, it is some unresolved feeling, perhaps attachment to the soil where I first saw the light of day. Yes, I do feel almost always when I am alone, a longing for all the remembered pictures of my boyhood, the people I knew. Or perhaps, I don't trust myself with a new passport—that it really does not signify anything, that I'll always be a second-class citizen in America. Look at the Indians and the Latinos who have been here long before the white men. Maybe, America is too much of an ideal, unreachable now, perhaps for a long time to come. And therefore, for someone like me, something to reach for, to fight for even. Maybe I'll have to wait, maybe for a long time, maybe forever, before I can say, now, I'll leave my native land behind and accept this America, which after all, is my second country.

Umingan had changed. My parents had long died, my brothers and sisters were all old. I had several nieces and nephews—they were all grasping, greedy, believing that in America, money could be picked up from the streets. I had to tell them how hard I had to work, how I was beaten for setting up unions. They did not believe me. I was Americanized, they said. I doubted that very much, but I am sure that in all those many years that I had lived in America, I learned truly the value of work, of saving, and education. And here were my young relatives, thinking of nothing but parties, good clothes, leisure, and going to America, too. They paired me

125

off with a distant niece—good-looking enough, who had finished college, but in my conversations with her, it came out that she was willing to marry me only because it would mean she could go to America and be an American citizen and that she would probably dump me the first thing after she had set foot on American soil. This, after all, is what had happened to so many such marriages.

After two months in Umingan, I gave up. There was a lot for me to do in America, to help the Filipinos already there, threatened as they always were by unscrupulous labor contractors that supplied the big farms with seasonal workers. Not just Filipinos, but Mexicans as well.

There was also something which I did immediately after World War II, something inspired by Laura for without her prodding, I would never have gone into it. She felt that I had undergone so much suffering, seen so much of life in the raw, life close to the earth, I should write about my experiences—not so much for publication, but as a record of a life, of a time.

The first essays I wrote were about my native Umingan, the rural life there as best as I could recall. She labored over them, corrected my grammar and also my use of slang which I should discard in formal writing. My second attempt related our lives in Hawaii, and even then, I could not but recall the harshness of the conditions, and how physically tired and abused we were.

She said I had to record my struggle, a tough and uncompromising writer in the finest American tradition, but I told her, I have always been a Filipino although I had lived most of my years in America.

She kept the essays and on occasion gave them to the local paper, or had them published in the union newsletter. I will never forget the first time I saw my name in print. Although it was just in a small town paper, it filled me with such gladness my chest could have burst.

The soil in California is the same earth everywhere—this is not a poetic or philosophical way of stating a truth any more than saying that men are the same everywhere. Those of us who have always worked the land know how precious it is—how it must be cared for, so that it will nourish the seed. The men who work the land shape it and in turn, are shaped by the land. In these men, although they may not be conscious of it, is a profound feeling of oneness with the land, not just the plot they till but the land as something to love, to worship—a church and a religion even. And more so, if this plot is theirs to hand down to their sons and daughters. That plot of land in Pangasinan which we tilled was not ours just as the lettuce and asparagus truck farms and the orange orchards in the West Coast and the cane fields in Hawaii were not mine; I cannot lay claim to them, watered though they were by my sweat.

126

So now, you hear the cry against the Mexicans pouring illegally across the border, Filipino immigrants like myself slipping in, but they forget, it is us who provide America with cheap vegetables because we accept the lower pay that the Americans will not accept. This is never in the perception of city folks when they go to the supermarkets. They must know of this. This is the real reason why we have organized, why we have promoted boycotts, and this, too, is in the American tradition. We had our quarrels, our differences in the union, but in the end, we have preserved unity for it is the union that makes us strong.

I remember all these now as I place all that I leave behind in this chest; here where memory is buried, and all the hopes I have nurtured, the labor I have dedicated to the union so that the workers—my countrymen—will not be abused, so that they may live in freedom and dignity.

14

IN HIS MIND, Japan had always loomed, exotic and savage, beautiful and brutal, recalling as he often did the death of Apo Tale and Inay Mayang, and that vague, dismembered memory of his separation from his father, the Japanese soldiers who had shot at that mass of jostling humanity into which his father had melted. Buddy's earliest knowledge of the front-line war was what he had heard from his American father, but Captain James Wack was in the rear, and could only talk about a starving population, the ravaged and burnt remains of villages and towns. There were pictures, of course, and accounts, but they had seemed so unreal, for what Buddy remembered of the Philippines were not ruins, but trees, a mountain, the olive tents of soldiers, and the heaps of food the Americans ate or gave away.

In the winter of 1980, Buddy took Jessica with him to Japan. She had arrived that Christmas morning, her blouse torn, her face swollen, her arms bruised. She had been out the whole night, which was not unusual.

Buddy was horrified. He told Porfiria to prepare a cold compress to apply to her swollen face. He followed her to her room where she changed clothes and then started to cry.

"The son of a bitch beat me up," she said between sobs.

"This is assault and battery," Buddy said. "He'll pay for this. Who is he?"

"Oh, it doesn't matter," Jessica said. She paused to wipe her eyes; the left was already swollen, the bruise would soon darken like eyeshadow on copper skin. She breathed deeply. "But I have had my revenge, if that's what you want to know."

Then she started to feel dizzy, and she collapsed on her bed.

"I better take you to the hospital," Buddy said, going to her and trying to hold her up. "Can you stand or shall I call for an ambulance?"

"It will pass," Jessie said.

"No," Buddy insisted. "You could have a brain concussion—you'll have to see a doctor."

Very much against her wishes, he took her just the same to the hospital where she stayed for a couple of days under observation. When she returned to the house, the swelling in her face had subsided and only the black eye remained.

"We have a doctor's report now, Jessie." Buddy said. "We'll have to report this to the police."

"Please, Buddy, no."

"Why not?"

"Then we'll have to go to court, and it will be embarassing for me."

"Why?"

"We were making love, Buddy. But the bastard, I had my revenge. I assure you, I had it."

Later that evening while they were having dinner, Buddy told her it was best that she stayed away from San Francisco, from the man—or is it men?—who were giving her all that trouble. Maybe, she should go east, a vacation in Florida—then he came up with the idea. "I will take you with me to Japan for three, even six months," he said. "That way, you can meet some Japanese men. They are ✓ usually more gentle."

Jessica turned away from her cereal and looked at her brother. "You're going to introduce them to me?"

"No," Buddy continued eating. "I will certainly not. You are going to do that on your own. I am not going to be your pimp..."

He was more surprised than hurt; Jessica had swung around and slapped him hard across his face. Stunned, he looked at the young woman first with incredulity, then with an anger that was quickly rising. Jessica had to know what she had done to herself, the wantonness, the casual embrace and rash enthusiasms that soon decayed into trivial infidelities. He had always tried to point this out to her, that they bespoke not just of an absence of depth in her personality, but a damning lack as well of personal integrity.

129

Jessica realized what she had done, and immediately, she embraced him, spilled his coffee on the table, saying, "Oh, Buddy, I am so sorry, I didn't mean to. Please forgive me, please forgive me," and she smothered his face with kisses.

That was when he made up his mind; if he left her behind in this state, he did not know what she would do, what the man would do. He did not even know what devious form of revenge she had taken.

Jessica was very happy—she wouldn't be left alone in the house. She detested being alone, even with Porfiria faithfully watching over her. She had become so dependent on Buddy, and furthermore, had never been to Asia, to Japan most of all, the most exotic country in her imagination although once in a while, she forayed with friends in nearby Japan Town to sample a bit of Japanese life. Again, she left the marketing job she had barely begun. It had been that way in the past, a new job almost every year for Jessica easily lost interest in whatever she was doing. Receptionist, copywriter, researcher, market analyst. She did not need to work, but as Buddy told her, if only for her own self-respect, she needed to.

They left immediately after Christmas. Buddy's fellowship at the Southeast Asian Institute in Kyoto was from January 15 to January 15—a whole year, with no specific requirements other than to write.

They arrived in Narita on a cold afternoon, patches of snow on the ground. The airport was new and coming out of it in the bus to the city, he was immediately aware of the many security precautions, the helmeted riot police in strategic places, the high wire fences, the barricades at the gates.

It was not his first time in Tokyo; he had been to a couple of conferences, one sponsored by the Japan Foundation at the Imperial Hotel and at the International House of Japan in Roppongi. His master's thesis on the impact of Japanese modernization on Southeast Asia had provided him with a glimpse as well into the Japanese ethos, how Japan had broken out of its isolation to accomplish within so short a time western modernization with the Japanese spirit.

Jessica took in everything with curiosity and enthusiasm. They had reservations at the International House and were met by Hiroshi Kato, the managing director whom Buddy had met earlier. That evening, they had dinner with him, a couple of Japanese sociologists and two old acquaintances, Ivan Hull, a Harvard Japanese Ph.D., and Edouard Senseiker, perhaps the foremost American scholarly translator. Jessica had long been exposed to the kind of dinner talk that academics and writers indulge in and she brought it to her level with

130

her questions about Japanese life, why for instance, was she the only woman in the party—didn't Kato-san have a wife?

Ivan explained it, that the Japanese woman usually stays at home, running the family, that Japanese salarymen spend their early evenings with their colleagues drinking whiskey.

The Mamiana was a few blocks away from the International House, more than a century old, specializing in various kinds of soba, the noodle made from buckwheat. It was done in the manner of the traditional farmhouse, with its old wood accoutrements, its clay floor and wood partitions; having taken design classes, Jessica was amazed at the elegant use of wood, the dark hues that suffused the restaurant, something medieval in effect, and with the candles and the Japanese lanterns, it seemed as if she was in some feudal dream and that anytime now, one of those gorgeous ladies in radiant kimono would appear as a shoji screen parted. It was just the waitress, however, in the garb of a peasant woman, with their noodles. Jessica did not really like it but it was her brother's favorite and Kato-san had obliged.

They had two weeks to do Tokyo and Buddy was the guide although he himself knew little of the Japanese capital. On the street, they seemed like newlyweds, arm in arm, Jessie always laughing, noticing things—Buddy was glad, she was not as moody and easily given to acidic remarks and gestures of impatience the way she was in San Francisco. She also did some shopping, admiring the fine quality of Japanese couture, a string of beautiful Mikimoto pearls, and her pleasant discovery of Japanese eel which she could have for breakfast, lunch and dinner every day.

Then the bullet train to Kyoto, the smoothest, fastest train ride she had ever had, and slipping by, the green countryside, the endless huddle of small Japanese houses, their blue tile roofs glinting in the sun, the smokestacks of the industrial suburbs like a myriad pins stuck in the blue haze of sky.

Kunio Ishii was at the station to meet them, a man with a ready smile. He was a Southeast Asian specialist, having mastered Bahasa Indonesia and Thái, and as director of the Institute, he managed the activities of more than two dozen scholars, almost half of them visiting professors and researchers like Buddy.

There was not enough room at the Kyoto International House so he billeted them in a modest hotel near the railroad station; were it not for Jessie's luggage, they could have just walked to it. The trip to Kyoto had taken just more than a couple of hours. In the old days, Professor Ishii said, it took the whole day. They left their luggage in the tiny rooms then they walked to a nearby restaurant where they had another Japanese lunch, and luckily for Jessie the unagi was on display at the shop window.

"I want to show you your office and, of course, the Institute," Professor Ishii said.

There weren't too many tall buildings as in Tokyo, nor crowds in the streets. They passed through the entertainment district, Gion, the small shops and the Japanese inns, their fronts festooned with buntings, the women clad in their thick winter kimonos, then they drove alongside the Kamogawa river, which was gurgling noisily, and finally, a bridge, a driveway, and the Institute, a red brick, four-storey building. He was led through the staff offices and was introduced quickly and so was Jessica.

His office was on the third floor—wide, well-lighted and much bigger than the room in the apartment hotel which included a kitchenette, a bathroom and a washing machine. Here he had a big desk, a sofa, bookcases, a typewriter, a washbowl.

"You're on your own now, Jessie," he told his sister. "You discover Kyoto and tell me about it."

IT WAS easy to settle down in Kyoto. Like all Japanese cities, it was convenient, comfortable. His fellowship was liberal—he was under no obligation to present any progress report although toward the end of his fellowship, he would have to give a seminar for a day, perhaps to relate what he had done. There was much for him to do and now he wished he had studied Japanese so that he could read the papers and converse on a scientific and intellectual level. Though he knew about a hundred or so Chinese characters and the usual conversational Japanese to take him through the daily intercourse in the city, he had to rely on materials available in English, actual interviews, particularly in his effort to go into the background of Japanese interest in Southeast Asia, particularly the Philippines.

He had read how the Filipino revolutionaries had sought assistance from Japan at the turn of the century and how that indomitable Filipino general, Artemio Ricarte, had refused to pledge allegiance to the United States and instead sought exile in Japan. Now, the story of the old general excited him. How did he live in Japan? What happened to him when he returned to the Philippines with the Japanese imperial forces? Here was a story rife with tragedy.

He stumbled upon another interest, the Filipino workers in Japan just as they were in Hawaii and the West Coast of the United States a generation earlier.

One evening, Jessie barged into his room, angry, her voice terse. "There are three policemen in the lobby, Buddy," she said. "I brought them here because I told them my passport is in the room. I think you should talk to them, too, and bring your passport. They think I'm Filipino."

In the lobby, the policemen were talking with the receptionist and when Buddy and Jessie reached them, they were profuse in their apologies and were bowing. "Sorry. Big mistake," one of them was saying as they withdrew.

"I told them," the receptionist said in very poor English. "You are a professor at the Southeast Asian Institute, that she is your sister, and you are Americans..."

Back in her room, Jessie explained; she was stopped by the policemen while walking in a section of the neighborhood where there were many restaurants and souvenir shops, and the policemen had told her she was Filipino and they wanted to see her passport. "I didn't have it, of course. They wouldn't believe me when I told them I was American. And then I said my brother is here with the Institute; they didn't believe that either."

It all became clear what he had often heard about, the thousands of Filipino women in Japan working in bars and restaurants illegally, entertainers, dancers, prostitutes. How did this happen? Before World War II, it was the Japanese women who were all over Southeast Asia, working as bar girls and as prostitutes, and now it was the Southeast Asian women who were in Japan doing the same thing. Another topic for you, Buddy, in your relentless search for your people as travellers.

That same week, he started prowling around the neon-washed facades, the silver-dusted alleys of Gion, balustraded with artificial cherry buntings and plastic lamps, to look for the Filipinos lurking there.

By now, they had settled into a routine. Jessica would go around the city, taking the numbered buses at the railroad station as far as they went, and returning on the same route. She was also a frequent visitor to Takashimaya, the small shops along the major streets and in the evenings, Gion where all the restaurants and the bars and souvenir shops jostled, spilling into alleys and along the banks of the river.

The Kyoto trip for Jessica became some sort of revelation for Buddy. In Pacific Heights, they did not live as closely as they did now. Their tiny rooms did not entrap them and made them claustrophobic; instead, they were brought together every morning and evening if Buddy did not go out with his colleagues. Both did not want to cook, so they bought their dinners at Lawson's, the corner store which was open the whole night, plastic-wrapped eel for Jessica, and sushi or some other lunchbox complete with meat, vegetables, pickles and chopsticks for him. All Jessie had to prepare was tea or coffee to warm them. Their rooms had TV and while Buddy watched his favorite samurai serials, Jessie watched Yoko Tanaka, now her favorite Japanese actress, go through the domestic drama.

One evening, while Buddy was in bed reading, Jessie slipped in beside him. She said she wanted to go home, and soon. Outside, snow flurries lined the window sill with white, and the sound of traffic in the street below came into the room, muted and sonorous, a sweet potato vendor with his cart and plaintive music...

"I'm beginning to feel lonely here," she said. "Two months and I haven't met any man...or woman. And your colleagues, they don't seem to notice me at all. What's wrong with Japanese men, Buddy?"

He couldn't answer. "Times are not changing fast enough for the Japanese, Jessie," he said. "You will be surprised that even today, arranged marriages are the rule. There is a lot of romance going on, of course—you can see that in the movies, but casual meetings here do not necessarily become amorous."

She was silent for a while, then she started the old miserere, only this time it was more plaintive. "I'm getting old, Buddy. I want to settle down. You just don't know how hard I've tried. But I seem to screw everything up. I don't know what's wrong with me. Do you know, Buddy? You're a man, and you're my brother. So tell me."

He turned on his side and gazed at the dark, inquiring eyes, the smooth brown skin, the pert chin and that perfect nose. His sister was truly beautiful. "There's nothing wrong with you, Jessie," he told her, assuaging her doubts, nurturing her self-confidence. "You are very beautiful, everyone can see that. And you're talented and, most important, independent because you are rich..."

"Then why am I so unhappy and so lonely? Why don't I have friends? You know, Buddy, you're my only friend. My only friend!"

"Because you're rich, because you're beautiful and because you're black."

Again, silence. "I could sense it," she said quietly. "Are the Japanese racist, Buddy?"

"Yes," he admitted readily. "They are racist, but perhaps in another way. They think that they are a chosen people. And they discriminate against their own kin as well. The 'burakumin'—they who do dirty work..."

"Will I ever find happiness?"

"Don't try too hard. It will come and you may not even realize it until it is at your doorstep."

Then she asked him. "And you, you're pushing forty. And you aren't married yet. Will you ever get married Buddy? Have you met

134

a Japanese woman yet? I hear they are so docile, so accommodating, and especially so in bed."

He laughed and tweaked her nose. "You will be the first to know when I have found a woman I want to be tied down to for the rest of my life. As for a Japanese girlfriend," he paused, "I don't know. There are always possibilities especially since I am not Japanese and I know how to make a Japanese woman feel special the way Japanese men don't."

She kissed him then went back to her room.

THE LIBRARIAN at the Institute showed him their collections, wide and continually expanding, but almost all of it was in Chinese and Japanese, and the English publications, though substantial, could not quite approximate the collections in Newberry, New York or Berkeley. There were items, however, that the American libraries did not have. The librarian, Kage-san, like Doña Aurora in Seville, was very helpful. She showed him the English translation of a monograph on Ricarte done by a scholar in Tokyo, Motoe Iketa. He called her up and Professor Iketa had happily obliged, gave him the name of two other scholars who had worked on Ricarte. She also said it was possible there were still people in Yokohama who would remember the old general. Ricarte had lived there frugally for many years, teaching Spanish as well as running a small restaurant that had become a some sort of meeting place for the Filipinos in the area, and a port of call for visiting Filipino leaders, Manuel Quezon included.

Going home in the afternoons, he would cross the river and walk on the opposite bank, all the way to Gion and from there, through the maze of narrow streets that led to the railroad station where the apartment hotel was. The preludes of spring, the iron-cold winter in Kyoto, were ending. Jessie was getting bored; she had already seen so much of the city and Osaka and was suffering from what she called "temple fatigue"—the surfeit of visiting temples and shrines although some were the most fastidious monuments to Japanese architecture. They had also gone to nearby Nara where Jessie was bumped and knocked to the ground by a huge deer in the deer park there. Now, Jessie needed to go back home.

They went together to Tokyo and she accompanied him to Yokohama; Professor Iketa had sent one of her brightest students to take them to Sakura Gicko, the Chinatown of the port city, and they had spent a day there, asking around in the neighborhood where the shop used to be. The district was razed during the war and so many new houses and buildings had gone up. The old people did not know the Filipino restaurant, although they had heard that a Filipino general was in exile there.

Jessie was determined to leave. "Do you know that in these three months, I have not met a single Japanese who could become, at least, an acquaintance? They are one cold lot, Buddy," she complained.

At least, for three months, she had not gotten into trouble, Buddy consoled himself as he took the train with her to Narita for her flight to San Francisco. Again, good-bye, Jessie. Brace yourself, just remember your problems are infinitesimal, solvable, and ephemeral, too, but it can never be, America will never be color-blind as you want it, nor will other regions of the earth be freed from the distinctions that people impose because they are different. Accept! Accept and plod on, for that is the meaning of it all.

BACK IN KYOTO, in the early evening, he hurried to the restaurant in Gion whose owner he had met earlier, a woman perhaps younger than his own forty years. He was walking along the riverbank one early afternoon; spring was in the air, although the trees were leafless yet. College students practicing on their band instruments, and elderly Japanese relaxing on the wide shelf of the river. He had by now memorized almost everything along the way, the manicured backyards, the gardens walled with brush, and on the river, an occasional optimist of a fisherman.

He looked like a Filipino seated on a stone bench watching the river. Hungry for a Filipino acquaintance, Buddy went to him and asked, "Are you from the Philippines?"

The man looked at him, a question on his face, then he smiled. "Yes."

Buddy sat down beside him. "You are the first Filipino I have seen here. I was told there are quite a few women. I come from the Philippines but grew up in America." He felt it was necessary to introduce himself. "In fact, I am American. My sister was here with me—she is actually mestiza Negra, I was adopted," he explained. "And you know, the Japanese police questioned her. They thought she was Filipino because she is brown like you and me..."

"'Tang ina!" the man cursed softly. "They do that all the time. You must always carry your passport."

"I have an identification card," Buddy said. "I got it from immigration in Osaka..."

"That's good," the man said. He then asked where Buddy was staying and Buddy told him of the tiny apartment near the station, that he hoped he would be able to move to a Japanese lodging, perhaps a Japanese inn, so that he could learn more about Japanese life.

"Maybe you are in luck," the man said. "My boss, she is a woman, she lives alone in this house. She owns the restaurant where I work." He pointed to a building way down the riverbank, in the Gion area. "She was saying the other day, perhaps she should get a boarder so that one of the rooms earns some money. I told her I don't know anyone who would rent it. I know it will be expensive. If Filipinos take it, there will be eight in that room. I do not think she will like that."

Vladimir Ilyich Acosta came from Camiling, in the province of Tarlac. He could speak Tagalog, Pampango and Ilokano and he worked as a cook in this small restaurant. On his off hours, he idled at the riverbank, sitting there, wandering away in his mind to the places he had been. Until five years ago, Vladimir Acosta was a cook and had served in ships; he had literally seen the world. He had fled to Kyoto from the nearby port of Kobe and had at first stayed in a small apartment with four Filipinas.

The small restaurant was up a steep, narrow stairway, on the second floor of a nondescript building. It had those small chairs with wicker seats around a counter, and on an elevated floor, tatami mats with the usual low, wooden tables. At four in the afternoon, it was open but still no customers. Chika, who manned the cash register at the end of the counter near the door, was also the waitress. She wore an inexpensive blue kimono—by then, Buddy could note the difference; the more expensive ones were usually of finer material, with embroidery. A Japanese who peeped in briefly from the rear must be the other cook.

Vladimir was speaking to her in bad Japanese, meanwhile turning briefly to Buddy. Although it was quite dim, she wore dark glasses. When Chika finally faced him, she spoke in slow, carefully pronounced English, the kind which was taught in high school. "My English is not good," she said, her voice so gentle, it was as if she was not speaking at all. "Are you sure you want to stay in a Japanese house?"

He said emphatically, "Yes, of course. If I can find one."

She couldn't leave the restaurant then, but in the morning, if he would come back, she would take him to her house. Vladimir cooked chicken adobo for him and Buddy was convinced the cook was, indeed, very good.

A SHORT WALK from the hotel near the station to Gion; she was waiting for me, this time in a blue cotton dress with little white flowers. Over her slim shoulder, a heavy woolen shawl as it was still quite cold.

I learned later that she had retired early from the geisha life as she already had this small restaurant; it could not accommodate more than two dozen customers but was popular with the artistic set and was always full, one must have a reservation in the evenings. Then, too, as I later learned, with Vladimir as cook, the restaurant had attracted gourmets for Vladimir often had specialties, the tapas he had learned to do well, announced at the front of the stairs, the deep-fried squid, the slices of marinated dried beef, and the pickles done in the Spanish manner which went well with sake or beer.

Chika wore those dark glasses as usual and I wondered when I would see her without them. Did she prefer seeing things in the dim light and was more comfortable with the dark?

She wore no makeup and there was this paleness about her face, her lips which were rather thin, so pale in fact that she looked almost like a corpse, a tint of grey in her hair. I knew she was pretty except that her pallor, her whole demeanor was ghostly or was it ghastly? and by her looks, she convinced me that she was aloof, contrary to what Vladimir had told me, that she was very warm and kind.

In the spring morning, the people were out in the streets, the shops were open, and the sidewalks were decorated with plastic flowers. We left the restaurants and the shops and came to the residences by the river, wooden houses and Japanese inns with their simply decorated fronts. Chika's house near the end of a narrow lane with flagstones, both sides palisaded with dried reeds tied together with black vine. It was a small house with three rooms in the Japanese style, with tatami floors and set apart by shoji screens, except the room I was to have; it had wooden walls throughout. All the rooms opened to the back and a small garden planted to a lone cherry tree and bushes and, beyond the garden, fenced by a low hedge of azalea and a high wire mesh, was the river, pushing on to the sea.

Chika showed me the kitchen, a cubicle which she seldom used, a small refrigerator stocked with food, and down the short corridor, the Japanese-style toilet, and beyond it, the Japanese bath, with its shower and sunken tile tub which I learned to appreciate later.

I asked how much it would cost—I would have the house to myself almost the whole day as Chika came home late at night and left again early in the morning. This, every day even on Sundays and holidays for the restaurant truly was her life.

She said she had never taken a boarder before, never. I was the first and if it turned out all right, she might take in another if and when I left Kyoto. She did not look at me when she mentioned the price—it was more than what I was paying at the hotel, but I decided it would be more interesting to live in a Japanese house, in a Japanese neighborhood.

We went to the narrow alcove, the living room, which had an oversized sofa and a low coffee table of very fine polished hardwood—oak, its grain so beautifully brought out. She had set out two cups of green tea and jelly sweets.

"The middle room, the room between us," she said. "Please, do not enter. It is closed. Only I go. It is a holy place."

She was silent, trying to locate the word in her limited vocabulary.

"A shrine," I suggested.

She nodded, her lips slightly parted in what I hoped was a smile, but with those glasses on, I couldn't tell. I had this urge to take them off, but was not prepared to risk her anger, her displeasure, or whatever such an act would elicit. She had removed her shawl, revealing her shoulders, her arms wiry and veined, very much like the arms of a ballerina, her fingers long and tapering, as if she was never meant to do any kind of work, as if those fingers were crafted only to caress.

She noticed me looking at them—no ring on any of her fingers and her nails were trimmed and unpolished. "You have very beautiful hands," I said.

Again the slight parting of lips...

And then, "I am sure you also have beautiful eyes. Why do you always wear dark glasses?"

She evaded my question, her lips compressing as if she was angry.

"This room," she continued evenly, "it is not shrine, really. Maybe memory room, treasure room. Very personal—difficult for you to understand."

"I will try," I said.

"My father's room," she said. "I was very close to him. My mother died when I was a child. I never go in, just clean. Do you understand? He died during the war. His things are there. He was officer in imperial army."

I TOLD the Institute that I had moved and the secretary went with me to see my new quarters. She was very pleased—a charming area of the city, but was shocked when I told her how much it cost. She said it would have been possible for me to get a much better place for half the price; I was now paying double the rate at the hotel, but then there was nothing there but routine, aridity, commonplace.

Having told Vladimir well in advance, that same Friday evening, too, I invited the whole academic staff—there were fourteen of us—to Chika's restaurant.

An international menu, presented in the Japanese manner, in small servings in those exquisite lacquered plates and bowls, including what Filipinos call "crispy pata." Professor Maeda, who knew a lot about Southeast Asian cooking being an Indonesian specialist, said this was one of the nicest evenings he had ever had and was going back just for the food alone.

The sake flowed and soon we were singing, much of it bad, but who cared? I was asked to sing and I gladly belted out my favorite, a sad short song, "Hamabe No Uta," about a sailor on a beach in some distant region perhaps in Southeast Asia, looking across the sea, pining for his distant homeland being washed by the same waves that broke on the surf before him.

Then someone commented on Chika's dark glasses, why she wore them even at night, and one of the professors called across the room, "Chika-san, you are so lovely, why are you hiding your beauty?"

She smiled at us, bent down and rummaged through the drawer in front of her, drew out another pair of glasses and put them on; they were lighter, but we could not see her eyes just the same. We all laughed. She explained in Japanese that her eyes were very sensitive to light.

When everyone had left, I asked her how much the bill was. She said I was an exception and she would give me a twenty percent discount. Twenty percent was a lot but when I converted the yen into dollars, it still turned out to be an expensive evening. I didn't bargain or complain.

It was not the dinner though which was memorable; I went home enmeshed deeper into Chika's personality. Professor Ishii told me the following day, he thought he knew now who Chika-san was—that is, if he hadn't made a mistake. It was the first time for all of them to go to the restaurant but they had heard about it. As for Chika-san again, there was speculation that evening among them. Her dark glasses—they attracted attention more than giving her the anonymity that she perhaps wanted.

A very romantic story, Professor Ishii said, about this beautiful geisha and her patron, what she did to him when she found out he was cheating on her. One more item for your research on Japanese mores, he said, laughing, and thanking me again for a splendid evening.

I GOT a call the following morning at the Institute from Professor Iketa in Tokyo. The assistant who had gone with us to Yokohama had persisted and had found two old people who knew General Ricarte and if I wanted, I could go back and interview them.

Yutaka-san, the graduate student, met me at the Tokyo station; I had a room waiting at the Shimbashi Dai-ichi hotel which he said was convenient because one of my informants, an old woman, lived close by, in a neighborhood of wooden houses, with their ground floors transformed into shops.

She was in her seventies, and was expecting us. Like so many elderly people in Japan, she seemed bent. I cannot figure out how she was able to make a living with that small shop which sold so many things, hardware, stationery, even fruits in boxes all the way to the sidewalk. It was not her shop—it was her daughter's and she lived with the family.

Yutaka-san interpreted for me; I had brought along my tape recorder just to be sure. She and her family had lived next door to the Ricartes. They had set up a small restaurant in Yokohama but it was closed after some time. The old woman had been there only once—it was very small, more like a tea house, and there weren't too many customers either. She remembered General Ricarte's wife, a small hardworking woman, who ran the restaurant and did the household chores. Japan was not all that rich at the time, and many Japanese were poor. Sometimes, there were Filipino seamen who visited, musicians working in the nightclubs and cabarets of Yokohama. Sometimes Japanese who looked like they were government officials, or Filipino tourists, stayed longer in the restaurant and often talked with the general. Had she been inside the Ricarte house? Yes, several times. It was nothing special, just like any Japanese house. There was a small garden in the back planted to vegetables which the general was always watering. He also had a dog and he would often take it for a walk. Otherwise, he was at home reading or writing most of the time. He was teaching somewhere and he would get up early to walk to the station, in heavy snow or rain; he never took the bus.

The old woman was quite gregarious but unfortunately, she could not tell me anything more of interest. Since I was in a hotel close by, I asked if I could see her again, to which she said she would be very happy to receive me, and perhaps, she would also remember more details.

We went next to Shibuya, to an apartment block for low-income people, one of the several that had risen all over Tokyo the last few years. Our informant was not in; and we were about to leave when he arrived, saying he was sorry he had forgotten all about our appointment. He remembered it only when he was already at the train station, he had to rush back. He was glad that I could speak Spanish for that was what he studied under the general, when he was in his teens before World War II.

141

I no longer needed the interpreter but he preferred to stay on, for he had gotten interested in the story of this recalcitrant and stubborn Filipino who chose to defy the Americans and be exiled in Japan.

The informant apologized, saying his Spanish was rusty as he had not been able to use it for many years since he retired from one of the global trading companies as Spanish translator and interpreter. To the best of his knowledge, the general never absented himself from school, even in the foulest weather. Was he strict? He was like any Japanese teacher, which meant he was strict, this I concluded. Did he notice anything unusual about the general? The old Spanish translator gave the question some thought. Then he said, "Yes, the general always brought his lunch, and once I saw him eating just a potato. One potato for lunch."

I told him he was frugal because the general really had very little money.

"So I thought," he said. "The pay in the school was not much."

Yutaka-san, like the translator, wanted to know what happened to the general, so I retold how he went back to his country only to be reviled by his own countrymen, and eventually to be forgotten altogether. Those years of travail, of hunger, of suffering. Of what use were they after all?

There already formed in my mind the story that I would write, Ricarte denied his place in his country's history, denied the vision that he had for his benighted people.

In the university library, I found a copy of the dissertation and the master's thesis about him. I read them, how early on the Japanese influenced so much of the revolutionary movements in Asia. The tragedy of Ricarte is obvious enough—the failure of a man to recognize that his convictions had shackled him and made him not only irrelevant but also an object of scorn and hatred by the very people whose freedom he had fought for with devotion.

The other tragedy, perhaps more grievous because the Japanese did not recognize it, was their betrayal of a whole generation of Asian nationalists who had looked at them as the harbingers of freedom from Western imperialism. Sun Yat-sen, Chou En-lai the Chinese writer Lu Hsun, Sukarno, the Indian nationalist Subhas Chandra Bose, and so many others had gone to Japan to admire and to learn. Today, many Asians are looking again to Japan, more prosperous than before World War II. Will the Japanese recognize the great responsibilities that go with their wealth? If Ricarte were alive today, maybe he could suggest an answer.

15

HE IS one of Japan's greatest soldiers, a brilliant strategist, and had commanded in the early days of the war an army that defeated the British and conquered much of Southeast Asia. They called him the "Tiger of Malaya," but now, like me, he is in these mountains, the roof of the Ilokos, holed in, with no possible succor from Japan, his men sick with the afflictions of the tropics, hounded by guerrillas and an equally relentless enemy, hunger, and the superior airpower and technology of America. It is an honor to be invited by him for tea. But knowing him, I know he is not having much to eat, so very much like his men.

I am weaker now but I can manage going to his cave which is only a short distance from where I am bivouacked with my aide and relatives who have joined me.

These last few days, knowing that I am trapped, have given me some time to think, to reminisce about those days in Cavite when I was in the company of our illustrious leaders like Emilio Aguinaldo, Andres Bonifacio. I was young then, so eager for combat against the Spaniards. All of us had war names, like Apoy (fire), and here I was, a schoolteacher, and I was Víbora (viper).

Like the many young people who managed to get an education in Manila, an education that marked us as the privileged, I was filled with

143

dreams about my people, that we might achieve unity and strength as was already developing in Japan.

Japan had always fascinated me. It could very well be the nation we aspire to be. Look at the land—it is also an archipelago. And look at its history—for so many centuries, their warlords fought one another. But more than us, they were able to shut off the West for so many centuries and were thus able to evolve the basic characteristics which they now have— the social cohesion, the discipline and, most important, a sense of nation.

I have convinced the leaders of the Revolution that we should try and get assistance from them, weapons, most of all, if we are going to succeed in defeating our new enemy, the Americans, who had grabbed our newfound freedom from Spain.

After being abused for three centuries by the Spaniards, I cannot understand how easily so many of our leaders now wanted to collaborate with the Americans, merely because they have superior arms, merely because they also promised to the ilustrados and to those who chose to collaborate with them the highest positions. But we will not be masters of our fate. No matter how badly the war had turned out, I know that we will have to go on fighting till Filipinas is free.

I couldn't swear allegiance to the United States. And for this they exiled me to Guam.

It was not unbearable, and still after that, I endured six years in Bilibid prison in solitary. Six years! The terrible loneliness almost snapped my mind—as the wounds inflicted on the flesh heal quickly, but not the hurt that gnaws at the mind every day, lacerating it, but to those of us who are committed, strengthening it as well.

In that cell, deprived of anything to read, of pencil and paper, I let my mind wander. I tried to recall the past strategies of the few victories we had wrested from the Spaniards, our helplessness before the superiority of American weapons. In Guam, Mabini and I had agreed that we could only fight a guerrilla war, in the villages as well as in the towns and cities. On that blank stone wall, I drew a map of Filipinas and designated on this imaginary map the places where we could withdraw, the forests that would protect us.

In the mornings when I went out to the prison yard by myself, separate from all the prisoners, the guard up in his tower would shout his greeting, "Good morning, general." He would salute and I would return his salute with a wave of my hand. Those prison guards—they were all very good to me, but they were not allowed to talk at length with me. And when I passed the cells of the other prisoners, they would shout their greetings from their cell windows. Somehow, those six years seem lighter after all.

Six years—and what were the images that I always remembered? What else but what I saw of American barbarity, what they did to our soldiers whom they captured, what they did to the villagers who were helping us. Nunca! I will never forget these. It is this memory and this memory alone that has heightened my resolve to fight them to my dying day!

I had returned to my country in secret and under a new name, I visited my old comrades, hoping they had not flagged, that all I needed was to stoke the embers in their hearts, and again, the revolutionary fire would be fanned alive.

They had grown older—all of us had done so—but I was not prepared for their adamant refusal, for their rationalization—wait, the time is not yet. But when is it ever the time?

I had to flee again, to Shanghai under the name Minami Hikosuke; and finally, Japan. Thank God, a Japanese friend, Goto Shimpei, stood by me.

There were great difficulties. I had to learn the language, which I did not readily do, and earn a living as well. This was not so easy, for Japan was poor and many of the Japanese were trying very hard to survive— a time when their women, their workers and craftsmen were all over the region, which was then much more prosperous than Japan. But they proved themselves capable and strong. Imagine, a small country like Japan defeating Russia! I saw the triumph, the mood of resurgent nationalism which, all the more, endeared the Japanese to me.

After some years, I could speak the language very well, knew its nuances and the subtleties at which the Japanese are so adept if they want to be ambiguous. But living with them, I knew I was not part of the society.

I saw Japan change, saw its leadership become militarized, yet at the same time I felt this was necessary if they were to rid Asia of her shame, drive the white man out. In their dream, I found justification not only for my exile but for the long wait I had to endure.

We lived poorly. My ever-patient wife, she was courageous as well; during the Revolution, she carried on her head a basket with things to sell; underneath were messages, a gun, bullets.

Through the years, many Filipinos came to see me, my relatives who thought I was being foolish—Filipinas was changing and the Americans were not bad rulers after all. Officials, many of whom I did not know, told me to return; there was much I could do at home, which my background had prepared me for. But always, I demurred. There is something in the Ilokano that is stubborn, that is steadfast like granite. It could also be his undoing.

In 1935, my wife visited Manila and she returned with stories of how much the country had changed and progressed. Should I not return? I pondered long and hard but in the end decided not to return. The Americans were deeply entrenched. The country was a colony still.

Then the Japanese invaded China, and from there started to move towards Southeast Asia. I could understand what was happening, how nationalism was changing Japan. I felt that it was inevitable for Japan to expand, not so much for its own ambitions but as part of the ideal of driving away the west from Asia.

Then, Pearl Harbor. I was so pleased that Japan had finally humbled the United States, and that soon, I would be going home. Thirty years I was away, thirty anguished years, and I would finally see my homeland. The very thought lifted my spirit but at the same time filled me with some apprehension. Filipinas had changed, just as I, too, had changed and I was no longer sure about the nature of my return.

Indeed, Manila had grown, and the suburban towns that had seemed so small had developed, too. I was accorded some respect; I was not expecting to be treated like a returning hero, but just the same, I did get a very warm reception everywhere.

I had expected to be given a very high position. I was very disappointed when it did not come; the Japanese high command decided instead to depend on the same elites that the Americans had used.

My disappointment changed into outraged betrayal—how could they so easily disregard our history! They had given back to the oligarchy, my enemy, the enemy of my people, the very same power the Americans had given them! I saw it then—the necessity of being truly free, but it was much too late.

I had expected it, knowing how the Americans had so influenced my countrymen, how they had transplanted a lot of their institutions on to our soil—there was going to be resentment against the Japanese. It was the ferocity of such resentment that astounded me, frightened me.

Had my countrymen forgotten that they were brown, that they belonged to Asia? How soon they had thrown away their past, what they had suffered under the Americans, the insults, the tortures, the massacres inflicted on them? Where now is history? And memory?

Some groups believed in what the Japanese were doing; I had talked with them, but they were few, reviled by the people, and declared enemies of the guerrillas who had now proliferated.

I could understand why there was so much opposition now to the Japanese—they had shown themselves to be brutal. But part of that brutality was in keeping with the military code; it was not unusual, for instance, for soldiers to be slapped by their officers for ordinary offences. This the Filipinos never understood, for to be slapped meant the severest loss of face.

Yes, the Japanese were true to their word—they gave Filipinas independence, although it may not have seemed true freedom at the time. But that could not be helped; a war was raging, the United States was the enemy, and to defeat this enemy was more important to the Japanese than the niceties of independence.

It was now a matter of time. The United States was much too powerful, was too big an enemy to be defeated even by a nation as united and as courageous as Japan. I knew that the war was going badly.

For one, there was not enough food for the soldiers now, nor for my own countrymen. Soon enough, the Americans were in Luzon. The Japanese had to flee; I had to make this difficult decision, whether or not to stay with the Filipinos, even with those who had very strong pro-Japanese sentiments, or to join the Japanese retreat to the mountains of Northern Luzon—the very same mountains which General Antonio Luna and Bishop Aglipay had chosen as a redoubt from the Americans when they first invaded my country.

I had not realized I had truly grown old—I knew this now as I joined in the long march to the Cordilleras, those lofty mountains that had to be crossed, the many days that we had very little to eat.

I brought back to mind—how easily it all came back!—those days we were fighting the Americans four decades back and we were fleeing from them, superior as they were in arms and in number, and we were all so poorly equipped. I saw then how it was the same war all over again, except that now, it was my own people I was fleeing from, who would probably kill me without qualm for collaboration with the Japanese.

But was I really the enemy? What had time wrought upon the face of my land which in my absence I did not see or had the chance to stop? I was wearing the uniform of a Japanese soldier, yet I was not one, that I could never be one for it was to this land always, these brooding hills, that I had committed myself perhaps not too wisely.

I owed so much to the Japanese, they who had helped me in my time of distress and need. They were an inspiration to me, and I thought that inspiration would serve my countrymen as well. Why could they not see it my way? What had the Americans forced down their thoats, what lies had they embedded in their minds?

It was a harsh life during the Revolution. Now, it was doubly difficult. Thank God we had reached the recesses of these mountains and were not caught in the plains below now ranged by American planes.

THE GENERAL'S headquarters was a cave deep into the mountain; it could not be seen from the air and even if it was bombed or strafed, it could not be hit. But it was not just the Americans and the guerrillas now whom we had to fight—far more insidious was the hunger, the disease that resulted from malnutrition, for there was now very little for us to eat, camote leaves, some camote which the Igorotes tended and had left behind.

I last saw the General in Manila three months ago, shortly before Christmas, although it had been years since I last celebrated this Christian occasion. There was a lull in the air attack. We met near the mouth of his cave, hidden from view by giant pines. He was gloomy and after the stiff formal greetings, he asked me how my health was. He must have noticed that I had grown much thinner, and so had he, and I am sure, almost everyone. He also knew I was ill.

He always addressed me as "general," which I appreciated. I had always known the Japanese never to reveal their feelings—a trait I think I have taken on. But now, all that pride was shorn from him, as he asked me dejectedly, almost in a whisper, "Can you explain to me why we failed?"

Until now, I had not really looked at our condition with such finality. I knew we couldn't be rescued, I knew we could not escape this fate, but I felt that some way out must be found and I had by then, too, considered suicide as the last honorable alternative.

I did not want him to have more anguish than he already was burdened with. "I have been away too long," I told him. "My people have changed and I cannot understand them now."

"Your people," he said equably, looking away. In the distance, the boom of American artillery reached us, and the shells whistled overhead, then a series of explosions followed well beyond us. "Ah, your people, they do not know it, but the Americans have removed from their minds the knowledge that their destiny is here."

And what could I say?

"How do you explain this?" He peered at me through his glasses, his face a mask as always. Then he sipped his tea slowly.

I had to search my deepest being for some time; was he actually asking me what I, myself, felt now? I was still Filipino in spite of the uniform I was wearing, inspite of the many years I lived in Japan. And then I realized it—after all these years, we have not become a nation, and judging from the ferocity of the guerrillas who sought us, I can only think back to the old days, too, when our own guerrillas sought the Americans and killed them where they could be found. A nation is created out of the blood and the grime of war. Did Japan contribute then to Philippine nationalism by its very presence? And how about those who believed in the Japanese like I did?

I told him how in our war with the United States at the turn of the century, we had also selected this place as our refuge because in these mountains we could hide and fight for a long, long time. Did he know of the Battle of Tirad Pass farther north in these mountains? He was familiar with it but not with the details, so I recounted to him how the young general Gregorio del Pilar had delayed the advance of the Texas Rangers and bought with their lives time enough for the President of the first Philippine Republic,

General Emilio Aguinaldo, to flee, only to be captured by the Americans months afterwards, betrayed as he was by Filipinos themselves.

A continuous crackle of radio transmission heightened the urgency of our discussion; more than once, a messenger would come in, salute stiffly, and hand him messages. The answers he gave were brisk. I could easily gather from the exchange that our positions were crumbling, that the advancing enemy was closing in. Although it was still a long time before the sun would set, surrounded as we were by these lofty pine trees, some of them hoary with moss, it was always dark and gloomy. The tea—it has been weeks, too, since I have had it—settled in my stomach and warmed me. Again, kindness such as was shown me in Japan by my Japanese friends during all the years that I was there, living frugally, poorly, because I never earned enough as a teacher nor from the restaurant in Yokohama which my wife and I had set up. All those years of poverty, of hunger, and now here in my homeland, to be poor and hungry again.

I had to bid him goodbye. He went to the recesses of the cave and returned with a small package of rice crackers—*osenbei*—that is what the Japanese call it. I thanked him for the gift; I would relish it.

We have been here in Funduang for several days now. The malaria which has ravaged me is slowly depleting my strength. I don't think I can even get out of this forest on my feet. What can a seventy-five-year- old man, his life behind him, expect? There is no recognition from my own countrymen who now seek to kill me like a mad dog. And my Japanese friends—they have betrayed me, too, betrayed my expectations of them as allies in the war to rid Filipinas of the Americans.

I call Ohta-san, my aide, my trusted confidante, my student, my interpreter. He has also lost weight. His face is gaunt and he looks tired in the sunlight. He knows I have been with the general, but he does not ask.

I tell him candidly—when I die, bring my ashes to Japan. And my grandson, Besulmino—see to it he will study there.

My life flashes across my mind and I ask myself, what did I do wrong? I had acted not for myself but for Filipinas. I never wavered, not before their guns and torturers, not before the calumny they heaped on me, that I collected money and pocketed it. Against all the vituperation—I persisted for I saw so clearly the enemy, the powerful Filipinos who legitimized themselves by joining the Revolution. Mabini confirmed this and, poor man, he suffered, too, the vile gossip they spread about him.

I see it so clearly now, and it is so painful precisely because it is so clear. Nothing that I have done—the years in prison, the terrible home-sickness, my whole life—these have no value now. I ask myself, should I have succumbed to the blandishments of allegiance to America? To the wealthy ilustrados? Like Mabini, I had always regarded the ilustrados with suspicion. I knew they were the enemy. But how do you fight them? They are your own people, traitors though they may be.

And again, why did I do it? Was I trapped by my own beliefs? Have I so much believed in my country's freedom, or was it my pride that made me persevere? It is not just the failure that tortures me, it is the mockery of my own people—they for whom I had paid with suffering, and now with shame?

But I have nothing to be ashamed of. For Filipinas, I gave everything, this life worthless now because it has been lived in vain.

I remember the cherry tree I had planted in the yard. It was so sickly in the beginning I thought it would die. The first time it bloomed, it was such a beautiful sight it filled me with a longing for home, remembering as I did then our own flame trees, how they emblazoned our land with color.

Blood on the earth. Will it still be there when all this is over?

16

I FEEL most comfortable in Tokyo because I can go out late at night or in the deep, deep dawn without feeling unsafe like I would in any American city. Life does not ebb out of the streets the way American cities die after nightfall when the business and central districts are empty and desolate though the buildings are still garlanded with light. Not in this city, where shops and residences are crammed together, and here in Shimbashi, for instance, I go around in the early evening, feeling so alive, the restaurants, the streets filled with commerce, those pushcarts selling oden—boiled potatoes, hardboiled eggs, kelp, soybean curd and very strong mustard, with sake, of course. And the station close by, thousands of people always pouring out or pouring in, close to midnight when the trains stop running, and again at four in the morning when they start. But always, there would be someone in the street, a taxi, a late reveller singing, drunk, throwing his vomit on the pavement.

He visited Motoe Iketa in her office at the university, a cubicle jammed with books and pamphlets, tapes and newspaper clippings. They had met twice at an Orientalist Congress in Paris and in Mexico City, and she had also visited once at Berkeley. She was still youthful and good-looking in spite of her forty or so years, and her manner of speaking English, pronouncing each syllable clearly, slowly, had not changed.

With Yutaka-san, her graduate student, they went out to lunch at a Chinese restaurant, her choice, in the Dai-ichi Hotel where he was staying. She had heard that the restaurant in the basement of the hotel annex was very good, that a Japanese writer, Hirabayashi Taiko, frequented it when she stayed in the hotel to write.

Professor Iketa told him that the hotel was old, that the main building was one of those spared by the bombing during the war. The food was Cantonese, and greasy as usual, one reason Buddy preferred Japanese cuisine—it was so healthy, with so little oil in it.

Then without telling them that he was actually staying in the house of Chika-san, Buddy asked if they knew the story about a beautiful geisha who, in the fifties or around that time, had a lover— a very wealthy Kyoto businessman. He was unfaithful. And when she found out, she had applied a violent logic to the situation; while he was asleep, with a razor, she snipped off his penis. Now, that singular object that had given her so much pleasure was completely hers. He committed suicide afterwards.

"Why this interest?" Professor Iketa asked.

"Japanese manners, Japanese logic, and the geisha life—I am extremely interested in it, too," he explained.

She took him to the university library that afternoon. They found the clippings from the fifties—it had been such a big story, magazine articles, including running coverage of the trial and how Chika-san was sentenced to two years in prison. Two books were written about her plus a novel based on her story. They had all sold very well.

He asked for a Xerox copy of Chika's picture, one whole page of the magazine itself, a girl with clear innocence in her eyes, such piquant beauty, this thirty years ago.

He studied the picture, brought it with him to Kyoto, looked at it again before he threw it in a trash can at the train station.

AT FIRST, if he got up early, he would prepare breakfast, usually just coffee and toast. Japanese bakers were excellent; a French journalist whom he met at the Institute told him French bread baked in Japan is better than bread in Paris. One piece of toast was enough, with just a spread of marmalade or butter.

One morning, he came upon Chika in the kitchen preparing breakfast. She usually had it in her restaurant at ten. "You must eat big breakfast," she said.

She was wearing her dark glasses even in the kitchen which was quite dim.

She set the small table by the window, and asked Buddy to sit down with her, which he did. It was the first time he saw her in the morning.

The usual Japanese breakfast, steamed rice, raw eggs, seaweed, salted salmon, pickled radish and cabbage, and miso soup. It could have been lunch or dinner.

She said it without the usual innuendo. "I was geisha, Buddy-san. But I stopped because my restaurant. This house—my family keep for very, very long time. I have no children so it will go to distant relative, a young girl who is maiko."

He didn't know what a maiko was.

"Virgin," she explained, smiling, the corners of her mouth widening, her eyes most probably smiling, too, and he remembered again her picture. "She is training as geisha, and after long time training, she ready to entertain customers."

Then she asked him, "Would you like to see geisha class? Meet my niece?"

He nodded, pleased that Chika-san was thawing, that she was finally confiding in him.

This is the time, Buddy thought, to finally ask her. "Chika-san," he said, bending forward, "Please take off your glasses. They are not graded, I know. There are just the two of us. Just us. I know you are beautiful, that you don't have a squint..."

"My English not good," she said. "What is squint?"

He showed her. "Like this."

She laughed lightly. "I saw," she said, "much about life I do not like. Maybe I wish to be blind."

"Have you heard of the ostrich?"

She shook her head.

"It is a big African bird," Buddy explained. "It has wings, but it cannot fly because its body is too big. But it has very strong legs and can run very fast. When it sees an enemy, or something it does not like, it buries its head in the sand, hoping that that reality will vanish. You are hiding from the world, but does the world really care?"

She did not speak.

"Chika-san," Buddy said, feeling more courageous now, "I am sure you would like me to see you." He rose tentatively. "I would like to take off your glasses myself." He stretched his hands to her face but she quickly backed away.

"No, no," she said, alarmed, "you must not do that." But almost immediately, she leaned forward and said softly. "All right, only two

153

of us, and my father there." She thrust a chin to the empty room at their right. Then, slowly, she removed the dark glasses.

Just as Buddy had expected, it was the eyes that made the whole difference; he recalled quickly the picture he had thrown away at the Kyoto station, the Chika that was thirty years younger, and was very pleased that in spite of all those years, the beauty was still intact and it seemed, although afterwards Buddy thought it was his imagination, Chika had not aged at all.

THE SYBARITE that I am, I had become addicted to the Japanese hot bath and in the evenings, particularly in the spring and the fall, I would soak in it and squeeze the tiredness out of my bones.

The evening ritual, shortly before I retired, consisted simply of soaping first, then rinsing everything from the body. By this time, the sunken tub would be filled with water as hot as I could take it. I sink into it and luxuriate in that warmth. Sometimes I read in the tub, and more than once I had fallen asleep. Sometimes it was Chika-san coming home from her restaurant who woke me up.

Again, I had fallen asleep, and she had come in to bathe herself. The light was on, and she simply took off her yukata and hung it on the hook. She started to soap herself; it was as though I was not there. She was in front of me, Venus in ivory, her breasts glistening in the light, her long hair now encased in a plastic shower cap.

"Is water still hot, Buddy-san?" She finally asked. It had grown lukewarm, of course, and I hastened to rise and cover my nakedness with the towel.

"Stay there," she said. "I add hot water."

The water started to get warm, and soon the delicious warmth spread all over me again. She stood in front of me—all that glory, all that beauty—before sinking into the tub. I couldn't help it, and if I had risen at that moment, she would have noticed how well I expressed my manhood. Her face, like some mannequin's, was without expression, and it seemed I was not there at all.

"You are beautiful," I said, unable to leash the thought.

She smiled, a sad smile, a wan smile. "I am almost sixty, Buddy-san." Then she held my hand, "But touch," she pressed it to her breasts, one then the other. They were very firm.

"Like young girl, yes?" Pride in her voice, but then, I remembered her story, what she had done and everything that was romantic or sensual in my mind simply fled. I saw her as a vengeful old witch, and for an instant, I was repelled by her.

We had breakfast together almost every morning, and a bath, too, on those occasions when I took it late, and so whenever I could

154

I bathed early. I could see the reason why she joined me, she saved on water and gas. In any case, I was not supposed to drain the tub after soaking in it, so that whoever followed, there would still be warm water there.

One morning, she asked if I wanted to visit the school where they trained geishas so I could see her niece who was a maiko and who would soon join the ranks of the regular geisha.

A cultural excursion I did not want to miss, not so much because this ancient institution was still intact but because I wanted to know Chika better.

About four in the afternoon—there were few customers in her restaurant and Vladimir could easily take on the job as cashier and waiter. We walked over to Gion again, to one of those narrow streets which led to what seemed like a small theater. We were not the only visitors—there were also quite a few tourists and elderly Japanese ladies; in fact there were far more Japanese in the audience than foreigners.

We were led to the balcony, and when the curtain opened, we were shown several highly stylized folk dances. Chika pointed out one of the dancers, but with her face chalk-white with makeup, she looked no different from the others. After the performance, we were taken to a room where we were served tea in a traditional tea ceremony which I knew had been shortened. The girl who served us, who smiled daintily at me, was Emiko. But as I said, with that makeup on, I wouldn't be able to recognize her outside.

"You must see her again," Chika told me. "Next time, where she work."

This was a restaurant far from Gion, toward the mountain, up a winding road above the city. Its parking area was lined with big cars, some Mercedes-Benzes. We went by taxi. The restaurant had separate rooms, woodblock prints on the walls, and so many women in kimonos fawning over us. They knew Chika for they greeted her with a lot of bowing and seeming deference. We were led to a room which I soon realized was just for the two of us although it was as large as the other rooms. On the handsome low table were two places with the usual arrangement of chopsticks, small trays for the hot towels, and teacups. A woman in a kimono came in; she was a waitress. She poured our tea, placed the hot towels on their lacquered trays, and those daintily arranged appetizers, anchovies in salt and sugar. In a short while, Emiko came in, gorgeous in a dark blue kimono which I am sure cost much, her face made up with chalk, on her head the headdress of the maiko, with its small plastic flowers, hairpins and beads. She smiled at us, then she sat beside me.

155

"What do you want , Buddy-san?" Chika asked. "She can dance, sing, or say poem."

"But I won't understand a thing," I said.

"I translate," she said.

Emiko did not eat with us—she merely stayed by my side and, on occasion, removed the bones from my fish and tried to make me comfortable. Once, she stood before us, sang and danced with her fan which she opened and closed with extreme agility. Chika told me later it took years of training to do that, and the geishas are usually trained from childhood.

It would have been a boring lunch were it not for the atmosphere, the simplicity of everything. The food was not particularly good. I would take Vladimir's cooking anytime.

I did not bother with the bill—it was very expensive, only those men downstairs with their Mercedes-Benzes could afford it. The taxi was waiting at the gate. It was three-thirty—the whole experience had lasted three hours. A girl was waiting for us at the door and she joined us, slipping into the front seat beside the driver. She had a suitcase which she carried on her lap. "This is Emiko," Chika introduced her.

What a change indeed! She was like any teenager, a student, with her boy's bob and, without a touch of makeup on her face, there was this piquant freshness of a virgin about her, which Chika said again and again is what distinguishes the maiko from the geisha, the most important distinction. She was in a white summer dress, with lace at the neck, and like her aunt without those infernal glasses, she was pretty.

"How many more months before you become a geisha?" I asked.

"My English bad," she said apologetically. Even her voice had that quality of gentle femininity, part of her training, I surmised. She turned to Chika, then to me. "Two weeks," she giggled.

Two more weeks. It all became clear afterwards what Chika had in mind. Again, we were in the tub together, any sexual urge in me deadened by the chilling remembrance of what she had done to her lover.

"You live here three months now, Buddy-san. I know you have no woman."

I wanted to tell her that I desired her, middle-aged though she may be, but still very young, even virginal to me, yet every time the desire came, it quickly passed. I do not know if she knew or suspected it. Surely she could see that several times, in that tub, my loins ached for her. Vladimir had suggested that I should have a girlfriend, take my pick from any of the Filipino girls in the apartment. They were not bad-looking and they would be willing.

"I manage," I said.

And that was when Chika suggested that I become Emiko's patron and that I should do it happily, for it was always a distinction to be a maiko's first lover.

"It is not too much," she said. I made a hasty calculation, it would cost a fortune which, of course, I could afford. The money would not go to Emiko—it would go to her aunt, to Chika, as payment for all that she had spent and done for Emiko.

IN CHIKA'S PRESENCE, I paid Emiko in cash. I had not spent much of the Institute's stipend as I was spending my own money most of the time. I was reading in my room that same evening; anxious voices at the door and soon, Chika and Emiko were in my room.

"Every night," Chika announced, her face bereft of expression, "Emiko will come after work in restaurant. She belong to you." Then smiling gravely, she left us.

Emiko was in a leather jacket, blue jeans and red sneakers. She bowed, looked around the room with perfunctory interest; I was sure she had been here before. She had brought a suitcase which she hastily opened and proceeded to hang her clothes in the cabinet next to my clothes. I watched her silently, a college kid come for the weekend, or a holiday. When she was through, she undressed without any hesitation, and put on a yukata. It was around nine in the evening and warm. In broken English, she asked if I had eaten and when I said, yes, she asked if I had taken a bath. She was very anxious, it seemed, to serve me. When I told her I had not, she said she would prepare the bath. While the tub was filling, she looked in and asked if I wanted a beer. I was going to be pampered and I was beginning to feel uncomfortable. "I'll get it myself. Thanks," I said.

The bath was ready; the sunken tub, more than a meter long, is walled with small blue tiles; a narrow shelf is at the bottom for the bather to sit on. Emiko took me by the hand to the bathroom where she undid my shirt, then my pants, with such careful thoroughness I wondered if this was also taught in the geisha school.

She bade me sit on the low stool and started soaping me, scrubbing my back first then all of me with a hand towel. A feeling of coziness, of a pleasant and quiet peace came over me, I could have sat there forever. Her breasts were small, the nipples dark red against the lustrous skin, fair, too, like Chika's but tinted with the rose of youth. There was not a single sense of hesitation in the manner with which she washed me, as if it was the most natural thing to happen

157

to a man, and when it became turgid, she washed it, too, carefully, as if she had held one so many times in her life. With all that skill and premeditation, was she really a virgin?

In the meantime, she also soaped herself with some heady assistance from me. The rinsing over, we stepped into the tub together. She did not sit in front of me, she sidled close beside me so that our bodies touched. I asked her to sit on my lap which she did immediately. I hugged her lightly, kissed her nape, the lobes of her ears, and could feel her quiver. We hardly talked—there was no need to, and then it was time to get up, and rising from the tub, the tension eased, she rubbed me dry with a soft towel till, I think, my skin was red.

We went to my room. She had switched off the light except for the reading lamp on my table. Of Chika, no movement; was she there listening? Or had she gone back to her restaurant? It was still early, just a little over ten in the evening. Any movement, each syllable of speech carried clearly through those thin walls which were made of some flimsy material; when Chika was there, I could hear her move about, and moan in her sleep. Was she listening to us? From down below, the river murmured softly on its course, somewhere in the azalea bushes, a cricket declared itself, and wisps of quiet talk from down the narrow lane reached us. The room smelled of pillows, old tatami, and muted expectations.

Kyoto is colder than Tokyo in the winter and hotter in the summer; the mountains that ring the city made the difference. It was now midsummer, August, but it was not as warm as it was in the American midwest, New York or Washington. The window that opened to the river was open to let in the breeze; there was no airconditioning in the old house. I did not mind that too much.

Emiko had brought in a plastic basin with water, a thermos bottle, and some towels; we were to use them when we were through. She had also prepared the futon to which I was now accustomed, but not with the sand-filled pillow which the Japanese still used. I was in my summer yukata and so was she.

She lay beside me silently and when she turned on her side to face me, an expectant smile adorned her face, so elfin-like, so much like a child. I was twice her age. In hindsight, I realized it was a most impulsive thing for me to do, throwing away that small fortune so casually. There are impediments to desire, to lust which do not seem probable, even real until they confront us. Who was it who said that the best aphrodisiac is in the mind? It is all there, and so is the iron sensibility that blocks it. I had fantasized earlier, knowing she was very young, that this was any foreigner's supremely orgiastic adventure in Japan, to partake of a culture that has survived to this very day together with pizza and McDonald's. Indeed, as the days unfolded, Emiko showed herself to be no different from the other young Japanese in a country that was undergoing changes not just in its food habits but in the way the youth behaved as apart from their elders.

It was Chika who woke me up. Breakfast was ready. Emiko had prepared it. Another chair was before the breakfast counter. In the morning light, without any makeup, Emiko's skin was purer, lovelier, but her eyes were swollen. She had been crying.

"Why you not do it?" Chika looked at me accusingly.

"Does it matter, Chika-san? I paid in full, didn't I?"

"You don't understand," she said. "Emiko thinks she fail."

What could I say? I didn't even remember so much what transpired that evening; the hot bath had worked like an opiate but more than that, I think I was hindered by some recondite compulsion not to collect the salacious dividends of my investment. I do fondly recall, however, Emiko caressing me oh so gently, those expert hands wandering all over my body. She lulled me into a syrupy, hypnotic sleep instead. I wanted to tell Chika that it was she I desired, more than this sweet virgin but it couldn't be, and I think she knew it.

"She return your money," Chika said.

"No," I told her. "That is not necessary. There are still so many nights ahead—and you said she will not leave me for as long as I want her."

She explained this to Emiko who listened silently, nodding all the while. Then she broke into a smile and said "hai," she understood.

I have heard Filipinos say that even a green branch, just cut off from a tree, when brought close to a flame, would soon burn quickly. Thus did my Emiko become a full-fledged geisha.

THE THIRD ROOM devoted to the memory of Chika's father had fascinated me but since I respected her request that I do not intrude into it, I did not even ask what was inside. One morning, however, perhaps the only time that I recall her cleaning it, she opened the screen that faced the river; she was vacuuming the room. I was in the garden at the time, reading in the sunshine. I rose to watch.

Chika did not mind me. I just stood there in the terrace. She knew I was watching but she did not ask me in. A scroll adorned one wall, and on a low table, was a lacquered box in dark maroon. On the wall, too, was a photograph of Chika's father in the uniform of a Japanese imperial army officer. I learned later that he had the

159

rank of a colonel. Below his picture was his sword hanging from a red sash. On the table were several notebooks tied together with a piece of red string, and a small satchel, a leather shoulder bag for men such as those that had become fashionable in Japan.

In another moment, she was through and she closed the screens behind her. At least, she did not shoo me away.

Chika came home early that evening. Emiko was in the restaurant, managing it in her absence. Emiko was free and owed no debt except to me; she could do anything she pleased except to leave me, her patron.

Chika told me, "You take her to America, she can be your mistress, not necessary to marry."

I had no such plans and had already written away the money I had to pay for this unique experience; how many maiko are there in all Japan?

Chika said we should take a bath and talk in the tub. I had by then gotten used to seeing her, aging though she was but so beautifully preserved, and because she never had a baby, her stomach was flat and unmarked by the lines inflicted by childbirth. Emiko's stomach, because she was a little bit more stout, was not as flat, and her navel was half hidden by a fold of baby fat.

So we were there in the tub, warm and cozy. Her father was in Manila, she told me, that it was there where he was killed. The box in the middle of the table contained his ashes, the sword on the wall was his and the notebooks on the table, too, were his diaries, notations.

I had visions of possessing those notebooks, and indeed, had plans of photographing their contents while Chika was away, but I did not dare. She had trusted me, I was not going to betray that trust. They could say so much of the Occupation, how they regarded and subjugated people. There would be names even, and many Filipinos who disappeared during the war were never heard of again. Those notebooks could unravel so much. As an historian, my frustration was needling, profound. I had no answer to the question I often asked: Why are the Japanese, either as soldiers or as businessmen, so brutal when they are on top?

I also realized then how important to these people was the past, their own family history even. Indeed, although so many documents were burned during the war, many records of that period remained, and it was possible to trace the units, the individual soldiers even. If I knew Japanese, and could read it as well, I would have attempted to find out who were in the Mountain that fateful year and unravel completely, at least for myself, the murderers of Apo Tale and Inay

Mayang. But I was now being distracted; I was beginning to enjoy the polished ministrations of my chattel, my Emiko.

Sometimes, I would pick Emiko up at the restaurant. Chika would let her go and we would end up at one of those small coffee shops where she listened to rock music; in fact, she had a whole set of Japanese rock tapes which she often played in the morning while she cooked breakfast. She also prepared simple lunchboxes, bento they call it, rice balls wrapped in seaweed with pickled things inside, the thermos bottle filled with tea, and off we would go on one-day trips to Osaka, to Nara, to so many temples. She never really enjoyed the temples, I realized later, but had assiduously taken me there because she understood I was a student of Japanese culture.

At home, in the early evenings, she would be reading Japanese comics. Always mindful of her duties, she would ask me if I wanted her to sing, or dance. She said I was easy to please and she was forgetting the technique of those dances that geishas perform. She would turn on her stereo set and in jeans or short skirt, she would perform snatches of them, incongruous as it was. Then she would play another tape and would pull me from my desk to dance rock or sometimes the tango, which young Japanese barely knew. Her English was also improving and there were times she no longer had to consult the dictionary she always carried in her bag.

I DID not finish my one-year term in Kyoto. In early November when the leaves of the maple and beech trees had turned golden yellow and a delicious coolness had come upon the city, I received a call from Porfiria. Once again, Jessie was in the hospital. Porfiria told me the danger was over and I should not worry anymore, but that if I could, I should return to San Francisco right away. Two weeks earlier, Jessie had called and in a voice rimmed with despondence, she said she needed me truly. Would I please come home?

Now I deeply regretted that I had not heeded her urgent call for help, for that was what it was. She had attempted suicide, drank an overdose of sleeping pills. Thank God, Porfiria had gone to her room that morning and again, took her immediately to the hospital. They pumped her stomach, did everything to save her and it was some time before she was conscious again. I was the first person she wanted to see.

She came on the line, her voice weak, defeated. I asked her why she did it. Did she not think of me at all? Then my chest started to cave in, I was being strangled by feelings I could not control. I couldn't speak anymore. She knew I was crying, and she said, "I am sorry, Buddy. I won't do it again." But I couldn't stop crying so I had to put the phone down.

It was a sad wrenching away from Kyoto but I did not have to hurry. I just wanted to be with Jessie, protect her from herself, care for her. I went to the restaurant to tell Vladimir I was leaving, I told my colleagues at the Institute, too. With Professor Kunio Ishii, the simple truth; he would understand it better that way. On the last week, I gave a one-day seminar on Southeast Asia, its prospects, my perception of Japan's role in the region. They knew I had never been to the Philippines and I didn't want to sound like someone who knew the country explicitly. Besides, Marcos was in power and it seemed then that he had everything under his imperious heel.

Chika was silent when I told her about my leaving, and Emiko cried; the girl, I realized, had truly become attached to me, not just as a patron who paid for her freedom but as a human being, her lover, her husband, to whom she had given the gift of her innocence. Her affection, I realized with some sorrow, was certainly larger than a teardrop and I would not see her again. It could all be fine acting, of course, but that shudder of grief as she embraced me would have been difficult to fake, as was the tremor in her breast. She had learned more English but would not need more of it were she to pursue life as a geisha, or just be Chika's assistant at the restaurant. It would be hers someday.

"There is something I would like you very much to do for me, Chika-san," I told her. "Please, I want to see you in the kimono of a geisha, to see you in the radiance of what you were."

She agreed and that early evening, she showed me the large closet in her room which she flung open, revealing more than two dozen beautiful silk kimonos for all seasons. Although she said they were old, they looked like they were very new. They would all pass, she said, to Emiko. I watched as she prepared herself, the white paint on the face, the powder all the way down her back, the carefully applied eye shadow. Emiko helped her in every way, the adjustment of the wig, and finally, the purple sash and the gorgeous kimono that ignited the austere and arid room in a grand explosion of living red.

Even without her dark glasses, Chika was unrecognizable—a life-size porcelain doll, mannered movements of such dainty elegance; truly she was magnificently transformed. We took a taxi to the restaurant which was closed for the night; the whole party was just for us, for Vladimir and Anita and the three girls in the apartment. I did not invite anyone from the Institute. Also, they did not know about Emiko. Chika-san in her role as geisha sat beside me the whole evening, and she performed two traditional dances. I know she had not rehearsed them but just the same she did them, to my untrained eyes, perfectly. She also sang twice in that plaintive manner of the traditional singer. Emiko waited on us and at the same time watched her aunt like a maiko again, learning from every gesture Chika made.

Vladimir, freed from his chores in the kitchen, had drank a bit too much sake—he was silent almost the whole evening and there was this smile plastered on his face throughout. Only when the three girls and Anita started to sing did he liven up and he joined them in singing a Tagalog folk song about a butterfly which one could easily catch. The girls were at first very circumspect—they had obviously heard of Chika and her benevolence, and now, they were awed by her. They had never been to a party like this, with a real geisha in attendance. I wondered how it was at their place of work, the men looking at them as objects of purchase. Anita, most of all, and Vladimir waiting for her to return from the rigors of her nocturnal commerce. I realized with a pang of sorrow how tormented their lives were, and in a sense, I was happy that Chika had acceded to this party, and they were thus transported into this brief but exotic interlude.

It was perhaps the most memorable party I had ever attended and when I asked for the bill, knowing it would be expensive but well worth it, Chika said, "It is my farewell gift to you."

I thought of Vladimir, the lives of the illegal Filipinos in Japan—thousands of them, not just in Japan but everywhere. I recalled Vladimir's stories; the epic diaspora needed to be recorded.

17

VLADIMIR ILYICH ACOSTA—*my name was given to me by my father, who was enamored with the Russian revolutionary, Lenin. He had Lenin's picture in our tiny living room in Camiling, Tarlac, which Mother, I remember this very well, tore when I was a boy. They had quarrelled because Mother was worried the army would come to the house, see the picture and accuse my father of being a Huk, which in a sense he was, although he never really joined the Huks. In his own way, he was a rebel and he often told me that the Philippines needed a revolution.*

When I went to school, my classmates joked about my name particularly since Acosta, my family name, starts with A, and I was always the first to be called at roll call. It would have been better if I had a nickname but I did not, so it was Vladimir all the time, in school and wherever I worked later on.

My father, who was a schoolteacher, had scrimped, and my mother had taken odd jobs like selling vegetables in the public market, so they could buy a piece of land and build our house. But Father had sold his three hectares, which he thought he and Mother would live on when he retired and my mother would not need to sell vegetables anymore. College in Manila was expensive but he managed to send my two sisters and myself on the money from that sale.

My father was rigidly upright. He always reminded us that the food he put in our mouths was bought with hard-earned money, that even then, corruption was in the school: teachers passing students whose parents had given them gifts, the principal and the supervisor playing favorites with teachers—so many examples of what he called immoralities had seeped down everywhere and were now destroying the country. I suppose that a bit of that constant sermonizing had gone into me.

I hope he is happy. I did not disappoint him the way my sisters did; when they got married and had families of their own, they stopped sending money which our parents needed particularly now that they are old.

In the last five years, I always sent them sometimes six lapad (ten thousand yen, one lapad) each month. My employer, Chika-san, is very generous, maybe because of my name, maybe because I am Filipino.

I stopped going to college in my junior year because I saw no point in it, my taking up commerce and management when there were so many educated unemployed. My parents did not know that I had answered a job placement advertisement for a cook, and so I spent time in bookshops looking at the cookbooks, watching the cooks when I sidelined as a waiter in a Filipino restaurant. I said that I had three years experience and thank God they did not check else they would have found out I only worked there for a year as a waiter. I was so pleased when I was given the job on an ocean-going vessel, Filipino-owned but flying the Panama flag.

My father's surprise was total when I told him I was leaving to work on a ship, not as a stevedore but as some clerk. I couldn't tell him that I was going to be a cook. To join the crew, I flew to Singapore where the boat was loading cargo and we were there for a week. The chief cook was Filipino and when I started working, he immediately knew I had no experience. He was mad for he had hoped that with my arrival he would have more time on his hands, particularly in Singapore where he wanted to do some shopping and also visit with his girlfriend.

I begged him to keep my secret. I was twenty-three and eager to learn; I would do anything he ordered me to do, anything! and that I hoped he would also teach me. I was able to calm him somewhat. He was Ilokano and I spoke to him in the language, saying always, "Wen, manong."

Early Sunday, in our best clothes, we went to Orchard Road where his girlfriend was waiting. Lucky Plaza is a giant emporium, actually a conglomerate of shops, selling everything—dry goods, cameras, jewelry— and some Chinese and cafeteria-style restaurants. I was surprised when I saw them, hundreds of Filipino women on the sidewalk, everywhere talking and exchanging gossip. Orly, the cook, was forty years old, and his girlfriend was from Bontoc, a lovely enough girl, with broad hips and a dimple. He said it was better this way, the likelihood of his catching gonorrhea was remote, and because he was generous with his money, the girls entertained him every time he was in port.

"Look for one yourself, Vladimir," he told me. "It is also cheaper— you get a prosti and you will spend a hundred US dollars. My girl is happy if I take her out to a restaurant, buy her a dress, and thrust thirty Singapore dollars in her bag so she can take a taxi."

The Bontoc girl spoke Ilokano and she introduced me to one of her friends, a girl from Baguio, who like her was in college when she found a job in Singapore. I was inexperienced, shy with women and a virgin, so I spent the whole afternoon with her, just wandering around the shops of Orchard Road and afterwards eating at McDonald's. I liked her a lot, and she promised to see me again that Sunday, if the boat would still be in Singapore and I could manage shore leave. It was also from her that I learned for the first time of the life of our women domestics in Singapore. There were also construction workers, and they lived on the sites, sleeping on the floor, atop piles of building materials. Tough life, but at least they were earning more money.

The MS Bataan plied the Pacific ports, all the way from Sydney to Tokyo, and Seattle, et cetera. Its crew of thirty-six was all Filipino, which was good because I could be myself and did not have to adjust to other cultures as I had to do later on when I got assigned to other ships. There were four of us in the galley, including Orly who was chief cook. We did not just cook—we also served, did the dishes and kept the galley clean. We had more opportunity to go on shore leave than the other members of the crew for the captain was choosy with his food and, as much as possible, he wanted fresh vegetables, fish, meat, rather than rely on the huge freezer. So when we were in port, almost always one of us was sent to market with the chief cook.

Much, much later, I realized how important the cook is in the ship. When you cross the Pacific or the Atlantic, that means more than two weeks of monotony, nothing but that mass of water around you, squalls and mountainous waves and seasickness, or calm, mirrorlike waters all the way, but water all around just the same. And what relieves the monotony is lunch and dinner when there is something different and good to eat and also time for the crew to be together. So we really tried to cook the best that we knew, for the meals then became an adventure of sorts that relieved the crew of its daily tedium.

We went to Hong Kong, too, on this first trip and there again Orly had a girlfriend waiting. I was introduced to a girl from Bacolod, a sweet Ilongga, and, like our girls in Singapore, I heard the same stories, most of the time of ill treatment, of masters of the house who tried to rape them, and the generally bad conditions under which they worked. In most instances, being college students or graduates, they were often more educated than their mistresses and this contributed to the tensions in the household. Housing was often horrible; the girls slept on the floor, or atop tables or counters, wherever a body could lie down.

On my first voyage to the United States, I was almost tempted to jump ship in Oakland where we unloaded cargo. I learned that the captain expected this—always some crew member disappeared into the honeyed entrails of America to pursue the Filipino dream. We all knew it was easy to get a job in America if all that one worked for is food; God, the food that is thrown away, but as elsewhere, if you have no papers, you are going to be exploited. I did not want that.

I lasted in the Bataan a couple of years and when my contract was up, although I could have renewed it, I decided to go to the Middle East where the pay was much higher, for cooks anyway. If I had known it would be very difficult, I wouldn't have gone at all.

By now, I really knew how to do Filipino dishes, including such delicacies like crispy pata and kare-kare. Orly taught me these and I am forever in his debt. The firm that took me was in construction; they were deep in the desert and the nearest city, Jeddah, was about five hundred miles away, across that desolation of sand and rock. They were laying pipelines and building refineries.

The company I worked for was American, and there were some American engineers, but most of the workers were Filipinos with a sprinkling of Indians and Pakistanis. It was not just the heat that was unbearable, it was also the fact that it was absolutely boring. Thank God, I drank moderately, and did not have to suffer so much. The boys tried to make alcohol from grapes and fruit juice which they managed to drink in secret. Lechon and pork were completely unavailable, and one gets tired of chicken, chicken, chicken, with occasional lamb and goat meat thrown in. And camel, too. Many wild dogs roamed the desert and I heard that some of the boys would trap and cook them, but I never really saw it happen. I don't know how they did it, but one day, a lechon was smuggled into the camp and they took it to the kitchen for me to cut up. It was a big disappointment for the trip across the desert had spoiled it. We buried it in the sand, grieving.

Our quarters were airconditioned—that was an absolute necessity. Because I was also cooking for the officers, it was also with Mega Construction Company that I learned to do the usual American fare, Middle Eastern, too, which required a lot of condiments. The Pakistani cook helped me with such new dishes. I was beginning to get very good. I had also built a small library of recipes including those fancy ones which are supposed to contribute to a man's libido.

In the desert, however, sexual gratification was impractical if not impossible unless one was homosexual. This is one reason why most of the boys who could grew beards or moustaches because the Arabs had a penchant for kidnapping and raping them. In Saudi and Kuwait, many of our women suffered this fate; others were battered, and those who couldn't take it often lost their minds. To be in Saudi Arabia is to be in the middle ages. You'd get your arm chopped off if you were caught stealing; bringing the Bible into the country is going to cost you a jail term. And in my time, a couple of Filipinos were beheaded, one because he had killed a fellow worker, and another because he had fucked an Arab girl. If I knew it, it was not rape, but the girl's honor and that of her family had to be preserved.

We had VHS; when we were homesick we watched videotapes of Filipino movies, listened to Filipino records and read Filipino komiks. Sadness hovered our lives; some of the women—wives and girlfriends who were left behind—were unfaithful to their men who were slaving to send money home.

And boredom—that was our most difficult problem. No alcohol to balm the mind, certainly no sex for those of us who were out there in the desert, although I was told there were some Filipinas in the cities doing it as a sideline. So we had fistfights without gloves just so there would be a respite from this boredom that wrought us all. Sometimes, we went just outside the camp, to that seemingly rimless sea of sand, and screamed as loud as we could as if by doing so, we were expunging our loneliness, too.

We were all counting the days and finally, time to go home. Thirty of us were in the plane, and once up there, I opened a bottle of Black Label which I had bought at the airport. I did not down it in one gulp, I just took a little sip, letting the warmth of the liquor dwell on my tongue— ah, such a wonderful, beautiful feeling, telling me I was now whole again and not a machine without blood and intestines. Then another draught, feeling the silky caress of the liquor down my throat, that luxurious, lingering feeling of pleasure spreading from your middle to all parts of your body, your fingertips, the roots of your hair!

We changed planes in Bangkok. By then, time had no meaning and the airport was a blur. But I do remember going to the airport restaurant, found pork chops on the menu, and I ordered a couple, ate it like a hog— no more chicken day and night till I thought we smelled like chicken shit. I dozed off and was wakened by the announcement of the pilot that we were approaching Manila, that we would be on the ground in thirty minutes. We had all been forewarned about the dangers at the airport, in our own country, the thieves in police uniform, the bloodsuckers who feed on us, the little people, loaded as we were with dinars, the electronic geegaws we had bought—will these get to our relatives at all?

Just the same, we rushed to the windows and looked at the land we had not seen in two, even four, five years, the ricefields verdant and glazed

168

with water, the mountains laced with trees, the small towns with iron-roofed houses—how really small they looked from above. Then, someone in the back yelled, "Hoy, Vladimir, now you can fuck!" And the whole plane shuddered with our laughter.

I thought I would never go back to the desert and of course I did not return to Saudi. I went instead to Dhubai and worked there at a new hotel. Dhubai was better than Saudi—the Arabs in this small oil-rich country were not as conservative as the Saudis. And Filipino women all over Dhubai, in the shops as salesclerks, in the hotels as waitresses and even as masseuses. The airport tax free shop in Dhubai is manned completely by Filipinas, it is like shopping in Makati.

The hotel had two chefs, a Russian and a Frenchman, and again, I was able to learn French cuisine and, in keeping with my name, some Russian dishes, like piroshki, botvinya, bozbash and others. By then, I was also able to cook Chinese and Italian, and double as a bartender if necessary. We were using a lot of wine in our cooking and I was getting to know wines as well.

In Dhubai, I fell in love with a Filipina check-out girl at one of the big supermarkets. Every Saturday, my day off and also her day off, we would go out. There was very little opportunity for us to be alone; Perla was Ilokana, from Laoag—she was slim, in her early twenties, and she had these perfect lips that begged to be kissed. She was living in an apartment with four Filipino girls, all of them working as salesclerks. One afternoon when I took her home I realized that we had the whole apartment to ourselves. I think that was also the reason why she insisted we go home. I wanted so much to make love to her and I think she was also hungry for it. We were finally alone in her room and I had already started to undress her when she said, "Wait. I must tell you the truth." She was a mother, she said, of a five-year-old girl in the Philippines, that her husband was waiting for a chance to go abroad, and, all of a sudden, my hunger, my passion, started to cool. And though I still kissed her and fondled her, I just couldn't get truly excited anymore. I felt ashamed—I was thinking of my friends in Saudi, desolate in the desert, working themselves to the marrow, and their wives in the Philippines betraying them.

Perla, I said, more in sadness than anything else; I am sorry I cannot do it.

So she put on her dress, kissed me and said it was all right. I had to make some explanation that wouldn't embarass her, like some other time perhaps when I was not too anxious, or when I was not too tired, some other time—but there was no other time for I decided not to see her anymore.

I clipped this from the Manila Chronicle: "There is no ship in the oceans today that does not have a Filipino sailor. Five thousand international ships employ 62,000 Filipino seamen, as captains, chiefs and second and third mates, engineers, radio technicians. The luxury ships have Filipino musicians, pianists, waiters and, of course, cooks (like me)."

For us, the average salary on a ship is US$700 a month, which is an executive's salary in Manila. They take us because we are willing to accept lower pay, because we speak English, but I am sure the reason is more than these: we adjust easily to circumstances, it is easy for us to get along with other people, and we work very, very hard.

I was on this Norwegian freighter and the cook and two other assistants were ill—as a matter of fact, a kind of flu epidemic almost crippled the ship. We were in the North Atlantic, it was bitterly cold—and I had to man the galley by myself. I never worked so hard before in my life. The Norwegian captain recognized this and he gave me a bonus when we docked in Hamburg.

By the time we got there, the crew was healthy. The radio operator who was Filipino and I did the town, meaning we visited Reeperbahn, the famous prostitution district. For seamen to have "good" women is extremely difficult; it is always the professionals, the streetwalkers, the usual houses of prostitution. Orly, whom I mentioned earlier, had very good opportunities but they required nurturing and this was possible only if the ports are in our regular itinerary. This district in Hamburg is well known to seamen. The girls are on display in windows, as in Amsterdam, and we could proposition them right there. We were making the rounds when we clearly heard, "Pinoy! Pinoy!" And there, framed by one of the windows close by, were two heavily made-up Filipino girls.

They were very happy to see us, not so much as guests, but as countrymen who could tell them about home. The radio operator went upstairs with the smaller woman—he said he always liked them tight and small—and I was left with the girl from San Fernando, Pampanga. I told her that I was not going to do it and she said, "There's nothing wrong with me, I am clean." I said that was not the point; I was not in the mood for the truth is I was just hungry for some female company, someone I could talk with.

"I won't waste your time," I said. "I will give you what you usually get."

She said she could at least masturbate me, and she started fondling my crotch, but I told her that was not necessary. She ordered some beer and so, for the next hour, we just talked, two Filipinos away from home, stricken with homesickness, wanting to go back, but to what? the poverty, the filth and the corruption of the homeland? No, it is better in Hamburg, and certainly better, too, in the hot steamy galley of a Norwegian ship.

She said there were several of them doing the European circuit, and sending money home. She was not married and was the sole support of a family of eight; she was the oldest, her father was dead and her mother was taking care of the family, aged three to seventeen. She was nineteen. I do not think that the name she gave me was her real name, and I don't think she even came from Pampanga for when I tried talking with her in Pampango, she always replied in Tagalog. She had come to Germany on a tourist visa, hoping to get some work as promised by the Filipino who recruited her—and she paid him 30,000 pesos! But the job was not there, she and the others were stranded in Frankfurt. Fortunately, there was this available recourse else she would not have eaten at all. She had been at it now for a year, sending money regularly to her family who, all along, thought she was working in an office. She was hoping she may yet meet a good man who would marry her—it is not impossible, she said; look at all those prostis in Subic and Clark who were able to bag American GIs!

In Hamburg, we unloaded lumber, grains and loaded chemicals, Mercedes-Benzes, mixed cargo. I visited a social center set up and managed by a civic-minded Filipina together with a German priest, and every day, Filipina mail-order brides visited the center, bringing with them their mestizo children. A Filipina maid had declared herself a widow, although her husband and children were very much alive in Leyte, so that she could marry a German and get assured of permanent status. Oh, yes, so many such cases, and when I asked about their German husbands, they always said they were mabait—very good. Love was an alien word.

Where else are the Filipinos working? In the frozen tundras of Alaska, in the pampas of Argentina, in the mines of Africa, in the North and South Poles—Filipinos are there, and if the Russians will open up Siberia to Filipino workers, there will be thousands willing to suffer that arctic cold. All over the world, all over the world! Mail-order brides in Scandinavia, in Australia, where our poor women marry not for love but for money men who are drop-outs, outcasts in their own society. Illegals in Italy, in Switzerland, and yet more maids in London. It is difficult now for Filipinos to travel with their brown passports—everywhere, they are suspect. In Sydney where I went to meet my ship, I was searched like I was a smuggler, all my clothes, pockets, all my things, my airline ticket, my seaman's papers. And why not? TNT's, that is what most Filipino travellers have become, "takbo nang takbo," always running away from a land that denies them honor, always running, just as I am running now.

Five years ago, I was cook again on a Japanese ship, the Sendai Maru, which carried containers from North America to Japan. Again, the crew was almost all Filipino except for a few Pakistanis. This Pakistani crewman was always quarreling with Filipinos, and he crossed my path that day. He was much taller than most of us, with a beaked nose, a stubble on his chin always, and the general appearance of a man who seemed to fear a shower. We were having lunch, I was serving. First, some insults in English, and then he purposely spilled his coffee on me. It seemed he had lost some money in his bunk and was blaming the Filipinos. "All Filipinos," he was shouting, "are thieves. Like their leaders. All Filipino women are prostitutes!"

I couldn't let that pass. "*Putangina mo!*" I shouted back.

"What did you say?" he glared at me.

"Your mother is a whore," I said, ready to take him on, the whole world even.

He drew a knife and came to me. I grabbed a stool and swung with all my strength. His knife fell. I picked it up and stabbed him in the chest. My compatriots had let him get away with it because they didn't want any trouble. But I was mad; I was really going to kill him and stab him again, but he had collapsed, screaming, and the other crewmen held me back. I had never been so angry in my life, it was the first time I realized how capable I was of violence.

The other Filipino crewmembers were aghast but they didn't say anything. We were docked in Kobe at the time unloading cargo. I went to my quarters, got the little money I had saved and my papers. and jumped ship. Now, the Japanese police were looking for me and I did not know what to do. I wanted to get as far away as I could from Kobe, to Tokyo, anywhere in a big city where I could hide. The farthest I got was Kyoto. I wandered aimlessly around the city, got to Gion by late afternoon just as the clubs and bars were opening and the girls were going to their places of work. This girl was walking alone—she looked Filipina so I approached her, told her I didn't know anyone, that I was running from the police. Would she help me?

She doubted, I think, my story. I showed her my passport, my seaman's papers, and there must have been a tremor in my voice, that undeniable sincerity. It was one of those incredible coincidences—studying my passport, she knew I was born in Camiling, and she was from Camiling, too. Some questions, and it turned out my father had been her teacher in grade school and that she and her family lived in the western end of town. My identity conclusively established, she said, the club where she worked, maybe she could get a job there for me. And where can I stay tonight? "Come home with me, that is if you don't mind sharing a room with three other girls. They will be very delighted to have a man around."

So that was how it was; Filipinos really do help one another in times of distress; otherwise, it is each man for himself, like crabs, as they always say.

About Anita and the other girls—they never had to tell me what they did; I knew almost immediately. Anita was in her late twenties—she had finished high school and was a sophomore in college when she stopped as her family had no money left. She was fair, ivory skin and all that, and her guests must have drooled over her when she lay naked before them. She was soft-spoken, "mahinhin," as we call it in Tagalog, "mahindutin," as the girls joked. She could have passed for Chinese and I asked her if she had Chinese blood but she did not know—her father and mother were both fair. Unlike the other girls in the apartment, she was not noisy; she was some kind of leader to them for when she spoke, they kept quiet and listened. The illegals also had some kind of network and soon, Anita found out about this vacancy for a cook in one of the small Gion restaurants. That was how I started working for Chika-san.

As for the Pakistani I had stabbed, I heard afterwards that he was also a psycho. He was brought to a hospital. There was no charge against me; the Japanese captain testified it was self-defense. This didn't help any. I was now an illegal, like Anita who had helped me, my guardian angel, my savior. If the police found me, I would be deported quickly. But I want to stay on here—the pay is very good, I have little work really for Japanese cooking is not difficult. What holds me back, more than anything, is Anita. You will find this strange; she is what they call here, Japayuki—Japan girl. I really would like her to stop. Pride demands this of me, but she does not want to. She earns so much and sends so much to Camiling. She is also saving so she can go back, buy some land, build a house. I told her I would marry her and return with her to Manila and she said she would think about it. She is lucky, unlike so many of the girls who are victims of the yakuza, who are sometimes unable to leave their places of work for they are virtual prisoners. Anita is free, just as I am free, but both of us, if you want to be precise, are illegal aliens. I am always in fear, just as she is, of policemen coming to ask for my passport. When I see them in the street, I walk away. And in the restaurant, I keep to myself in the kitchen, I do not know how long my luck will run, Anita's as well. She sometimes is reckless, going out to public places, visiting temples, tourist spots for she wants to learn about this country. She already speaks good Japanese. I know because I speak a bit of it now. Five years on the run—that is how lucky I have been. She is luckier—she has been here seven years.

At least, I do not have to do heavy manual labor on a daily basis. I have a regular job, and my employer gave me this certificate which I should show to anyone who asks; it says that I am a cook in her establishment. Other illegals lead a much tougher life, working for daily wages, at jobs that are dirty and often dangerous, construction, stevedoring, jobs the Japanese do not want. "Standing men," they are called. Early in the morning, they stand with other illegals and some Japanese drop-outs in designated street corners in the city slums. There, they are picked up by labor contractors, then hauled off in vans to their jobsites. They live in crowded rooms piled with their purchases to be sent home.

173

Sleeping in that apartment with four Japayukis, I could hardly breathe. It was really small, almost airless, and it smelled of soy sauce and dried fish which the girls often cooked. I had very little money and had no choice. No sooner had I found a job when, fortunately, the apartment next to Anita's was vacated, and I moved in. It was much too expensive being by myself so I asked Anita if she wanted to have more space and help with the rent; by this time, there was this understanding already between us but we had merely embraced and held hands.

I avoided going beyond; I did not want to be a client. I am no prude, I am quite good-looking, I think, and it is not difficult for me to get a "decent" girl; it was therefore a bit of a shock for me to realize that I was falling in love with, I use the word now for this is what Anita really is, a prostitute.

It was not difficult to convince her to move in; for one, the girls had suggested it, and teased her for they knew how close we had become. In that tiny and airless room, it was obvious how much attention I paid her, how grateful I was. When I could, I cooked for all of them and there was always food ready to be eaten, in the refrigerator. For our new home, Anita soon enough bought a secondhand refrigerator, a color TV, and a stereo she would take back to Camiling. I also cooked whenever I could, kabutoni— that is her favorite—a big fish head, steamed with soy sauce, sugar, tofu, and noodles.

I went to work at around ten to help prepare and clean the restaurant. Anita spent the whole morning and early afternoon in the apartment; I usually returned home at eleven p.m. and she would come in long past midnight, sometimes in the early morning, sometimes not at all, and she would lie on the futon which I had already prepared and, wordless, go to sleep.

The first time—it was really she who started it. We had been living together for two months and no one, absolutely no one, would ever believe that in those two months, eight weeks, fifty-six days—we had abstained. I think she told the girls, and how they teased me! It was midsummer and warm and our apartment had no airconditioning. I was sleeping in my shorts, and did not know she had arrived. I must have had an erection for in a while, she was on top of me, kissing me, and murmuring, "You never ask for sok-sok (the slang for it) and you know very well I would do it for you for free. Don't you know that?" There was this delicious scent about her, this softness and tenderness in the way she touched me—I realized then not what I had missed, but that I truly loved her, that I wanted her to be my wife if she would only marry me.

She did not let me wear rubbers because, as she said, there was something between us. With her customers, rubbers always, and there was always a supply in her bag, in her wallet, as a matter of fact, in all her bags, just in case there was a sudden need for them. The girls in the other apartment looked at me differently soon enough, an older brother they could confide in, who would help them, advise them, tell them again and again to take care of their health for, in their kind of job, it was their most important asset. This they knew.

Anita made much, much more than I did and the following fall, she bought me a Benetton sweater and a down jacket made in Taiwan. I needed both for when I jumped ship, I had brought with me just a small bag of clothes. I thanked her; her gifts meant more money for me to send to my parents who were now living on a tiny pension and the money I sent.

Life is good in Japan; I do not doubt the horror stories I have heard from my father—there is enough of that in our history books. But the Japanese are good, kind and very helpful.

And now, the big question. Why am I here, or what is the purpose of my life? I have been busy trying to make a decent living, working hard to make money for my parents and myself, I have no time to think about such high and profound matters. I am, of course, very fortunate because in my country, so many people can only think of where they will get their food that evening, or the following day, a continuous struggle to survive, to scrounge, to steal—these are the compulsions that rule our lives. To philosophize is a kind of luxury we do not have.

Perhaps, the future I have in mind is not attainable. I would like to continue earning good money so that I can fulfill my obligations to my parents, to buy back the land my father sold, to see to it that they will not be hungry, that they will grow old happy in the thought that I have been a filial son.

But most of all, I would like to go back home, take Anita with me and get her away from all that demeans her here so that we can have a happy life, raise a family that will not know what she had done, what I had done.

My father is a rebel—as a schoolteacher he was warned many times not to make so much of our revolution, of the crimes of the landlords and the rich Filipinos. He had read a lot, and seen a lot of suffering, too, now and during the war, and he tells me every so often that our country is oppressed by its own leaders, that this form of colonialism is more pernicious and hateful because it is Filipinos depriving their own countrymen of their dignity.

There is nothing more shameful for a human being than to be hungry. In those times that I did not have a job and was studying with the little money that my father sent, or when I was running away, I had known this hunger. In my country, there should be no hunger at all—so many lands that are not planted, so many men without jobs because they have no land. My parents do not have a single hectare of land now, other than

175

*the lot where our small house stands. I fear for them. If they do not receive
the money on time they may go hungry.*

*How do you banish hunger from a country which has so much
land, so much wealth? Why aren't those multitudes of Filipino doctors
and nurses in the United States ministering to the poor and afflicted in
their own country? How do you bring home our thousands of women
who are shamed in Hong Kong and Singapore where they work as
housemaids? How do we stop our women from becoming prostitutes in
Japan? Our thousands of skilled workers in the Middle East—why are they
not building our country instead?*

18

MY LAST night in Chika's house will always haunt me with its bizarre unreality, and all the more convince me about how different the Japanese can be, this difference being a constant feature of their self-definition which is encrusted in their psyche. I will tolerate this definition, but only up to a point. I had gone back to the house alone—she and Emiko had to close the restaurant and they did not want me idling there. I was lying on the futon, trying to finish Mishima's *Confessions of a Mask* when Chika arrived. I could tell by then if it was she who came in, for soon after she would go to her room. With Emiko, it was to ours.

In a while, she slid my door open. She was in a yukata, slightly apart in the front, revealing the rise of her breasts, her thighs. Although she had appeared naked in the bathroom in my presence, she had not been that careless with her housecoat. "I have something to tell you, Buddy-san," she said. "Emiko not coming home tonight—she visit her sister for weekend."

I considered that very strange, why Emiko did not tell me in the first place, but I let it pass as one of those oversights which can only be explained by the "difference" I had mentioned earlier. It occurred to me quickly though that Chika had arranged Emiko's absence because I could see it then, her unlikely presence in my room late in the night, in her casual disarray, that she was going to seduce me. It was not an altogether unpleasant expectation.

She sat on the futon by my side. "He is homo," she said, noticing the Mishima novel that I had laid aside. There was hardly anything by now about the Japanese and their sex habits which surprised me; having read so many of their novels, I recognized their innate kinkiness that bordered on the perverse—a matter for inquiry and psychological speculation. Chika's manner was definitely provocative but I was not responding.

"I tell you about my father," she said. Then, she lay beside me, her yukata now wide open in the front. I did not touch her and, as if she was suddenly conscious of her undress, she drew the yukata to cover herself. "He was very good father and we were—" she raised her hand, two fingers pressed together.

At this point, may I now relate, dear reader, her story as I understood it that evening, and extrapolate some questions which came later on. This, to avoid the ambiguities and the faulty grammar of her English. In this telling, I may have committed some misinterpretations but I am sure, memory being very lucid and stringent, that I have not missed the important details. This is Chika-san now speaking:

"My father and I had a very intimate relationship, maybe because I was an only child as my mother died when I was six years old. I was in the care of an aunt, a retired geisha, a sister of my mother, who came to live with us while Father was away. He was a very gentle person, extremely helpful and kind—all our neighbors here know this. Then he went to China for three years, and when he returned I was already sixteen, grown up, and our relationship became even more close, he told me I reminded him so much of my own mother. (*Could there be, at this time, more than just a father-daughter relationship? Her narration convinced me there was.*) But those three years had changed him—he had become very quiet, reclusive and, at times, in his sleep he would scream and knowing him, the screams were not of anger but of fear. I knew so little of the war, other than many of our young men were in the army, that we had to make sacrifices for the war effort. Then he was assigned to the Philippines; by then, he was a colonel in the military police. His office was in a place called Fort Santiago. I used to look at him in awe and affection when he put on his uniform, his sword by his side. He really took good care of that sword—many a time he would unsheath it, the blade gleaming in the light, and clean and oil it, his hands caressing it—at times, I felt as if the sword was alive, that it was a woman who competed with me for my father's love. Sometimes, when he was lavishing care on it, I wished it was I he was touching instead. So he went to the Philippines, and he would write long letters, telling me about the country—they are all there, as you had seen them, bundled together with his notebooks. And then he stopped writing, and in three months, this officer came to the house and delivered his sword, his uniform and his ashes. I was told that he and a junior officer were in a bar near a church called Kiyapo. A guerrilla walked into the bar and shot them both. The officer told me that almost immediately, they roped off the area where he was killed, that they took a dozen male hostages and killed them all. (*Fort Santiago was the Japanese military police headquarters during the Occupation; Filipinos considered those who were taken there as executed for rarely was anyone brought to Fort Santiago released. I asked her what her father was doing at Fort Santiago, and she answered simply: he was the chief of the Kempeitai— the military police.*) I visited Manila ten years ago, simply to see the street where he was killed and, of course, to visit Fort Santiago, but it was destroyed during the war, and so is much of the Walled City where it is situated. I saw the dungeons where the prisoners were kept, the cross surrounded by many lighted candles—it was the Day for the Dead when I got there, and everything I saw confirmed in my mind what is in those notebooks. The day that I learned of my father's death, I decided to be a geisha, and with my aunt's connections, it was not difficult for me to be one. I had no one now to take care of me but myself, and when the war ended and many Japanese were hungry, I was not. (*Because you are very good- looking, Chika. Because you are also passionate. You didn't tell me though of the patron to whom you applied the ultimate feminine logic; poor man, as I see it now, so much can be traced to those notebooks and your relationship with your father!*) I was very fortunate—I had this house all to myself. I could have sold it then for so much, and now, if I sell it, I would be very, very rich. But what will I do with all that money? But going back to my father, I did not read the notebooks till very much later. I felt they were very personal testaments of his past and I should not trespass. He had, after all, written to me so many times, repeating in all of them how much he missed me, that when he returned, we would make up for the time that we had lost. He described the Philippines, what a beautiful place it was, the fire trees in bloom— how very much longer the flowers adorned the trees before they fell, unlike our sakura which bloom then quickly fall. How different were his letters to me, as compared to what he had written down in the notebooks about which I must now tell you. They are all there—the details of torture, and the many men and women who were sentenced to die—how their heads were cut off! He did not do the torturing himself, but he supervised it, watched it carefully, and was always searching for refinements. Even when the information he needed had already been given, the torture still continued. How many kinds were there? So many, each one suited to a particular individual whom he studied first before the torture was applied. The most common—they would push a man's head into a basin of water and hold his head down till he could no longer breathe and then they would pull him out by the hair, or as it often happened, held down his head until he drowned. Or fill a man's stomach with water, and then pump it out of him. His favorite was the electric rod which had variable current. It was applied to the head of the penis or the female clitoris. The pain is so intense, it cannot be endured. The victims would be screaming all over the place, and fainting. Then there were the more physical forms, the cutting off of ears, of fingers, the pulling of fingernails, or nailing a hand to a board. Beatings were common. A man's stomach was slit open, his intestines spilling onto to his lap. And the penis head was also cut. Psychological torture—the relatives of the victim, his sons, daughters, wife, even the very young, were brought to him and in his presence they were harmed physically, or the women were raped...It's all there in those notebooks, all there. And then, the final verdict which he usually made himself, the executions...with his sword, the sword on the wall. It is his favorite sword, forged by Kyoto's most famous swordsmith and handed to him by his grandfather who was one of the last samurai. The sword is alive, that is to say, it had killed even before my father inherited it. He used it sparingly, he said, only when the doomed man showed great courage, dignity or stoicism—all the qualities that the Japanese warrior admired and respected. I had taken it out of its scabbard slowly, most carefully, maybe there was a speck of blood on it but I saw nothing except the tiny beginnings of rust because it was not cleaned or oiled well after use. If I had a magnifying glass, perhaps I could see bits of bone embedded in the shallow ridges of the blade. No matter how well-tempered its cutting edge, it is so sharp and thin that it is always damaged when it cuts the bone. It has to be sharpened again, maybe after the third kill. (*So then, my favorite TV samurai serial, "Abarembo Shogun" is nothing but a heroic myth the Japanese foist on themselves. Every week, Ken Matsudaida, the incognito shogun, performs a precision ballet with his sword and disposes of two dozen "evil men" in the conclusion of the serial. As an instrument of feudal justice, toward the end of those glorious swordfights, he must be swinging a very damaged weapon indeed!*) Do you know how many men and women have been decapitated by it? It is all there, too, how a head would fall to the ground or the pit, sometimes with the face up, an eye winking at him, a mouth cursing him in some language—the head still alive although already severed from the body. A body kneeling without its head stood up, turned around and walked to him—it collapsed before he could strike it again with the sword, a neck that was too tough it required two strokes to separate the head from the body, a headless body kneeling and refusing to fall until he kicked it...So many such descriptions. I read them all, not just once but many times. Not that I enjoyed reading them—it was some form of compulsion, maybe because he was my father, maybe because he came alive in them, his handwriting. And reading his words, I could imagine him, his presence, like I always knew him..."

I had listened shocked and silent, and while she was telling me all these, I could imagine the man in his colonel's uniform, his cruel sword raised over those doomed, kneeling Filipinos. I decided then that I must see Fort Santiago. When I kept still, when I didn't say anything, Chika rose slowly and went to her room. I lay for some time, feeling oppressed, as if the whole house had become alien to me, a cell in Fort Santiago; I must leave quickly, and could hardly wait for the morning to come. I could not sleep anymore, so I started packing my things, all the while wondering how Chika could live in peace with all those ghosts hovering about her, her house, her country.

I had to see Vladimir, Anita and the girls again. Vladimir said he was leaving Japan very soon, too. Anita had gotten pregnant and they would go home together, get married. They had surrendered themselves at the police station in Gion and the police there had told them to go to the Osaka immigration office.

Vladimir was jubilant. He said the immigration people did not seem to bother about their status; that he and Anita could return to Japan in six months and to their old jobs.

But Anita would not return to Japan anymore, just him. His father had already regained his land. Anita's parents had opened a sari-sari store, and also bought some land.

JESSICA HAD fully recovered when he arrived in Pacific Heights but she was still very pale and she had lost considerable weight. He rushed to her and embraced her, mumbling, "Oh, Jessie, why did you do it—a stupid thing like that!"

They looked at each other, wordless for some time, then Jessie shook her head. "I can't explain, Buddy. I was so depressed, I saw no sense in living."

"We cannot change some things," he tried the old blah; "We just have to accept them and continue living, counting our blessings which millions of people do not have."

She explained it so simply, the series of social snubs, being left out. "The whites don't want me, the blacks don't want me either. Where do I fit in, Buddy? Would it be better if I were much, much darker, like the darkest black? With really kinky hair? No, the blacks don't just not want me, they resent me. Buddy, I don't have a single friend. Only you. So you have to be here for me. Always."

He shook his head. "That is impossible, Jessie. First, I will get sick and then I will die. But even if I lived to be very old, I would still have to leave you, and you will have to leave me, too."

She was silent for a while. Then she brightened up, "But at least, if I need you and call you, promise you'll come..."

"If I can," he said, and hoped to God that he could for now he was really afraid that leaving Jessie for a long time would end again this way.

ANOTHER ATTACK came—a deluge of fatigue, and listlessness. It was as if he had done some chain gang labor and now all strength, all desire to move had fled him.

Porfiria, ever faithful, drove him to the hospital; he was going to have a checkup, a complete series of tests; he was healthy, there was nothing to worry about.

But he was worried because he did not know what was wrong with him; the doctors had told him they did not know—they were not sure, they wanted to know more about his nervous system, if and when he would have another "attack." How could he foretell when it would come? There were no signs, no premonition! What tormenting shape and manner would it take and God, how soon?

Jessica visited him on his second day at the hospital. She was much better, the color returned to her face, the lilt in her voice as well. At least, Jessica recovered quickly. She brought a bag of cherries which they ate together.

"What's wrong with you, Buddy?"

He held her hand, pressed it and assured her he was all right, that the tests were not conclusive, as yet, and there were more that day and the next. She visited him every day, asked the same question. On the sixth day, when the fatigue seemed to have ebbed, she took him first to Sausalito for lunch.

He wondered if he should tell her what the doctors had said, their suspicions, what he should expect in the future. The worst could be total blindness, total loss of locomotion, paralysis, the loss of speech but, he was assured, the mind would remain clear. Meanwhile, since their findings were inconclusive, he should just learn how to relax, to exercise often, to take good care of his health and not engage too much in work that would tax the mind and depress him.

Watching her across the table enjoy her filet mignon and the baked potato and white asparagus spears, somehow he felt comforted. Jessica was all he really had now, and to see her so pretty, so at peace with the world, sent a surge of bliss coursing through him.

19

IN JANUARY 1981, Buddy arrived in Honolulu for a six-month fellowship at the East West Center to look at the remnants of the communities set up by the early Filipino migratory workers. Much earlier, at an Asian Studies conference in Boston, he had met a charming Filipina teaching Tagalog at the University of Hawaii. Buddy had told her he was trying to learn Tagalog—there were so many Tagalog documents he could not understand. The problem had really cropped up when he was reading the letters of the exiles in Spain in the 1880s to their homeland. Lena Mabango told him he could join her classes; more than that, she would accept all his invitations to coffee if only so they could converse in Tagalog.

He had a suite at the Lincoln Center, a comfortable arrangement with its own kitchenette and two bedrooms, for the suite was intended for a scholar's family. He arrived on a perfect morning, as unblemished as any San Francisco spring morning. He had looked forward to swimming at the fabled beaches of Hawaii, which is what he did the very hour after his arrival; he boarded a bus and was soon lolling at Waikiki.

In his third week, a convocation sponsored by the Filipino students was addressed by the Filipino senator, Benigno Aquino Jr., who was then in exile in Boston with his family. The imposition of martial law by Ferdinand Marcos had forced into exile hundreds who opposed him. Aquino, jailed by Marcos, was given permission to leave for the United States for heart surgery and had decided to remain there after the surgery to mount a campaign against the

Marcos regime; where but in the United States after all did Marcos get his support.

Buddy had moved within the periphery of the exile community in California and once, in New York, he even listened to a speech by Raul Manglapus, a former Filipino foreign secretary now in exile, too. He sympathized with their lot, but for so many of them, exile was a most convenient explanation for staying away from the Philippines, where, if they were really serious, they could do the most good.

The talk was given in one of the lecture halls of the center—the last in a series that Aquino was giving in Hawaii, his audience composed mostly of Filipinos from the university, sympathizers and, Buddy was sure, some Marcos lackeys who were there to monitor everything Aquino would say and do.

The hall was already full when he arrived, but there were still a few seats out front, to which he immediately went. He wanted to get a truly close-up view of this man whom every Filipino he had met expected to succeed Marcos.

The lecture was at ten a. m. and five minutes to the hour, Aquino arrived with Guy Hawker, the American professor at the center who was one of the foremost specialists in Southeast Asia. There was no fanfare; the professor went straight to the podium and introduced Aquino; they were very old friends, he said, and he had known Ninoy for more than two decades, having visited him often in his province where he was once governor, and yet again as Ninoy rose in political stature.

From the very start, Buddy had expected the usual anti-Marcos verbiage; this was where the exiles he had heard excelled, but though there was great sincerity in their talk, somehow they did not seem to relate to the American audience, insulated, uncaring, although certainly, liberally inclined to listen to whatever complaint was presented to it. But Aquino said more which now fascinated Buddy. Aquino mourned the death of the American dream, the beliefs of the American founding fathers which have lost their meaning, not because the American people no longer had vision, but because they had become too comfortable with their status and with the dictators with whom they forged pragmatic, opportunistic alliances.

He then went on to describe his plans, that it was just a matter of time when he would go back, because in the recesses of his soul, he knew that exile was not the solution. In fact, he said, every Filipino exile who felt passionately about his native land should go back if he could, to help rebuild that nation from the rubble of the Marcos dictatorship.

185

It was then that Aquino asked the Filipinos to stand and start singing; Buddy had heard it before, in Berkeley, at another Filipino convocation—"my country, even the bird has the freedom to fly"—a sad kundiman, and when the song ended, he looked around. Many of the Filipinos were in tears.

How could such a simple tune evoke so much emotion? Even when they were filing out of the hall, many eyes were still misty. He felt envious of these people, brown like him, for they could feel so much about a place, now torn apart by politics and one man's ambition, and he wished he could do the same, having already known so much of that country's painful history.

He waited till the crowd around Aquino had thinned, then he went forward to tell him how much he had learned from the speech. Aquino's face was mobile and, by now, his easy enthusiasms had truly affected everyone.

"I wish you had something written down, Mr. Aquino," Buddy said. "Do you mind sending me some of your recent speeches?" He handed Aquino his card which Aquino glanced at, then he stepped back. "I know you," he said with great enthusiasm, his face wreathed with unabashed, even boyish pleasure. "I admire your essay, 'Exile and Revolution.' I liked it very much because it agreed with my own conclusions—that I must return to the Philippines."

How could he have known about the essay? He had given the revised portion of his dissertation only the week before to Professor Robert Scapini who edited the *Asian Journal*. To the quizzical look on Buddy's face, Aquino said, holding Buddy by the shoulder. "Bob sent me a copy for comment, and I wish I had my comment here now so I could read it to you. We talked on the phone, too, and he said it is coming out in the next issue of his journal. Congratulations!"

He said thank you and turned to leave, but the Filipino politician held him back. "I must have a long talk with you," he said. "I will be leaving in the afternoon, but I can cancel my flight. Are you busy tonight?" It was more than flattery, of course, and spoken before all those Filipinos he felt that though he was a stranger to all of them, it would seem that now, he had not only joined them, he was also anointed, picked out of the whole lot, to talk with this man who would be Philippine president.

Aquino's Waikiki hotel was modest, about three blocks from the beach. Buddy had pizza near the campus, and was not particularly hungry, but Aquino was so they went to a McDonald's near the beach where he ordered a Big Mac and a large Coke. A cool Hawaiian night, the stars swarming like jewels all over the cloudless sky. Night swimmers were in the water and couples, many of them Japanese honeymooners, were reclined on the sand, listening to cassette radios. Aquino had refused to talk about anything except inanities when they were in the hotel and had suggested this walk

"I am not paranoid," he explained with a laugh. "But I know I am being watched—could be Americans, or Marcos people, I don't know. I have my own man following us. He keeps himself inconspicuous—and he knows how because he is a military man. Are you surprised, Dr. Raza, that I have many friends in our military in spite of the fact that it is supposed to be completely loyal to Marcos?"

Buddy had not expected the question. "Yes," he said.

The next question astonished him further. "I take it you are an American citizen. Have you ever thought of becoming a Filipino— your academic interest in the Philippines is very strong."

He had not expected to be interrogated like this, not that he resented it, but he had flattered himself that, perhaps, this politician would like to gain some insights from him, some practical lessons which he could use in his climb to power. Politicians are a self-centered, self-seeking breed. Surely, this Filipino was not going to be an exception no matter how well and sincerely he spoke.

Buddy was silent.

"I know," Aquino said casually. "You have not given it enough thought or, perhaps, you are too comfortable to even think about it."

The sand yielded under his feet. To the far right, the lights of Ala Moana sparkled and on the freeway, the steady thrum of traffic was muted. Laughter, young voices all around. He must tell the truth; this was no ordinary politician, judging from the questions that he had asked. "I am very sorry to disappoint you, Mr. Aquino..."

"Call me Ninoy," the politician said.

"Buddy."

The politician paused briefly; in the semi-darkness, the smile on his face broadened; he shook Buddy's hand.

"I was going to say," Buddy continued, "I have no loyalty to the Philippines, no deep feelings for the place. Maybe because I left when I was so small. I grew up in San Francisco, Ninoy."

"Your American accent reveals that much," the politician laughed. "But your writing, your views...you know, I agree with you so much, that the exile really has no place, other than where his heart truly is."

There, just the two of them, an affinity was struck. There were some questions that had bothered Buddy, questions that perhaps this Filipino would be able to answer; didn't his father collaborate with the Japanese? Wasn't he himself a member of the oligarchy which had condemned the Philippines to penury? Weren't they who were proposing solutions the problem themselves?

"I have looked around carefully," the politician said softly, as if he wanted his replies to be private, to be listened to by no one but Salvador dela Raza. "I know my countrymen will not believe me, even my relatives. But there are a few Filipinos to whom I have revealed these feelings, intellectuals, some trusted writers whom I meet every so often. We all agree that it must be a revolution—and nothing less—that will banish the inequities in my country."

Buddy was silent.

"I have in mind only one kind. There is so much facetiousness about definitions and the word is now dropped so carelessly. I am fully aware of its implications. I was in Vietnam several times, in Cuba, too. And, of course, China. I really envy these countries. They have resolved their internal contradictions."

Buddy remained silent, absorbing everything.

"You don't believe me," the politician said. There was now a quality of humility in the man, childlike in its intensity. Why should Buddy believe him? A total stranger revealing himself so openly to someone he had just met?

"It is all right if you don't, Buddy," he said simply. "I am telling you this whether you believe it or not. For the record, a footnote in a future paper you may write. You are perhaps asking why a man like me should destroy the very ladder he used in reaching for the peak."

They had paused; Ninoy had finished with the Coke and the hamburger and he put the cup and wrapper inside a nearby trashcan. In the afterglow, his face was open, vulnerable, waiting for approval.

"I believe you," Buddy said, acquiescence borne out of instinct.

They continued the slow, even pace. "I have done something to advance this belief—you will see. It is not true that our poor cannot wait—they can, and they persevere." He was now talking in a quiet monotone, as if in reverie. "But we cannot afford another Vietnam, a million Filipinos dead. What a horrible loss..."

"That was about the number of Filipinos killed during the Philippine-American war," Buddy reminded him.

"But where has American democracy taken us?" Ninoy asked with a sneer. "Even now, do you know that I am not welcome in Washington? I am on the other side—they do not look at me as a champion of Filipino freedom, only as someone who wants to destabilize the harmonious relationship between Washington and Marcos. It does not matter that Marcos is a fascist plundering the country—he is in power. I am a leper shunned by Americans who declare themselves to be our friends, and by Filipinos who do not want to be seen with me for fear that their fortunes at home will be in jeopardy."

After a while, Buddy spoke. "It was Asian nationalism which the United States confronted in the Philippines; and nationalism again—not communism—which it encountered in Vietnam. We never really learned from our own history." There flashed vividly in Buddy's mind the pictures of the dead insurrectos in their trenches, barefoot because they were farmers; only the ilustrados could afford shoes. "You are suggesting a solution that may not end the way you like it. Revolution has a way of acting out its violence and its logic unpredictably because the actors have a way of intruding when they should not."

"I know what you mean," Ninoy said. "And that is why I have to go back, and soon. I cannot be here while my countrymen are there, dying. Already, the Marcos people are calling us 'steak commandos.'" He laughed bitterly.

"You will be killed," Buddy said simply. "Not because you will lead a revolution, or that you will campaign against Marcos. You will be killed because whether you act or not, you are his foremost rival."

They had reached the Ala Moana complex; the shops were closed but the other buildings were adorned with necklaces of light. They turned back to walk to Waikiki, its towers gleaming monoliths against the night sky.

IT WAS NOT the last time Buddy saw or talked with Ninoy. That same year, Ninoy went to San Francisco, and he sought Buddy again. Three times, too, he called Buddy, reiterating his wish to go home, and asking Buddy to return to Manila or just simply visit—isn't it incredible that someone like himself had never been to the Philippines. "But it is all right," Ninoy said; "Blumentritt, Rizal's intellectual friend, who wrote so knowingly about the Philippines, had never been there. So with the foremost Russian scholar on Philippine affairs, George Levenson, and the East German Helmut Fessen." Buddy was merely joining a tight fraternity of illustrious men.

The foreign affairs group that had invited Ninoy to speak in San Francisco had billeted him at the St. Francis on Union Square and on the day he left for Boston, Buddy invited him for lunch at the nearby Clift whose Redwood Room served the finest roast beef in town.

On the sidewalk, before entering the lobby, a group of Filipinos had recognized the politician and had crowded around him, shaking his hand.

"At least," Ninoy said once they were inside, "there are still some countrymen who are not afraid to be seen with me."

When they had taken their seats, Ninoy started immediately. "This is it, Buddy. I am going home next month. August. Friends have been telling me not to go back—I know you think the same way, but I must."

"Marcos is very ill," Buddy said. "Why don't you just wait till he dies. Here, at least, you will be safe. They won't try and get you here—the risks are too great."

"Ill or not, I have to be there," he said firmly. "And you, I want you to go back, too, with me if possible. You can do so much to help—with your background, your insights..."

Buddy shook his head. Go to Manila for a visit? He toyed with the idea. What was keeping him back? Certainly not time or money.

Ninoy took a notebook from his briefcase and started writing names and addresses. When he was through, he tore off the page and gave it to Buddy—there were about half a dozen names on it, with telephone numbers for three of the names. "These are my trusted friends. Trusted, remember that. All of them underground, all of them in fear of their lives. Memorize these names and addresses, and when you are through, throw it away. If you cannot see me when you get to the Philippines, look these people up. Tell them I gave you their names. And I will certainly tell them of your coming. I want you, Buddy, to be involved with the people of your country, your birthplace. We need you. America does not."

When he read of Ninoy's death the following month, he was stunned; it all came back, their conversations, the piece of paper Ninoy had given him, the names like sacred scripture. He had them etched in his mind, the addresses, the telephone numbers. It was not easy but he had always been good at recalling the minutiae that others missed. He held on to the piece of paper, wondering if he should really destroy it as Ninoy had told him. The man was dead; he decided to keep it, it would be secure in his desk; who would ever make a connection between him and Ninoy? It was a memento, priceless to him now, of the man whom he had perhaps nudged unerringly to his grave.

190

20

HE DREAMED of Ninoy that very week the politician was killed; he read everything about his death that he could get in the newspapers and magazines, and could imagine him, his voice urging him not just in the dream but in the stern silence of his own conscience, go home, Salvador dela Raza. Go home!

Why he should dream of a man he did not know too well was easy, of course, to explain. Ninoy was now embedded in his subconscious. On waking up, he would lie motionless, lost to all the sounds of living, of San Francisco even. On New Year's Eve in 1985, this time, the dream was so vivid; Ninoy was right there, in his bedroom, seated on his bed and, again, they were arguing—he could remember the discussion almost word for word and when he woke up, that was the first thing he did, write everything in his journal so that the dream was no longer an ephemeral fragment of sleep, but an obstinate reality.

Buddy: Why do you intrude so often in my life? Not only in my sleep do you bother me now, my waking hours as well.

Ninoy: It is not I, Buddy, who is bothering you. It is your own conscience, your own past, your race and your nation.

Buddy: I am American.

Ninoy: With a Filipino dream.

Buddy: No such thing. I am comfortable here, I have a good job, a meaningful one.

Ninoy: All the more then that you should go home.

Buddy: I have no loyalty to Filipinas. I told you that. Yes, I have written a lot about it—it is my career—but I do not know anyone there. And what will I be if I went back? A voyeur? Just as I have always been? I will be insecure there, afraid even. So much crime in the streets, poverty, oppression, a dictatorship that is vicious, greedy beyond satiation...

Ninoy: You are arguing precisely for the reasons that you are needed there. Who was it who said, Where there is oppression, and injustice, that is my country.

Buddy: Tom Paine.

Ninoy: He's American, right?

Buddy: Don't entrap me with that crap. This generation does not believe in it anymore. Look around you—in our campuses, the young now simply want to go on with their lives, to study, to get jobs, to be comfortable.

Ninoy: And live like pigs?

Buddy: Your words...

Ninoy: Is that what this great country has become? If you belong to this breed, why did you even bother going into your own past?

Buddy: So you want to know the reason. I was an adopted child! I wanted to be very much in my father's grace, to grow up in his exalted image, in a manner that would endear me to him. And I succeeded. Besides, it was interesting, getting to travel, meet all sorts of people, and women. Ah, the women!

Ninoy: But when he died, you didn't stop. You went on, travelling to Japan, writing. No, Buddy, you are not being honest with yourself because you cannot face the truth. And that truth, American though you may be, is that you love Filipinas and the freedom and justice our motherland longs for, just like the many men whose lives you have studied. You are one of them, Buddy, a traveller, and now you must go where your heart is.

He had gotten up at four in the morning, wrote everything down as he remembered it so distinctly, Ninoy in a white suit seated on his bed. When he was through, he walked to the window, to a San Francisco still asleep, the Golden Gate Bridge to his left strung up with lights, and across the dark expanse of the bay, Marin County, its hills softly shaped against the golden glow of the night sky. Standing there, it came to him again, those silver mornings in the Mountain, Apo Tale, Inay Mayang—their faces as vivid as he would always remember them, and this feeling, this longing so intense as that fragment of his life came like a whirlwind, engulfed him, and tears burned in his eyes but he couldn't explain them, nor the quickening desire to see that distant and unhappy land of his birth.

IT WAS NOT difficult getting a visa for the Philippines for a year; better to have a long one so that way he had a choice to stay on or he could always pack up and leave if the return turned out to be traumatic. In a sense, he was a "balikbayan" and the regime was enticing all Filipinos in the United States to go home, bring their dollars, their expertise, to build Marcos's New Society.

He had left Jessica a few instructions, how to get in touch with him, send him money if he should need it, insurance payments — all those details that make American life so easy and uncomplicated. She had finally stopped taking drugs, an effort to which he had greatly helped and for which Jessica was so grateful. She had become more dependent on him and did not want him to leave. She had also found a job as a social worker and was spending so much of her time on it.

His last breakfast with her, hash browns, sweet ham and eggs sunny side up. And at every opportunity she asked him not to stay away too long.

There was time; so she parked her BMW then joined him at the departure lounge. "Write to me often, Buddy. Tell me what it's like, how it feels to go to a country you've studied so well."

She kissed him at the departure gate and started to cry. There were just the two of them now, and she would be alone in that huge and empty house.

The Filipinos in the university had warned him about the airport, the touts and the thieves, and policemen allied with them. But he was travelling first class, and a Manila Hotel representative at the gate was waiting for him, so he had it easy, clearing immigration and customs and reaching his hotel.

January is cold in San Francisco, and though the Filipinos said it was cool, to him Manila was really warm. In the airconditioned hotel Mercedes, he finally saw the country he had abandoned. Here they were, the weed-choked sidewalks, the cratered streets and seemingly listless people everywhere, decently dressed, but so many beggars in corners, the discordant array of houses, buildings, and in between—he could not miss them—the squatter dwellings. Tokyo where he had stopped for a couple of days was pell-mell, a cacophony, but Manila was bedlam, hideous and pitilessly scorched by the debilitating tropic heat.

Then the boulevard and the sea, the palm trees; the driver who was in white uniform turned to him and said that the boulevard was one of Imelda's beautification projects, as was the Cultural Center and the complex of cement blocks around it. And then, it assailed him slowly. The stench of Manila, its squalid bay—it seeped into the car in spite of the airconditioning. He knew that smell of perdition, decay and filth which pervaded the gutters of any city slum, but it would hover all over Manila with loathsome permanence.

The driver pointed out to him the American embassy on the left, and soon, they were going past Rizal Park and up ahead to the left, the Manila Hotel declared itself, dazzling white in the January sun.

He could cash checks at American Express and he had a pack of credit cards but, just the same, he brought along travellers checks and cash. He deposited these together with his passport in the hotel safety deposit box, and carried his spending money in a special canvas wallet worn like a necklace. He put a few hundred pesos in his wallet; he had been warned that if he was mugged, he should simply hand over his wallet and his cheap Casio watch.

His first two days were taken up with city tours; with a map, he wanted to master the city first. On the third day, he asked the concierge to get him a taxi which he could use the whole day. Now, he would go visit the people whose names Ninoy had given him.

THE FIRST NAME on the list was that of a priest. His parish was in Barrio Magsaysay, a district of Tondo. Buddy had done enough reading to know that Tondo was considered the toughest slum area in Manila, but it was also here that one of the first Indio rulers whom the Spaniards met and respected—Rajah Sulaiman—ruled with fastidious dignity. He had told the Spaniards that they were welcome to visit, but that they should abide by the regimen of conduct that was respected by the natives.

Tondo was also where the revolutionary Katipunan was born and because it had always been considered out of bounds for tourists, when he had asked the tour guide where it was, she said it was across the Pasig. She had pointed it out to him when they were touring Fort Santiago. Beyond the grey, untidy wall of stone buildings alongside the other bank was Tondo.

Alex, the taxi driver, asked what he wanted to do there. "Not many tourists go to Tondo, sir," he said, "unless they want to see how our poor countrymen live. Besides, many consider it unsafe. But sir, it is not all that bad. I also live in a very poor place. Would you like to see it sometime?"

He was, by now, accustomed to the easy confidences, the casual friendliness of Filipinos. Was it because they were so poor, they had to be ingratiating, fawning? He did not want to conclude, particularly since Alex, he was sure, was used to dealing with foreigners who may be persuaded to be generous with their tips if some form of solicitousness was shown them.

They drove again across the Pasig, now dark with pollution and silt, and once across the bridge, they descended upon the vibrant cacophony of Manila's biggest slum. Alex pointed out to him the cosmetic attempts of Imelda to change the face of this district, the confectionery frontage of small apartments which still could not hide through the alleys the sorry constructions within, the driftwood and cardboard houses, and so many, many children everywhere.

To the left, the ships that plied the southern waters sat in the morning sun and to the right, the unending line of hovels, the laundry flapping in their fronts, the unruly roofs held in place with stones and old rubber tires and, above the rusting tin, a thicket of TV antennas.

All over Tondo, the rot and stink of a bay that had become a cesspool seeped into the airconditioned cab. The driver said it was worse in the wet season when everything seemed to decay with the rain and the sun alternating their savagery upon the hapless slums.

The taxi driver told him what this barrio was during the short, peaceful years following World War II, this part of Manila Bay is reclaimed land; the government had intended it to be part of an ambitious port development, but it did not reckon with the thousands of homeless people uprooted from the rural areas who soon flocked to the vast expanse of mudflats and erected in it the first postwar squatter colony, Pampangos and Tagalogs from the war-ravaged areas of Central Luzon where the Hukbalahap rebellion had already decimated thousands, refugees from the typhoon belt in Samar and other Visayan islands, and just plain landless agricultural workers who wanted to flee from the poverty of the provinces.

"It is much better looking now," Alex said, a chin thrust at the sorry constructions which did not seem to have any clear demarcation from the other poor sections of Tondo.

The taxi driver knew exactly where they were going. They skirted the seaside boulevard, past the same dreary amalgam of squatter houses, children everywhere as if they were spread upon Tondo—blessings upon the land? or a curse that would drag the country deeper into the nightmarish swamp of poverty?

"Sir, if you are going to see this part of Manila, I might as well take you to Smokey Mountain."

He had read about this, too. This garbage dump where hundreds of Filipinos lived, salvaging scrap and whatever bits of plastic and empty bottles they could find. They parked on the shoulder of the bridge and Buddy got out. To his left, the bay was muddy and dark with sewage and it stank. And to his right, this broad dishevelled hump smoking in places where the dry garbage was being burned. On top of the heap and on the shoulders of the rise were perched the scavenger homes and, close by, big-bellied children played. He had long been convinced that children everywhere will always be children, capable of enjoying themselves even under the most onerous conditions, just as these slum children were playing now, indifferent to the stench around them. He got back into the taxi, quickly assailed not so much by the odor of poor living, as by revulsion. How could people be so degraded—again, the old malaise, the realization that he could have been any of those unfortunate people destined to this hell.

They backtracked to the same precinct of decrepit surroundings, and turned left to a rutted street, dusty now that the rains had stopped but still muddy in places where the ruts were deep. In a while, they came upon a narrow plaza, cemented and transformed into a basketball court, where some young men, some of them half-naked, were playing. They drove to the front of the small church at the other end, a wood and cement construction of unambitious design, but brightly painted in greens and reds. It stood apart from the drab buildings surrounding it.

It was airy within the church and a group of young men were scrubbing the floor, dusting the neat wooden pews which seemed new. Directing them was a half-naked man with round surfaces, his arms tattooed as were some of the other young men who were busy at work. He went to the man who was supervising the cleaning. "I am looking for Father Jess," Buddy said. "Is he around?"

"What you want to see him for?" the man asked, his buck teeth yellow with nicotine.

"I am from New York," Buddy said, surprised that he was asked such a question. "I am a professor and I want to ask him several questions."

"You wait here." The man pointed to a pew. "I will call him."

He sat down; the church smelled of floor wax. Up front in the altar were the usual religious images. Garlands of small white sampaguita laced many of them and the whole altar, though simple and without the rococo adornment of churches in Spain, was decorated with vases of red bougainvillea and poinsettias.

A big man—he could have been a sumo wrestler—sidled up to him. He did not look like a priest. In his blue denims, black T-shirt, and sneakers, he could easily have been mistaken for a stevedore.

He had a very homely face, a bulbous nose, thick lips and a dark complexion. But his eyes, when he introduced himself, were those of a man who was very sure of himself, as was his tone, which was friendly. "I am Father Jess," he said quickly, extending a hand. The handclasp, too, was warm and tight.

"Salvador dela Raza," Buddy introduced himself. "I hope you don't mind if I ask you some questions. Benigno Aquino said I should meet you." Everyone called the politician Ninoy—he must now get used to that, too. He dug into his airline bag and brought out a copy of the *Asian Journal* article he had written. And at the end, the brief but eloquent comment which the Filipino politician had appended. "I wrote this," Buddy said.

Father Jess stroke his thick mop of short-cropped hair. His grin had broadened. "I will try to answer your questions as best as I can. I can see that you are a scholar. But it is noisy here," he said, noting the scrubbing of the floor and the babble of the young men busy with their work.

"They are tidying up everything; they do this once a week," the priest explained hastily. "You are perhaps wondering who these men are, their tattoos—they are members of the Tayo-tayo gang, one of the many gangs in the city. A former sacristan of mine conned them way back into doing this service for the church."

The priest rose—he was also very tall. Having watched sumo twice at the Osaka stadium and on television in Kyoto, he wondered how a priest this corpulent would perform in a sumo match where not only bulk is necessary but agility as well. But Father Jess carried his obesity with easy grace and, in a sense, even his blue jeans became him—just like any other huge black man strolling on the streets of an American city.

They proceeded to the sacristy which adjoined the rear of the altar, equally airy though cramped; through the open window, the life in the alleys obtruded, the babble of children, the blasts of radio or TV sets. Father Jess offered him a chair—one of the several that were set four to a table. The sala was a kind of reception area, the cement floor shiny with polish. At one end of the room, bookshelves, and on the tables, he was surprised to find not just the usual religious magazines but all sorts including government information materials from the United States, the two Chinas and the Soviet Union.

A fat, middle-aged woman looked in from the adjoining kitchen. "Two cups of coffee, Petra," Father Jess told her.

"I want to know what is happening, Father," Buddy began simply. "Ninoy told me you would be a very good informant and not only that, you can also put me in touch with people who are trying to get Marcos out of the way. This is my first time in the Philippines—" he proceeded to talk about himself, to tell the story all over again without any superfluous embellishment and, most of all, how he would like very much to understand the people.

The question of the priest was simple, direct, and because of its simplicity, he had to give a simple answer.

"Why are you doing this, Professor? Why leave the comfort, the sanctuary of America to be with us? You can see it is not comfortable here."

"I got fascinated, Father," Buddy said. "As you know, I am in history and I have done a lot of reading. I must tell you how very much the Filipinos all through the centuries have impressed me. I have even imagined myself as one, in those difficult times when the challenges were also physical. The little people. Then Senator Aquino killed. I met the man—his death affected me very much. We had a discussion when we met in San Francisco." He couldn't go on for there seemed to have suddenly lodged in his throat this rock that suppressed speech, and this vise that tightened his chest.

The priest took a sip from the coffee that had come in; he poured some cream into Buddy's cup and would have put a heaping teaspoonful of sugar hadn't Buddy stopped him.

"Thank you for thinking highly of my people," the priest said softly. "Right now, the whole world thinks ill of us, of our leaders. But you must not romanticize us. There is so much cussedness in this country, so much hypocrisy and, yes, so much poverty. The future is very bleak indeed."

Buddy was silent; he had already seen enough of that poverty and the obscene contrast of those Makati villages which he had passed through on his first tour of the city. "I am very careful and I try to be very objective. My training dictates that. But I really got interested. No, attracted is the word!"

"And now, I suppose that your attraction has diminished your academic dilletantism?" Suddenly, the priest challenged him. "Now you want to belong, to be part of this brutalized nation, to be a Filipino, Professor dela Raza? Is this where you are headed?"

How neatly the priest had put it! Honesty was now demanded of him. "I'm not too sure, Father," he readily admitted. "As you said, I am comfortable. Yes, this could be just a passing academic interest— but it has hounded me all of my life, first to please my foster father but now, basically to please myself."

"Ah, so it is pleasure then! All of us look for pleasure and we then define this pleasure according to our needs. I seek pleasure, too..." the priest laughed, baring a set of nicotine-stained teeth. "It can be addictive. And here, I must warn you, it can also be self-defeating. The frustrations, the unvented angers will corrode not just the mind but the heart. Keep that in mind, and remember it was said by a priest who has served in this Godforsaken parish for twenty years!"

"Just the same, " Buddy said. "I want to know. Not from books, but from you. What happened to this country? From what I read, it wasn't like this before..."

"There is no mystery at all about how this nation deteriorated, how it has been colonized by its own leaders. But this internal colonization wouldn't have happened if the Filipinos did not want it, but they permitted it through their ignorance, their incapacity to look at the Filipino elite as their exploiters. Many Filipinos are stupid, Professor. You will see soon."

But then, what elite in history has not done the same thing to perpetuate itself? It was the capacity of this same elite, however, to recognize the basis of its longevity, its own wherewithal for survival that enabled it, also, to change? To be where we are, we have to change— thus says Tancredi in *The Leopard*, and if the Filipino elite has survived, it is because it was able to change, too!

"No!" Father Jess proclaimed vehemently, shaking his ponderous head. "This is why there is this call to revolution, this is why this very day, hundreds of our young men are in the mountains, in the recesses of this city, waging war. Here in this barrio, when you go out, you do not know who among the people you meet are revolutionaries or sympathizers of the revolution. I am echoing an old friend, a very young man who joined the revolution many years ago—he believed this revolution is not only inevitable but that it is also feasible and righteous!"

"What makes you so convinced of its righteousness?" Buddy asked, disturbed that a priest could talk so quickly, impulsively and perhaps, lightly, of revolution. It came to him quickly, his favorite quote from Judge Learned Hand, "The spirit of Liberty is the spirit of never being sure you are right."

Outside, a medley of Christian hymns playing on a radio floated in, here in this corner of the country punished by unkindness, a kindly morning sun pouring its warmth upon everything, the big-bellied children, the emaciated mothers, the old men in tatters.

Father Jess looked at his inquisitor. "Because I know whereof I speak. Would it surprise you, Professor, if I told you that I come from the same class I condemn? I was born very rich, in Negros—you know where that is. I do not have to be here, if I may brag about it."

Buddy leaned forward. "There is also another name Ninoy gave me—a name which he said I should not mention too often, but that you could lead me to him. I would like to meet Pepe Samson, Father."

A scowl crept over the priest's face quickly; was it anger? or resentment? But the scowl gave way to another sad shaking of the head. "You are asking me about a man I love like my younger brother," the priest said. "Pepe Samson was my sacristan, he lived here for a couple of years—the best sacristan I ever had—but I really cannot say where he is now. Who knows? Not even the army knows! He comes here sometimes to see me, briefly, like the wind—then he is gone. A brilliant man—he could be a success in any environment—but he has elected a life that is without reward, perhaps even without honor as we know honor to be. Do you under-stand what I am trying to say?"

Buddy nodded.

"Give me your address, where you are staying, and I will tell him to get in touch with you. I will have him read this article you have written, too."

ON THE WAY back to the hotel, Buddy asked Alex, the taxi driver, a new set of questions, all of which the driver answered with alacrity. How much did he make in one day? Roughly, Buddy calculated its equivalent in dollars—ten on a good day. How much was his rent? It was a small, dingy room in a squatter area—ten dollars a month. His wife sold ricecakes to augment the income; his three children in grade school were not earning. How much did that boy selling cigarettes in the street make? Four dollars a day, on a good day. And the people in the barrio which they had visited, what did they eat? Boiled bananas with fish sauce when the earnings were little, rice three times a day, or twice when times were bad. Hospitals—they can go to the government hospitals, but they have to pay for their medicine, which sometimes they could not get. And how about the people in the rural areas? And that was when Alex told him how so many people from the provinces had flocked to the city because life was more difficult there. Someday, he hoped he would be able to go to Saudi, too, and earn more. Or to Japan—if he ever got a visa. Could Buddy help him get away? He was willing to take any kind of work in the United States, any kind, and accept very little pay; his dream is for his kids to be able to finish college, perhaps nursing for his two girls, so that they will then be able to leave for the United States.

As they neared the hotel, Alex said, "I am not so sure who they were—they did not look like Tondo residents—they seemed to be more like military men..."

"What are you talking about?" Buddy asked.

"As I was parked there waiting for you, these two men came and asked questions. Who you are, what you are doing in Barrio Magsaysay."

"Muggers?" This was the first thought that came to mind.

"No," the taxi driver said; "if they were, they would have just waited for you to come out and jumped you. No, they wanted something, information about you, more than anything."

HE DECIDED to see Professor E. Hortenso next. It was nine a.m. and Recto where Alex had taken him, throbbed with hordes of students. He had no difficulty looking for the office of the dean to whom he was directed by a receptionist. She had looked at him glumly and he thought suspiciously when he told her he was looking for Professor Hortenso.

The dean was balding and stout. He also sounded and looked equally grave when Buddy introduced himself. "May I know why you want to see Professor Hortenso?" he asked, looking at the name card which Buddy handed to him.

He must treat this man with deference. "I have heard of his reputation, sir, from a colleague in the States. That he is a man familiar with the political situation. I simply want to know his views. I am an historian."

"Yes, yes," the dean said, pointing to the empty seat before his desk. Buddy took it and the dean sat down. "I am sorry you won't be able to see him here," the dean said. "He is no longer with us. He was, for many years. A very bright man, but he gave us a lot of trouble...if I may call it that, although it may be unfair. Well, I suppose he got what he deserved..."

"Is he dead..."

"No," the dean said quickly. "It is not as bad as that, although we don't know, of course, what Marcos will do. He was picked up last month here at the university by the military. It was not the first time; he is in jail, but I really don't know where. I wish I could tell you where his family is, but I don't know."

The next was Leo Mercado, Mercado Tailoring, Bilibid Viejo.

"That is not far from here, sir," Alex told him. Alex came from Ilokos Sur, a big town called Candon. Remembering how the Ilokanos in Honolulu had defended Marcos and blamed his excesses on his Visayan wife, Buddy thought the taxi driver would also be a Marcos supporter. But the very first hour they were together, Alex had fulminated against the dictator, saying that he would even have the devil himself as president as long as food was cheap.

The tailoring shop was in an old battered apartment. Its simple shop window had a faded male mannequin, cracked and stained, in a double-breasted blue jacket. A large table was in the center of the shop and behind, in the poorly lighted interior, three men were working with antique sewing machines.

"I am looking for Mr. Leo Mercado," he told one of the tailors who stood up when he entered. The man went up the flight and soon came down with a young man about twenty-two or so, in blue jeans, white T-shirt and sneakers.

Buddy handed him his card. He must be discreet so he told the young man, almost in a whisper. "Before he left the United States, I had a long talk with Ninoy. He gave me several names. And you are on the list."

"Who are the others?" came the quick question. Should he answer? Should he not play it safe?

"I am sorry—I am not sure if I should give you the other names. Can we go somewhere and talk?"

The young man smiled. "Sure," he said, "there is a beer house close by."

It was not even noon but already, the place was full. The waitresses were good-looking and provincial and they seemed to be on the friendliest terms with all the customers, mostly young men who were, judging by their countenance, either clerks or students.

The young man ordered San Miguel and halo-halo—the innards of a pig. He seemed hungry and he finished his beer quickly. "What else did Ninoy tell you?" he asked.

"He tried to convince me to come back. I had written quite a few things on the Philippines in academic journals. He said I was wasting my time in America, that at heart I am Filipino."

"Are you?" The question was abrupt, demanding.

Buddy smiled wanly. "I don't know. I'd like to find out. Are you really a tailor?"

The young man laughed. He was really gorging on the pig intestines and had ordered another beer. More questions, where

Buddy was staying, where he was born, what was it really tha.
wanted to find out.

Of course, he was being asked all these questions because he was
not trusted; he had dropped out of a clear sky and expected people
to open up, to accept him. These people are not fools. They were
surrounded by traitors, spies and opportunists who would betray
their mothers. He could go no further, so he paid the bill. Alex was
outside waiting.

Before leaving, he gave the young man his room number at
the Manila Hotel. "I hope you will call me," he said. "I can't stay
at the Manila Hotel forever."

At least, he had already made contact. The next was a writer
and journalist, who told him he would meet him at the hotel coffee
shop that evening.

At eight, the phone rang. "I'm in the lobby," Mario Dolce said
in a small squeaky voice, "Tell me what you look like, so I will
recognize you."

He put on his only red shirt and in that blaze of color, he would
stand out. He walked around the expanse of marble, the capiz
chandeliers above in a mellow glace, eagerly waiting for someone
to approach him, but no one did. He decided to wait it out on one
of the oversized maroon sofas. On the left, a musician was playing
a medley of Filipino tunes on a grand piano; again, the plaintive tune
of that popular song flowed into the lobby, and after the tune died
down, desultory applause. That song—it had become the symbol of
the opposition, the anguished cry of the people, right here in this
magnificent hotel which Imelda had rebuilt.

After fifteen minutes or so when nobody approached him, he
stood up to go back to his room. The man who was seated across
from him stood up, too, walked up to him and smiled. "I really need
that cup of coffee, Mr. dela Raza," he said brightly, then guided him
to the coffee shop.

"I'm sorry if I kept you waiting," Mario Dolce said. He was
slim of build, with a thick mop of greying hair and eyes with
huge bags dangling from under them. His voice sounded faintly
effeminate.

He handed the writer his card.

"Yes," Mario Dolce said. "I have not read anything by you, but
some friends at the state university did talk about your articles—that
major piece on Enrique of Cebu, for instance. You don't know it, but
it elicited a lot of interest here. Now, what can I do for you?"

He hadn't had dinner yet and he invited the writer to have one
with him. Dolce wanted just a cappuccino and ricecake.

"Ninoy gave me your name," Buddy said. "That if I ever made it to Manila I should see you, and learn from you."

"Oh, Ninoy, trusting so much in people, always opening his mouth and talking too much."

"But he talked sense," Buddy objected.

"Yes," the writer agreed quickly. "But a little discretion, silence even, is of greater value in the end. I should not be saying this—before we part, you will also note that I talk too much. But that is my trade, words, words. I am a writer after all."

"Now, are words enough?" Buddy asked.

The writer shook his head but did not speak. He sipped his coffee slowly. He asked finally, "Well, what are we to do, Mr. Raza? What will you do?"

By then, he had some inkling of what could be done, what he himself could do.

ON HIS seventh day at the hotel, early in the morning, his phone rang. A girl downstairs—she was the daughter of Leo Mercado and had a message for him. Buddy just could not believe that Leo Mercado could have a grown-up daughter; the man was not even twenty-five. If a trick was being played on him, he was well prepared and had nothing to lose.

He went down and this time did not have to wait for someone to approach him. She was standing near the elevator, a slim girl with a boy's bob, a perfect Malay face and very clear skin. Her sneakers, blue jeans and denim jacket had seen a lot of use. She could very well pass for Inay Mayang, particularly with her eyes which, as he got to know her better, were so vibrant, alive.

She went forward and shook his hand. "I am Namnama Mercado," she said. Her palm was rough and when he looked at her hands, he was surprised; they were hands that eloquently showed she had done hard work. To his unspoken incredulity, she smiled again, "The man you met—he is Junior, my younger brother. I hear he ate a lot in that beerhouse."

So, they had checked him out finally. "I should have come earlier, but I was away, in the province," she continued. They walked out in the morning sunshine to the green park before the hotel. Joggers were making the rounds, and knots of people were doing calisthenics. They walked slowly, the sun warm on their skin. Manila Bay, now turquoise in the light. A few ships were anchored in the water, mostly freighters. At the pier to their right was the white Marcos yacht, and a Japanese passenger boat. As they approached the sea wall, a man seated there rose to meet them. He was middle-aged, with patrician features, much too tall for a Filipino, taller than Buddy himself. He was in his seventies.

"My father," Namnama introduced him. They shook hands.

"Ninoy must have trusted you so much to give you my name," Leo Mercado said. "Tell me what we can do for you. Why you are here."

They continued walking on the grass, away from the sea wall. He was now extremely interested in Namnama; she was sharp, no doubt, but more than this, she was physically attractive. He felt he could tell them his story, and he proceeded to do so. "In a way, perhaps a very romantic way, I am really here to pick up the lost threads of a life..."

They hadn't had breakfast yet and Buddy suggested they back-track to the hotel, but Leo Mercado said it was too expensive there and they wouldn't be able to talk. The tailor brought them to Maxim's, a Chinese restaurant at the other end of the Park. They ordered congee with fish and siopao.

"You have a very unusual name." Buddy turned to the girl.

"I am from Concepcion, Tarlac," her father explained, "but my wife is from Vigan, that is in the Ilokos. Namnama is named after her mother. I've known Ninoy since he was a boy."

Leo Mercado also spoke about how he had been a member of the Huk movement, but was now too old and without saying it, it was his children who were continuing the revolutionary tradition.

No more subterfuges, no more probing questions, nothing now but the truth. "I came to the Philippines because I want to look up my beginnings," he told them simply. "But more than this, as Ninoy said, it is here where I belong, where I should be able to contribute something..."

He told them of his earliest memory, of his father and mother always running, running, from an unseen enemy, from danger, and in the telling, it suddenly occurred to him that his father was a guerrilla, and that the Japanese who were after him shot him because he had dared fight them.

"It is all so hazy. I was very young. But I remember I was in some plaza, in some church, that was where my father left me, hoping he would come back. There was a big procession which the Japanese broke up. So many people, almost all of them men, and there on this carriage a black figure with a cross, and men pushing—"

"The Black Nazarene!" Namnama cried. "You were at the procession of the Black Nazarene. Had you arrived earlier, you would have seen it. Every January, during His feast day, there is a fiesta in Quiapo. We live there."

They boarded a jeepney at the next street. His heart was thrashing so hard it seemed as if it would break his ribs. So this is what it means to finally know who you are—oh, my father, that I should have at least known you, absorbed your courage, defined your cause. He exalted in the knowledge, tenuous though it may be, that there in his blood, after all, was a tenacious strain of continuity, that his father had shed his blood for Filipinas.

They reached Plaza Miranda. In midmorning, the fumes of a thousand jeepneys befouled the air and tightened his chest. This was the pulsing, raucous heart of the city, pumping out its listless humanity and, here, Leo Mercado explained, some of the biggest demonstrations were held in the past, but they could not surpass the giant demonstrations that preceded the elections the other year, an election which everyone was sure Aquino's widow won.

Buddy gazed at the church before him, not as imposing as the cathedrals in Spain, its trite architecture, but it seemed oddly familiar. Then he recalled the women walking on their knees to the altar, beads in their hands, lips moving silently in prayer, their eyes lifted in supplication.

It was not Friday so there were not all that many people. How many prayers are necessary to atone for our sins, to assure us entry into heaven? But heaven is what we make it—here and now, the cauldron heat of the country, the acid breath of the city; this could be the hell that Filipinos have made without Marcos helping them.

They went in and as his gaze turned to the altar at the other end of the aisle, his heart leapt. There he was, the Black Man, and on his shoulders this cross, the wanton sins of the world.

I am here, I am here! Buddy cried within him. Black Nazarene, help us, your children who wipe your feet and your brow, who carry you on our shoulders in penance and in hope.

Again: Memory, help me!

I was here as a child, right here by the door, pushed to a corner where the crowds could not touch me, pressed against the wall; how easily was my body bruised. I hear again the boding rattle of guns, imagine again my father fallen, my mother gone.

He knelt in the front pew, Namnama beside him. Leo Mercado had left them, saying Namnama would tell him everything he needed to know and, perhaps, show him, too, now that he had been to Quiapo, the way Ninoy would have followed if he were alive.

Back in his hotel, Buddy was restless. That night, he couldn't sleep. Early the following morning, he went to Leo Mercado and asked the tailor to accompany him to the rectory of Quiapo Church. "There must be someone who can tell me, someone who perhaps may have even kept a record."

They found the oldest sacristan in the sacristy, cleaning the church vestments; the parish priest to whom Buddy first presented himself was much too young to know and he took them to Mang Carlos.

Even during the war, the Black Nazarene procession was held—that must have been in January—during the feast day of the image. Japanese soldiers came shooting, scattering the crowd, killing several people.

All at once, the old sacristan's face brightened, memory burned bright. Two Japanese officers were killed in one of the bars close by. One of them was a colonel of the Kempeitai. Very high-ranking. They had zoned the place—zona, they called it—stationed soldiers in strategic corners and alleys, then conducted a house-to-house search. They came upon some guerrillas who fought back, then ran. He was, the old acolyte said, on the platform of the image, together with three other sacristans, wiping the Nazarene's face, his hands with the handkerchiefs and towels the devotees threw at them, when the Japanese—he could see them even now—came in the direction of Evangelista Street running after some men who had merged with the crowd.

Mang Carlos remembered very well; twenty were killed, and the Japanese hauled about fifty people in trucks. The dead had no identification on them; they were all buried in the church cemetery in La Loma.

And lost children in the church? Several, because times were difficult, sometimes the children were just left in the church, and were passed on to the Hospicio. "We had no way of caring for all of them," the old acolyte explained.

21

THE FOLLOWING week, Buddy moved to a modest residence, a pension, in Ermita, recommended by Namnama not only because she knew the people who were running it; the Manila Hotel was simply too conspicuous.

He had entered the Philippines at last and the circle which he avidly sought was ever-widening. He wrote to Jessie that he had already experienced, too, his first demonstration; Leo Jr. had taken him—a march from the University of the Philippines where he had studied, all the way to Malacañang, the presidential palace, although they did not reach Malacañang for at Mendiola Bridge, barbed wire and tanks stopped them.

It was so unlike the demonstrations in the United States, he wrote; there was much singing and chanting. And discipline was kept in the ranks. I was the oldest in the group, and I was there only because Leo Jr. took me, saying I was a friend from the U.S., and they called me Cano, and joked about my accent and inadequate Tagalog. It seemed like fun, but it was serious business, for many had been killed precisely for joining these demonstrations.

Sometimes, Mario Dolce would arrange meetings, and Buddy would meet with young men whose faces and names he couldn't remember. They were all, it seemed, completely absorbed with their politics. Many a time, he would be embroiled in arguments with them about definitions but, in the end, they seemed to be thinking about what he said; he had, after all, the authority of knowing this nation's history. He could easily see that so many of them were very doctrinaire, and he tried to dissuade them from clinging to barnacled positions, that always they should be aware of the people's sentiments. They committed, he told them, a tactical mistake by boycotting the elections the previous year—and now, they had come to accept their error. It could have been avoided if, as he told them, they had been more aware of what they themselves called the "objective reality."

IN EARLY February, Namnama finally took him to the Mountain. After their visit to Quiapo, he had shown her the map of Luzon and pointed out the exact place where James Wack had found him, a village called Raza, after which he was so named. With great surprise, Namnama said she knew the place and was often there. At the moment she had work to do in Manila, but when she was through she would take him to Raza herself.

It was not a calesa this time which took them, but an aircon-ditioned bus; they had started out at dawn. The night was just ending, and the city had already begun to stir, the brightening streets already raucous with jeepneys and people rushing to escape the traffic mess that surely would come with the daylight. He strained to remember, the fallow fields, the little towns, but the pictures that came to mind were indistinct. At the end of the bus route, a big town, they transferred to a jeepney—the mountain now clearly ahead of them—until they reached the foothills. They got off at a village, wooden houses lining the road, none of which he could remember. Shops were announced in a flurry of Coca-Cola and Pepsi-Cola signs, Maring's Store, Old Martin's Place, Drink Seven-Up, Atang's Canteen and on and on. This is Raza, Namnama said.

Indeed, Namnama knew the place. They stopped for lunch at Atang's Canteen and she talked easily with the waitress who owned it, who cooked the meals. His Tagalog had improved and he understood almost everything. He was introduced as a visiting professor, and the woman had joked that, perhaps, he would take Namnama with him to the United States to escape the poverty of the country. To which Namnama, brown though she was, blushed so beautifully. "It's not such a bad idea, you know," he told her later, "in spite of the difference in our ages."

He was very pleased when she objected, saying he did not look that old.

The food was cold, chunks of pork swimming in grease that had coagulated. The Coca-Cola, too, was warm and it curdled his tongue; he had not yet fully adjusted to the drinking water except in Manila; with his delicate American stomach, even Namnama had warned him against diarrhea. But he was hungry and in his hunger, he recalled his first meal up in the Mountain, the fragrant rice and the nameless greens that tasted so sweet and, afterwards, with James Wack, the mashed potatoes, the powdered eggs and all the butter he could slap on his bread.

It occurred to Buddy then that here, in the last village before the Mountain, there would be some who knew of Apo Tale and Inay Mayang. "Let's look for the oldest people here," he said. "I want to ask questions, if they remember anything about my people at all."

They found the oldest man in the village, in his late eighties perhaps, feeding the chickens in his yard. He was bent with age, and hard of hearing. Namnama asked the questions: before the war, did he ever know of an old man who lived in the Mountain? who had a daughter? They lived alone and they had a clearing planted to crops and vegetables. The old man shook his head and went on with his chore. They were about to leave when he called them back, yes, there was such an old man who came to Raza every so often, leaving his calesa with a farmer at the end of the village. But that farmer had long gone, he would have been the best person to talk with. The old man had a daughter, yes, very pretty but very few had seen her for she seemed like a spirit of the forest, disappearing into the trees at will...

"You can see," Buddy said brightly, "it was no imagination. It was all very real." A small group of young men walked up to them and, again, she introduced Buddy.

Sitting there in the shadow of the Mountain, he felt the compulsion to move on. "I want to go up," he said.

They boarded a tricycle and went farther up the street. The old schoolhouse was there, its roof rusted now, its wooden sidings which had fallen apart, replaced with galvanized iron. And beyond the schoolhouse, the market—the same low open building, with many stalls.

The ride was bumpy, but he did not mind it too much; with Namnama beside him again, closer now, this was what he truly wanted. Up the slow rise of ground, they passed small knots of houses. Children waved at them, and they waved back. A man who was going up the Mountain sat in the front, a farmer who was silent all the way, until he got off and Buddy realized that he, too, knew Namnama as he bade them good-bye. By then, he did not have to ask—he realized that, as she had earlier told him, she really worked here.

The tricycle could go no farther; ahead of them was a wall of trees, a steep path, boulders as big as elephants. They had covered so much distance, but this was not yet his destination, instinct told him that.

"We have a camp over there," Namnama pointed to the right, to the far distance, what seemed like an inaccessible part of the Mountain; it would be a good day's hike to reach it. "Shall we go there?" she asked.

"No," he told her tentatively, wondering if he could ever find the place where Inay Mayang and Apo Tale lived. The trail was no longer visible, if they had to move on, it would be through foliage, and thicket that tightly enfolded them.

They pushed through the trees; sometimes, they came across what seemed like the beginning of a new trail but after some distance it disappeared again in brush and more trees. Then they came to the first stream and, beyond it, what seemed like a trail again. "I have passed this way," Namnama said. "Beyond, there is a cave with a spring, a holy place."

She was right, they had cut through the forest. The beating of his heart quickened. I know now, I know now, he exalted, as if he had never really left the Mountain.

They had been here before, motley pilgrims searching for peace and that elusive alchemy which banishes callousness from the heart and cobwebs from the mind—a sweet, opiate-like quality of grace dispensed not by promise of salvation but by faith, unquestioning and personal; they came hopeful like children unsullied yet by failure, by adult hypocrisies, their eyes undamaged by the cataracts of despondency. And they also came as malevolent destroyers, seeking sanctuary from their pursuers, men as violent as they, fighting not for themselves or for beliefs but for their masters who had paid them.

Could there be piety here? It was piety after all with which their movements were measured, the tones of their voices, the depth of their sincerity. Piety was everything—a pervasive incense in the atmosphere, even when it was tense with uncertainty and danger.

But it was not necessary for him to be pious for he was already that, not for himself but for those who would ask him to answer them with words dripping with holiness, not the holiness of the afterlife but of the life in the near future, of tomorrow—as close as that—that had yet to come with all its effulgence and plenitude.

I am so close to reality and if I will pass as all of us must, perhaps the next life will even be closer to the reality that we all seek, the eternity of our station.

It all came back, no longer a disordered dream but sensuous and continuous recollection, culminating in resolve. I was here, this is home, at last. Home—the sweet and honest word sank into his consciousness, his very flesh suffusing him with the brightness of discovery and belonging, as if in all his travels, he had finally found the end of it all. Here.

It was already late afternoon and the sun, hidden by the trees, broke in pale bursts of light upon them. They ascended a steep slope and came to a plateau bordered by even bigger trees, and in the middle was a clearing with shorter trees, a second growth and still higher up, the narrow margin of the ridge.

It was as if his feet were led to this spot. He dropped to his knees and scooped the ground—saw how dark it was, and after all these many years, some ashes had remained, apart from the soil. He was now convinced of where he was, this hallowed ground. And bending on his knees, he kissed the earth in thanksgiving, in prayer. Apo Tale, Inay Mayang—this is Badong returned to your embrace. He took a deep breath, inhaled within his lungs that were close to bursting this ineffable scent. I feel its life-giving potency spread out to my entire being, my arteries, throbbing, pulsing; the Mountain had become a part of me, or perhaps it had always been a part of me and I had merely reunited with it. These leaves, this aroma of green—the juice of the fores —everything has commingled with me; I am the present, no longer bound by scabs to the past. I am home at last.

He rose slowly, silently. How can I describe this to Namnama? This final sense of belonging, this end to my travelling?

"There was a house here," he told her, "and down there was the vegetable patch. And ahead, a ridge."

"There is no ridge," Namnama said.

He assured her there was, and that higher up was another spring. He took her to the top of the ridge. She was surprised to see it, hidden by trees. They pushed onward, away from the ridge, and soon enough, the stream was before them, shallow, quiet and clear. It had a long time ago watered Apo Tale's clearing.

Dusk was upon them, and they had a long walk back. The night would be cool and dark. "We can find the way, it is not difficult," Namnama said. "I am used to walking distances in the dark. There are always the stars, the evening glow, sometimes the moon."

212

He was very tired. He had never walked this far before and, perhaps, he told himself, I am really getting old.

"But we can sleep here—I am used to sleeping under the night sky. Have you ever done it?"

"No," he admitted easily.

They ate the supper which she had the foresight to order wrapped in banana leaves in the canteen, fried catfish, vegetables and cold chunks of rice. When they were through, they went to the spring, drank and washed their hands as well. A small patch of ground was by the spring and they decided to sleep there, their backpacks as their pillows. Namnama's backpack contained so much, a nylon jacket, a plastic sheet which could work as a raincoat and which they shared, even a flashlight.

"We are high up. There will be no mosquitoes, but it will even be cooler in the dawn," Namnama said.

"It's all right," he said, holding her hand. It was rough as he already knew it to be. "You are with me."

They could not see the sky and the stars—the trees hid them all. But sometime in the night, a swarm of fireflies crowned one of the tall trees; Namnama woke him up. "Our guardians," she said.

She was sorry, interrupting his sleep, but he was rested and couldn't sleep anymore. He wanted to know more about her and she readily told him, that she was a civil engineer, having passed the board exams the previous year. Leo Jr. had just finished a course in animal husbandry at the state university, too. "So you can see," she said proudly, "we will be ready to build, to work, when this is all over."

"It's almost like starting from scratch," he said. "Some societies can do it quickly because there has already been a very strong foundation laid down by tradition, culture, whatever. I do not see this in the Philippines. There are so many beginnings but there is no consistent follow-up. You know what I mean. Maybe because there is not enough sense of nation, of purpose, particularly among those who lead." It was one of those questions he should not have asked because the answer had already become obvious. "And so I ask, why do you fight?"

She drew away and though her face was indistinct in the dark, he knew she was looking at him, perhaps wondering why he asked the question at all.

Her reply was not pat, a well-learned rote. "I want to live, Buddy," she said simply, clearly. "To live in freedom and I am not talking in the abstract because this freedom, this justice, are not just words

213

to so many of us. You have been here for sometime, you know our history, too. I need not explain further."

Buddy was silent and, certainly, he could feel the slight belligerence in her reply.

"So then," he continued after a while, "that strong foundation I have mentioned, where is it in this country? To put it another way, are there things now, today, which Filipinos can be proud of?"

Her voice pitched. "Not things, Buddy. But people. Me, I am very proud of my mother. Oh, yes, I am proud of my father, too, but my mother, most of all. She is my inspiration and I am hoping that I will be able to live even just a little of the way she lived. And fought!" She rose immediately and from her pack, she brought out a well-worn leather frame. She opened it and beamed her flashlight on the picture of a woman; even the faded brownish image seemed to exude character, the eyes as luminous as her daughter's.

She switched off the beam and returned the picture to her backpack. It had really become cool and he was glad he had worn a jacket and a cap. They lay back and in a while, resumed talking.

She told him about her dreams of the future, her people free, who will never go hungry, and while she spoke he could feel himself flowing out to her, and she in turn was being welded into the very tendons of his flesh.

He moved closer to her and knowing what he wanted, she lifted her head so she could rest it on his arm, wordless, her warm-scented breath on his face. "Thank you, Namnama," he said.

In the morning, after they had washed in the spring, shivering in the cold, he told her he had made up his mind. He would come back, build a house where the old house used to stand, up there on the ridge. He would also clear the land and plant.

"Will you help me?" he asked.

A shard of morning light was on her face; it was radiant when she said, "If you want me to."

HE HEARD IT first on the Walkman radio in his room and was about to go down and check with Mrs. Ramos, the landlady, but it was she who had gone up knocking furiously at his door. "Professor Raza, there's a coup!"

It was five in the afternoon, and the details were coming in. Downstairs, several tenants were watching the developments on TV, but there was not much to glean from it. There was more on the radio which was on full volume.

He hurried to his room and got his travelling bag, his Walkman, and hailed a taxi to Bilibid Viejo. Leo Mercado Sr. had left, Junior and Namnama were also out. Everyone in the tailoring shop was listening to the radio.

"How far is EDSA?" he asked no one in particular.

In Quezon City, he was told. He rushed out and waved down a taxi; the driver was also listening to his cab radio. "It could be dangerous, sir, to go there," he said. "Maybe, we can just go somewhere near the place." Mario Dolce had told him of the possibility of a military coup against Marcos and his gang. Many officers were angered, not just by Marcos' favoritism but by the fact that the army was being used by ranking officers to enrich themselves. That was obvious enough; at the Manila Hotel, he had seen generals swaggering about and the entire Marcos crowd acting as if their day of glory would never end.

The traffic was tangled as usual. It was already dusk when he reached Cubao. The driver said that would be the farthest he would go—he did not want to be caught in the crossfire. He pointed out the general direction, up the highway, of the military camps. Buddy could walk there.

The highway was now wide open, traffic had simply stopped, and up ahead were groups of people. He listened to his Walkman; the stations were not reporting what was happening but there was one, Veritas, which kept a running account of the attempted coup, and Cardinal Jaime Sin went on the air several times, urging people to go to EDSA and help the beleaguered rebels by building a human wall around their camps.

Dusk had come quickly; the mercury lamps were on, and people had started to arrive on the highway where traffic had now completely ceased. The air was cool, and gone was the acrid smell of burnt oil and the pollution that had hovered over the city; here in Quezon City, on the broad cemented highway that went around the eastern rim of Manila, the cacophony of traffic was now muted and on street corners, barriers had sprung up, buses with deflated tires, piles of hollow blocks, anything that should be able to stop vehicles from coming in. But would these puny barriers hold if the dictator decided to send in his tanks?

Looking at the stretch of highway brightly lit by mercury lamps, Buddy recognized immediately that it could very well be a battleground, but this did not seem to deter people for they came in, slowly at first, then as the night lengthened, the trickle became a flood.

He listened to the radio, the bewildering welter of information coming in, the Marcos propaganda machine trying to tell another story, and Radio Veritas reporting the huge crowds that had by now gathered at EDSA; this cannot be refuted, he was there, he saw the people come.

Instinctively, he knew that the situation was dangerous; Marcos was not going to accept this—a man with no moral compunctions, he would surely order the forces loyal to him to scatter this rabble that dared side with the "traitors" to his regime. Buddy was not going to be involved, he was not going to be part of it, much as he sympathized with it, this was a Filipino cause—not his.

He walked away from the quickly thickening crowds, back to where the taxi had left him, and took another cab to Ermita. He had asked the driver to drive around first, to Sta. Cruz and the Quiapo districts, all the way to the port area, to the boulevard by the sea, to antiseptic Makati, precincts of the rich quietly asleep, the shuttered banks and business buildings on Ayala Avenue like any American business district once the day is over. The taxi driver drove, too, as near as he could get to Malacañang where Marcos and his family waited out their fate; the place was barricaded but everywhere, too, were the signs of preparation for the dictator's inaugural, his pictures plastered everywhere, the buntings of his proclamation emblazoned across the streets. Everything then was normal, the city was not endangered by a wildfire; it was only on that strip of highway, EDSA, where history—and hope—were being written.

At the pension, every tenant seemed to be in the living room, watching the announcements on television, Marcos decrying the infidelity of his former lieutenants, vowing retribution. On Radio Veritas, however, the news was different; close to midnight and still Cardinal Sin exhorting the people to go to EDSA, "this is the time we have been waiting for and we must all contribute to it..."

He went to sleep wondering how it would be if Filipinos were finally able to stand up.

HIS VISITOR came with the morning that splashed into the room with the bray of jeepneys in the street. Another Manila morning, rife with the malodorous smells of the city, the uncollected garbage on the sidewalks, the sweaty effusions of the early rush. He opened the door to a man grown dark with sun, a blue baseball cap on his head, his eyes protected by thick eyeglasses. "Good morning, Professor," he said, entering the room without being asked. "Father Jess said you wanted to see me."

This then must be Pepe Samson. "Please come in," he said; he was in his underwear and he proceeded to put on his pants which were hanging behind the door.

"I am very sorry," the man said, "that I have to come here without any announcement. But you know how things are. I did not come here just to see you. Of course, you know what is happening at EDSA—it's all over the country. I couldn't resist coming to Manila."

Buddy had put on his jeans and shirt. "Excuse me," he said, "I need to use the bathroom. Please wait—we can go out and have breakfast."

When Buddy returned to the room, the man was nowhere. He went immediately to his desk; his passport and travellers checks were all there in the drawer, and there was not a single peso missing from his wallet. He shrugged—he needed a cup of coffee. He went down to the tiny coffee shop in the lobby. The man was there, seated at one of the tables facing the entrance and the street.

"You said breakfast," he told Buddy who was quickly relieved that his visitor had not left. "I heard it on the radio yesterday afternoon and I hurried immediately to Manila, saw Father Jess first, then went to EDSA. I haven't slept, and now here I am."

"Thank you for coming. I heard about you from Ninoy and Father Jess—nothing but good things. I was very impressed."

"So now," the man smiled; "I should impress you some more." He had good teeth, very rough skin, and a confident demeanor. He was also handsome, his brow wide, a high nose and eyes brilliantly alive. "Father Jess said you wanted to know more about the Philippines. I will try and help you get that knowledge, even take you to places where I think you will get facts firsthand. Now, questions."

Buddy glanced around him, wondering if the man had truly come alone, but everyone seemed busy with their pan de sal and bad coffee, and no one seemed to be looking their way. He had been told by Namnama and her brother that this place was all right, but he was now in the company of people who would be imprisoned if Marcos could lay his hands on them. He would be suspect, an accomplice. Would his passport be of any help? He doubted it. He wanted so much to know what was happening at EDSA; Radio Veritas had been silenced, but there was now a clandestine station that had taken over and it came on the air clearly, the woman who had been making the announcements so sure of herself.

"Maybe," Buddy suggested, "we should go to EDSA and talk along the way."

Midmorning, and the highway was already awash with people; this was no massive display of opposition to Marcos; it was a fiesta as well as all along the whole stretch of the highway, there had sprouted all sorts of food shops, stages, and altars with religious images. Coveys of nuns in their religious habits, people praying the rosary with them. He had listened to the radio on the way here, through the streets alive with normal commerce, news of the tanks that were rumbling towards EDSA, truckloads of soldiers with guns on the ready. A massacre was in the offing, but the mass of people did not seem to care.

They had approached the highway from Makati, and now, it was impossible for the cab to go any farther. They got out and walked, and halfway toward the crossing at Ortigas, they saw their first fleet of armored personnel carriers rumbling toward EDSA.

"They must be from Fort Bonifacio," Pepe Samson said. The machines thundered ahead then after a while the column stopped. A line of nuns and civilians had formed a human barricade on the highway, they were all praying, most of them kneeling on the pavement; and around the huge machines, the puzzled soldiers on top of them, the people milled, greeting them with smiles, some of them handing the soldiers sprays of flowers, roses, sandwiches in wrappers. An officer was shouting at the people to give way, and the crowd roared at him, shouting peace, peace. Shaking his head, the officer slunk back into the bowels of the machine, shouting into his radio transmitter.

Buddy watched, wordless, his throat dry, his heart knocking against his ribs. He knew then that he was witness to history in the making. "How long can they hold on before the shooting starts?"

Pepe Samson shrugged. "If the soldiers shoot," he said calmly, "all these people will be dispersed immediately."

"Do you think Marcos will order his soldiers to shoot his own people?"

Pepe Samson looked at him incredulously, "That is what he has been doing all these years! Of course he will order them to fire—it is just a matter of when."

It was difficult squeezing out of the crowd that had now gathered around the tanks. Someone started to sing the song he had heard so many times, stirring them into one vibrant voice, the song filling the air and picked up all along the highway, "Even the bird has the freedom to fly..."

Perhaps, it was time for him to fly, to flee this spot where people had flung themselves before the tanks and dared Marcos's soldiers to run them over. Just one soldier with his hand on the trigger, unable to control himself, disturbed and confronted by his countrymen who may not understand how it is to be a soldier—just one finger on a trigger.

The sun rode high and makeshift shelters sprang up. Some of those who had stayed the whole night had spread pieces of paper, plastic, and were lying on the pavement, on the grassy islands. Food was being distributed in boxes, softdrinks, Chinese siopao—Buddy recognized it—in tin cans.

"Let's go somewhere else," he told Pepe Samson. "Away from this, to a restaurant that serves Filipino food."

They walked to where the people thinned out, where traffic had started to move, and hailed a cab.

"How far do you want to go?" Pepe Samson asked. Buddy turned to the east and pointed to the foothills of the Sierra Madre; he had studied the map very well—Antipolo, Angono—these were towns he had never seen.

THEY ARRIVED at the Filipino restaurant at noon; they had passed Manila's developing industrial site, the scatter of new houses along the stone highway. The taxi driver had suggested the place; it served, he said, beautiful catfish, duck, and other Filipino delicacies.

A sprawling, nipa-roofed building, in two or three levels, with an artificial pond in the middle, and on the walls primitive paintings and native cooking utensils. They were immediately served appetizers, half-ripe mango slices with salted shrimp paste. The menu was very interesting. With his limited Tagalog, he was pleased that almost every word was clear to him. They had talked about inanities in the cab while he took in everything, the slow ascent to the foothills, and now, to their right, the clear and placid lake and in the distance, the towers of Makati and that black, dreadful pall of pollution that hung like an implacable fate over the city.

Very few people were in the restaurant. A radio was tuned to what was happening at EDSA. In their corner at the far end, they had all the privacy for the many questions that Buddy wanted to ask.

Pepe Samson had taken off his blue baseball cap and the thick-rimmed eyeglasses which apparently, were more for disguise than better vision. He looked younger without them, more serious, too, and when he gestured with his hands, Buddy noticed they were rough, like any farmer's. Pepe Samson took a sip from the beer that he had ordered. "Now," he said with a grin, "shall we start the inquisition?"

"I am very self-conscious about asking so many questions, but as Father Jess must have told you, I am a student of this country. More than a student, I see that now. I didn't grow up here, perhaps I am really American in spite of my skin. This is one of the things I have come here to find out."

"You will be making a big mistake," Pepe Samson said, biting into the slice of yellowish mango after spreading shrimp paste on it. "Everyone wants to leave for America you should see the long lines at the American embassy, Filipinos fleeing the poverty, the dangers of living here. And you want to be here. To share the suffering, Dr. dela Raza, or to assuage it?"

"Stop calling me doctor, Pepe. I already told you, call me Buddy."

"At least you are a real Ph. D. I once knew someone who wanted so much to be addressed as 'doctor' although he was phoney."

"Call me Buddy," he repeated.

"You must look deep into your heart, really deep into your heart, and ask if you are willing to pay the cost. It may be something that you will not, in the future, want to bear."

"Did you do that?" Buddy asked. "What made you decide to be what you are now?"

Their food came, the rice fried with garlic, the catfish broiled, with sliced onions, tomatoes and yet more shrimp paste, and broiled porkchops, too. Buddy explained that the catfish was from the bay, raised there in the pens he had pointed out on the way to the restaurant, as was the milkfish cooked in vinegar and pepper that was yet to come.

"To me this is a feast," Pepe Samson said, looking at the generous spread with delight. "Where I come from, I will be lucky if I can have some fish, or a scrap of meat. Most of the time, it's just vegetables and vegetables. I had my fill of that when I was young—I thought when I grew old, I would have more variety, but—" he smiled wanly, "this is one of the things we have to endure."

Buddy was silent; he remembered the old injunction, "in my poverty, I have shamed you." "Please, help yourself," he finally said, embarrassed. But Pepe Samson hardly heard for he had begun to eat the porkchop with such relish, it was as if he had not eaten for days. Maybe, he hadn't.

He could not get his mind off from what was happening at EDSA. Up in the air, six helicopters rattled on their way to EDSA—were they going to gun down the people there? He hurriedly put on the earphones of the Walkman. The woman, June Keithley, was still on; she must have been at it for hours now, without sleep, but she was there hanging on. In a while, her terse voice—no, the helicopters had not fired at the people. They had landed instead in the middle of the camp where the rebels were holding out. In the field, more units were joining the rebels—Marcos was losing his men, their loyalty most of all.

He told the news to Pepe who did not seem too interested. "I am a pessimist," he said. "So we will get rid of Marcos, but will we also get rid of all the powerful Filipinos who have enslaved us?"

Buddy joined him; the broiled catfish was, indeed, tasty, the flesh soft and ample.

"At least," Pepe Samson said, "if this succeeds, that's one Filipino tyrant that will be removed. But when will Filipinos realize that it is themselves who are often their worst enemy. My people, Buddy—they are vindictive, they do not know how to save, to produce, to innovate. They are petty, and they pride themselves in baubles which they love to show off. We are a nation of show-offs, and Imelda has captured all that is in the Filipino character—she is the epitome of the Filipino."

"You are asking for a cultural revolution," Buddy said.

Pepe Samson smiled. "Yes, and even now, the revolution, which people like myself seek, is not here, and we delude ourselves but we cannot stop because we have to hope."

Father Jess was right, this was a thinking man, perhaps rethinking even now his premises, his revolution.

"I should not be talking like this. It can get dangerous. It is necessary to conform because conformity brings protection, a sense of comfort. I do not think you understand what I am saying." Pepe Samson stopped eating and looked his inquisitor in the eye.

"I do," Buddy said.

"Would you like to come with me one day to see the rural areas in my part of the country? The trip would make your education more rounded," he laughed quietly.

But the suggestion had already set in Buddy's mind; he would finally see the stern reality that Ninoy had told him about.

"I will come again and see you. Be ready anytime, I will not tell you in advance," Pepe Samson told him.

After Buddy had paid the bill—it was so triflingly little—they returned to the cab. "One more question. I have read of the brutality of the Philippine-American War. But through the years, the Americans tried very hard to do what the Filipinos themselves wanted. Why are you so anti-American? Most Filipinos have forgotten and have become instead pro-American."

"That is the party line," Pepe Samson explained. "Personally, I am not anti-American. Never have been although I know all the reasons for the line. I myself believe that the American presence here perpetuates the teacher-pupil relationship, the dependency on the United States. This inhibits our development. And the cultural influence of the United States is so pervasive it stifles Filipino creativity, originality. There is also the American-Filipino elite alliance which works for the elite, but not for the people. The sugar quota, etc."

"I know," Buddy said sadly in agreement. Pepe Samson had summarized it neatly.

He dropped Pepe Samson off in Quiapo, where the man immediately disappeared into the squalid warrens of Plaza Miranda. He was sure Pepe Samson would return.

He hurried to the pension in Ermita, eager to find out if there was any message, any newspaper in which he could read about what was happening but there was none. All there was to know was from the clandestine radio station, all there was to do then was to go to EDSA again and immerse himself in the fiesta, the liturgy and the hope that EDSA had become.

When he went out he was very glad to find Junior on the sidewalk, apparently waiting for him. "Would you mind if I went with you?" he asked ingratiatingly. He suspected that Junior wanted to go with him, not just to guide him but, as he surmised, because he wanted to eat. And it came out without any urging, in open and friendly candor. "With you," Junior said with a disarming frankness, "I know I will get something good to eat."

Late afternoon; already the neon lights of the bars in Mabini and del Pilar were ablaze, the jeepneys jostling the streets, office clerks hurrying to get a ride home—everything in the city was normal, as if there was no EDSA broiling, and the Marcos regime tottering.

To please Junior, they went to a nearby restaurant, a turo-turo or, as Junior explained, you point out the food you want from a line of trays. Junior had pork adobo and another beer, and fried chicken after the adobo, and another beer, and Buddy was introduced to mami. The big lunch earlier had sufficed. They ordered siopao to take along. It was already night when they reached EDSA and the massive crowd had now spilled onto the side streets; it would seem as if all of Manila was there, the radical chic from the exclusive villages, their big cars tucked away in the side streets, people from the provinces who had arrived in buses, and plain young people. The whole place exuded an atmosphere of gaiety and, on occasion, cascading applause, of continuous chatter and speculation. In that gathering, there was no place for tension, although as Pepe Samson said, it could be dangerous. What if any of the Marcos artillery fired at this mass? If one air force plane took off and strafed it? But that did not happen—what did happen was an air force plane did fly over the palace and dropped a bomb which did not do much damage. The news was greeted with cheers.

Buddy went home past midnight, leaving Junior in Quiapo from where he would walk home to Bilibid Viejo close by. They would go again to EDSA the following night.

The fourth day of the EDSA "revolt" was, to the city, another normal business day. Every so often, Buddy tuned in to the broadcast—it was only a matter of time now, most of the units of the army were joining the rebels. Enrile, the former defense minister who started the revolt, was on the line, rejoicing at the pledges of support he was continually receiving from armed forces units in the field.

In the morning, he wrote, what he heard on the radio, what he saw on television, Marcos, his family and the generals loyal to him in the palace, then even that channel was shut off. Some fighting around a government radio and TV station, but it was an isolated encounter; everyone seemed to have massed only at EDSA.

In the afternoon, he went for a walk around the area, down to the boulevard and in front of the American embassy. No unusual activity there, just a helicopter coming in for a landing on the embassy grounds. He went back to the pension to wait for Junior.

There is no lingering twilight in Manila; darkness drops quickly, a massive curtain on the city, the west a flurry of colors, magenta and deep purple. Then the sun sinks and the world is suddenly dark. Day's end came to EDSA, the mercury lamps were on, the floodlights, the makeshift altars lighted with candles; the news came at dusk— Marcos had fled the country; it was final, absolute—and from that mass of people, a joyous shout as he had never heard before, more than a new year's celebration. Strangers were embracing one another, shaking hands, greeting the world effusively, and it came to him the realization that he had finally seen one great event in history; it had unfolded before him in all its human glory and he was grateful that he was here, and long afterwards he would always remember this moment of freedom, not for himself for he had always been free, but for his people.

ONE AFTERNOON, a few days later, Leo Mercado Sr. came to the pension, his face radiant with happiness. "We are going to the Luneta," he announced. "You will see Cory—there is a thanksgiving demonstration."

Even before they reached the park in front of the Manila Hotel, people were already everywhere and the side streets were blocked with cars. It was now late afternoon and the sun was kind but even if there had been a typhoon the people would still have come. The green was simply aswarm with people—a million perhaps? two million? He had never seen so many massed together as they were now; there were so many, too, at EDSA, but they were hemmed in by the width of the highway, unlike now where they spread out, people with their yellow ribbons and buntings and their hastily painted placards denoting who they were. Up ahead on a well-lighted stage, this fragile woman was in the center, her voice coming dully through the loudspeaker, the people hardly listening to what was being said, for every so often, they would break out in a chant, "Coreee — Coreee — Coreee — " so deafening, so unanimous and heartwarming, it reassured him not just of their unity but of their capability for creating a nation.

He wanted to go near the stage to have a good look at this woman, Ninoy's widow, who had unified and inspired her grieving people, but the crowd was an impermeable wall, he couldn't push through. Briefly, he looked at the old tailor beside him. Tears were streaming down his face but he didn't bother to wipe them off. Buddy looked around—it was not just Mercado who was crying, there were others, too, weeping and smiling in this, a nation's thanksgiving.

HE KEPT REMEMBERING Pepe Samson's words, so we have gotten rid of Marcos; will we now be able to free ourselves from the oligarchy that has enslaved us?

The answer came to him, ironically, a few days afterwards; euphoria was pervasive and everyone seemed so hopeful, so expectant, that now the Philippines would move. Cory was on television, making her first major statements. And there she was, confident and motherly, announcing, "I will not accept any unso-licited advice..."

He jumped from his seat; he was not the only one shocked by what she had said; the rest in the pension living room who were watching TV with him murmured in disgust. This cannot be—but there she was with her natural presence; still again, a few days afterwards, she announced with presidential finality, "I will make this office an eight a.m. to five p.m. job."

They had called her a housewife who did not know anything, but it was Marcos and the enemies of the people who had spread that lie. Buddy realized quickly she was more than a housewife— she was a cacique housewife, imperious, unfamiliar with the heat of the kitchen because she had a hundred maids doing her work. He did not want to admit it that early, it was too soon to make crass judgments, but somehow, again, the words of Pepe Samson came to mind, insistent, irrevocable. He must see the man again and voice to him his suspicions, that Pepe Samson, Namnama, Father Jess and

224

all of them who had waited for a new dawn upon this blighted land had misplaced their hopes in Cory Aquino. There would be no land reform, no change in the encrusted system of privilege and power, that the darkest days loomed ahead. He must now have a really long talk with Pepe Samson, so that he himself could make the right choice, whether to return to the saccharine comfort of America, or linger in this hell hole which was his birthplace.

22

IN MID-APRIL, Pepe Samson visited Buddy. Five in the morning, and sweaty as all Manila mornings are in the dry season. The pension was closed but apparently the guard knew him so he let him in. He knocked softly but with the airconditioning on, Buddy did not hear. Again, this time louder, and Buddy, his body not yet fully attuned to the contours of reality, came to the door to be instantly shaken. Pepe Samson said, "If you want to come with me, we leave now, before it gets light."

As he started dressing, Buddy asked: "How long?"

"A week, if you have the patience. Or just a couple of days if we bore you."

In five minutes, he was ready—his jeans and T-shirt, aspirin and the tranquilizer that would put his mind at ease in case the recurrent ailment attacked him again, his camera, and all the five thousand pesos in his drawer.

They boarded a cab on the street which had begun to stir with jeepneys and people going to work; from down the street, night people were picking their way to the all-night restaurants for their early breakfast, or very late dinner. Pepe Samson had wanted to take a jeepney, but Buddy dissuaded him—they could get to the Pantranco bus station faster by taxi.

It was not yet daybreak when they got there and the first bus to eastern Pangasinan was about to leave. Pepe Samson sought seats in the rear, away from the bales of merchandise clogging the passageway and the babble of passengers on their way to the Central Plain. They eased out of the station into a wide avenue and onto what he recognized as a portion of EDSA.

Pepe Samson had a canvas backpack, and this time a shapeless denim hat and the same thick-rimmed glasses. They talked in Tagalog and Buddy was glad that he understood everything and didn't have to parade his American accent. By now, he recognized Pepe Samson's carefulness, how he glanced around him first, imprinting in his mind the people within hearing, observing their movements, a carefulness which seemed to be instinctive. Buddy had learned, too, to watch him, to decipher those signals, a nudge, a look telling him that it was better to be silent.

Along the unlighted highway, the traffic was already heavy and the pollution, too, which he had become accustomed to. Trucks with produce were coming in from the provinces and unloading at the intersection where the bus turned right, and they were finally on what was considered a Philippine expressway for there was a tollgate before they entered it.

Pepe Samson had told him he came from the Central Plain. "That is where we are going, so you will see what we do."

In a while, the mountains to the right took shape, the dawn slowly brightened into a flood of light that submerged the land, the stubbled fields of brown, and where there was irrigation, the second rice crop, large patches of green on the otherwise withered plain. Across the fields were villages, new houses with iron roofs, and old farmers' homes with nipa roofs, an unimpressionable landscape, the approaches to small towns slipping by with their endless impieties of soft drink signs.

"We need land reform very badly, anything to improve the lives of our rural people," Pepe Samson was saying in a low voice, "Maybe, Cory will do it. But I doubt it very much. She is herself a very big landlord. Ninoy had some ideas about it and I am sure if he had become president, he would have done something. He was a populist. Cory should be doing it now, while there is no constitution, while she is ruling with what she calls a revolutionary government. With congress, you will have the same landlords back, and they will surely oppose it. Not even Magsaysay could do it in his time, and he was very popular."

Land reform—indeed, it was what the country needed most; it was what the Huks demanded in their time, and it was now being demanded again not just by the left but by the people. Marcos did get something going, but it did not include the sugar and corn lands and, certainly, when he abolished tenancy in the entire country and substituted it with leasehold, at least that was some beginning and all that Cory had to do was go one step further.

"It had never been really adopted as a nationalist platform," Pepe Samson was saying. "The bourgeoisie nationalists—" he smirked, "Recto and Tañada—they merely hated the Americans. They did not plead for land reform, they did not understand its compulsion. They opposed it instead."

He was now talking in the language of the schoolroom, about a host of things, Filipino movies among others, and Pepe Samson said it was very rare that he saw one; it has been more than two years since he saw a movie although whenever he came to Manila, which was not often, he would slip into a movie house on occasion.

"They are so asinine," he said. "There is this Lino Brocka, who tries to honestly mirror the social conditions, but he is less an artist and sometimes, he lays on the message so thick it gets in the way of entertainment. You know, Buddy, these movie people do not know the psychology of their own countrymen, particularly the very poor. The poor do not want to be reminded of their poverty— they want to escape from it; romance, comedy, anything that will drag them away from the tedium of their lives into a world of fancy and light."

"And the actors and actresses?"

"Most of them do not know how to act. There is one very good actress, Nora Aunor—she acts from her guts, a common-enough singer, but when she plays a role that she likes, she lives it. Incidentally, she is dark like any atsay."

Buddy did not know what the word meant.

"Housemaid," Pepe Samson explained. "An exception. Most of our actors and actresses are pretty boys and pretty girls, usually fair-skinned mestizas and mestizos. The Filipino is racist, did you know that? As an old professor friend used to say, in this country, the higher you go, the whiter it becomes. Spanish white, not American. The Americans did not stay here long enough."

Buddy noticed the signs on the highway, the road to Malolos, to Calumpit, names he had come across in his reading, the Malolos Republic and, finally, Tarlac, where they stopped in midmorning for breakfast.

The restaurant, like the bus, was not airconditioned; another turo-turo with uncovered food trays, the meat swimming in gravy, the vegetables overcooked. There was pan de sal and instant coffee. The rice was steaming, though, and Buddy had rice and vegetables and that abominable coffee while Pepe Samson had adobo and rice.

"Nothing like this where we are going," he said, explaining his choice. He asked Buddy about his sister, if she was planning to visit the Philippines, too, and it occurred to Buddy that he had not asked her, that to do so would expose her to the agony of the Filipinos and she already had so much of her own. "I haven't even thought about asking her," he said defensively.

He was surprised at Pepe Samson's comment. "Don't ask her. Maybe some other time, in the future, when there is peace and justice here. It may not come at all, though."

He told Pepe Samson a bit of what he had done; the man had already read his essay on exile and revolution and Buddy wished he had brought his book, all his historical articles, a kind of life-work, of travel and travail, about this land to which he was now inexorably drawn.

They reached Carmen before midday and it being mid-April, the heat permeated everything; it was not just the heat and the sweat, it was also the dust, a dull white patina on the ramshackle buildings, on the buses parked along the highway, their diesel engines throbbing. Dark-skinned boys and women crowded around the buses, selling bunches of eggplants, bottles of shrimp paste and coconut sweets wrapped in cellophane. Their bus merely paused for it soon turned to the right, to a narrower road. They passed a decrepit town called Rosales. "I was born here," Pepe Samson said simply; in half an hour, they were out in the open again, the mountains ahead, distinct blue-green with gashes of amber where the range had eroded. The foothills were brown with dead grass and were shorn of trees.

The road was no longer asphalted. The gravel was uneven—and the bus slowed down, huge billows of dust trailing behind it. Dust covered the houses, their shuttered windows, the banana trees, the shrubs by the highway. He could imagine how it would be in the rainy season, mud everywhere.

They got off in an hour at the fringes of a village, before a sari-sari store. Pepe Samson knew the owner and he asked her, a stout middle-aged woman, for Coca-Cola which as if by some good fortune was cold for she had a gas-fed refrigerator in the back. After that bumpy ride, in this broiling heat, the drink sank into his stomach like benediction.

A jeepney rattled by, shaking and rolling with the indentions on the road. It was overloaded; three passengers on the hood, a couple on the roof, and four people hanging by the sides. It seemed as if any moment, the whole contraption would break down and expel in a sprawling mess all its cargo.

"There is always room for two more," Pepe Samson said, urging Buddy to climb up to the roof which he did with great difficulty. "Like they say," Pepe Samson continued with a laugh—"even in a full suitcase, there is always room for a handkerchief."

Pepe Samson knew some of the passengers and he greeted them effusively by name; he introduced Buddy as a relative from the city who had come to visit, a relative—he was now assured of welcome, of security, of belonging.

If the gravel road was bad, this barrio road was worse; the jeepney banged and swayed so much he thought he would surely fall off. They passed stray sitios with four or five houses, all roofed with grass, so tiny the people in them must have the barest of needs. He could see through their open doors the meager property, the earthen jars, the firewood under the houses, a few pigs and chickens roaming about their barren yards. This was the rural area he had read so much about, truly different from the rest of the countryside.

As they went along, people got off the jeepney, and soon enough there was room for them to sit. A schoolteacher going to her post was inside; she was middle-aged and her hair was white. Pepe Samson greeted her politely. She got off next and soon there were just the two of them and the driver, the last village on the route, for beyond it, the mountain already loomed.

"This isn't it yet," Pepe Samson told him. "Now, we have to walk."

Buddy had expected to climb the foothills and continue up the mountain, but beyond the village they followed a trail that skirted the foothills, past cogon wastes. "This is ranch country," Samson explained.

It was still hot and Buddy was sorry he had forgotten to bring along the light khaki hat he had bought at Eddie Bauer's way back.

Pepe Samson started to talk. "This is what we call a liberated zone—actually, a misnomer because the army can come here anytime. But the people here, they are our friends, they know us—as you saw."

"I didn't see any army checkpoint," Buddy noted.

"Oh, yes, they are there," Samson said. "They are usually in the towns. They don't want to go on patrols and get shot at, or led into areas where they do not know anyone. And we—we avoid encounters with them. Where we have some contact with them, we try and win them. They are our brothers after all. And the soldiers, they are the children of farmers, of workers like us. They know this and I think, in a way, they understand and even sympathize with us."

The cogon grew lush and thick, hiding anyone walking even just a few meters ahead. In some places, the grass had already been burned, and the green sprouts would soon rise with the first rains of May, good food for the cattle. They climbed a low hill and at its summit, they looked down on a narrow valley, unusually green, rice plots, vegetable rows, and a dozen houses of bamboo in the midst of all that astonishing verdure.

"There is a spring in the mountain," Pepe Samson explained. "We helped the people channel the water so they could farm the valley floor."

They went down almost in a run, and at the first house were greeted with broad smiles and questions about how their hike had been. Again, spring water, cooling and sweet. It was now very late in the afternoon, the sun had sunk below the hill but daylight still limned the horizon. Supper was cooking in the kitchen.

"We will sleep here tonight," Pepe told him.

They came after Buddy and Pepe Samson had eaten a farmer's supper, rice and greens and sliced tomatoes with salted fish, nothing more, but everything had tasted so good—that was what a good hike always did to the appetite. They were all very young. No lamp was lighted but in the afterglow, he could make out their faces. They were squatting in the yard, on a couple of logs, houseposts for a bigger house, perhaps. A guitar materialized, and soon they were singing, not in Tagalog but in Ilokano, songs that were sad yet melodious, and he listened with some regret that he had not learned enough of the language from Old Tele in San Francisco or from the workers he had met in Hawaii.

Pepe Samson joined them, his voice resonant and clear, distinct from all the rest. He also talked to them, more as a teacher than as an equal, Buddy could see that in the careful attention they gave him. Manong Peping, they called him. Ka Peping, too, was his other name. They stayed for some three hours, perhaps more, during which there was much laughing. Everyone who wanted to speak out seemed to do so without any difficulty, without any restriction, and if there were discussions, they were often forceful with some haranguing. Ka Peping listened patiently, made his comments. The guitarist started playing again, this time they sang in Tagalog which he understood, not a love song, not a kundiman, but a song that exhorted them not to flag, that their lives were now committed to

231

Filipinas, that they should be prepared for the ultimate sacrifice. There was no clapping when it was over—just that stern and rigid silence of soldiers before they set forth to battle, and looking at them, these kids who perhaps still had their mothers' milk on their lips, a warm and kindred feeling came over him.

THEY LEFT by midnight, he could see that in the luminous dial of his cheap Casio watch. They drifted away, like fireflies at the inevitable approach of dawn, with their knapsacks, their guns.

"Where are they going?" he asked

"To where they came from," Pepe Samson said.

"They are all so young."

"Many of them are old," Pepe Samson assured him. "You know what I mean."

He could not sleep. Out there in the yard, the star-strewn sky clear and luminous above, the mountain rising behind them, it seemed as if the whole world had receded, and here they were, encircled by the hush of phantoms that were not to be feared, by the vastness of the land itself. He should feel lonely now, away from Pacific Heights, from Jessica, how he missed her! From all that was familiar, all that he remembered, the sprawling house, their walks around Chinatown when she was a kid, their picnics on the Pacific beaches, and all the splendor and glitter of America. A sliver of loneliness stabbed but briefly into his heart. He recovered quickly, and was glad that he had come here, seen the poverty of the people as well as the promise of their salvation.

They continued talking far into the night. Pepe Samson told him how they had organized the villages, how they help farmers in their work during the planting and harvesting seasons. "They have been so dependent on their landlords, they must learn most of all how to be free from them—a process that is not easy, but which they understood after we had talked with them. Those kids you saw, they are from here, most of them are the children of the peasants themselves."

Pepe Samson was a learned man, he was also a practical man. Was Pepe haunted by the same thoughts that had badgered him? Buddy asked the old question, for him such a boring cliché, but a question that needed to be asked if only so that the path ahead for him would be more clear. "Have you ever thought about who you are, where you are going—you know, that question about identity which so many are asking? I ask because, if you must know, this is one reason why I have returned..."

Pepe Samson was silent for a while, then he laughed silently, the laughter turning into a patronizing cackle which Buddy resented.

"You academics, you Americans—you are no different from our middle-class Filipinos wondering about who they are. Did it ever occur to you that this is a kind of luxury you are indulging in?"

Buddy resented being made fun of. "It is a real problem, not a luxury," he said hotly. "It gnaws at the spirit, diminishes a man's worth if he does not know who he is..."

"That's a lot of crap, Professor," Pepe Samson said, then immediately apologized. "I am sorry, but look at me, I have no time to ask such questions. None of us bother with that. We all know who we are, what we are trying to do, where we are headed. I think it is those who have all the leisure, who are not concerned with society or people—they are the ones who have that problem."

Buddy let the words sink in. They were a challenge, a description of what he was and even now, what he had always been, a voyeur, a spectator.

"I am Jose Samson, I come from a small village in Pangasinan. I am Ilokano but, above all else, I am Filipino. I am also certain it is here, in my unhappy country, where I will die. It really is as simple as that."

Another of those silences; in the east, across the cloudless night sky, a falling star traced its descent with a streak of light. Somewhere among the farmhouses, a cock crowed and it was soon followed by the crowing of other cocks.

Buddy asked how they raised money, since they paid for their food, for the medicines that they dispensed, for here there was no doctor, no public health facilities. In the dark, he could see Pepe Samson smile. "The poor have money," he said, "All over the country—have you seen them? The Iglesia Ni Kristo churches? They were built by the poor—twenty-five centavos during each church service, that's how. And if they don't have the money, we raise the money for them." Buddy had seen them, of course, how could anyone miss those churches, their needlelike spires so uniform in their ostentation.

Buddy had read much of the underground literature that the movement had published. "Pepe, do you hate Americans?" The question was candid and in reply, again, a seemingly mocking laughter.

"I don't," he said. "In 1898, if I had been around then, I might have. It is too late to make amends, to ask the Americans to undo their alliance with the Filipino oligarchy. That is no longer their problem, it is ours. All that I want is for them to keep away, not to interfere. I have never been to the United States, I would like to, but I cannot go now. So much work here..."

"I understand," Buddy said.

"No!" the man objected bluntly. "You do not understand, you are not one of us. You will never be hungry, without a single centavo in your pocket. You can always leave anytime and go back to the comfort of your past." Pepe Samson stopped, and his voice became plaintive, soft, weary. "I am sorry, Buddy. But it has been so long. Almost twenty years of this kind of life. You get very, very tired, and you want to stop, to rest, but you know you cannot, until you are killed, or imprisoned, and even there the longing won't stop. How will it end for me? There's a price on my head. So I'll probably be betrayed or I'll walk into an ambush. Whichever way, I sometimes hope it will be soon. It's such a cliché, about death losing its sting. But because I—we—expect it, it is not so fearsome anymore. I have seen so many of our people die. And I often ask myself, what right have I to lure them away from the safety of their homes, poor though they may be? I can promise them nothing and I am not even sure that we will be different from the tyrants we seek to destroy, that is, if someday by some miracle we will ever come to power." He sighed, then continued: "How I long for a future that is just, I hate this present that is so difficult to change. I hate..." he paused and a lilt came back to his voice. "It is strange, but it is precisely this hate that keeps me going, keeps me alive..."

"The other side of love," Buddy said quietly.

In the dark, Pepe Samson nodded.

"I asked about America," Buddy continued.

"Ah, yes, it is uppermost in the Filipino imagination. In fact, we have tried to create a nation in the American image—but we have failed miserably. It is the most powerful nation in the world, the most trusted. And why not? Look at your history. Americans can do so much, but they don't realize it."

"What then can Americans do? What can I do?"

Again, one of those silences. When Pepe Samson finally spoke, his voice was so clear, his words were like crystals suspended in the air. "In this country, so many things seem strange, bizarre to others, funny even. But not to us because we live here. Imelda's three thousand pairs of shoes! Remember, millions of Filipinos go barefoot! What then can I ask of you? Of the world? Nothing! Nothing, but your compassion!"

MORNINGS slide abruptly into the villages in the foothills of the Caraballo Range with burnishings of gold that quickly turn to silver as the sun goes up, splashing on the barren hillsides and on the wooded mountain. In the green, fecund valley, with its few houses, work starts early, even before the light breaks. Buddy and Pepe Samson woke up with the farmers starting out to work. They had slept without a mosquito net; the mosquitoes in the beginning had been a bother, but Pepe Samson told him there was no malaria here so he need not worry about catching it.

Breakfast was ready; the leftover rice the night before had been fried in fresh coconut oil and again, the usual plate of fresh vegetables from the plots outside. And salted fish sauce with slices of ripe tomato and diced onions. It all tasted so good he could eat it the whole day.

As they went down the ladder, in the corner of his eye, Buddy saw Pepe Samson giving the farmer's wife some money, and pills which he said were for fever and headaches. The two young boys of the family were also getting ready for school—they had to hike at least three kilometers to the nearest barrio school below.

"We will go to another barrio," Pepe Samson said. "This is a rich village, a demonstration village if you may call it. We showed the people there how to use a spring—but in the other places, there are no springs, just deep wells, or a creek we could perhaps dam up. Cooperative effort, we are also showing this to them. So you can see, Buddy, it is not always organizing, or fighting. Most of the time, it is education which, I think, is the real solution to our problems." He pointed out the distance they would cross, a long walk in these treeless hills; no roads, just trails, cattle paths that led high up to the crest of the mountain, much of it barren now although the deeper ranges beyond, more difficult to reach, were still caparisoned with forest.

"This is so far away from the towns," Pepe explained, "and it is here where the very poor, the landless, have been flung, but even these lands, you see, are titled to cattle owners, to rich politicians and, yes, to generals."

"There is very real hunger here," he continued. "There is no irrigation, and so there is only one rice crop a year, planted in the narrow hollows, on the hillsides. During the rainy season, before the harvest, many people here eat only once a day, bananas roasted in the fire or boiled, with fish sauce, or coconut meat flavored with salt, or sugar—if they have it."

They paused in the spare shade of a solitary tree. Pepe Samson's face became thoughtful. "I want to tell you," he said, "that we avoid as much as we can encounters with the army. It is very, very sad— the soldiers come from the lower classes, from the peasantry; they are soldiers because there are no other jobs available to the poor.

235

And the officers—especially the young ones—many of them sympathize with us. This is a different breed of officers altogether although I would not say it is incorruptible. There was an encounter over there, in that sitio, a day before I left for Manila. It was one of those things that could not be avoided because they came upon one of our education units conducting classes—we retreated, but not before one of their officers, we learned later, was killed. But they got two of the cadres." He inhaled deeply and, after some silence, they walked on.

They had reached the next hill and were on its summit; below them, more hills flattened out into the plain, wide and shimmering in the noonday glare. Then toward the right, down the gentle slope, the loud chatter of gunfire; no mistaking it, two long bursts, and in the still midday air, the crackle seemed so near, echoing, rocketing across the hills. Pepe Samson stopped. There was no more gunfire— just those two long bursts. A gun battle?

"No," he said; "if it is a gun battle, there would be more shooting, response, sporadic."

In a while, a plume of smoke far to the right rose to the sky, whitish then greyish and finally black, but he could not see the source of the fire as a line of trees blocked the view.

Pepe Samson gasped. "They are burning Lupao," he cried. "They are burning Lupao!" and ran, headed to where the smoke had now risen high in the heavens.

He slowed down when Buddy had caught up with him. "Follow my signals, do not talk. We might walk into an ambush," he said.

Buddy's throat tightened; soon they were on level ground, the cogon wastes around them. A few more steps, and they could see the burning village although it was still a distance away.

"I wish I had binoculars," Pepe Samson said as he crouched before a stand of grass. He instructed Buddy to do the same. In a while, from the village, men in single file moved out—they did not proceed to the villages higher up in the hills; they seemed headed back to the town far below where they had come from.

"How many? Five?"

"No," Pepe Samson said, "A platoon—they don't go this far if they are only a squad."

Now they ran when they could, and walked when they were out of breath. In a while, they were in the approach to the village. The fires of the burning houses were dying out.

The villagers were huddled on the ground, the women wailing, and before them, the bodies of the dead—ten men, five women and a couple of children. A woman who was wounded lay on the ground, blood oozing from the wound in her chest. A babble of voices, grief-stricken, angry, confused, beseeching help. Pepe Samson went directly to those who were laid on the ground, lifeless all of them, and to the woman who was wounded. They prepared some boiling water and as he washed the wound, they told him what had happened, that the soldiers had come, surrounded the village and shouted at the rebels inside the houses to surrender. The men came out and were immediately shot. Then the houses were fired upon—that was the second volley—and set afire. An officer was with the platoon and they had with them a man, a spy whom the villagers didn't know, who told the soldiers that this was a rebel village. It was true, of course, as were all the villages that lined the foothills, but the men who were killed were all farmers, there was not one whom Pepe Samson could claim as his.

"Your camera, Buddy."

He took out his old, faithful Leica and immediately started taking pictures of the dead, the cindered remains of houses, the survivors. In death, there was a calmness in their faces, the blood on their clothes starting to dry. He couldn't look at the man whose face was disfigured by his wounds, his head a gaping hole. Nausea started to knot his stomach and fog his senses, so he drew away, having finished the roll, and loaded the camera again, this time to focus on the ashes of the burned houses, on the grieving villagers, their faces distorted in disbelief and sorrow.

"You have met Mario Dolce," Pepe Samson told him. "Go back to Manila, give him your film. He will know what to do."

Three young men had arrived—all were armed. They said the rest were nearby, waiting for orders.

Buddy could not follow the farmer talking to Samson, but he could catch the drift. The soldiers had come and destroyed their homes because Pepe Samson and his men were here. If they had never come, the village would have been spared. Now it was a battleground. And who else would be left to suffer?

"And you think we do not suffer at all? We do, far more than you know. We have worked with you through the years, we are always here, the soldiers just pass by." Pepe Samson spoke to them in Ilokano and Tagalog. "Some of your children are with us—they joined with your permission because they will be protecting you. Who helped you in the planting and harvesting? Who helped you build your houses, rid this place of cattle rustlers and thieves? And your landlords, can they drive you away from this land now as easily as they did in the past? No, because they are afraid. Have the soldiers been on your side? Never, always they were for the landlords. Who gave you medicine when you needed it, advice? When we come, do we tell you to catch your chickens and butcher your pigs for us? We don't; always we give you something in return. Ask yourselves, my dear brothers and sisters, what the soldiers, what the government has done for you! Ask yourselves. And now, you think we are the enemy!"

From the villagers sullen silence, then a slow nodding of heads, and again, wailing. Pepe Samson went to them, embraced them, held their hands to comfort them, but what in the name of the Almighty who dispenses with holy justice, who promised the earth to these, the meek and the humble, could Pepe Samson do now to assuage this immense, unbearable pain?

On his instruction, they made a stretcher from a rattan hammock for the wounded woman; she will be taken to town, to a doctor or to a hospital—if she survives the trip. The wound had stopped bleeding.

Pepe Samson turned briefly to Buddy. There was sorrow in his face, a quiver in his voice. "What is identity to these people, Buddy? This is their life, and you may ask, is it really worth living? But they will go on, just as I will go on, because we have something to live for."

And in that moment, Salvador dela Raza realized what it was all about, that he had really shut himself off in some impermeable cocoon, some comfortable prison, and that now he must break free.

To one of the young people from the village, a boy of fifteen or so, Pepe Samson gave specific instructions. "You will go to Manila to tell the people what happened here."

"He is too young," the farmer who had spoken earlier said. "Let me go instead."

Before they parted, Buddy gave Pepe Samson his overnight bag; it contained two changes of clothes, soap, toothpaste and his toothbrush; he retrieved the toothbrush and put it in his pocket. Out of the villagers' hearing, he told Pepe Samson. "I am very sorry, this is all I can leave behind. There is five thousand pesos here—the villagers need it. I will send you some money through him,"—he thrust his chin at the farmer who was saying good-bye to his family.

"He is a good man," Pepe Samson said, "I understand his feelings." Away from them all, from the rancid smell of death, Pepe Samson shuddered; he was crying though no sobbing was wrenched from him.

All the way back to the highway where they squeezed themselves into a jeepney, and all the way to Carmen and the bus back to Manila, Buddy's mind was numb. Never before had he seen blood

238

so fresh and so copious drenching the earth and, for a while, fear strangled him. What if they had been in that village when the soldiers arrived? The anger that coiled in him swelled, and his chest ached because he could not release it, could not express it.

I have seen death and looked at the faces of the innocent, touched their living blood which is also mine, understood the silence of their passing, for I too shall pass like them. They cried for justice; will their unanswered cry be mine to repeat and proclaim?

IT WAS in all the newspapers, and he would have gladly testified to the authenticity of the pictures, of the massacre, but Mario Dolce said it was best that he stay detached. The farmer who had gone with him was witness enough. In afterthought, he realized this was for the best. He also learned quickly how short-lived the interest in the news was, how so soon the newspapers—even those who had sent their writers to the scene—forgot everything, and how the government did nothing in the end. Now, he understood clearly— it was not so much that a weak government had misgoverned, but that absence of government had destined barrios to neglect and oblivion.

What then could someone like him do? He was drifting in this dismal swamp called Filipinas—how he loved the name! the sound, the image of a mother—now shorn of the delightful vagaries of his imagination. He did not expect this bewildering poverty which misted the eyes and clotted the chest. How could people live in those slums, those villages which he had seen, what could they be eating—if they ate at all. He had seen poverty in Mexico, in the outside reaches of American cities, but not like this. Who had condemned my people to such a pitiable fate? But Salvador dela Raza, you do not belong here. Leave, flee this accursed land, these stunted people and their malignant leaders. No effulgent morning will ever break here— nothing but the night which shrivels the soul. Can you not see? The rich and the poor are yoked together!

23

WHEN THE APARTMENT beside the Mercado tailoring shop was vacated, Buddy immediately rented it. He had been looking for one; the Ermita pension was becoming too crowded. With his new connections, he did not feel comfortable in it anymore. The other reason was deeply personal. The apartment would keep him close to Mercado Sr. and to his family, Namnama most of all.

He had it tidied up a bit by two carpenters from the town of Mexico, in Pampanga, whom Mercado Sr. had recruited, and when it was ready, he had an airconditioner installed in the bedroom, and the usual cooking facilities, a refrigerator, living and dining room furniture, a color TV, and a bookcase. He asked Junior if he wanted to move in and sleep on the ground floor and watch the apartment, to which the young man immediately agreed. He had been looking for a job for almost a year but could not find one, and it was just as well for he had maintained his ties with his university friends and, they were, like him, in constant demonstrations and mass action now.

Buddy had access to the UP library and the national library with his credentials. Whenever he could, he did a lot of reading on the Huk movement, on peasant rebellions, and on available underground literature, the publications of the old communist party, the Maoist party and the scattering of socialist, non-communist pamphlets, some

240

of which were available at the libraries. In all of these, there was so much ideological posturing and jargon, he decided to go to the original documents and all the materials he could amass on land reform and the Filipino peasant. In much of these efforts, Junior proved to be an excellent assistant, as well as a most expensive watchman, for the refrigerator was always stocked with beer and his favorite pig innards, halo-halo.

Junior gave him, too, what he wanted most to know, what Namnama was doing, where she was (that was not easy to track), and for his particular interest, developments within the movement.

Provided with "democratic space" as the movement called it, many of its leaders had surfaced and had come to Manila to participate in the Cory government's peace initiatives. The president had gone to the south to meet with the Muslim rebel leaders, and to the Cordilleras as well.

"But she does not want to meet with the peasant leaders—and they are not even armed," Junior wailed, all the more strengthening Buddy's belief that there would be no land reform under Cory. Couldn't the people see that she is one of the owners of the huge Hacienda Luisita in Tarlac—more than six thousand hectares of prime agricultural land planted to the colonial crop, sugar. These were not the only properties of the Cojuangcos; there were others in banking, in communications, in real estate. She was not going to give away such vaulting privilege.

And yet, it was all hers—to give shape to what Ninoy wanted, a revolution that was bloodless or, at least, with the minimum number of Filipinos killed. She had a revolutionary government, with her tremendous popularity, she could do almost anything, if only she understood not just the opportunities at her doorstep but the fact that such opportunities might never come again to any Filipino leader.

One morning, Junior told him not to leave the apartment; a big demonstration, he said, was to take place in the afternoon and if he wished, he could join. A peasant gathering at Malacañang to force Cory to look at the agrarian problem which she had failed to do although during the election campaign the previous year, she had promised that she would.

They went out together for lunch at Ma Mon Luk on Quezon Boulevard—the usual mami and siopao which he had grown to like although the noodles tasted a bit soapy. For Junior, this was a feast. He was in the uniform of a demonstrator, blue jeans, grey T-shirt, rubber shoes, and the usual backpack. After a leisurely lunch, they walked over to Morayta where they were to form ranks together with the others who were coming in from different directions. As Junior had told him, they were farmers, workers; he would recognize them, just as he saw them in Hawaii, in Old Tele, the rough sun-darkened skins, the thick hands, fingernails rimmed with dirt, the shabby clothes and the odor of a humanity perpetually drenched in sweat. Some of them did not have shoes—just the cheap Japanese rubber sandals which now the poorest peasant could afford, unlike in the past, as Mercado Sr. had explained, when most farmers were barefoot. Again, Buddy remembered the yellowed pictures of the Philippine-American War taken by Americans, the dead Filipinos in uniform, but barefoot.

By three in the afternoon, the crowd had swelled and had begun to march towards Malacañang, the red flags lifted and waving in the breeze, a canopy of red over the throng, the bullhorns exhorting everyone to keep their lines. Junior knew exactly where his colleagues were. They were there not as individuals now but as a group, and everyone knew everyone else so that it was close to impossible for an outsider to break into their ranks. They marched up Recto talking noisily, walking purposefully, the wide street emptied now of traffic and the hordes of students who usually crowded its sidewalks.

Buddy wanted to see how it was out front, so when the marchers finally reached Mendiola, he and Junior moved up to the front. The afternoon had waned, and tension was rife—he could feel it as if it was something solid but permeable wherein they were all immersed.

So this is Mendiola—nothing but a short bridge barricaded with barbed wire, fire trucks and armored cars. The bridge spanned a dead estero, a drainage canal which extended to the Pasig, on the left the old Benedictine college, San Beda, an elite school in a proletarian part of the city, close to the diploma mills, the womens' colleges, too, and on the right, the pink buildings of Centro Escolar. Up the broad avenue lined by trees was the white east gate of Malacañang, manned as in the Marcos regime by a squad of soldiers. He recalled television images, how the gate was breached during the EDSA uprising, the people jostling their way into the palace and stamping and tearing apart the pictures of Marcos and his wife.

Many demonstrations during the dictatorship—they all ended here, then the ritual confrontation, the police and army officers decreeing the marchers could go no farther, the marchers ranting their demands, Marcos should go, the Yankees should go.

Now, the farm leaders were asking: Why did Cory not want to see them? She had passed on to her agrarian reform minister the duty to look after the peasants' demands, but the minister had not done anything. Where is land reform? Why has Cory betrayed the trust of the people? The shouts were getting furious, the exchange of accusations rising in pitch.

No one among the policemen, the soldiers, would admit it afterwards. It would have been so easy to make a list of those who were assigned to Mendiola that fatal afternoon, to have all their guns examined, to hold them for trial for it was plain murder and, because it was plain murder, the crime could be ascribed not just to the police but to Cory Aquino who had refused to see the demonstrators "because they had no appointment." She dismissed them with imperial disdain; now that image of a Joan of Arc, of a faultless and incorruptible leader was forever dashed to the mud—Cory Aquino had blood on her hands.

The first flurry of shots from the barricade struck the phalanx of demonstrators. The bullets whistled above him and where it struck human flesh, it came as a thud. Again, that sound of gunfire roiled in his ears. Junior, who was beside him, collapsed, screaming, and when Buddy looked at the young man, a spot of red had blossomed on his chest. Before Junior could fall, Buddy caught him and dragged him away from it all, to the safety of the sidewalk, behind the walls and columns of buildings. There, among the many who had fled, he ripped open Junior's T-shirt; the young man shuddered and became still. He is dead, he is dead, his mind told him but he refused to believe it, this young man who was so full of life, who had been friend and companion.

Some of the demonstrators, young men all, had now crowded around them, and they carried Junior to a jeepney, to the nearest hospital in Morayta. He prayed as he had never done before, hoped to God as he had never beseeched God before, that Junior would live but in the emergency room to where Junior and several others were rushed, the verdict was final.

"You should change your shirt," the nurse told him, and for the first time, he realized that the front of his shirt was wet with blood, Junior's blood. Touching it, looking at it as if it were some precious emblem, Buddy started to cry, the tears scalding his eyes, and wrenched from him were these unspeakable, almost unendurable spasms of pain and anger.

The wake was held at the tailor shop; they cleared the big table in the middle and Junior's coffin lay there for just a day. His blood-soaked clothes were not removed. Friends from the university came. Among them, a very pretty girl who was Junior's girlfriend; when she arrived, looking at her loved one in death, she fainted.

They told him that not even during the most virulent demonstrations under Marcos were so many people killed—nineteen of them,

243

and for what? Cory Aquino was waiting to be awarded the Nobel Peace Prize. What supreme irony now if that were to materialize.

Namnama came the following day, shortly before they carried Junior to a crypt in La Loma cemetery. Her face was pale and when she looked at her only brother in the coffin, Buddy thought she too would collapse but she quickly regained her composure. She did not cry; perhaps she had seen too many deaths, perhaps the grief that coursed through her was beyond physical expression now and must be expressed in other more telling ways, in more commitment to the ends to which her family had devoted itself.

WHAT MUST I do? He had seen what had appeared so ordinary, so trite to millions of Filipinos because they have come to accept the harshness of oppression as part of life itself, that this was destiny. But like Pepe Samson, he knew it was not. Must I then heed the thunder of the urgings in my heart, the quiet, insistent voice of conscience which demands that I do something? What was that five thousand pesos I left in Lupao? Nothing, not even five hundred dollars, but it would feed the whole village for more than a month. Yet, as Pepe Samson had said, it is not so much money they need as the strength to stand alone. With what? On their bare feet? Their frail bodies? What can I do for them? I see my brownness in their own skins, myself in themselves had I not left. Truly, I am a peasant, too, like them.

IN THE APARTMENT, the sound of living permeating everything, the clangor on the sidewalk, the snort of jeepneys; he could still be truly by himself, thinking, wondering now what he must do. The mountain was waiting, just as it had waited for generations for the faithful, the young people who were willing to forego the easy journey in the plain.

Mario Dolce sometimes dropped by, and would take him to the libraries, the private collections, the Gopez Collection and Buddy would continue his reading there, an occasional dinner in China-town—all of Manila is Chinatown!—or at the Comedor in Ermita, a Spanish restaurant which served gazpachos and paella, his favorites, reminding him of Spain. When Mario Dolce came along, the discussion always turned to the past, to the beginning, how it all started, this legacy of Spain that had a more lasting impact than what the Americans or the Japanese had left behind.

For all his knowledge of the world, Mario Dolce had never left the Philippines; he did not have the money to do so, what he earned as a journalist and writer hardly enabled him to support a family and, like Mercado Junior, he relished Buddy's company, his spending for the kind of food he could not afford.

This, Buddy realized early enough, was one test of a democracy. Does the taxi driver have the same food as the president of the country? Mario Dolce, thin, anemic-looking, with a perpetual stoop, agreed with him. "The forms are here all right, free elections, a free press, but what have they brought us?"

Then, between spoonfuls of gazpachos, Mario Dolce asked him. "Buddy, what did we really inherit from our colonizers? You have been here for some time now, you have done a lot of reading, you have been with the people, what do you see? You can be objective, I know that. Why are we like this? Incapable of uniting?"

The string quartet at the other end of the restaurant had started playing "Reloj" and the headwaiter came up to Buddy, asking him if there was any particular Spanish tune he wanted to hear. He smiled and said, "Nothing in particular."

"Three hundred years of Spanish rule," Buddy sighed, "and the Spanish character has been indelibly imprinted in the Filipino elite which, as you very well know, is Spanish mestizo. Isn't it so?"

"There was so much cruelty during all those years, and we were denied so many things. Have you ever heard of the garrote?" Mario Dolce asked.

Buddy had read about it.

"The Spaniards executed Indios with it in public. They strapped a man garbed in white, a hood over his head, to a chair with a metal screw clamped on the neck. Then, slowly, the screw was tightened, until the poor man's neck was broken or he was strangled. They left his corpse on the platform the whole day for everyone to see. The guillotine is kinder. Why were they like this?"

Long before Mario Dolce asked, he had already asked himself, too, about the Spanish character which, after all, had masterminded an empire. A country with hardly any arable soil had a handful of adventurous conquistadors who laid barren the proud civilizations of the South American Indians. The Philippines was a different case altogether—the islands had no civilizations of such cohesive magnitude; big towns, yes, trading centers with highly skilled artisans, even a scientific culture, but small fiefdoms more at war with one another; it was easy to bring them to heel.

"The Spanish Inquisition, Mario," Buddy said firmly, "it was different from the European Inquisition which started in the thirteenth century. It was autonomous, free from the control of the Pope, and it lasted many centuries, from the fifteenth onwards to the middle of the nineteenth. Confiscation of properties, tortures, executions,

There was a death penalty for booksellers who were selling the prohibited books in the Index. And you know something, the Spanish people accepted it wholeheartedly and they regarded heresy as a national evil to be eradicated. You see in the Inquisition the Spanish compulsion to authoritarianism. In spite of all that piety the Spanish Inquisition warped the Spanish personality, made them cruel, racist. They even twice imprisoned St. Ignatius of Loyola, condemned St. Theresa of Avila..."

"All in the name of God," Mario Dolce sighed."The Hispanistas here, they are so proud of Catholicism. Spain's legacy, they say. If it was a success, then there would be uprightness in our leaders. How often does Cory Aquino go to church? It is this moral decay that is our most serious problem—religion, how many crimes are committed by the religious themselves!"

"It was more than that." Buddy said. "It was for limpieza de sangre."

"Limpieza, what is that?"

"Purity of the blood," Buddy explained. "It is the most basic of Spanish laws. It evolved out of the Inquisition. You have to have pure Spanish blood to gain public office. One drop which is not Spanish—and you are out. Even the nobles were subject to this mindless scrutiny. And, of course, the Jews, the Moslems, who were forced into Catholicism; they were never trusted. It didn't matter that they had lived for generations in Spain."

"This explains so many things," Mario Dolce said. "Why the Indios were never really given an education because they were not Spaniards." He sat back and laughed. "This also explains," he added, "why the Spanish mestizo elite in Manila send their kids to Spain, not just to polish their accents, but also so they will not intermarry with Indio mongrels like us—this more than a hundred years after the bastards were driven out...And you know, there are still some Spanish mestizos in our midst who, because of their Spanish ancestry, think brown Filipinos are not capable of creativity, of leading organizations. Our skulls, they say, are not big enough to hold more brain. And mind you, they say this out loud."

"They said that in Rizal's time. But it's Indios now who run this government, who make the laws, Mario," Buddy reminded him.

Mario Dolce was silent. Then, "The Koreans and the Taiwanese are coming up very fast. Sometimes, I wonder if it would have been better if we were colonized by the Japanese. They leave behind a work ethic, and because they were such cruel rulers, we would have had no hangover with their regime, unlike this terrific hangover with the Americans. Forty years in Hollywood—you have heard of that."

"But the Japanese, like the Chinese, are racist, too. To them, every foreigner is gaijin—and that's not complimentary. As for the Chinese—all non-Chinese are barbarians. I must also remind you that I am very proud of my country. I am American, Mario, do not forget that. There are many problems in America, but attempts are made to solve them. And the Washington taxi driver can eat better than the president..." He remembered Alex, the poor meals the taxi driver usually ate at home and at work.

AFTER DINNER, Mario decided to take him to nearby M. H. del Pilar Street to show him the line of bars and pick-up joints there. And again, visions of the pathetic exile in Barcelona, the spartan life, the anonymous death; what would he say now if he were alive and could see this squalid street, its sexual commerce, its child prostitutes?

They went into a brightly lit restaurant, Rosie's Diner, done in the manner of American diners frequented by truck drivers, the counters filled with Caucasians and girls in shorts and high-heels. The coffee was American and so were the servings of hamburgers, noodles, temptingly big, but the paella and the gazpachos had filled him. Coffee would do.

It was ten o'clock when they went out. They walked across the street to where Buddy could hail a cab to Quiapo and were waiting on a dimly lit part of the sidewalk when a white car stopped in front of them, and two men rushed out. In the dimness, Buddy could see that they had drawn guns aimed at them. But they were not interested in him; they pounced instead on Mario Dolce, the poor, thin man, his voice a squeak. "Who are you, what wrong have I done?"

To which one gruffly said. "Come with us and if you refuse, we will shoot you right here." A third man had opened the car door. Before they shoved Mario Dolce in, he cried out to Buddy, "Tell my wife, Buddy, please, tell her..."

As they sped away, the light of passing traffic shone on the car; its license plate was smeared with mud, or dirt, and was unreadable. He stood numb, wordless, bewildered, on the sidewalk. People who saw did not even stop or ask, just another incident here on M.H. del Pilar, here in this city where people have become callous, inured to the raw wounds inflicted on them...

He did not know where Mario's wife lived. And the newspaper where Mario Dolce worked did not seem interested in following up his story; he was not a regular staff member, just a stringer. There was not even an item in the newspaper about his disappearance. Through Mercado Sr. Buddy was able to have word sent to Mario's wife. He never saw Mario Dolce again, or heard anything about him—one of the many who had disappeared in this widening miasma that is Filipinas.

Would he be picked up, too? That was now a possibility he must deal with; he could flee this country now and be safe from the bizarre dangers that threatened anyone with conviction. He had already seen so much persecution against which he could do nothing. Should he persist? This was not his country, the cause of the Filipinos not his cause. He could be comfortable if that was all he sought, but from the depths of his own being was this feeble stirring of concern, of compassion, as Pepe Samson had so passionately defined, and the stirring was gathering force, drawing him into its centripetal vortex, determining now his future action. He was a free man, but at the same time he shivered at the thought, for he could feel an invisible, and perhaps inevitable dragnet closing in.

24

THE DECISION was not difficult to make; he was pushed to it by circumstance, by the city itself, and most of all by a desire to belong. But when he raked avidly into his own motives, he realized that Namnama possessed some dulcet talisman and he had succumbed.

I had thought that the city—any city—with its crowds and its crannies could be an amorphous haze into which any man could disappear, but now, niggling doubts crowd my mind; I was safe and I had not been involved but I began to question my assumptions. Uninvolved? What was I doing in Lupao? In Mendiola? What was I doing with all those thousands of cheering people at the Luneta? And, yes, EDSA—now nothing more than a euphoric memory that expands the chest and gushes blood to my temples. I was there! I was there! That was enough to lift me up from this prosaic self to swagger among the clouds.

But it was all over, all over, and time again to walk the cratered streets and soothe the bruised spirit.

Namnama and three of her friends, young men who smiled easily, came to the apartment, and they helped carry my things—the rest we left in the tailor shop. It had been raining, Manila's sewers were clogged and Quiapo was flooded. The clouds, however, had lifted and the city, newly washed, seemed bright, a thin veneer over the shabby buildings, the jeepney morass in the vitriol streets.

We arrived in Raza in mid-afternoon, trundled ourselves in three tricycles, then onward to the Mountain. We got off where the tricycles could no longer climb and walked.

I knew it—I was truly going home. Birds who migrate to other climates know the way back, and so it was with me. Follow this tiny stream, it will lead you to where you will be happiest.

I stepped over the smooth, moss-covered stones, splashed the cool water on my face, feeling refreshed so that there seemed to be new strength in me, climbing now over boulders and thickets. Trees crowd around me. I was walking alone, although Namnama and her friends were there behind me.

I came to where the spring began, gurgling out of the earth, an immaculate pool surrounded by small boulders, the same spring from which Apo Tale had hauled water, unchanged, pristine; I was home again.

Up the sharp incline, to the clearing, to where the house had been, I thought I heard my name called from the forest fastness, Badong, Badong, but there was no one there, just trees and the sun daubing them. The call of birds, the rustle of leaves in the wind, the thumping of my heart—these are the sounds that told me life could be nourished here. I listened carefully, my ears keen and ready to receive the slightest sound, a worm turning in the ground, a cricket perched on the canopy of green above. What were those that moved close to the spring? A doe looking at me as if it knew me, unafraid of my presence? I motioned to Namnama, to her friends, but they couldn't see it. O Apo Tale, Inay Mayang, you have welcomed me!

Now I am at peace with all this green surrounding me. In the mornings when I wake up, wondering when I will be paralyzed again, or rendered blind, I am eager to see the sun range over the foothills in its brilliant ascent. I stand in the light, breathing deeply, savoring everything for this very day could be my last.

My little house is finished. My needs are few and whatever I need from the city, my tailor friend and guardian gets them for me. I can never thank him enough.

They start coming to me, and they ask questions. I tell them what I know, relate to them stories about Filipinas, and they are all so eager to learn. God and nation, people and justice—these are the givens in the equation. I go back to my reading of the Colorum Uprising in eastern Pangasinan in 1931 and repeat what the Colorums have said, that God created earth, water and air for all men, that land belongs to them who till it—and that it was against God's laws for one man, one family, one group, to own so much while the rest of the nation starves. I tell them that enlightening men's minds is the most difficult of all endeavors, much, much more difficult than violence and killing.

I go to sleep early. Although they never bother me at night, someone always drops by, the women who cook and do my laundry, the men who help with my plot of land, my vegetable garden.

Most of the time I go to sleep wondering if I will wake up, but sleep comes just the same, a balm to my mind. They know now that there is something wrong with me, and that is why they try to be by my side always, ever solicitous. Have I become their teacher? What is this man doing among us? Why does he not go back to America? He suffers here.

I will tell you, Namnama. I am tired of a complex world, I long for simplicity, for choices not shrouded with moral ambiguity.

You have asked me, too, what is history. I echo now my father: Our lives, no less. But more than that, it is our capacity to remember, to make the past useful and more so for Filipinos who have permitted themselves to be lobotomized by their own willfulness. They have done this to themselves because they are weak, because they did not know any better. I hope I can give them memory, which will exalt them and give them hope.

But this, I do not tell her: I am here, Namnama, because you are here.

MY FIRST YEAR, my first Christmas in the Mountain, and I would have missed it entirely the days having slipped by so quickly, I had even forgotten to look at the date that automaticaly pops on the screen of my laptop when I turn it on.

As early as October, many of the shops in Manila were already playing Christmas carols. I visited Father Jess in Barrio Magsaysay; his church was freshly painted on the outside, and in late November, it was already bright with Christmas decorations. He also had the church choir—all of them young people from the neighborhood— rehearsing Christmas carols; he said come the season for carolling, they would range over the city in a couple of jeepneys to raise gifts for the many in the barrio who were poor. I gave him money to spend as he saw fit.

The house had long been finished, the plots planted to vegetables, attended to by the young people who come to visit. I have not tried to dissuade them from what they are doing, from what they believe in. Who am I to do these things? An intruder in the sanctity of their idealism, for I always told myself, I have so many alternatives, I can leave anytime I want to, and I did not have, as all of them did, to live harshly.

I have not seen Leo Mercado for weeks; he had always helped me with the things I needed from the city, and now he was here. He had brought along my recharged laptop batteries, one whole roast duck which, he said, since it was the twenty-fourth of December, we would have for noche buena, and for the Christmas lunch the following day, lechon—a suckling pig was squealing in a sack. He was going to sleep in the house tonight, if I would let him, a matter of formality, because he need not even ask.

He had grown thinner and had a slight cough. His face was paler, too, and his hair had greyed in such a short time. I asked if he was sick, but he smiled and said, "It is just the change in the weather," for indeed, it had become much cooler, and more so because we were high up. I suspect he has tuberculosis.

The roast duck was more than enough for the three of us, and was extremely welcome, a change from the daily diet of my own vegetables and the canned food with which the larder is well stocked. They are not only for me—it is for them when they arrive unannounced, tired and hungry, and there was no time to cook.

I had put on a sweater and so had Namnama and her father. Namnama did the dishes, and Leo Mercado and I sat in the yard, on the circle of benches that the young people had built from branches of big trees.

Around us, the night is hushed, then the crickets sing, and the smell of leaves and moss and the warm earth fills our lungs. Leo Mercado was pensive.

I could never get him to call me Buddy; always it was Professor and because he wouldn't change, I let him. "I am very troubled," he said. "I see no change in our people, and I can see—because I have lived this long—so many sorry events repeat themselves. I was in the Huk movement, did you know that?"

"First time we met, you told me." He was looking at me, and in the semi-darkness, his eyes were serious and probing. "I heard about it from Junior, too."

He bowed and in a voice that cracked, softly: "My son, my son...now, it is only Namnama. And I fear for her, that I will lose her, too."

What could I say? This is what we must expect, what she herself was prepared for.

"I know her kind of life," Leo Mercado continued. "I have lived it. And I am glad I have children like her. But she has been at it for eight years now. Eight years—and I think they are wasted years. Is it strange for me, being what I was, to be talking like this?"

"No," I said. "It is actually the pessimists who are the optimists. We try to look at the very dark side, so that we can get at the bright side..."

"There is no bright side," he said sadly. "Hindsight tells me so. I am an old man, Professor. Seventy-six years old, ten years in jail, years and years in the forest, and what have I to show for all those years? At least, my two children were able to finish college—one has to be optimistic..."

"I wish I could be more positive, tell you not to lose hope, for I know there is a possibility of redemption here. Look at all these young people, look at your own history..."

"You are wrong!" he said with a sudden outburst of passion. "History does not confirm you. We fought the Japanese, the army, the collaborators of the Japanese. We fought tenaciously, despised them and, look, after the war, who became rich, who did our people elect back to power but these traitors, these collaborators? Look around you in Manila—they are all back, the panderers and the plunderers who worked with Marcos. They are in the newspapers being feted, writing columns, justifying themselves. I see them on television, grinning, preening. No, Professor, I have very little faith in my countrymen, because they have no memory, because they have forgotten their exploiters, their torturers and murderers, because..." he paused and breathed deeply.

How could I argue with him? History was on his side but he didn't know it? It all came back, too, what I knew, the ilustrados who joined the Americans and profitted for themselves, the wealthy mestizos who collaborated not just with the Americans but with the Spaniards before them, and as Ka Leo now confirmed, with the Japanese as well.

"Hindsight again," Mercado continued. "And after all these years, I see how wrong I have been. Even if we did win, there won't be any change because the leaders would be the same. Hostage to relatives, old habits of mind, personal vanity...I have tried to dissuade Namnama, argue with her. Tell her it's all wrong—but she says we were wrong, too. My country is hopeless, Professor. There will be no change, no revolution as I see it now, if we don't first change ourselves. Tell them..."

But what right had I to tell them otherwise? After they had sacrificed so much, must I tell them now that they are wrong? Yet, Leo Mercado was voicing a truth. There must be more than faith, a restructuring of the old beliefs, a passion undiminished and unfaltering for the freedom of Filipinas and the dignity of all Indios— that much history, at least, had impinged upon me.

The old Huk continued, "I tell them to learn from our mistakes, but they have not done so. Did you notice, Professor? They were not at EDSA! And now, these assassinations of unarmed policemen, soldiers doing their marketing. We are all tired of this violence. Why don't they assassinate the crooks and crooked politicians, the cronies of Marcos instead? Marcos is gone. They say the enemy is still there— and I agree. But the tactics must change..." Then, after some silence, he asked: "What's wrong with us. Professor? You are a learned man. You must know the answer."

I have, of course, been troubled for so long by such a thought.

Yet, as I have written, these people have always been imbued with a sense of duty, of honor, but on that quiet evening, surrounded by the placid majesty of the forest, it occurred to me that there was a granite truth in what this old rebel said. He was right— collaboration with the enemy, with evil, was never recognized and condemned by the Filipinos. Collaboration in World War II with the Japanese, for instance, was settled as a political issue when Laurel ran and got so many votes. But as a moral issue? The collaborators were never ostracized. I did not want to say it, I couldn't say it, that the modern Filipino has no morality which, after all, is the basis of politics, and the populist state. Am I now dealing with a people who have lost their ethical moorings? How could I explain this to someone who had fought the enemy? The revolution then that was being preached would not succeed, unless it was grounded on a very strong moral principle. Unless collaboration with the enemy, with Marcos and his rapacious oligarchy, was considered the ultimate crime against the people.

"A lot of changes have to be made, Ka Leo," I said. "You have done your share, so the young are now doing theirs..."

Then he asked me. "Namnama tells me you are helping them so much. It is dangerous, as you very well know. Have you decided to remain here—stay here permanently?"

I had, of course, decided way back. "Yes," I said simply. I did not expect the next question and could not reply immediately.

"Do you love my daughter?"

I knew only too well my feelings. Namnama was the most important reason why I chose to stay in this Mountain.

"I do," I said, "Very much. But I think, she does not know."

"Then," he turned to me, eager for my reply. "Why have you not told her? I asked her. She says there is nothing between the two of you...but I know. I know!"

"Is it necessary? I am old enough to be her father. What future can I give her? As you must have been told, I am not well..."

He was silent again, as if he was searching for one thought he had failed to express. "Please do not be embarrassed by my questions, Professor. Forgive this old man, this anxious father. I don't want to lose her, Professor. My only child now. She has done enough—more than enough to prove herself, her commitment, as they say. May I ask you a very great personal favor? Just one."

"I will gladly do it for you," I said, wondering what it was.

"Marry Namnama. Take her away from all these. Take her with you to America. She will be safe there. You said you love her—then there is no hindrance. I know she cares for you very much, too. She tells me. And she worries so much about you..."

In an instant, I was lifted from this night, this mundane earth. Ka Leo went on talking, I was listening, but my spirit was high up in the perfumed ether.

"She is a good girl. An engineer—and she is here. She will make a very good wife. So very much like her mother. My dear wife— she was devoted to me, she followed me even when I was in hiding. She cared for me, just as Namnama will care for you. My wife—" and he paused. He could only mumble as he quavered, recalling the woman he loved. "She knew what sacrifice was. Her life was one..."

25

I WAS CALLED Commander Toothpick—the name was not given to me by the leadership; it was spontaneous because I am tall and thin, like a toothpick. They also called me Nardong Sastre because of my occupation.

Filipinos really have a way with nicknames. A person's personal appearance soon becomes part of his name: kalbo (bald), payat (thin), pilay (cripple), negro (dark). Imagine a grown-up man still being called Baby. Dong, Ding, Ting, Bing, Jing—are common nicknames now. But very Filipino names are still given by traditional Filipino parents. Liwayway (Tagalog for dawn), Liwliwa (Ilokano for joy), Waywaya (Ilokano for freedom) Lualhati (Tagalog for glory) and Namnama (Ilokano for hope).

My wife's father was Ilokano and her mother Pampango. Both were extremely wealthy and they maintained houses in Manila, Vigan, Ilokos Sur, and San Fernando in Pampanga.

Shortly after I was released from jail in 1978, I took the children to Vigan. Namnama was then in college and Junior in high school. Vigan is the old capital of Nueva Segovia—that is the name the Spaniards gave to Northern Luzon. They also named Vigan Ciudad Fernandina.

She had described the house to me so well and although I had never been in it, it was already clearly imaged in my mind, the wide grounds surrounded by a high brick wall, the tall tamarind tree by the gate which she said bore sweet fruit. As a little girl, she was awed by the bigness of the house, its many rooms with their keys hanging from a chain in the kitchen and those giant wooden cabinets where she used to hide, seeking solitude in their darkness and space.

The house is still there, cared for by my wife's youngest sister who is an old maid. Its tile roof is so old, grass is sprouting on it. The ground floor is wide but dim because it was where the carriages were kept. You go up this wide staircase to a large living room with thick wooden floors and equally thick panels. Old, greying family pictures on the walls, and antique cabinets with china and silver, and in the bedrooms, four-poster beds of woven rattan—no mattresses.

I had asked permission to see the house on the excuse that my daughter was an architectural student—actually she was taking up mechanical engineering—and she wanted to see how the old houses were designed and built.

My wife told me her picture and that of her parents were above the piano. It turned out to be a grand piano. Namnama and Junior were silent as they looked at the picture of their mother when she was about six years old, dressed in a sailor suit, with knee-length stockings, and that unmistakable beauty in her eyes. Their aunt did not know who we were. She explained that the doctor and his wife in the picture were dead. And that little girl? She did not speak for a while, then she said she remembered very little of her oldest sister; she had disappeared during the war.

All through our history, our women fought beside us men; sometimes, they fought alone or led in the struggle. When Diego Silang was betrayed and the Spaniards killed him, it was his wife, Gabriela, who infused new life into that rebellion. My grandfather took part in the revolution against Spain; my grandmother was there by his side. Women who were wives, daughters and sisters of the revolutionaries were called "camp followers" by the Spaniards and the Americans, but they bore arms, mended clothes, cooked and washed for the men in the trenches. During the Japanese Occupation, many of our women gave their lives in that guerrilla war, Josefa Escoda among them, and Yay Marking and Lydia Arguilla, among those who survived. Our women were called Amazons by the constabulary propagandists but, like my wife, they were just Filipinos who truly believed in their cause.

Look at the map of Central Luzon. During the Japanese Occupation, we controlled much of it at night, not the Japanese who were holed in the towns in their garrisons. It was the same during the rebellion against the American puppet regime. Remember how, in the late forties, so many checkpoints were scattered all over the Central Plain, how traffic through Central Luzon went in convoys, with armored cars and tanks as escorts? We ranged over this vast area—from the Zambales mountains, across the plain and the Candaba swamps to Mount Arayat, then to the Sierra Madre Range all the way from Rizal and Bulacan down to the Bicol peninsula, or all the way up to Cagayan Valley. My wife and I walked these great distances, these forested mountains, on blistered feet and lived as poorly as the people we were trying to help. Who were our enemies then but the oppressive landlords and civilian guards.

Yes, Namnama lives in the shadow of her mother. Thinking about her now in this old age makes me young again, makes me relive again not so much the dangers we had faced but the joys of being together in those times when our togetherness was dearly sought and made precious. She was very fair but the difficult life, much of it spent in the open and in the sun, had so darkened her. In a gathering of peasant women, she was easily one of them. Look at my daughter now, those eyes are her mother's, and she too is fair but, like her mother, she has grown dark as she is no stranger to hard work in the fields.

All through time, there are "moments of truth," when the mettle and nature of a people are subjected to the greatest stress. Then the true character surfaces. My generation may be judged by how we acted during the Japanese Occupation, if we collaborated with the enemy or not. For this generation today, its moment of truth came when Marcos became a dictator and Filipinos collectively and as individuals acted out their character.

For my wife, this moment had come when she was barely out of puberty. The family lived in Ermita which, as everyone will tell you, was the most elegant district in Manila before the war. As a girl, she was what they called an "interna." Although their house was just a couple of blocks away, she lived in the convent school on the assumption that living with the nuns she would master her French and Spanish more easily, and she would be safer, particularly during the war.

What they did not know, what the Japanese did not know, was that there were some Filipino nuns in the convent who were in the guerrilla movement, that one of the nuns brought her along when she was carrying messages to other parts of the city, and at times to the province. She was twelve at the time. By the end of the war, when she was fourteen, she had become a courier herself.

Ermita was devastated by the Japanese. The family home had been burnt down, but the convent school was spared. She stayed to finish high school, and on to college. But she did not finish college. Instead, she continued working with the guerrillas—they turned out to be with the Huks.

Those who live by the gun—the policeman, the soldier, the guerrilla and revolutionary—if they lose their moorings, the same guns that are their implements for justice may easily be the weapons for oppression. They deteriorate into hoodlums and kidnappers as we see happening now; they who are supposed to uphold the law have themselves become the robbers and kidnappers. This was true in the latter part of the Huk rebellion, when some guerrillas made violence their way of life.

There were many dark episodes in the guerrilla war. As the resistance heightened, soon it was one guerrilla unit fighting other units, each one jealously protecting its territory and area of influence. Personality conflicts, the acting out of ancient grudges at a time when there was no law became commonplace. Many Filipinos died in this fratricidal conflict.

We should have been happiest when Liberation came; we had, after all, fought for so long, we helped in the Liberation itself. We regarded the Americans as friends; the pilots who parachuted in our areas were treated as heroes. But the landlords who had fled to the city returned to reclaim their lands. They had allies among the Americans; most of all, they controlled government and the armed civil guards whom they paid, many of them former Japanese collaborators. The American army disarmed some of our units; we were now called communist bandits, the new enemy. Thus, the Huk rebellion began.

But though we lost in that rebellion, we always kept alive the ideals we were fighting for—justice most of all which should be made real with land reform. If we fought the Japanese for our freedom, now it is the same freedom we seek from the greedy landlords.

Have times really changed? I was a sophomore in college at the outbreak of the war, fully ten years older than my wife, when we in Central Luzon were inspired by the words of the socialist leader, Pedro Abad Santos.

It was I, myself, who found her one December evening in 1949 when we were marching towards Arayat.

The night was already upon the land but in the afterglow, it was still easy to recognize the shapes of things, of men. She was lying on the edge of the cane field. Had they tried to hide her and dumped her inside the cane field, I would not have noticed her at all. She was very fair, and there she was on the grass with no clothes. Her face was bloody and bruised, and there were wounds on her shoulder and waist. The blood had coagulated for some time, there was no more bleeding, which was just as well, else she would have bled to death. She had almost no pulse but was still alive and breathing. We improvised immediately a stretcher from the branches of ipil trees close by—we have had plenty of practice in this, and carried her to our base camp, a village where the people were friends. In the meantime, one of the men had turned back to Angeles to get a doctor. He arrived about midnight; by this time, one of the women had already washed her but she was still unconscious. She had lost a lot of blood. Someone had to rush back to Angeles to get plasma and other medicines. She regained consciousness the following day. I had been keeping vigil by her bed when this happened, and she looked at me then closed her eyes again and lapsed into unconsciousness. In the evening, she opened her eyes again and asked for water. The following morning, after she slept the whole night without once waking up, she finally asked where she was and who we were. I did not know who she was so I did not tell her anything. We had to move every two days to other villages. To stay in one place for a long time would be dangerous. I suppose she realized soon enough who we were and that was when she asked if Ka Luis (Taruc) was anywhere close by. That was the time, too, when I realized who she was.

I never really asked her about what had happened. She did not seem comfortable talking about it. It was not the constabulary, that much I knew—it was the civilian guards. When she was already well, I told her she was free to go, back to Manila where she came from, but she said that was over. Now she wanted to be one of us, to be a soldier and not a simple courier. I told her being one was just as important, but she said, not as important as those who fight, who take more risks because they are the people who get shot at. Would I take her? I tried to dissuade her—yes, we had women with us, that was true, but they all came from the village. She said I had insulted her, but that she would forgive me if I took her in. It was, of course, just a matter of time. By then, although there were sanctions against it, I had begun to love her. I think she knew that and, eventually, my entire unit knew about it, too.

She was reticent about her family, her upper-class background, but these could not be hidden; the way she conducted herself, her speech, revealed so much. As I learned more about her, I was truly humbled by the difficult choice she had made and I loved her and respected her all the more for that.

I did not get to read the newspapers every day but later, on those few occasions that I did, I often came across items about her sisters in the society pages, the cultural and charity committees they were involved with, all of them looking pleased with themselves. I wondered aloud how she felt about leaving that easy life. She would rebuke me lightly, saying there was no turning back on what she had decided her life would be. And when we had nothing to eat, or had so much hard work, I chided her about the fine meals she was missing. She would shake a finger at me as if I were a misbehaving child. I truly appreciated her for that, for the sacrifices she had made not just to be with us but to be my wife.

And so I ask myself again and again, what was her reward? In fact, I ask this of my daughter and, maybe, I should also ask this of myself. Was it all worth it? We have not succeeded, and the enemy has grown stronger and invincible instead.

And like my dear wife, I would be unflinching and sincere, I'd say the act of trying, of fighting, is in itself the reward. Nothing more than one of those fancy phrases, but she felt it deeply as I do even now.

Before the children came, she was captured once in a village where she had stayed to set up a grade school. She was in detention for more than two years; it was not prison like it was with me. There were no charges, no court sentence. She was in military custody for questioning. Yes, you can be held in detention for years without trial in this country. She did not tell them anything other than she was an orphan—they could go to the Hospicio and look at the records, that she was a "manang" in the convent school. They could check on that, too, but I think they didn't because they simply did not believe her. Two years, some of it in solitary confinement, against all the threats and trickery her captors used to make her talk. When they released her, she proceeded to the convent school immediately, and spoke with the nuns, convinced them she was in mortal danger and could she stay for a short time? They trusted her and her request was so simple. She knew the army was watching her. Two weeks after she went to the convent, a group of nuns in their habits went in a van to Tagaytay. On the way back, she changed clothes, got off in Pasay, boarded a bus to Pampanga and went to one of the villages where our movements were known. I did not hold much hope of seeing her again. I was so grateful I cried. I saw soon enough her breasts and her torso were covered with dark spots, scars almost. They were burns; they had tortured her, too.

When the children came, I wanted her safe, in a village among friends. Junior was about a year old; she had breastfed him and he was already weaned. Namnama was four—even as a little girl, she already had so much of her mother's beauty. We had a little house in this village and during the many days that I was away, she looked after it and the vegetable plots close by. During the planting season, almost all of us helped with the planting; and in the harvest season, we were out there in the fields reaping the grain. Rain or scorching sun, she worked perhaps harder than so many of us. And in those times that there was meat—which were rare—she cooked it in such a way that you would think we were eating very well. Truth is, it was vegetables most of the time. And on the march, there was very little food. We did not eat any better than the peasants in whose homes we rested.

In her messages, she said the children could now be left in the care of my relatives, that her place was beside me. Long afterwards, I often thought she loved me so much she wanted to be by my side always. But that was not so, she wanted to be where she could do the most good. She was, after all, a soldier. I have often wondered too, in fact, I have never stopped wondering why she chose to suffer our kind of life. My daughter had answered that question for her; any person who sees what is happening to our poor, to our peasantry, would do the same—if she had the will and the heart. With my wife, she saw early enough the wide and deep chasm between her family and the common people with whom she identified.

261

Maybe there was some feeling of guilt, but I know it was not so, that all the while it was love.

Her family never stopped trying to locate her, to know most of all if she was safe. I could understand their anguish not so much as parents but as wealthy landowners whose child had turned against them and all the privilege and security they offered her. It must have made them wonder no end, search the very dregs of their soul, why their oldest daughter had betrayed her past, her class. But in fairness to them, they were not abusive; their tenants in the Ilokos and in Pampanga were better off—though not by much—than most tenants in Central Luzon.

It was not just farmland, however, that was the source of the family's wealth. As I already mentioned, her father was not only a successful doctor, he was also an astute real estate investor, having bought large parcels of land in Makati and other suburbs when they were cheap and held on to them, or built houses and buildings for rent.

On occasion, she would get a letter from her parents and her younger sisters. They'd pass from hand to hand in that circuitous way messages outside our communication channel would get to us. Letters several weeks old, splotched with dirt and by too many hands. I had watched her read them, the wan smile on her face, the wistful look. Not once did she cry, not once did she reply.

It was one of those rare events. Both of us went to Manila—a meeting but also, for us, a respite. We saw the movie, "The Sound of Music." We also went to the restaurant, D & E in Makati, and gorged on pancit malabon, fresh lumpia and chicken barbecue. She was enjoying herself, I could see that in the glow on her face. Before we returned to the safe house—an old apartment—in Sampaloc, we boarded a cab. I told the driver to take us to Forbes Park. She whispered to me that she didn't want to—but the opportunity was at hand.

"Are you testing me?" she asked. I shook my head. She needed no testing. She had already burned all the bridges to her past, of this I was sure, but I felt it might give her some pleasure to see the house again where, after all, she had also grown up. She had described it to me, although not as nostalgically as the old house in Vigan which she had truly loved.

At the gate to the Park, we were stopped by the security guards, and the driver surrendered to them his driver's license. "We are visiting relatives in Tamarind Street," I said.

She hadn't forgotten, she gave the driver instructions. We drove slowly, making a few turns. The magnificent houses that flanked the roads awed me—I had never before seen so many of them in one place. We finally reached the street. We drove past the house twice, slowing down, but couldn't see much because it was dark—it was nine in the evening, nothing but that closed iron gate, a high ivy-covered wall and the red tile roof.

"How it has grown," she sighed, pointing to the fire tree in the yard. "And so many houses here now."

That night, as we lay on the floor and before going to sleep, she held my hand and said she was glad I took her there.

"But you didn't go in and you didn't see any of your sisters or your parents."

She was silent for a while, then she spoke, at once tender and sad: "I love them very much. But I am all the more sure now that I cannot go back to them and live there. Those big, big houses—what do they really give to people. Happiness? Fulfillment?"

When she died, I knew I had to tell her parents. I had thought of going there myself. Maybe they could still claim her body if the army had not buried her, another unknown casualty in this peasant war. I thought against it, though, and sent instead one of the men who last saw her alive. I gave him a few photographs to give to her parents, some of her old clothes, and an old and tarnished silver hand mirror which belonged to her mother— her only concession to feminine vanity. He told me when he came back that it was only her mother and father whom he saw; her sisters were still in school. Both had cried; they tried to get more information about her, but the announcement of her death was all that he was instructed to give.

SHE HAD come to join me in the mountains of Laur, Nueva Ecija. That unit was ambushed by a constabulary patrol. Was it carelessness on our part? or was one of us a traitor? I do not know.

Four were killed in the first volley. She was hit in the thigh and was immediately crippled. We always carried our dead and wounded away from the battlefield but, this time, she urged her comrades to flee. They did not want to leave her or the dead, but she shouted at them, their lives were more important. She asked that they leave her some grenades and a 12-gauge shotgun which was good for close combat. As they ran away, they listened to the continued firing, the garands and carbines in clear volleys, the louder report of the shotgun, the whump of grenades, a few scattered shots, then silence.

The squad which survived that ambush never tired of telling and retelling the story of her courage. It was not I who made her a legend— she did that herself and I only bask in her glory, remembering that she was not just a good soldier but a dutiful wife and mother.

26

LOOK AT WHAT time has done; no longer do I look sickly, dissipated. There is a peasant roughness now to my skin, the work in the sun did that. Work? It gave me joy to till the old plot, planting it to bitter melons, cassava, okra, eggplants—food that I can eat. It was not difficult work; thank God there was Namnama. In the morning when the sun is out, sparkling on the grass, shining through the canopy of trees, I hurry down to see how fast the green things have grown.

And I am now utterly confident with my Pilipino—that's the euphemism for the Tagalog of the sidewalk. I can now lecture in it although it is extremely inadequate when it comes to scientific and philosophical terms. In which case, I revert to English which they understand anyway. The coffee sessions with Lena Mabango in Hawaii had helped and then there is Namnama, always ready with the appropriate word when I falter.

I know now that I can be on my own.

I haven't been to Manila in weeks and the telephone operator in the substation cannot quite believe what she sees; she says I have grown so dark, I look like the farmer which I had become. These Manila phones, they are so unwieldy, but I now have all the time to wait.

It's two hundred pesos for three minutes. Jessie comes on the line, so pleased that I had called her. "Buddy, do write more often! I get so worried when I don't hear from you."

I had brought out a wad of hundred-peso bills and told the operator to let me talk for as long as I wished and forget the three-minute minimum. "There's about a thousand pesos there," I said to her.

It was almost noon in Manila, and eight p.m. in San Francisco. She had just returned from some reception. "I have very good news for you, Buddy," she said brightly, and I could imagine her, eyes shining as she spoke. "Finally, I am truly in love. And I'm marrying him."

How would Jessie know? How many times had she felt she was truly in love only to be shattered again? I couldn't speak for some time.

"I know you don't trust me with such a feeling, Buddy. But this time, I'm sure."

"How, Jessie. How?"

"I've always been, as you said, self-centered. But I could sacrifice for this man. Money is important to him, it is to all of us, but he wants to spend money not just for himself but"—a meaningful pause here—"for others, for his own people."

"He's not American?"

Laughter on the other end. "He is. Sammy Neqwatewa is Hopi."

"Beads, feathers, can he do the snake dance?"

More laughter. "He is here in San Francisco, Buddy, in a business suit, working for a foundation."

I was very pleased. Jessie would be able to hold on to something now, meaning and all that sort of thing which had eluded her all these years.

"There's more, Buddy. I'm pregnant." When I didn't say anything, Jessie continued evenly, "No, this is different. I'm going to keep her, love her."

"Are you sure?"

"Yes," she said happily, "two months. I'm so, so happy! Now tell me about yourself. Letters can be so impersonal. It's much nicer listening to you."

"I called to say good-bye."

For a moment, silence. "What do you mean? We can't say good-bye, whether I'm married or not."

"You will be in very good hands now. So saying good-bye is easier." Yes, there would never be an end. We are both orphans, and the bond between us has solidified, permanent and strong. I continued evenly: "My dear Jessie, I have decided to stay. And I may not see you again."

"But there is so much for both of us. We—you, you don't even need to work, you know that. What do you want to stay there for and suffer. I know you're suffering..."

"You get used to the inconveniences, Jessie. No plumbing, no running water, no electricity. But there is a spring close by, and at night when the fireflies adorn the trees..."

"Oh, Buddy, it's all poetry for you. I love you!"

"I love you, too," I said quickly, and in my heart, I emblazoned the words. Who is Jessie but the woman who has been closest to me all my life; we were truly brother and sister now. "But this is good-bye, Jessie."

"No!" she was emphatic. "Just good night. I will come and see you very soon, just to be sure you are all right. Very soon, Buddy. Maybe this month, or this week."

HE MISSED HER at the airport; there was such a mess of people there and because he came in a taxi, he was shunted to where the welcomers were packed behind a grilled barrier, each one straining to look at the passengers squeezing out of the two exits with their bulky boxes of homecoming gifts, travellers in their winter clothes, now sweating and uncomfortable in the tropical heat. He had reserved a suite at the Manila Hotel—Jessica always deserved the best. Surely, the hotel had sent a car to pick her up.

He hurried to the hotel. The suite was on the top floor of the new annex. She had arrived only minutes earlier. The guest relations officer was instructing her on the use of the facilities. When she saw Buddy she rushed to him, embraced him and kissed him noisily. "Oh, God, it's really you! How you've changed!"

He looked at her and all those exultant feelings of family and shared experience swept over him, and they embraced again. His cheek was soon wet with her crying.

He pushed her gently away; she had aged a little and now a shallow wrinkle or two lined her forehead, hinting at maturity rather than hardness. It became her.

Buddy glanced around him. He was no longer used to this luxury, this surfeit of living. "You have a lovely room," he said, noting the four-poster bed. She started unpacking, talking about San Francisco, what she was doing. From the suitcase, a tin of his favorite honey-flavored cookies which she had baked. Beyond the wide window, the bay was placid and shimmering in the noon-day sun.

How was it then? To the right, the wooden ships from China and Japan wallowing in the shallows, the subjects of Sulaiman bartering their rice, dried fish and ropes of hemp which they had made in exchange for the implements of agriculture, the plow, the harrow, and the precious silk. And Tondo across the river—a large village with nipa-roofed houses clinging to the shore and, above them, the palisade with its cannon mounts. And beyond, inland into the forest, and across the serene and unchanging expanse to the left, Cavite; the wide basin that had been Spain's base for its battle fleet, a naval station for the Americans, abandoned now with no viable plan to make use of it.

Jessica shattered his momentary reverie. "I want you to come home with me, Buddy," she said, sidling close to him. Her skin was much lighter than his now. "Look at you," she said, appraising him. "What kind of life do you live? You have grown so thin, and look at your hands—they look rough and bigger." She took his right hand and pressed it to her cheek. He embraced her again, smelled her, too, all sweetness compounded with the sweat that the tropics had squeezed out of her skin. When was it last that he held her like this? Some timeless parting, unremembered as their partings had always been for there was always a meeting again.

She drew away. "But otherwise you look well. Why, there is a look of contentment on your face—the look of Buddhist monks, as you yourself once said."

She remembered; once in San Francisco, four Siamese monks gave a talk on Buddhism and, said Buddy, studying their old but unwrinkled faces, their contented countenance, "There's peace in them."

"Maybe," Buddy said, "I have found my monastic calling."

"And your teeth are perfect."

Like the people in the villages, he used the end of a crushed guava twig to brush his teeth. Yes, the many days in the sun had roughened and darkened his skin and the wind had whipped his hair so often it had become dry and unruly.

"I could never quite get it from letters, your getting involved with the life here. Just what is it you do? What keeps you here? What is so important that you can't leave? A woman?"

Certainly, Namnama was beguiling reason enough, but it was more than Namnama now. Jessie, ever imperious, wanting everything her way—there was only one way to argue with her. He would have to show her.

"Well then, come with me," he said. "See how I live."

"I will! I will!" she cried. "It's all a riddle to me. All that money waiting for you anytime you need it, and you've hardly touched it. I have more than enough, Buddy."

To him, it was no riddle. Maybe twenty years ago, if he had acted this way. It was all so inchoate then. He had found it finally, this sylvan sanctuary where his feet were sunk long ago without his knowing it. Indeed, he had drifted away, and yet never really left.

But would Jessie understand? It was her first trip to this part of the world and even now, it was obvious that the heat had simply enervated her. She would now be taken to some jungly retreat, and her suspicions would become truth, that Buddy had become ascetic, an hermit who would in time let his hair grow long, be garbed in saffron to chant in street corners.

He was very pleased to take her on a tour of the bedraggled city, first to EDSA where he was witness to the grandeur of a people's uniting in ringing expression of national will, to the short bridge in Mendiola where, for the first time, he truly learned the meaning of Revolution, but he did not tell Jessie of the blood on his clothes. He did not tell her, too of the villages at the foot of the Caraballo Range where Pepe Samson had taken him, to Lupao where he was witness to a massacre—all these would simply be too much for her. Jessie had wept when he took her to Tondo, to that mound which they call Smokey Mountain, and she saw the poor living on the garbage of the city and, finally, to Forbes Park, to the antiseptic and privileged ghettos of the wealthy. Buddy said very little, letting the places describe themselves profoundly in her mind.

On the fourth day, in midmorning, they took the airconditioned bus part of the way, the drab countryside slipped by like some sensuous dream in the heat. It was early afternoon when they reached Raza, the foothills. The jeepney to which they had transferred would go no farther, so they took a tricycle to the farthest it could go— the rest of the way, they had to walk.

He wanted to know more about what she was doing, her social work in San Francisco, which was how she met Sammy Neqwatewa. "He's going back to New Mexico," she said. "With me. We'll work together—there's a network there helping the underprivileged get education. Indians, blacks, poor whites. Oh, I'm sure we'll have many difficulties, but I'm willing to learn."

As she explained herself, he became more confident that it would not be so difficult to explain himself to her now. To her eager questioning, he related what had happened in the Philippines these many years, how the peasants had always been exploited and the land despoiled. The Mountain, he said, had become a redoubt of faith for those who believed there was salvation still.

"It was here where Dad found me, Jessie," he reminded her, glorying again in the retelling, as if it was only yesterday that it had happened and those battered images that had littered his boyhood were finally retrieved and made whole.

He did not want her needlessly tired—her baby, but she assured him her doctor said exercise would do her good. They had climbed slowly in the afternoon heat and the gradual ascent had made the height appear deceptive till, through a clearing in the foliage, Jessie looked back. The plain was well below them, rolling away in varying shades of sepia and green. A small stream, clear and sparkling, ran between the folds of the earth. It was strewn with huge, mossy boulders. The trail crossed the same stream in places. Where there was no boulder to step on, he carried Jessie, her khaki skirt tucked under her. Buddy's sneakers and jeans were now wet. She clung to him, her scent swirling pleasantly around him and he remembered the touching letters she had sent asking his advice in her many unhappy love affairs, her bouts with drugs.

They crossed the stream again, deeper than elsewhere and when he set her down the hem of her skirt was wet. Her blouse was also wet with her perspiration, her face flushed and damp. They had already climbed halfway up the mountain, across two hills, and his house was still far away. A few clearings came into view for they were now on a narrow plateau, and the huts of farmers stood in the clearings which were, like his own little farm, planted to cassava, sweet potatoes and vegetables. He could tell from her heavy breathing that she was already tired, but being strong-willed, she kept in step with him.

He decided to stop in the shade of a tall narra tree and laid his backpack and her overnight bag on the ground so she could recline on them. She told him about Sammy Neqwatewa; he was teaching at a small college in New Mexico, and it was there that he was recruited by the foundation. With his background, he would be ideal for some of the projects that the foundation had set up.

Above them, the canopy of leaves hid the sun. He stretched on the grass, rested his head on his backpack which contained his purchases from Manila, alkaline batteries mostly, and the occasional luxury of a large can of Cheez Curls for Namnama. He shucked off his shoes and wiggled his toes. Jessie sat beside him, her back against the tree trunk.

"I have never walked this far," she admitted. It was growing late in the afternoon, and there was still a way to go. From Buddy's pack, a can of soda water which he opened and handed to her. She took it gladly, and after a long draught she finally spoke out. "I don't get it, Buddy, you coming here, walking all this distance to be on this mountain, in the wilderness, a man who has seen so much of the world. I don't get it at all!"

"You'll have to see for yourself, Jessie," he said, getting ready to walk again. "How I live, where—and this Mountain, too."

In a while, they passed the first cave on the mountainside; she would have missed it completely—it was half-covered with vines—hadn't Buddy pointed it out to her. A mossy boulder at its maw was dotted with candle stubs, the side of the boulder streaked with candle wax.

"What's this?" Jessie asked.

"There's a spring inside." He pointed to the rivulet that flowed down beside the boulder to merge with the larger stream which they had crossed. "We are on sacred ground, Jessie," he said. "People come here to worship." He pointed to a stub of candle that seemed newer than all the rest. "They come in a trickle because this part of the Mountain is not easy to reach."

They continued to climb, the gentle slope beckoning to them. Now, the trees were truly huge, almost primeval, their broad, dark trunks veined with thick vines, like pythons in repose, and it seemed that the trail which they were following had vanished altogether. They must now walk on, guided only by instinct. Then the trees seemed to thin, to open up. They were before a tiny clearing planted to corn, the young plants already flowering. And on the neatly tended land were a variety of vegetable rows, tomatoes, squash, bitter melons, string beans, all supported by trellises. And beyond the clearing, up on a sharp ridge almost hidden by trees, was his cottage, solitary, merging almost with the surrounding green.

In the fading light of afternoon, Jessie took in everything, quietly, purposefully. Would she want to live in such splendid isolation; yet, she could immediately sense the serenity, perhaps even the awesome sanctity of this place.

"This is very difficult to locate," he told her. "People come looking for me, but they don't know how to get here. In a sense, this is also hallowed ground, Jessie. Remember the stories I told you about the blind woman whom I regarded as my mother, and the old man who found me in the church and brought me here? Their ashes are commingled with this soil and every time I breathe, I am breathing into myself their very essence." And again he told her how he had lost them both.

Up the small bamboo house at last. She took in everything, the spare furniture—the writing table with the laptop, the diskettes, the multi-band radio. Up on one side was a pile of pillows, a rolled mat and his few clothes on hangers. Books all over the place. The adjoining kitchen was just as bare, a small eating table, two chairs, an open cabinet filled with canned food and condiments, and on one side two big earthen pots which contained his drinking water.

"I sleep on the floor, Jessie," he said. "You'll have to sleep on the floor tonight, too. You'll get used to it."

Jessie just could not accept it. "You are giving up Pacific Heights for this! The house is all yours now, because I have decided to live in New Mexico. But this..." She shook her head vehemently.

Buddy went to her and kissed her. "But, my love, you're giving up Pacific Heights, too!"

The air had turned cool and birdcalls from the forest came to them in sonorous trills. Jessie shivered and asked what they were. He told her not to get frightened—there was absolute safety here. As she could see, the door was wide open when they arrived. She had to know, she wanted to be assured that he was well, that he was not wasting his time most of all.

She had taken a drink from the jar. Spring water, Buddy explained, and water had never tasted this sweet. She was tired, she wanted to lie down, so Buddy spread a mat in one corner; it would get colder, he told her, so he gave her a sweater and a blanket. Soon she was fast asleep.

SHE WAS wakened by voices which at first she thought were imagined, indistinct, as in a dream, but they persisted. Fully conscious now, she turned to the fire that was brightly dancing on the kitchen stove, and to the woman tending the pot. Jessie was under a huge mosquito net that occupied almost the whole house. She rose, and went to the kitchen. The woman turned to her—Buddy's woman? She smiled at Jessica, greeted her with a pleasant good evening, then went on with her work cutting up vegetables and washing them. For a while, Jessica watched her, a young woman in jeans and a shapeless blouse, her face brown with sun and, in the light of the kitchen stove, effulgent with youth and the easy charm which, by now, she recognized as an attribute of her brother's people. The vegetables— mostly greens which she couldn't recognize—were fresh, unwilted, and when she asked where they had come from, the woman pointed to the plots outside the house. "Buddy grows them," she said, and at once, Jessica knew this was the woman her brother had spoken about with fondness.

People were talking in the yard; she could make out their shapes, squatting on the ground, sitting on benches. She could make out, too, Buddy before them, speaking in their language which she could not understand, although on occasion English words interspersed their discussion—pragmatism, faith, imagination and several more—but she could not follow what was being said.

The young woman who was cooking went down to the group with a storm lamp which she placed on a stool and the indistinct faces took shape; there were four women in the group of ten. They went up the house and brought the food down, the rice in a big plastic bowl, and the vegetables in the pot. They asked her to join them.

They were subdued in their greetings, and when they talked with Buddy, it seemed as if they addressed him in some venerable form. He certainly was older than all of them. As she looked clearly at their faces, she realized that most of them were hardly out of their teens. Only the woman who had done the cooking seemed older. They ate quietly with their hands, seldom talking. The rice was hot and steaming and the vegetables which were ladled onto their plates tasted sweetish; there were scraps of fish in the vegetables and Buddy told her to be careful lest she would get bones in her throat. Their dessert, Buddy explained to her, was sweet potato boiled in syrup. After the long, tiring hike, she realized how hungry she was, how she could eat anything.

She stayed with them even after they had eaten and they asked her some trite questions, how she liked Manila, when she would return to America, that they wished her well. Upstairs in the kitchen, the clutter of dishwashing, of cleaning up. Then it was time for the meeting to end, and the girls joined the group; it was then that Jessie was surprised, for now, they picked up what they had on the ground, their backpacks—and guns. In the semi-darkness, she had not noticed the guns which all of them now carried.

What is Buddy doing with these people? He had a lot of explaining to do.

In a while, they were alone. "You have met Namnama," he said. "She is the oldest in the group. She means a lot to me, Jessica."

They were lying on the bamboo floor, and now that she was rested, she felt uncomfortable with its hardness. It is good for the spine, he told her. Buddy had extinguished the storm lamp that hang from a rafter. She had never known darkness like this before, so complete and so still; there was no sky above them, from the open window the outline of trees against the night sky, and the sullen quietude of the Mountain. It was lonely, it was also frightening.

"I am very safe here, Jessie. And so are you," he reassured her. She moved closer to him and held his hand. It was indeed cool, high up in this Mountain, but the blanket was thick enough.

"I think I saw a lot tonight," Jessie said softly, as if there were eavesdroppers beneath the house, around it. "You must still explain to me why you chose this kind of life, Buddy. Please make me understand. I don't want to lose you to them!"

"After you told me of your plans to go to New Mexico and work with the Hopi? Jessie, you know why I chose to be here!"

For some time, she did not speak. Then: "Fuck your revolution! You are risking your life! That's the difference. There's just the two of us now. And don't you forget it."

"Risk my life, "he repeated sadly. "What little of it that's left." He had never told her of his visits to the hospital; it had always been, he had decided long ago, in her best interest if she had less problems to think about, her life being already ridden with so much anguish.

"I don't understand," Jessie mumbled.

In an instant, it was all before him again, this night, this deeper forest that is seldom probed, and again, too, Inay Mayang, the animals nuzzling her hand, her beautiful but sightless eyes looking at him, beyond him, and Apo Tale, the wisdom of the earth entwined with that ancient and withered frame. What do we live for but to be a happy witness to a will more powerful than ours. The Mountain had laid its claim on me because it had sustained me even when I left it, fed me even when my stomach was full, embraced me even when my arms were locked in the arms of women loved and remembered.

To Jessie's question, he had no simple answer. "All of us, we do a lot of wandering, but in the end we have to return to where we came from. In a sense, that is what life is all about. An endless searching. Some find what they are looking for, others are destined to drift in space, rootless. Didn't you get what you wanted? Finally? And I—this! Aren't we both lucky?"

She squeezed his hand, then let go. A host of contrary feelings and doubts clogged her mind. She was angry at Buddy for leaving her, but at the same time she had begun to understand what it was all about. She loved him and she would lose him; it would hurt but she had been hurt so many times before and, because she was much older now, she knew she could cope. And to whom would she run to if the future turned bleak? Steady girl, grow up as Buddy has always told you. There's yourself first of all. Then there's Sammy Neqwatewa. Can't you see how, in many ways, he is like Buddy? Oh, Buddy, my dear brother, how right you are! We are, indeed, truly lucky and God up there is smiling at us!

She had not fully recovered from the rigor of the long hike and very soon, she was gently snoring.

27

I CAN hardly move now; my body is weighted down, my arms and legs feel like inanimate wood—to move them would drain me completely of strength. I think of del Pilar starving in Spain and I know I am much better off than he was. There is food in the kitchen but, in a sense, I am truly poorer because I have not done anything.

What are words? I've spun them out of the phantoms that inhabit my mind, formless but tangible and, having shaped them, could they also shape the hour? I am threatened by an immense gloom, which should bring forth passion and action from my very marrow, but all that I am capable of are words, mere words, and they will be lost, recorded though they may be like the trillions of words uttered before.

But the word, the only word, I knew it even before I was born, heard it then, not whispered but shouted from every mouth, and even from those who were mute, they spelled it in signs so it could be understood. I read it in my mother's womb, and it gushed into me, air in my lungs compounded with sun and starlight brighter than day and truer than right. I know who spoke it first—this incandescent word in my remembered past.

Even if the Coleman lamp and the flashlight were lighted, it would still be dark, a complete blackness that merges with the totality of night. The sounds of the forest reach me, the music of cicadas, the arrhythmic beating of my heart, but my body is formless, it has melted and become insensate and fluid with time.

I close my eyes but I don't have to for they are unseeing anyway. The images jump in the vast hollow of my brain, so clear, so vivid, if I could, I would reach out and touch them—multicolored escutcheons etched in slabs of newly minted gold, evanescent faces, my dear Jessica when she was just a small girl in pigtails.

How will it be with me? Will there be lizards, too, that will devour my carrion and scatter my flesh to the secret folds of this mountain so that I will nurture the seed? Now here is Apo Tale bending over me, his hair all white, his face ridged with wrinkles, and when he smiles, there are almost no teeth in his mouth. There's Inay Mayang now, her long black hair neatly combed, her beautiful eyes, unseeing but smiling nonetheless, her lips move but I cannot hear what she says because she cannot speak anyway. I wish I had learned how to read lips. Sleep comes, the images fade, and my last thought: Will I wake up?

I do, with gladness flooding me, immersing me. I can see again, I can move again, and I bounce down the ladder to my vegetable plots. How long have I been asleep? The string beans have grown so long, and the squash, too, is much bigger now. I stretch my hand to the sun—I am so happy I can do it—and see how bony my hand has become.

But in the afternoon, a sudden dizziness again, the trees suddenly seem to whirl around and collapse on me. I close my eyes and lie down on the wooden bench by the ladder and wait for the earth to balance itself, for the sky to stay in place.

I tell them to leave me alone at night; they may come and visit in the daytime, and they respect my wish. I need solitude more than ever to think and to write while I still can.

Namnama comes in. Whenever I am lying down, she always covers me with a blanket for I may sleep on through the evening which, up in this Mountain, is cool. Her boy's bob is gone—she had let her hair grow, only because once I asked aloud how would she look if her hair was long. She sometimes stays the whole day—she is now my nurse, my keeper. I know she is worried. She turns around and disappears into the kitchen. The clay stove sits at the far end, the fire is lighted, the smoke from the burning wood curls and disappears through the window and, at the same time, the stealthy onrush of dusk.

Then the big thoughts come.

What is the enduring vision of ourselves? What do we leave behind, a book of poems, a pillar of marble, a snatch of song?

The implacable night descends and with it the wraiths that commune with me, the immemorial and unresolved anxieties, the meaning of my days. Who is it who has no time, who bothers not with the broken, abandoned hours and daylight that does not come? Always I wait, as if waiting would tell me of its own essence so that I may also know mine. How I wish it were possible to know the very precise moment when sleep does come, when the self disappears and the dream begins. Then, perhaps, the riddle of memory will unfold and reveal itself as just another dream!

The thousands upon thousands who died for lost causes left their corpuscles in this soil so it will be firmer, impervious to the visitation of blight, of plunder, the greasy leavings of machines. They planted these trees in an act of redemption, knowing they will not sit in their shade, or harvest their fruits.

I sleep and wake and wait.

Again, it came without prelude; this is what they told me in San Francisco, the terminal regression. I fight it, fight it not for the love of life but for what I must still do.

When I cannot walk, they come and place me on a chair, a palanquin as if I were some potentate, carry me down to my squash and bitter melons so I can pick the fruits myself. They take me to the spring and I sit there, gazing at the water bubble, a miracle from the recondite bowels of the earth.

My tissues now warmed by the sun, they take me back to the house, to my study. Every day seems to bring an insight, unseen before because I was not close to my own kin. I am now.

All history is a lie—how could I have missed this! There is so much that is not in the books, documents, frayed or well-preserved though they may be. Their lives are not described in these at all— Vladimir, Anita, the helmsmen of yore, and now, those thousands in the desert, those maids strewn wantonly all over the world; it is they who have supported all these years the profligacy of the rich, the creaky functions of government. I can see them so clearly, the dead soldiers in the trenches felled by American guns; they are barefoot because they are farmers. Who will tell their story, recognize their ultimate devotion to Filipinas? And here, around me, are the great grandchildren of the same farmers, burdened with the sustenance of the Filipino dream.

When they flag, their niggardly meals souring their stomachs, their tiredness curdling their minds, I remind them of the many

276

peasants earlier in our time who fought, Pedro Calosa and the Colorums in 1931, Luis Taruc and the Huks in 1949. I quote again and again General Salud Algabre of the Sakdals in 1935: "No rebellion ever fails—each is a step forward in the right direction!" Yes, I tell them they are a sterling continuum of a revolutionary tradition for they are, above all else, a heroic people.

It is they who will redeem Filipinas, bestow on her the honor that was squandered, the future that was betrayed by the demons of colonialism and the cupidity of her own native sons. All this is now here, engraved not just in my mind but in the record, incomplete though it may be, their forebearance.

I am seated on the lowest rung of the ladder. This dizziness starts again so I close my eyes and struggle up the house. I lay on the floor and wait for the world to keep still, for the roof to stay in place. How many more weeks? Or is it days? I dare not tell anyone, not even Namnama.

I can still move my hands. I do not want them to see me like this but it cannot be helped. Thank God, my mind is clear. The doctors said, the spinal cord, the nerves are scarred, but not the brain; the body cannot respond to any command, but the brain is free.

What will I lose? My Jessica, but she is safe now. Namnama— I will never lose her for she will be here long after I am gone. It is so easy now to accept a physical death because I will surely leave behind a life, a memory. Memory, written or unwritten, preserves a people. How fortunate that I have looked beyond myself and come to know the beginning, and to know this is also to know the end.

I have watched them who will live after me, quiet in their talk, the fires burning in their bellies. They will weather all seasons, they will march beyond the emerald brow of the Mountain, and reach the verdant and sunny plain.

Again, this infernal darkness. It shrinks everything that is encompassed by my vision, the bamboo walls are blurred, the grass roof turns even more brown and is soon reduced to a narrow slate. The thick black ropes are my eyelashes, the pin of light diminishes. Again, I am immersed in a bog of total darkness and I am truly alone. Alone with my thoughts, as if now these thoughts are ever-widening vistas of reality slowly taking shape, enthralling and commending me.

Here I am, a waif in tatters, barefoot, hungry and sick, and this gentleman with curly hair, this tall American officer in khaki, two silver bars on his collar, picks me up. Oh, my father, look at your wandering son returned to his home, to his first memory. He tells me to put on an olive-green T-shirt and shorts, both army issues.

They are the smallest he could find, but the T-shirt hangs loosely on my tiny frame, and he has to tie a string around my waist to hold the shorts up. He looks at me and starts laughing. In the afternoon, he takes me to the village, to a woman who has a sewing machine—an old and rusting relic whose wheel she twirls with her hand. He gives her a couple of uniforms. Cut them up, he says, and make him some clothes.

He and his men scrounge Raza and the next town; they barter cartons of canned food and army boots for a pair of boy's shoes. They return with three used pairs, all of them a bit too large, but my father says they will do. And for the first time, I wear shoes.

I strut around the camp, in khaki and olive green, my feet encased in some boy's black leather shoes. In the afternoon, I take them off, wiggle my toes which have lost their freedom, and try to endure the barbed sting of blisters, knowing I have to wear the shoes again for that is what Captain James Wack wants.

When I limp the following morning, he asks to see my feet and I show him the raw blisters which, he says, will heal. His eyes are merry, he tousles my hair. "This is the price you have to pay for civilization," he tells me, then hoists me on his shoulders. I am very glad for up there, I can see much more.

278